BRING ME BACK

MICALEA SMELTZER

BRING ME BACK

Micalea Smeltzer

Cover Art designed by Hang Le

Edited by Ready, Set, Edit

Formatted by Indies InDesign

DEDICATION

To Wendi and her fecking swirls.

May you love each other until the end of time.

1

"Ben." My giggles carry through the kitchen. "Stop, stop," I plead as his fingers assault my stomach. "That tickles!"

His laughter is like music to my ears. "That's the point." He grasps my hips. "You need to loosen up some."

My body relaxes now that he isn't tickling me. He turns me around to face him, and then he cups my face in his hands.

"Ah, there it is." He grins. "Your smile. I missed it."

"I'm stressed," I defend. My eyes fall to the mess cluttering our kitchen counters. We're supposed to arrive at his mom's house for Thanksgiving in the next hour, and I've yet to finish making the pie I promised to bring.

"Don't stress," he murmurs, ghosting his hands down my cheeks. "It's just a pie."

Such a guy thing to say.

"It's not that simple," I say. There's no point trying to explain it to him since he won't understand.

"Is this another one of your crazy notions where you think you need some kind of approval from my mom?"

I frown. Maybe he does understand.

"Babe." He lifts me onto the counter. "My mom loves

you, and you know that. You're already part of the family." He nuzzles my neck. "I mean, we're getting married in three months. You have nothing to prove."

"I know." I frown and duck my head so he can't see my eyes.

He notices and grabs my chin, forcing my head up. "Obviously you don't, or you wouldn't be going to this much trouble. We can pick up a pie at Wal-Mart or something. They're always open."

I gasp, flummoxed that he'd suggest such a thing. "We can't bring a store bought pie."

He chuckles. "No one will know the difference."

I smack his arm lightly. "Oh, yes they will, and if they don't, then I'll know."

"Okay, okay," he says, hanging his head in mock-shame. The dimples in his cheeks appear, making him look more boyish than normal.

Ben exudes boy-next-door with his all-American good looks—blond hair, blue eyes, charming smile—and while I admit that his looks are what attracted me to him in the first place, it was his heart that made me stay. I'd never met anyone as kind and caring as Ben.

Kissing the end of my nose, he lifts me off the counter and sets me on the ground.

"We'll do it together."

I smile at that.

I know that attempting to bake a pie with Ben will make the whole process take a whole lot longer, but I suddenly don't mind it; I know he'll make it fun.

With all the ingredients needed already strewn across the counters, I begin to boss Ben around.

We work side by side, our laughter filling the kitchen.

I look up at him, and for a moment I'm taken aback by the fact that this guy is mine. We went to high school together, but while he was the popular jock, I was the mousy band geek. Cliché, I know, but love is. We ended up at the same college and ran into each other at a local coffee shop. He recognized me, and I'd been shocked he'd known my name. From there we started hanging out—one thing led to another and we ended up together. Now, we are in our late twenties, have bought our first house together, are getting married soon, and Ben is working to complete his residency to become a doctor while I have started my party planning business.

"Blaire?" He grins at me.

I duck my head, embarrassed that he caught me staring at him.

"Blaire," he says again, this time more sternly. I feel his cool fingers on my chin and powdery flour sticks to my skin. His eyes roam over my face, almost like he's searching for something. Finally, he says, "I love you."

"I love you too," I whisper back.

He lowers his head and kisses me.

A fire ignites deep in my belly, and soon all thoughts of pie flee from my mind. His fingers dig into my hips and my body arches into his. My fingers wind into his hair, tugging him closer as his mouth dances over my lips. My insides are doing the cha-cha. Kissing Ben never gets old. Every time feels new and I swear I fall more in love with him, like his lips are tracing a road map straight to my heart.

"Fuck the pie," he growls against my lips, and I giggle. He swipes his hand behind us, knocking everything on the counter to the floor, then lifts me onto the surface once more.

He fits himself in-between my legs and presses his lips to my neck.

My head drops back, giving him more access. His fingers skim under my loose t-shirt as he lifts it up over my head and drops it to the floor.

When he looks into my eyes, his are a dark blue, heated with lust.

His mouth is on mine again and his hands are pressing into my hips, keeping me from moving.

I know I should stop him, remind him that we need to go, but I don't.

Life is about living in the moment; I know this one is about to take me to the highest form of pleasure.

Breaking his lips from mine, he bends down and jerks my yoga pants and underwear off where they join my shirt in a pile on the floor. His eyes flash with a devilish glint before his mouth latches onto me. I cry out and my back falls to the cold counter top. You'd think it would be uncomfortable, but if anything, the cold only adds to the pleasure he's giving me.

My eyes close, and I hold my breath as my toes curl.

Oh, yes.

"Ben," I pant. "Oh, God."

His tongue swipes against me faster, and I can feel his eyes on me even though I'm not looking at him.

I hold my breasts, pinching my nipples between my fingers

as my hips rock.

I scream out a moment later, and then his mouth is on mine quieting my cries.

As I come down from my high, he steps back and pulls off his clothes—all the while his eyes are glued to me spread out on the counter before him like a feast. He grabs a condom from one of the drawers and rolls it on before climbing onto the counter with me.

He lays me down on my back with my hair spread around me. I'm sure the dark strands are covered in flour by now, but I don't care.

He guides himself inside me and my hips rise to meet his. I touch my fingers to his stubbled cheek and rub my thumb over his plump bottom lip.

How'd I get so lucky?

He puts his hand over mine where it rests against his face, then intertwines our fingers together and pins my hand above my head. He does the same with the other.

His chest presses into mine.

Heart to heart.

He kisses me the way he makes love to me. Slow. Deep. Hard.

He lets go of my hands, and I press my palms flat against his muscled chest. They fit perfectly there, like the curvature was carved just for them.

When I come again, I wrap my arms around his neck, trying to get lost in him.

He's not far behind me, and when he comes, he cries my

name and whispers "I love you," in my ear.

We lay together on the counter—a tangled, sweaty mess. He rests his head on my chest, his ear pressed to my heart. I rub my fingers through his messy hair and roll my head to the side. I'm completely spent.

"That's my favorite sound," he breathes into the quiet.

"What is?"

"Your heartbeat." He rises and cups my face in his hand, angling my head so I'm looking at him. "Every day, I'm thankful for you; for what we have together. It's special, Blaire. Once in a lifetime."

I smile at him and let out a small laugh. "You're always at your most romantic after we have sex. I think it turns your brain to mush." I wink.

He grins, his eyes crinkling at the corners. "I'm always romantic."

"You wish." I jokingly smack his shoulder.

He brushes a piece of hair off my forehead. "Okay, so maybe not always," he agrees, "but I try."

He's right. He does. I know I'm much luckier than most women. Ben's always surprising me with my favorite flowers, gift cards for my favorite stores, books he thinks I'll enjoy, date nights, and notes.

Every day he leaves me a note inside a paper crane.

He wants to make a thousand before our wedding so he can wish for us to have happiness in all our days together. After that, he says he'll start again, because there's always another wish to be had. I hope he makes them forever. They're always the best part of my day—finding them in the random spots he's hidden them in and reading the heartfelt words he's written.

Ben kisses me quickly and slides off the counter.

I sit up as he ties off the condom and throws it away.

He lifts me down, even though I'm perfectly capable of getting down myself. We then take turns dressing each other—a few kisses stolen here or there.

We clean up the mess together and then completely forget about the pie. It's a lost cause at this point, and I resign myself to the fact that we're eating Wal-Mart pie.

We head upstairs to get ready, each taking separate showers since we know what will happen if we take one together. When my hair is clean, I blow dry it and curl the shoulder-length strands. I shake them out, trying to make the curl appear more natural.

Ben steps out of the shower and wraps a towel around his waist. His chest glistens with droplets of water, and I stare.

He chuckles and kisses my cheek as he passes.

My cheeks blossom with a red hue.

Even after seven years together he still manages to make me blush.

That's how you know he's a keeper.

I finish my hair and apply my makeup, using a smoky gray around my whiskey-colored eyes and magenta on my lips. I'm normally more subdued in my makeup choices, but I feel like being adventurous today.

Ben comes back into the bathroom dressed in a pair of slim-fitting jeans and a maroon-colored sweater. He steps up to the other sink to try to tame his wavy hair.

Leaving him to finish up in front of the mirror, I move out of the bathroom and over to our walk-in closet.

I step into a pair of dark-wash jeans and pull an oatmeal-colored sweater over my head then add some bracelets to my wrists and my large gold watch. I opt for a pair of chestnut colored boots to dress up the look more.

By the time I step out of the closet, Ben has finished in the bathroom and is sitting on our bed waiting for me. Our Siamese cat, Winnie, sits on the bed beside him. She gives me a murderous look. I don't know why, but that cat has always hated me.

I pick up my purse and fluff my hair.

Ben stretches and stands from the bed.

"Ready?" he asks, looking me over.

I nod. "Yes, but knowing me I'm probably forgetting something."

"Pie." He winks.

My blush returns, and I duck my head. I'll never think of pie in the same way ever again.

We head downstairs and we each shrug into our coats. Ben locks up behind us, and then hurries to open the passenger door on his Mazda SUV for me.

"Thank you." I smile graciously and slide inside.

He jogs around the front of the car to get in the driver's side.

His blond hair sticks up from his brief jog, and I reach over to smooth it down. He smiles at me in appreciation.

He drives over to the local Wal-Mart and I sit in the car while he goes inside to get the pie. I feel bad that there are people working on the holiday when they should be with their families. It doesn't seem fair.

Ben returns a few minutes later with a pecan and apple pie. Surprisingly, they don't look that bad. He sits them in the back and starts the car.

"Ready?" He waggles his brows.

I laugh and smooth my hair back. "You bet."

An hour later, he parks in the driveway of his mom's house. It's a decent size, Cape Cod style, with white siding and red shutters. A porch wraps around the front.

My parents used to live a few neighborhoods away, but when I left for college, they decided to pack up and move to Florida. I can't blame them since lately the Virginia winters have been brutal.

Ben slips from the car and grabs the plastic bag. He meets me at my side of the car and entwines our fingers together. He smiles down at me so big that his dimples make an appearance.

"Next Thanksgiving we'll be husband and wife," he says.

I smile as my stomach is flooded with warmth at the thought.

Ben. My husband. I love the sound of that. I feel like I've been waiting forever to call him that. He proposed to me our senior year of college, and I was the genius that decided it would be best to postpone the wedding until his residency was complete or close to it. I regret that now. I should've made him my husband a long time ago, but the day is fast approaching.

"Why do you want to marry me?" I ask him in jest.

He pauses on the porch and looks down at me. "Because I love you."

"Good answer." I lean up on my tiptoes to kiss him.

He rings the doorbell, and the door swings open a second later.

"Benjamin," his mom cries, throwing her arms around his neck.

Even though we live close, we rarely get to see his mom or his brother, Jacob, and his family. We're both too busy with work, especially Ben.

His mom lets him go and pulls me into a hug. Loraine has always treated me like the daughter she never had, and for that, I'm thankful. Sometimes I go overboard trying to please her, like with the pie, even when I don't have to.

"Come in, come in." She steps back to let us inside. "It's cold outside."

Almost immediately, Ben is attacked by his six-year-old niece, Bella, and two-year-old nephew, Jackson.

"Hey, guys." He bends to hug them. "I've missed you guys."

I smile. Seeing Ben with his niece and nephew always melts my heart.

"Mom, take the pies before they get squished." He holds

out his hand with the bag.

She takes it and chuckles when she looks in the bag. "I think it's a bit too late for that."

Ben sighs. "Well, we'll all know they were squished with love." He picks each of the kids up in an arm and cries, "To the kitchen," before running with them down the hall. The children's laughter trails behind them and my smile widens.

"How have you been?" Loraine asks me.

"Good." I shrug. "Busy with the business. It's taking off."

"That's amazing, Blaire. I'm so proud of you." She beams. "How's Ben? Is he getting enough sleep? I worry about him working these crazy shifts," she rambles.

I frown slightly. "He's doing okay, I guess. They're taking a toll, but he doesn't complain. This is what he wants to do, and it's part of the job."

She nods. "Still, it's hard on a person."

"It is," I agree.

With a sigh, her shoulders fall like she has accepted defeat to the situation. "I just put everything out on the table before you guys arrived. I hope you're hungry."

"Starving," I tell her.

She smiles up at me and then moves on into the kitchen with the pies to sit them on the counter. Everyone is gathered around the counter eating from a vegetable plate.

Bella runs over to me then and wraps her arms around my legs. "Aunt Blaire, look." She points to an empty gap in her teeth. "I lost a tooth and the tooth fairy came. She left me five whole dollars."

"Wow," I say, bending down to her level, "that's awesome, Bells."

Her nose crinkles when she smiles and she hold her hands together while swaying slightly. "Daddy said I could buy a candy bar." She frowns and adds in a whisper, "But mommy said that will rot my teeth." She looks torn. "I really love candy, though."

"Maybe you can get a piece of candy and not eat it all at once?" I suggest.

Her lips purse as she thinks this over. "I can live with that."

"Dining room, everyone." Loraine begins ushering us into the space.

Ben's brother sits at the head of the table, with his wife and kids to his right. Loraine sits on his left and Ben and I take our spots beside her.

We bow our heads to say grace and then Jacob stands to carve the turkey. While he's doing that, Bella begins to rattle off facts about Thanksgiving and the Pilgrims that she's learned in school. Once the turkey is carved we pass around the food in a circle until everyone's plates are full.

A glass of water already sits beside my plate, but I decide to pour a glass of wine.

"I'll have some too," Ben says and takes the bottle from me when I finish.

"No drinking and driving." Loraine points her fork at him and her eyes narrow. "House rules."

"But, Ma—"

"No buts," she counters.

Ben shrugs and takes a sip of wine. "Fine."

She smiles.

Knowing Ben, he won't drink any more than the glass, and it'll be worn off by the time we'd leave, but I can tell Loraine wants us to stay. I feel bad. Her kids are grown and gone, and while Jacob and his family live nearby, they're usually busy. She substitutes at the local high school some to pass the time, but I know she gets lonely.

"This is delicious, Loraine," I say, taking a bite of homemade macaroni and cheese.

"Thank you." She smiles.

"How's it goin' at the hospital?" Jacob asks Ben around a mouthful of food.

"Manners." His wife, Melinda, smacks him softly in the arm. "You're worse than our children."

Jacob makes a dramatic show of swallowing his food and smiles at her. "Better?"

She nods, and I can tell she's trying not to smile.

"It's good," Ben answers him, bringing a bite of turkey to his mouth.

"I don't know how you do it." Jacob shakes his head.

Ben shrugs. "It's my passion. I like helping people."

Jacob grins and shakes his head. "You're something else, Ben."

"Hey, Mr. Big Shot Lawyer, look who's talking."

Jacob chuckles. "True."

Melinda turns to me. "One of my friends has a baby shower coming up, I told her you're the best party planner around, so I'm sure she'll contact you soon."

"That would be great." I nod. "I can give you some of my business cards too."

"Oh, that would be perfect," she replies.

Bella and Jackson begin to argue over a roll and Melinda sighs before interjecting and breaking up their fight.

I smile despite their bickering. I'm happy here, with Ben and his family. It feels like home.

2

The house grows quiet without Jacob and his family there.

Thanksgiving was a raging success, even if the pie was from Wal-Mart.

Loraine flicks off the hall light, and Ben and I look up from where we rest on the couch.

"I'm going to bed," she says, her hand on the railing of the steps. "I'm exhausted."

Ben yawns and rubs my shoulder. "I think we're going to head up soon, too, Mom. Goodnight."

"Goodnight," I echo.

"Night," she says and we watch as she goes upstairs.

I lean into Ben and he wraps his arm around me. The light from the TV screen flickers across us. An antique Corvette appears on the screen and a bunch of old guys begin bidding. My eyes widen with the increasing price. When the car is sold for over seventy-five thousand, my mouth drops open.

"For a car," I cry incredulously. "That's practically a down payment on a house."

Ben chuckles and his thumb rubs soothing circles against my arm. "It's a collector's item, babe."

I wrinkle my nose. Collector's item or not, I would never spend that much on a car.

Another car is brought out and with it my lids begin to lower. Ben might be fascinated by this, but it's one big snooze fest for me. I stretch out on the couch and rest my head on his leg. He rubs his fingers through my hair and then rests them against my neck where he begins to massage it. I'm pretty sure I start to purr like a cat.

Before I completely fall asleep, he turns off the TV and I sit up.

"You look tired," he comments.

"Thanks," I reply sarcastically.

He chuckles. "I didn't mean that in a bad way."

"I'm pretty sure there's no way to say that and have it sound good."

He ducks his head. "Okay, you're right. I take it back."

"Nope, too late now." I stand and frown at him. I'm not upset about the comment at all, but this is how we are. Always messing with each other.

He takes my hand, and with puppy dog eyes, says, "Tell me how I can make it up to you."

I shake my head. "You can't make this better, Benjamin Carter."

He winces. "The whole name. That hurts. Gunshot straight to the chest."

I press my lips together to suppress my laugh. "You deserve it."

He dives at me suddenly, and I squeal when he picks me up

and I land over his shoulder. "And you deserve this." He slaps my ass and jogs up the steps carrying me.

I laugh so hard that tears fall from my eyes. "Ben, put me down!" I plead.

"Shhh—" he smacks my ass again "—my mom's sleeping."

I slam a hand over my mouth, mortified that I forgot about his mom.

Ben opens the door to his childhood bedroom and drops me onto the bed.

His room is painted a shade of blue that almost looks gray and the walls are littered with posters of sports figures and trophies. His old helmet from high school football sits on a shelf along with other memorabilia from that time period. Basically, his room is a time travel to the decade before.

His bedspread is a navy blue, but the best part is his sheets covered in footballs. They make me laugh every time I see them.

Ben stares down at me and there's a glint in his eyes. One that tells me I'm in trouble in the best possible way. He lowers, covering my body with his, and I shiver.

"You're a bad girl."

I raise a brow. "Am I?"

"The worst." He grins and kisses me. I melt into the kiss, but just as quickly as he started it, he ends it. He stands and declares, "Bedtime."

Jerk.

I pout. "But—"

He shakes his head and grins at me.

I stand and shrug. Fine. Two can play at this game.

I kick off my shoes and remove my sweater. I then wiggle out of my jeans, purposely swaying my hips. His eyes follow my movements and the hunger in his eyes grows.

Gotcha, I think to myself.

His Adam's apple bobs and he stares at me as I stand in only a tiny pair of black lace panties and matching bra. It isn't my normal sleeping attire since I hadn't planned on us staying the night, but it is certainly doing its job in tantalizing Ben.

"Goodnight," I say with a grin and pull back the covers on his bed, slipping beneath them. I purposely pull them all the way up, hiding my body.

Ben's eyes darken and a second later he pulls back the covers. I lie almost completely exposed on his bed and blink up at him.

"Ben?" I say, fighting a winning grin.

He jumps onto the bed over me and I giggle but quickly quiet my sounds. The bed bounces and he holds himself above me.

"I love you even if you drive me crazy," he growls, pressing his lips to my neck.

"Love is crazy."

He kisses me. "That's true."

He presses his lips together, almost nervously.

"Ben?" I prompt after a moment when he says nothing.

"I want to talk to you about something." He rolls off of me and settles onto the bed beside me.

"Okay?" I question, his nerves making me nervous.

He smooth's his fingers over my cheek and his eyes flicker to mine. "You're going to think I'm crazy."

"Ben," I plead, "you're killing me here."

My mind is running through a million different scenarios.

He's being transferred to another hospital and we need to move.

He wants to postpone the wedding.

He doesn't want to marry me at all.

He—

"I want to have a baby."

My mind stops—completely shuts down.

"What?" I gasp. A baby? I couldn't have possibly heard him right. We've talked about kids, but always said we'd have our first child a few years after we were married.

"I know, I know," he says, almost like he's reading my thoughts, "this isn't what we talked about. But it feels right, don't you think?" Before I can respond, he continues, "We're going to be married soon, and people say it usually takes a few tries to actually get pregnant, so I think we should start."

He looks at me with big, earnest, blue eyes. "B-But our plan. My business. Your residency. Nothing is complete yet."

"But it will be," he says, toying with a piece of my hair. "I want us to have a family. Don't you want that? What if it takes a while? What if we're one of those couples that has to go an alternate route? Wouldn't you rather know now and not when we're in our thirties?"

I sit up and press my fingers to my temples. "You're freaking me out," I tell him.

It's not that having a baby is a bad thing. I want kids, but I've always been someone that's terrified of the unknown.

"Blaire." He takes my face in his hands and forces me to look at him. "Breathe. Just breathe. If you want to wait, we will." His tongue slips out to moisten his lips. "Just think about it, okay?"

I nod. "I will."

As I settle back on the bed in his arms, the idea of a baby lying between us doesn't seem so bad. Ben will be an amazing dad; it's me as a mom that scares me.

3

We arrive home a little after ten in the morning the next day and Ben immediately has to leave for the hospital. After a quick peck on my lips, he's gone for a twenty-four shift. It sucks that he has to leave so soon, but I can't be too glum since he had the holiday off; I know we won't always be that lucky.

Which brings me back to the topic of a baby.

Can I handle raising a baby right now with Ben gone most of the time? I think I can, but thinking and knowing are two different things. What scares me the most isn't that, though—I'm more afraid of losing everything I've worked so hard to build the last few years. My business is only beginning to take off and a baby might halt that—if it did, would I resent Ben or the child? I don't think so.

All my jumbling of thoughts keeps circling back to the same thing: I think we can do this.

It won't be easy—but it won't be easy to have a baby on our hands a few years from now—however, since he brought it up, every time I come up with a negative against having a baby right now, I can't help but see one in my arms and suddenly I want that. I yearn for that little piece of us. It's crazy, completely nuts, but I think—no, I know—I'm going to tell him I'm ready.

Since I'm still wearing the same clothes from yesterday, I decide to take a shower and then tackle our ever-growing pile of laundry. Ben and I might be adults, but we're not always the best at the whole adulting thing—resulting in piles of dirty laundry and dishes. The house wouldn't even be that clean if we didn't have someone come in twice a month to vacuum and dust.

It takes me a while to catch up on the household chores and when I'm done I make a peanut butter and jelly sandwich for lunch.

It's quiet in the house—too quiet—so I end up turning on some music. Almost immediately, I begin to sway my hips to the beat. I can't seem to help myself. Soon, I'm dancing through the house, singing at the top of my lungs.

Winnie watches me with shrewd blue eyes. She doesn't approve of my silliness. Most cats are like that, though—so judgmental.

Even though I don't have to work today, I find myself in my home office. Most people would probably say their office is their least favorite place to me. Not for me—it's my happy place.

Three of the walls are painted white, except for the focal wall, which has white and black stripes. It adds sophistication to the room. My desk sits in the middle of the room and is solid black, made out of some glossy material, and my chair is fluffy and white. There are a few black bookshelves, filled with books, files, and other odds and ends. One of my favorite pieces in the room is the wooden swing hanging from the ceiling. Ben surprised me with it because I was always complaining about how I needed to be moving to think clearly. Whenever I was stumped with how to pull together an event, or I just needed a breather, I would sit on the swing and let all my thoughts disappear.

Right now, I bypass the swing and took a seat at my desk. I begin answering emails—mostly inquiries about pricing—and then bring up my design board for an event I am currently working on; a birthday party being thrown by a daughter for her mom's fiftieth birthday. The daughter gave me very strict instructions, stating that her mom is conservative and won't want anything outlandish. I have a feeling this is going to be one of the harder events to plan. Even though it is the daughter throwing it as a surprise, I've already picked up on her opinionated tendencies, and I figure she'll be one of those clients that likes to change their mind at the last minute. I'm not complaining, though, and I'm up for the challenge. Life is boring if it's easy.

I call it quits a few hours later and decide to watch a movie—but not before popping some popcorn, that's a must. I dump the overly-buttery popcorn into a large mixing bowl and call for Winnie to join me. She hisses from her perch on the dining room table, jumps off, and runs under the couch. I wish I knew what I did to piss her off so badly.

I sit down on the gray sectional and tug the cream, sweater-material, blanket onto my lap before setting down the popcorn bowl. Winnie hisses again from beneath the couch—I guess because I moved the blanket and blocked her view.

I turn on the TV and hit the button that starts the DVD player. I already have the movie in there from a previous day where I didn't get to watch it completely. The movie comes on and I start it over.

Winnie eases out from beneath the couch—I know because I feel the blanket move.

"Come on, Winnie. Get up here," I coax. "I have popcorn."

Winnie loves popcorn.

I get a hiss in response.

Apparently she only loves popcorn when Ben is feeding it to her.

My phone chimes on the coffee table so I pause the movie to check it. I stupidly think that it might be Ben, but instead, my best friend's name appears on the screen.

Casey: Lnch with the girls 2morrow? And Ben?

Me: Sure. Ben's working tho.

Casey: 2 bad. Bean & Gone at 12?

Me: Yeah, I've been craving their avocado sandwich.

Casey: Weirdo.

Me: :P

I set the phone back on the table and resume the movie. I find my eyes growing heavy, and soon, I fall asleep.

By the time I wake up, it's late and I've missed dinner.

I sit up and rub my eyes as my stomach growls angrily. Winnie is nowhere to be seen and the movie is back to the start screen. I sigh. Maybe one day I'll actually watch the movie the whole way through.

I stand and stretch before making my way into the kitchen. I don't feel like making anything outlandish so I end up grabbing a box of Mini Wheats and pouring a heaping pile into a bowl along with too much milk. I open the utensil drawer, and immediately, I smile. I pluck the paper crane from the drawer and hold it up. My hunger forgotten, I unfold the carefully-crafted origami bird.

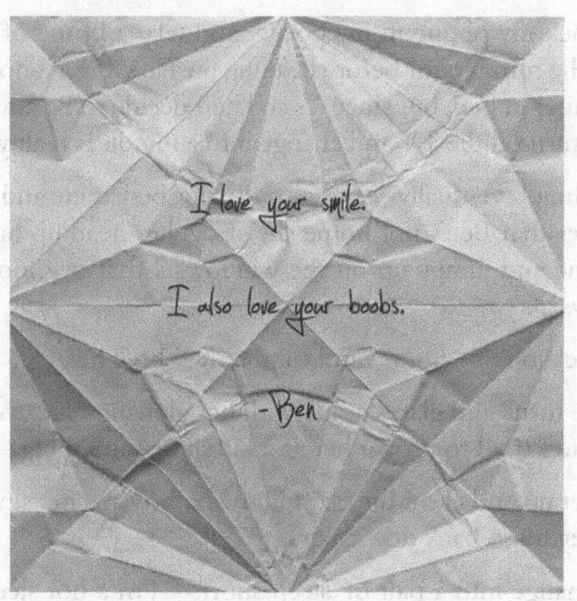

I laugh and shake my head. The things he writes in the notes vary from romantic, to silly, to completely sappy. I love each and every one, though.

I fold the note back up into the shape of the crane and add it to the large glass vase in the foyer. I don't know why I started collecting them in the vase, but it makes a pretty display. I also can't help but feel my heart flood with love and affection whenever I pass it. I'm as much as a love-sick fool as he is, but the fact that we're still that way gives me hope. We haven't always had it easy—with school, jobs, and too much of a workload—but we've been able to withstand every storm thrown our way, so I have no doubt that we'll continue to do so.

I grab a spoon and my bowl, frowning at the now soggy cereal.

Oh, well.

I tuck my phone in my pocket and take a bottle of water from the refrigerator before heading upstairs. I don't normally eat dinner in bed, but since it's so late I decide to be adventurous. I turn on the TV and change it to a mindless reality show.

Winnie eventually wanders into the bedroom and when she sees that Ben's not home she sticks her head up haughtily at me and jumps up on the windowsill that overlooks the front yard.

"He won't be home until tomorrow," I tell her.

She turns and glares at me with her glowing blue eyes. She acts like I tried to drown her as a kitten or something.

I get up and clean the bowl in the bathroom sink since I'm too lazy to go back downstairs.

I change into a pair of sleep shorts—I'm a hot sleeper—and one of Ben's old school shirts. It's gray and so worn you can nearly see through it, but I love it. He's tried to throw it away, but I won't let him.

I turn off the lights, but leave the TV on for the time being. I'm one of those people; when I'm by myself I start imagining all sorts of creepy things—like some man living under the bed waiting to eat me, or something else equally as silly.

Winnie moves from the windowsill to the doorway and lies down, making this displeased harrumph of a noise.

I settle beneath the mountains of blankets, and I drift off to sleep.

I wake up early, a little after six, and pad downstairs to make myself a cup of coffee. I grab my laptop and sit with it at the kitchen island. I'm all caught up on work emails, but there's a pile of junk mail waiting for me. Delete. Delete. Delete.

I hate how quiet it is in the house when it's only me, so I turn on the TV to a news station and let it play softly in the background.

I don't have anything important to do this morning since it's Saturday, and I still have hours until I meet the girls for lunch, so I end up grabbing a book, one of those historical romances with the woman draped over a guy and her bosom on display. As cheesy as the covers might be, I can't help but love these books.

I settle on the couch and begin to read. Ben makes fun of me for my love of historical romances, but there's just something about them.

The sun is up now and I make myself a quick breakfast before showering. I don't feel like doing much with my hair so I end up styling it in a messy bun. A few short pieces of hair fall around my face. Keeping my makeup simple with eyeliner, mascara, and a nude lip., I move to the closet to dress in a pair of black jeans, a loose white top, and my army-green jacket. It's fairly warm out, so I'm not worried about being too cold.

I'm slipping my feet into a pair of brown boots when I hear the front door open.

From the closet, I can see Winnie jump from the windowsill and run from the room.

Ben's home.

I grab my purse and head downstairs to find Ben rummaging through the refrigerator. He grabs the bottle of orange juice, unscrews the cap, and lifts it to his lips.

"Hey," he says when he sees me, and smiles bashfully knowing I caught him drinking from the bottle. It's a pet peeve of mine but I can't be mad when he's so exhausted. His eyes boast dark circles beneath, but despite that, he's grinning.

"Hey." I smile at him and stand on my tiptoes to kiss his dimpled cheek. "I'm meeting the girls for lunch. They wish you could come."

Ben grins. "It's because I'm hilarious, right?"

I pat his chest. "You wish. Your jokes suck."

He puts a hand over his heart. "You wound me, babe."

"Actually—" I twirl past him "—I think they keep hoping one day you'll show up with some hot doctor friends."

Ben laughs loudly and his eyes sparkle. "Is that so?"

"It's a hunch." I shrug. "I made you something to eat." I point to a plate, give him a kiss, and say, "Get some rest."

He nods and stifles a yawn.

I start for the door and turn back to him. "You look good in those scrubs." I wink and then cup my hands like I'm squeezing his ass.

He throws his head back and laughs. "I love you, Blaire."

"Love you," I say. "Oh, and Ben?" I linger in the doorway, suddenly feeling nervous. He looks up from the plate of food he's uncovering. "Yes."

"Yes?" His brows furrow in confusion. Before I can elaborate his eyes widen with clarity. "Yes, yes? You want to have a baby?"

I nod.

He rushes to me, and before I can blink, I'm in his arms and he's spinning me around. His lips latch onto mine and he kisses me like I'm the ocean and he's the moon. His lips taste of orange juice and the promise of great things to come.

He sets me down and holds my face between his hands. "Yeah? We're doing this?" He grins so big that both his dimples pop out in his cheeks. He suddenly doesn't look so tired. Just happy. So happy.

I nod and smile. "Yeah, we are." He kisses me again. "I thought about what you said," I continue, "and you're right. It usually takes a while to get pregnant, and our wedding is so soon—"

He cuts me off with yet another kiss. "I love you," he whispers, his eyes glimmering. "Let's start right now." He sweeps my legs out from under me.

"Ben." I laugh and push at his chest. "I have to go and you need to go to bed."

"Oh, right." He sets me down. "Later." He waggles his brows.

I pick up my fallen purse and lift it to my shoulder. "I'll see you later."

Ben kisses my cheek and disappears into the kitchen.

I hop into my Honda Civic and drive over to the coffee shop. I'm late, but not by much. Despite that, I'm still the last to arrive.

"Blaire, you're always late," Casey calls when I breeze into the shop. Bless her, she's already ordered my coffee and sandwich.

"I'm sorry, Ben came home as I was leaving and we were

talking."

"Aw, did you tell him to come?" she asks as I take a seat.

I hold the coffee mug between my fingers. "He just got off of a twenty-four-hour shift, he needed to sleep."

"Oh, right." She shakes her head. "Blond moment." She waves off the words like they're nothing. I find it funny since Casey is one of the smartest people I know and on the fast track to becoming one of our state's most powerful defense attorneys. "Anyway, how were the holidays, ladies?" She lifts her mug of coffee to her lips and takes a dainty sip.

"My brother and his girlfriend were totally doing it in the bathroom before dinner." Hannah wrinkles her nose. "It was gross."

Chloe snorts and sweeps her glossy dark hair over one shoulder. "If I was dating your brother I'd want to sex him up all the time."

"Ew." Hannah cringes. "He's my brother. I don't need to hear this."

"Your hot brother," Chloe and Casey say simultaneously.

Hannah looks to me for help. I shrug and sip my coffee innocently. "He is hot."

"Ugh," she groans. "You all suck."

"Didn't he model for Abercrombie once?" Chloe asks, leaning toward Hannah like she wants to soak up every word.

Hannah frowns. "Once, when he was eighteen."

"You don't model for Abercrombie if you're not ungodly hot. It's a fact," Chloe argues.

Hannah sighs. "You guys should start calling me, That-

Girl-Hannah-With-The-Hot-Brother."

Casey snorts. "It has a nice ring to it."

"Rolls right off the tongue." I laugh.

"You guys are taking me right back to my high school days." Hannah sighs, staring down into her mug of chai tea.

"Oh, stop it." Casey takes a bite of her blueberry muffin. "You're the one that brought it up."

Hannah blanches. "Nope, I'm pretty sure you guys brought up his supposed hotness all on your own."

"It's not supposed, honey—" Casey pats Hannah's hand "—it's the truth."

Hannah rolls her eyes and tucks a piece of strawberry-blond hair behind her ear. "How was your Thanksgiving?" she asks me.

"Good," I say with a smile. "It was nice seeing Ben's family."

"That's all we get?" Casey raises a brow.

I laugh. "There's not much to tell. My Thanksgiving was more low-key than Hannah's. Less banging around," I joke.

Hannah sighs. "You're as bad as them."

"Well, my Thanksgiving was a nightmare." Chloe leans forward and lowers her voice like she's letting us in on a secret. "My mom burnt the turkey, I dropped the pie on the floor, and my sister caught her hair on fire."

"What?" I gasp. "How'd she catch her hair on fire?"

"Candle." Chloe shakes her head forlornly. "I don't think she'll ever go near a candle again. The poor girl is traumatized."

"I would be too," Casey says.

"How was your Thanksgiving?" I ask Casey.

Her lips thin into a straight line. "Fine."

We all stare at her. "Fine?" I question. "That doesn't sound good."

Casey sighs. "James," she begins, referring to her boyfriend, "spent the whole day on his phone answering emails, which means I was left to endure his insufferable mother all on my own. The woman is insane." She adds when we laugh, "I'm not kidding."

"That's what you get for dating another lawyer," I tell her. "There's only room for one in a household. I think there's some sort of rule for that or something."

She frowns and brushes crumbs off the table. "You might be on to something."

"I take it this means there's trouble in paradise?" Chloe prompts before taking a bite of her sandwich—I'm currently devouring mine like someone is about to come along and snatch it from my hands.

Casey nods. "I don't think he's the one. He's not my Ben."

I choke on my sandwich, practically coughing up a lung. "What does that mean?"

"Nothing bad." She waves a hand dismissively. "I just meant that you guys are perfect for each other. I've never been around another couple like you guys before. You're kind of magical to watch because you're both so in tune with each other. It's like you're soulmates or something."

"Soulmates," I snort, "yeah, right."

Hannah nods. "No, she's right. You guys are…" Her lips twist in thought. "Special."

I laugh. "And you guys are nuts."

"Are we?" Casey asks. "Come on, I've known you forever, B. You had like two serious boyfriends before Ben and you never had the kind of relationship with them that you do with Ben. It's different—rare."

I shake my head, but there is truth to their words. Ben and I are different. It's funny how perfect we are for each other, but I also believe timing is everything. We went to the same high school but I think if we'd been together then, it wouldn't have lasted. Sometimes you have to find the patience to wait for good things instead of seeking it out.

We finish our lunch and agree to meet up next week. It's sort of our thing to meet up at the local coffee shop every week and catch up. Ben joins us when he can—we all went to school together so it's not like he's the odd man out.

I end up running a few errands while I'm out. When I arrive home it's practically dinner time. I park in the driveway and notice that there aren't any lights on. I frown. I hope Ben isn't still sleeping. He likes to sleep for a few hours, then get up, and go back to bed at a regular time.

I lock my car and head inside with my few shopping bags.

When I open the front door I notice a few dim lights flickering from the area of the family room.

"Ben?" I call out hesitantly, stepping further into the room. I don't know why, but I suddenly feel like the dumb girl in a horror movie who is about to get her head chopped off while the people in the audience yell about what an idiot she is. I set my bags down by the stairs and round the corner into the family. "Ben," I gasp.

He's pushed the coffee table out of the way and the fluffy rug in the center of the room is covered in what looks like every pillow we have in the house. The flickering lights come from all the candles he has lit. Tall candles, short candles, fat candles, skinny candles: every kind of candle you can imagine. The effect is a glittering kaleidoscope of orange flames.

Ben sits in the center of the pillows, holding a bottle of wine and two glasses. There's a plate with cheese, crackers, and fruit beside him.

"What's this?" I ask, kicking off my shoes and stepping onto the pillows. I stumble and fall, which makes us both laugh. I end up crawling the rest of the way over to him. When I'm beside him, he finally answers.

"I'm trying to woo you."

I snort. "Woo me? I'm pretty sure you already do that?" I point to the glittering princess-cut diamond on my finger.

He shrugs. "The wooing should never end. It's my job to always show you I love you."

I smile at him. "And what's my job?" I take the glass from him and he pours a little wine into it and his before re-corking the bottle and setting it aside.

He grins and my beloved dimple winks from his cheek. "Just to love me."

"I already do," I tell him, taking a sip of wine.

He leans over and kisses my cheek, then nuzzles his face into my neck. I feel his lips against my skin, when he says, "Then be happy."

"I am happy." I twine my fingers in his thick hair and he tilts his head back to me. "I've never been happier," I tell him honestly. "Things aren't always easy. You're tired and busy with work and so am I. There's the stress of bills, and life, but at the end of the day I'm thankful, and that's what matters. I wouldn't trade our life for anything."

He nips playfully at my chin before sitting back. "To us." He clinks his glass to mine.

"To us," I echo. "Now, tell me, what is this really all about?"

He ducks his head and smiles almost bashfully. "You said you were ready to try to have a baby—" he sweeps his hand wide "—and this is me trying to be romantic."

I raise my glass to my lips to try to hide my growing smile. "So you're not going to fuck me on the kitchen island this time?"

He groans and his blue eyes darken. "You know it turns me on when you say fuck."

I laugh. "I don't know why. It's a word."

"Yeah," he agrees, "but you never say it, and when you do your voice always goes really husky and sultry."

"Is that so?" I reach for a cracker and cheese, popping it into my mouth. He nods. "What else turns you on?"

"When we're having sex and you say my name. You say it so breathless and desperate. And when you lick your lips like that." He points at me and my tongue quickly darts back inside my mouth from where I'd been licking away cracker crumbs. My cheeks redden. "And that." He sweeps his thumb over my cheek. "I like that even after all these years I can still make you blush." He lies back, propping his body up on his elbow. "Now tell me, what turns you on?" I duck my head.

"Don't get shy on me now, Blaire," he scolds.

I swallow thickly. I don't know why I always find these kinds of things uncomfortable to talk about. Ben and I share pretty much everything. "I get really turned on when you're rougher…possessive, like you can't get enough of me. Like in the kitchen the other day. Don't get me wrong," I hasten to add, "I like slow and sweet, too. But sometimes there's this look in your eyes like you want to devour me, and I love it."

He reaches for my hand. "Don't be embarrassed."

"I'm not." I am.

He chuckles. "What else turns you on?" he asks again, going after me the way I did him.

I shrug. "You. Everything about you, really."

He smiles and his eyes twinkle. "Elaborate."

"I don't know how to explain it, but even when we're doing simple things—like cooking dinner together—I find myself so turned on and just…lucky to have you."

He sits up and takes my chin between his thumb and forefinger. "I'm lucky to have you, too."

I lean my head on his chest and listen to the steady pounding of his heart. My eyes close and I breathe in the unique scent that is Ben—clean laundry and hints of oak. I feel his fingers smooth through my hair and I inhale a small breath.

I pull away and Ben slides the plate in-between us. He picks up a chocolate-dipped strawberry and holds it out to me. Opening my mouth, he feeds it to me.

I moan—I totally don't mean to, but I do.

When I open my eyes and lick away a bit of the juice, I find that Ben is staring at me with darkened, lust-filled eyes.

Before I can blink, his lips are on mine and the food is scattered around us.

We both move frantically, tearing at each other's clothes like maniacs. We're a clash of hands, teeth, and quiet gasps. His skin is heated beneath my palms, and his lips taste like the wine. He kisses his way down my body and rids me of my jeans. They join the pile with my shirt and bra and his shirt. Luckily, even in our haste, we remember the candles and didn't toss our clothes around haphazardly.

He hooks his fingers into the sides of my panties and slides them down. He stares at me with wide eyes, like he's never seen anything more beautiful, and what's more is he makes me feel beautiful.

His large hands settle on my legs and he bends his head, kissing my inner thigh. I mumble something unintelligible. I'm not even aware of what I'm trying to say.

He makes his way back up my body, paying special attention to my breasts and his fingers find their way to my pussy.

"Fuck, you're so wet," he growls.

"Kiss me," I beg, tugging on his shoulders. He obliges.

The kiss starts out slow and then deepens. His tongue swipes against mine and he makes this rumbling sound in his chest that makes me clench around his fingers.

He slides his fingers out and rids himself of his jeans and boxers.

When he slides into me I have a brief moment of panic that he forgot a condom, and then I realize that's the whole point. Trying to have a baby equals no condom.

He holds my hips up at an angle that allows him in deeper. I moan so loud that the whole neighborhood probably hears me.

"Yes, right there," I plead, my fingers sliding weakly down his abs.

He leans forward and kisses me. "So good," he murmurs.

"Oh God," I moan. I feel like a firework about to go off. "Almost there."

When I come, my nails dig into his back, like I'm trying to hold onto him to keep from floating away.

He presses his lips to my neck. "Beautiful," he whispers so low that I wonder if I imagined him saying the word.

He cups my breast and rolls his thumb over my nipple. I can already feel myself building back up when he pulls out. I'm pretty sure I whimper like a kicked puppy.

But then he flips me over and slides in from behind.

"Yes," I pant, "fuck yes."

He rumbles at the word fuck.

"I-I'm gonna come again," I breathe out each word.

When I do, Ben comes only a moment later and we both collapse onto the pillows. He pulls my spent body on top of his, and I drape my limbs across him, my eyes growing heavy. That was amazing, albeit exhausting.

I feel his fingers skim over my arm. "Do you think we made a baby?" he asks softly.

I force my tired eyes open and peek up at him. "I don't know. I guess we'll know soon."

He nods. "I hope we did." He kisses me quickly.

I nod and snuggle closer to him. "Me too."

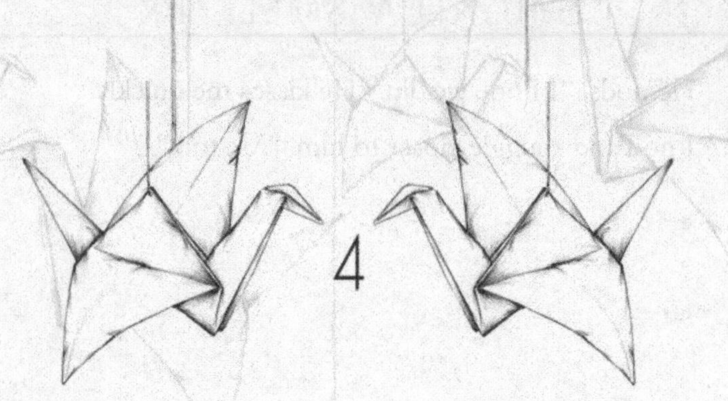

4

I'm late. Only by a few days, but my period is never late.

Ben is sitting on the bed when I walk into the room with the plastic-wrapped box. When I told him my period was late this morning he nearly jumped out of his skin for me to take a test. I'd been putting it off, waiting for the proverbial shoe to drop—in this case, for my period to start. I didn't feel pregnant, but then again maybe you didn't feel any certain way this soon. It wasn't like I'd ever been pregnant before and none of my friends were having babies.

"Hurry up," he says, bouncing on the bed like an excited kid.

"I just got here," I remind him, walking into the bathroom. He follows me and I mock-glare at him. "Back to the room with you, buddy. You're not watching me pee."

He pouts. "Please, this is a monumental moment in our lives."

"Out." I point back at the bedroom. "We won't see any results for a few minutes so there's no reason for you to be in here."

He sighs and leaves me alone.

"You know," he says through the door, "if you're pregnant, that would be the best Christmas present ever."

"Christmas is over," I remind him.

"Not by much," he argues, "it can count."

I shake my head and ignore him as I shimmy out of my jeans and open the box.

My heart is racing a mile a minute. I've never been so excited and nervous at the same time. I feel jittery and my stomach is rolling. I unbox the magical little stick and pee. I might cry, "Hallelujah," while I'm peeing because I've been holding it for so long. When I hear Ben laugh from the bedroom I know for sure I said that out loud.

I finish up and put the cap on the end. I wash my hands and Ben knocks on the door. "Come on, Blaire. Let me in."

I unlock the door and open it, so Ben practically falls inside. I shake my head at him. "What does it say?" he asks.

"I don't know." I hop up on the counter and he stands in front of me. "It takes a few minutes." I purposely covered the screen on it with the directions so neither of us can peek.

Ben places his hands on either side of my thighs and leans forward, nuzzling his head into my neck. His stubble scrapes my skin, but I don't mind. He presses a kiss to my neck and pulls away. "But you've never been late before, right?"

"No—" I shake my head "—I haven't. But it doesn't mean this isn't a fluke."

"Do you think that night…in the family room on the pillows?" he asks, putting his hand on my stomach like he truly believes a baby is hiding in there.

"I don't know, maybe." I nervously bite my lip.

I know there's no way it happened that night, but there's no point in trying to explain my period to Ben. He might practically be a doctor but he's still a guy and there's no point wasting my breath trying to explain how a period works. Unless you have one you don't understand.

"How much longer?" he asks.

I glance at my phone. "Two minutes."

He groans. "I never knew minutes were so long."

"Me either," I agree.

We both grow quiet, waiting. Hoping. Possibly even praying.

Ben looks at me and I stare right back. We both take a breath and I knock away the papers so I can pick up the stick.

"No peeking," he warns.

I hold it out so we can both see.

I squint, but the gesture doesn't change the outcome.

It's negative.

I feel crushed. Devastated. Like I was handed a gift and then someone said, "Oh yeah, sorry, this isn't for you. I need that back."

"Blaire—"

His words come too late. I break down, a sob shaking my whole body.

"Blaire, I'm sorry." He wraps me into his warm, strong, capable arms. He kisses the top of my head. "We'll try again. We knew it probably wouldn't happen the first time anyway."

I try to tell him that I know, but I can't seem to speak around my tears. I cry into his shirt, smearing mascara all over the blue cotton. I don't even know why I'm so sad. I was more reserved about this than Ben. More time is a good thing, but it doesn't feel that way. Suddenly, I feel fearful that it's never going to happen. What if there's something wrong with me? Or him? Or both of us?

"Hey, hey, none of that." Ben forces me back and takes my face between his hands. "I know what you're thinking and there's nothing wrong. These things take time."

I nod, but more tears come. "I really thought I was pregnant," I confess on a hiccupping cry.

Ben pushes my hair away from my face. "I know, baby, I know. It's okay, though. We'll try again; that's the best part, right?" he tries to joke, but I don't feel like laughing. Or smiling.

I stare down at the white stick lying on the bathroom counter. I feel like it's a bright neon light glaring at me, crying: You're not pregnant. You're a failure.

Ben wipes my tears off of my cheeks. He looks pained, and I feel bad. I'm completely breaking down and he's trying to remain strong, even when he's as bummed as I am. I lean forward, pressing my head into his solid chest, and hold on to the sides of his shirt. I'm not crying anymore, but I need to hold onto him a moment longer.

His arms wrap around me fully and he rests his chin on the top of my head. Neither of us says a word. We don't need to.

Eventually, I pull away and lift my head to kiss him quickly.

"It's going to happen," he says with so much hope.

I hop off the counter and grab the pregnancy test to toss it, and the box, in the trashcan. It feels symbolic somehow.

"It will, Blaire." He comes up behind me and hugs my back

to his chest. “I know you’re still thinking all kinds of negative things, but it was only the first month.”

I know that our chances of getting pregnant are good, but I can’t shake this ominous cloud that seems to be forming above my head.

“It will,” I echo his words, but not with nearly as much conviction.

5

A week later I find myself standing on a podium in the dress shop for my final fitting. Casey and Ben's mom are joining me. I wish my own mom was here for this moment, but at least she'll be coming to the wedding next month.

February twentieth.

"That dress is so beautiful on you," Loraine says, dabbing at her eyes.

"I can't believe you're getting married," Casey adds. "Who let us become adults?"

I turn, admiring the dress in the mirror. It's gorgeous—everything I ever imagined for my wedding dress. The top comes up high, with thin tank-top straps, but the dress is fitted all over with a small train. The dress is covered in lace detailing and the back boasts a million tiny white buttons—okay, so not a million, but a lot.

"I don't know," I speak to Casey, "it's pretty weird."

I haven't told her that Ben and I are trying to have a baby. We haven't told his mom, either. I think we both would rather surprise everyone if it happens. When. When it happens. I'm doing my best to think positive.

"Hold still," the seamstress admonishes me.

"Sorry." I'm careful not to move.

She finishes marking the places that need adjusting and then I change out of the dress and back into my regular clothes.

When I walk back into the main room, Casey is frowning at her phone.

"Ugh, I just got a work email, I have to go." She hugs me. "I'll talk to you later. Bye." She waves at Loraine as she passes.

I pick up my purse and Loraine waits for me by the door.

We step out into the cold winter air. We'd had a mild winter, until the last week or so when Jack Frost decided we needed arctic temperatures.

Loraine loops her arm through mine and we walk down the street.

"Would you want to get lunch?" she asks, nodding at a small bistro-type place across the street.

"Sure." I shrug. "That'd be nice."

We cross the street into the restaurant. It's bigger than it looks from the outside—the interior expanding back instead of out. I've never been to this restaurant, but I've heard good things. I remember Chloe saying something about it. The walls are painted a dark shade of blue, and you'd think that would make the space seem too dark, but somehow it works. The floors are a dark wood and all the tables and chairs are in a similar color. There are splashes of golden yellow in paintings and vases used as decorations.

We're seated almost immediately and handed menus in the same deep blue as the walls with the name of the restaurant spelled out on the front in a gold cursive.

"Fancy," Loraine comments with a smile, looking around.

"It is," I agree, perusing the menu. Luckily, it doesn't appear to be outlandishly expensive.

Our waiter comes by for our drink order. I ask for water and Loraine requests a red wine.

I pick the dish I want—some fancy pasta that I have no hope of ever pronouncing—and set my menu aside.

"Thank you so much for being here today," I tell Loraine. "It means a lot since my mom can't be here." My throat grows tight. I always imagined sharing these kinds of moments with my mom, but I know my parents are much happier in Florida.

"Of course, sweetie." Loraine pats my hand where it rests on the table. "I love you like a daughter—and soon you'll be a permanent part of the family."

I smile. "It's a bit surreal."

"More like, it's about time." She snorts. "I've been waiting for you guys to get married since the first time Ben brought you home to meet me."

"Really?" My heart warms. I hear so many horror stories about mother-in-laws not getting along with their daughter-in-laws. I've never had any animosity with Loraine, but me being—well, me—I'm always a bit nervous around her.

"Really." She nods. "I know most mothers would probably be the complete opposite—not wanting to see their baby boy grow up and move on, but when I saw the way he was with you, I knew he'd found his other half, and I've been so incredibly thankful for that. I just want him to be happy and you make him happy."

Tears pool in my eyes. I dam them back. I do not want

to cry in the middle of a crowded restaurant. "He makes me happy too," I tell her.

"I know." She smiles. "And Blaire?" She waits for me to nod. "Happiness is the number one thing we should strive to have in life. Not money. Not houses or expensive cars. Happiness is true wealth."

I absorb her words. They hold so much truth. I understand that nothing means anything if you're miserable.

The waiter appears at our table with my water and Loraine's wine and takes our order before disappearing again.

Loraine taps her red painted nails against her wine glass. "It's funny," she begins, staring down into her glass like it holds all the answers in the world, "how one minute you're young with little children and then you blink and they're grown. I always thought people were dumb for saying that—I mean, you have a child and they're with you for the first eighteen or so years of their life, but they're right. They're gone in an instant."

"Loraine—" I reach for her hand.

She shakes her head and sniffles. "I'm not sad—okay, maybe a little. I'm just telling you this because I assume you and Ben are going to have kids one day and..." She looks off to the side for a moment. "Things were bad between my husband and I, more times than not, and sometimes I look back and I feel like that overshadowed moments I should've been sharing with my kids. Not that I think you and Ben would be like us," she hastens to add, "but work, and stress, can make you forget to stop and appreciate the little things. And trust me, when you get to be my age it's the little things you remember the most." A smile touches her lips. "Like this one day, the boys knew I had a rough day at work so while I was showering they made me dinner. It was only cereal, but they'd even gotten a flower from the yard and put it in a vase on the table." She shakes her head. "And it's one of my favorite memories of them now."

I smile. "That's sweet. You raised good boys, Loraine."

She nods and tears pool into her eyes. "I did, didn't I?" One tear falls to her cheek, and she wipes it away. "I don't know why I'm telling you all of this, but I guess with the wedding coming up I've been thinking about my own and the years that followed."

I get up from my seat and move around the table to hug her.

Loraine is a good woman. She's always been kind to me, and I know she's been an amazing mother to Ben and his brother. But I also know from Ben that his father wasn't always the best. He never hit her—as far as Ben knows—but he was verbally abusive and he says it was hard to watch his mom go through that. I think both boys were relieved when their parents finally split up.

Loraine hugs me back, and I feel her tears dampen my shirt.

When I pull away, she laughs and dabs at her face with her napkin. "Here I was telling you how happy I am about the wedding, and now I'm crying."

"It's okay," I assure her. "Thank you for sharing that with me."

She nods and takes a sip of her wine. "No more tears, I promise." She crosses her hands and lays them on the table. "Tell me what you have in the works for your business."

I immediately launch into the details on a big account I recently landed, planning a five-year anniversary party for a local business. I'm sure Loraine is bored by my details on colors, arrangements, food, and other things, but she doesn't show it. She listens intently and lets me drone on as our food arrives.

Finally, embarrassed, I begin to quiet. "I'm sorry," I tell her, swirling my pasta around the fork, "I'm rambling."

"Ah, no, I find it fascinating," she says. "I never had your kind of drive. I find it remarkable."

I smile. "Thanks."

We finish eating and say our goodbyes. I head home and Ben's already gone for work.

I open the front door and Winnie comes running toward me. When she sees it's me, not Ben, she immediately turns tail and runs the other way.

I shake my head and drop my keys on the entry table along with my bag.

I kick off my shoes in a haphazard pile. I'll put them away later.

I grab a bottle of water and head into my office to work. I crank up the music—I hate the silence—and go through my emails. I reply back, answering questions, and booking dates. I still can't believe how fast my business is growing. Maybe in a year or two I'll be able to run my business out of a building and not our house.

I open the side drawer of my desk and rummage through it for a new pack of sticky notes. I smile when I find a paper crane hidden among my junk drawer.

I pull it out, forgetting my search for the moment.

I unfold the note and find Ben's boyish handwriting

scrawled across the paper.

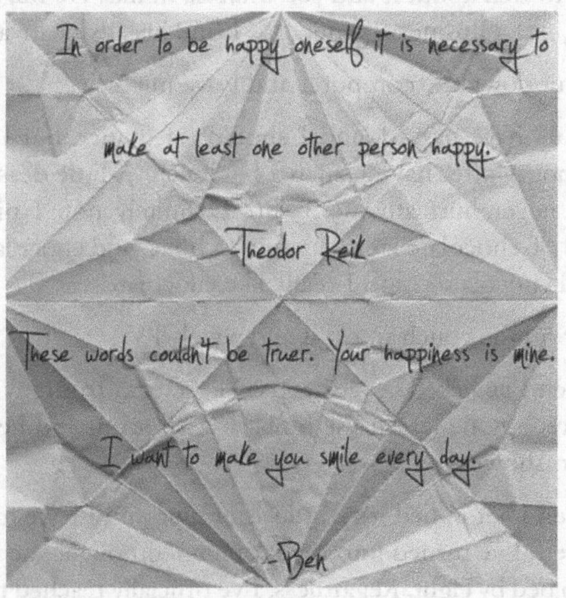
In order to be happy oneself it is necessary to make at least one other person happy.

-Theodor Reik

These words couldn't be truer. Your happiness is mine.

I want to make you smile every day.

-Ben

"You already do," I whisper, and I am, in fact, smiling. I fold the paper back into the shape of the crane and set it on the side of my desk to add to the growing pile of others. There's nearly a thousand of them already—I'm missing about fifty, though, plus the days that are left. Ben says he's written them, and they're hidden, waiting to be found. I don't make a habit of searching them out every day. I like being surprised. Sometimes I go days without finding one, and other times I find three in a day. Lately, he's getting better at hiding them from me, and that's okay; I always seem to find them when I need them most.

I finish what I'm doing and make a few phone calls. Before I even consider moving my business into a building I should probably hire an assistant. I could use one now so that I don't have to spend so much time answering emails and phone calls. It would be nice to focus solely on the planning part. I'll have to talk to Ben about it and see what he thinks. He might be a doctor, not a business owner, but I find his advice invaluable.

I shut down my computer and leave my office.

Hours have passed, and I should eat dinner, but I'm not very hungry after having such a big lunch. A little dessert for dinner never hurt anyone, right? Definitely not. I pile two scoops of chocolate ice cream into a bowl, add chocolate syrup, and chocolate chips. I really like chocolate.

I sit on the couch to eat it and watch TV.

When I've licked every drop of ice cream from my spoon and there's none left in the bowl, I wash it out and head upstairs to shower.

When I get in bed it's a little after nine and I have to laugh to myself. I've turned into my mother—although, she usually goes to bed by eight. Regardless, I've officially reached the level of adult-adult where you never go out anymore and you're asleep before ten. It's kind of pathetic, but it's the circle of life.

I fall asleep clutching my pillow, and sometime in the night I feel Ben climb into bed and slip his arms around my body.

I smile even in my sleep.

6

I wake up to the smell and sound of bacon cooking.

I sit up and rub my eyes, blinking at the clock. Lit up in green the numbers flash 7:10. The bed is empty beside me—no surprise there.

I slip out of bed and shuffle my feet into a pair of slippers. I'm always cold when I wake up so I grab my sweatshirt from the chair and tug it on before I pad downstairs.

I round the corner to find Ben standing at the stove with his back to me.

He's shirtless and the muscles in his back flex as he moves. He hasn't heard me yet, and he's intent on what he's doing—popping a piece of bread in the toaster.

I finally decide to make my presence known. "Shouldn't you be sleeping?"

He looks at me over his shoulder with an impish smile. "I didn't eat before I went to bed, so I'm hungry. I'll catch a nap later."

"Why didn't you eat?" I frown and step up beside him.

"I was too tired." He yawns.

"Here, let me make breakfast."

He shakes his head. "No, let's do it together."

Ben always prefers for us to do this kind of stuff together, and I find it to be sweet and endearing.

"Okay." I nod.

He lets me take over with the eggs and he adds more bacon to the other pan.

We work side by side in companionable silence.

One of the best pieces of advice my mom gave me was when she said, "Find a man that even in silence you're comfortable with. That's a telling factor, B. If someone makes you nervous to the point that you have to chatter endlessly, then they're not the person for you. You need to be able to communicate without saying a word."

As if to demonstrate this, Ben turns away from the stove to grab a plate. He hands it to me to put the finished eggs on.

He finishes the bacon and I begin to put together our plates. I add the eggs and toast—buttering the toast, of course.

Ben adds a pile of bacon to each of our plates. He doesn't indulge in it often, but when he does, he has it in excess.

We sit at the kitchen table and Winnie comes out of nowhere to jump on the table beside Ben. Neither of us wastes our breath scolding her to get off. She never listens and only turns her nose up at us when we do.

"How did yesterday go?" Ben asks, chewing on a piece of bacon.

"The dress is perfect," I tell him. "They're making a few alterations, but it's almost ready."

"What does it look like?" He winks.

He asks me this all the time. He wants to know what kind of dress I picked, but I refuse to tell him out of some sense of tradition.

"I'm not telling." I mock-glare at him with narrowed eyes and pursed lips.

He chuckles. "It was worth a shot." He rubs his hands on a napkin. "I actually got you something for your dress." I must make a face because he laughs and says, "It's nothing bad, Blaire." He stands and walks over to his work bag. He returns with a small black box. "Open it." He slides it across the table.

I pick it up and twist it back and forth. I lift off the top and set it on the table. Inside is white tissue paper, further hiding the item from me. Whatever it is, it has to be small to fit in this box. I fold back the tissue paper and gasp. Inside is a pin, but not just any pin. It's in the shape of a paper crane with glittering blue jewels.

I look up at Ben and he smiles boyishly, his dimple flashing when he shrugs. "Something blue. It seemed fitting so I couldn't pass it up."

"It's beautiful." I remove it from the box and hold it in my palm. It's about half the size of my pinky and beautifully detailed. It had to have cost him a lot, but I don't comment on that. "Thank you." I set it inside the box and lean over to kiss him. He kisses me back, his hand resting on my cheek to hold me there a moment longer.

"I understand if you don't want to wear it on your dress," he says when I slide away, "but I figured you could pin it inside and we'd both know it was there."

"It's perfect. Thank you so much." I smile at him. I'm trying not to get choked up and cry all over my breakfast. I delicately wrap the pin up in the tissue paper and tuck it back in the box.

I put my hand on his knee and lean over to kiss him. He smiles against my lips.

"You really like it?" he asks.

I nod and sit back. "I love it. I can't believe you found something so perfect."

He shrugs.

"Ben?" I urge, raising a brow.

He rubs his chin and grins sheepishly. "I may have had it custom made."

"Ben," I cry. "That must've cost a fortune."

"It was worth every penny," he assures me. "No need to worry."

"You're crazy," I tell him.

"Crazy in love." He winks.

I roll my eyes. "And cheesy."

"You love my cheese," he counters.

"I do," I sigh, fighting a smile.

"Pretty soon you'll be saying that while I slide a ring across your finger." He lifts the glass of orange juice casually to his lips.

I shake my head. "Cheeseball," I tease him again.

He simply smiles and goes on eating his breakfast.

We finish eating and wash the dishes side by side at the sink. He bumps his hip against mine, and when I look up, he lifts his hands from the soapy water and sprinkles the droplets all over me.

My laughter rings through the kitchen. His much louder, deeper laughter soon joins mine. He wraps his arms around my waist, with my back to his chest, and spins me around.

I lean my head against his shoulder and laugh until I cry.

I love that I've found someone that makes me laugh this much. He goes out of his way to make every moment special. Every look. Every touch. I'm aware that Ben and I share a special love and bond—one not many people have. I'm not saying that other couples don't love each other, but I think there are different kinds and ways of loving.

Ben sits me down and I spin around to face him, wrapping my arms around his shoulders. His tongue slides out and glides across his lips. He smiles crookedly.

"What'cha lookin' at darlin'?" He feigns a thick—and truly appalling—southern accent.

"That dent in your face." I surprise him by poking his dimple.

He throws his head back and laughs. Tipping his head down, his blue eyes shimmer with mischief. "I happen to know for a fact that you love that so-called dent."

"And how do you know that?" I raise one brow when I step back and cock my hip.

He leans against the counter casually. "Not only have you told me on numerous occasions, but you also frequently mumble about it in your sleep." He crosses his hands together and lays his head on them, pretending to be asleep. "Oh, Ben, your dimples are so cute. I just want to lick them," he says in a thick voice.

I swat at his arm. "I do not."

He laughs and straightens. "You don't but I wouldn't mind if you boasted about me in your sleep." He winks.

I shake my head. "Silly boy."

He pinches my ass. "Man, B. All man."

I skitter out of the kitchen and he laughs behind me. "You're cleaning up on your own now."

"Not a punishment," he yells back.

I pad into the bedroom and take a shower. I don't take long, and when I'm done I apply some makeup and part the front part of my hair—braiding a section of it and pulling it back into a bun.

With my robe secured around me, I step into the closet and flick on the light, searching the racks. I settle on a pair of black jeans, a short-sleeve black shirt that dips low with several cutouts, and since it's chilly out, I top it with a black leather jacket. I try to mix up my wardrobe, but I have to admit that most of the things I own are black. It's my go-to.

When I enter the bedroom, Ben is just coming back in.

"I'm going to see if I can get some more sleep," he says with a yawn.

I nod. "Good idea." I grab my phone off the table and see a text from Casey. Ben is slipping beneath the sheets when I say, "Hey, Casey wants us all to meet up for lunch at the café. You wanna go?"

He yawns again. "I can do that. I don't go back into work until tomorrow night."

"Please tell me you have a shorter shift?" I ask him.

He nods. "It's twelve-hours."

"Better than twenty-four," I mumble. I understand the need for such long shifts, but it really sucks and I hate the toll it puts on him. "Have a good nap."

I ease out of the room and close the door—not before I see Winnie jump on the bed beside Ben and snuggle close. She's such a whore.

I busy myself with cleaning the house and work. Always work. I'm not complaining, though. A year ago I would've never imagined I'd have so much interest in my little planning business. Especially in such a small town. But word gets out and that's been my best ally. It's not like I have a lot of money to spend on marketing.

Ben comes downstairs a few hours later. His blond hair is ruffled around his head and he's still shirtless. I'm pretty sure he's trying to kill me—only so he can restart my heart.

"How was your nap?" I ask him, turning down the volume on the TV.

"Good," he says and opens the refrigerator door, bending to grab a bottle of water. "What time are we meeting them for lunch?"

I push the round button on my phone so it lights up. "We have an hour."

He finishes his sip of water and lowers the bottle. "You know what we could do in an hour?" He waggles his brows.

I roll my eyes. "I think I have an idea."

He sets his bottle of water on the counter and runs over, jumping into the air to make it over the back of the couch.

"Ben." I laugh when he practically lands on top of me.

He rights himself and drapes an arm over the back of the couch. "Blaire," he says with the same infliction I used for his name. He leans over and kisses me. I'm slow to return the gesture, but he soon coaxes one from me.

My hand rests on his shoulder and I duck my head. His lips move to my forehead. "Blaire?" He questions, his hands sliding up my back. "Talk to me."

"I'm scared."

He knows immediately what I'm talking about. "It's only two tests Blaire. It doesn't mean anything."

"We have sex all the time," I counter. "With that much sex it seems unlikely that we wouldn't get pregnant."

He chuckles and takes my face between his large hands. "True," he agrees, "but we're also both stressed with our jobs and stress is known to affect fertility, and now you're stressing about this…" he trails off, letting me fill in the blanks.

I take a deep breath. He's right. He's always right. But it doesn't dissuade the nagging thoughts in my mind.

"You're overthinking this, B." He taps my forehead and blinks earnest blue eyes at me. "I'm a doctor, remember?" He cracks a smile, and when I laugh, he continues, "If I really thought something was wrong I'd tell you. I know on TV shows and movies, and even those romance books you love to read, men look at women and boom they're pregnant." He snaps his fingers for emphasis. "But that's not the real world, babe."

I nod and he cradles the back of my neck. I cuddle into his side and tuck my head into the crook of his neck. He rubs his fingers through my hair, murmuring sweet words under his breath until he has to get up and get ready.

He drives us over to the café and the other girls are already there.

Casey waves us over from the regular table—as if we didn't know which one it was already. Hannah and Chloe sit on one side of the table with Casey at the head of one end. Ben takes the other head, his usual spot, and I sit beside him.

"What do you want to eat?" he asks me.

I eye him.

He sighs. "Of course. I'll be right back. Nice to see you, ladies." He nods his head at the girls before heading over to the counter.

Chloe sighs dreamily and leans forward, propping her head in her hand and biting her lip. "Would you look at the way his jeans hug his ass? Mmm."

"Hey, he's practically my husband," I scold her.

"I know, but you did good, girl. Man, I wish he had a single brother. If only dreams came true."

"You're a mess. You'll find someone when the time is right." I wrinkle my nose. "On that note, you need to start dating the right guys. Stop going for the bad boys."

"But they're so delicious in their dark jeans, sunglasses, and leather jackets. It's even better when they have tattoos and spank me."

I snort.

"Who's getting spanked?"

Chloe lets out a squeak at the sound of Ben's voice.

"Apparently Chloe," Casey says with a smile, twisting a piece of blond hair around her finger.

"I hate you guys," Chloe pouts.

Ben slides my sandwich and coffee over and sits down with his own.

I take a bite and it's like heaven in my mouth.

"I don't know why you'd hate us," Hannah chimes in. "No one made you say it."

Chloe purses her lips and mutters, "Well …"

Casey laughs and brushes crumbs from her muffin off the table. "So the wedding's soon, are you getting cold feet?" Casey asks Ben.

"Casey," I hiss. "Why would you say something like that?"

She shrugs and flips her hair over her shoulder. Wrapping her hand around her mug of coffee she says, "You're overreacting, Blaire. It's just a saying."

Ben places his hand on my knee in an effort to calm me, and the gesture does help a little. I'm sure I'm being a little testy what with the baby thing, work, and a wedding.

"No, no cold feet here." Ben smiles. "My feet are nice and warm."

Casey gives me a look as if to say: See, it was an innocent question.

Casey's been my best friend for a long time, and we've never fought over a guy, but lately little comments she makes have me wondering if she has feelings for Ben. I know she's dating James, but I don't see that making it much longer, and I do know she had a brief crush on Ben when we were in high school. Regardless, I can't see her doing anything to sabotage my happiness but … but, you never know.

"How's work?" Ben asks Casey, leaning back in his chair.

She makes a face. "Same old, same old. I used to love law, but lately I want to throw a book at everyone I work with. They're all a bunch of idiots." Her voice spikes with irritation. "Even the old people that have been at the firm forever go around asking the dumbest questions. Sometimes I want to say to them, 'I'm not the adult, you are. Get it together.' But then I realize I am an adult and I'd probably get fired if I said that." She takes a deep breath after her long-winded rambling.

"Whoa," Ben says, holding his cup of coffee midway in the air. "That's intense."

"I should probably find another firm to work at, but they're really all the same." Casey makes a face like she tasted something sour. "Anyway," she lays her hands flat on the wood of the table, "let's talk about you guys. Any of you," she adds, desperate to get the attention off her.

"I'm moving," Hannah says.

We all grow quiet and stare at her. "Um, what?" I'm the first to speak.

"Not away," she clarifies. "But, man, thanks to the look on your faces I know I'd be missed if I did. Anyway—" she waves a hand dismissively "—I'm moving into a new apartment. The lease on mine is up and I can't take the roaches and rat poop anymore so I'm out of there."

"It was that bad?" Chloe asks, completely appalled.

"Yep." Hannah lifts her napkin and begins to break it apart. "It sucks."

"Now I understand why you've never invited us over," I add.

She nods. "The new place is really nice. It's a studio apartment, so it's small, but clean. It has exposed brick walls which I thought was cool."

"Do you need help moving?" Ben asks her.

"God, yes. Would you help?" she begs. "I really don't want to have to pay someone to help me. My brother already said he'd help, so another set of hands would be great."

Ben nods. "Sounds good. I'll let you know what my schedule at the hospital looks like and you can let me know what day works for you."

We finish eating and chat for a little while longer before heading out.

Ben takes my hand on the way to the car. "Want to go shopping?" he asks me, and I shake my head. "Movies?" Another shake. He laughs. "What do you want to do then?"

"Just go home, I guess." I shrug. "We can watch a movie there and resume your conversation from earlier."

"Conversation?" His brows wrinkle in confusion. I wink and it's all the answer he needs. "I like your idea." He opens the passenger door and offers me his hand as I get in. He's a gentleman, for sure. I tell him often that his momma raised him right.

We head home and pick out a movie to watch, getting cozy on the couch. I know I should've probably taken him up on his offer to go shopping, but I'd rather be here, in our home, with him.

I lay my head on his lap and he brushes his fingers through my hair. It's soothing, and I'm tempted to fall asleep, but I don't. It's not about missing the movie—it's this I don't want to miss. Life itself. I'm scared of blinking my eyes and finding these little moments seldom happening. We're both bound to get even busier with work, and throw in a baby …

It doesn't matter, though. None of it. This is where I'm happiest. Right here with Ben and I hope that love and happiness never ever fades.

7

I lie sated in bed while Ben gets ready to go off to work. I'm not going to lie, we definitely took advantage of last night and today since his shift doesn't start until eleven PM.

He steps out of the closet in his scrubs with a heavy gray coat over top. "Behave yourself." He winks at me when he sits down in the chair to lace up his white tennis shoes.

"No promises when I have this big bed all to myself." I rub my hand over the sheets.

He groans. "I have to go and you're not helping."

I smile slowly. "Stay."

"I wish life worked like that." He shrugs and stands. "Alas, I must get to work."

I snort and clutch the sheet tighter to my chest. "Who says alas?"

"Me, I guess." He grins, and there are those dimples I love. He walks over to me and bends, kissing my forehead and then lips. I hold his smooth cheeks in my hands, drawing out the kiss.

At last, he pulls away. "I've gotta go."

"I know." I sigh as he heads for the door. "Bye. I love you."

He pauses and looks back at me. His eyes peruse my body and he dips his head in acknowledgment. "I love you too."

I listen to the heavy fall of his feet on the steps and close my eyes. It's late, but I'm not really sleepy.

I hear the front door open and the alarm dings before it can close.

Winnie comes wandering into the bedroom and gives me a scathing look, like I personally sent Ben away.

"Don't look at me like that," I mumble at her. She merely swishes her tail and jumps up in the window to watch Ben back out of the driveway.

I unwrap the sheets from my body and pull on my robe, standing by the window with her. Ben happens to look up and sees me. He grins and waves. I wave back, pressing my hand to the window.

When his taillights disappear around the corner I head to the bathroom to take a bubble bath. My muscles need it after the day I've had. I add a heaping pile of bubbles and salt then light a few candles and turn on some soft music.

I dim the lights in the bathroom and tie my hair up. Letting the robe fall, I step into the warm water. Almost instantly I begin to feel my muscles loosen. I lean back in the water and rest my head on the back of the bathtub. There are so many bubbles that I can't see anything, and that's just the way I like it. I take a deep breath and close my eyes.

When the water begins to feel cold I step out of the water and dry my body. I change into a pair of pajamas and climb into bed. I open the drawer to my nightstand to grab the remote, but I smile when instead I find a paper crane.

I open it slowly, like it's a precious treasure—which I guess to me, it is.

My smile grows at his messily scrawled words.

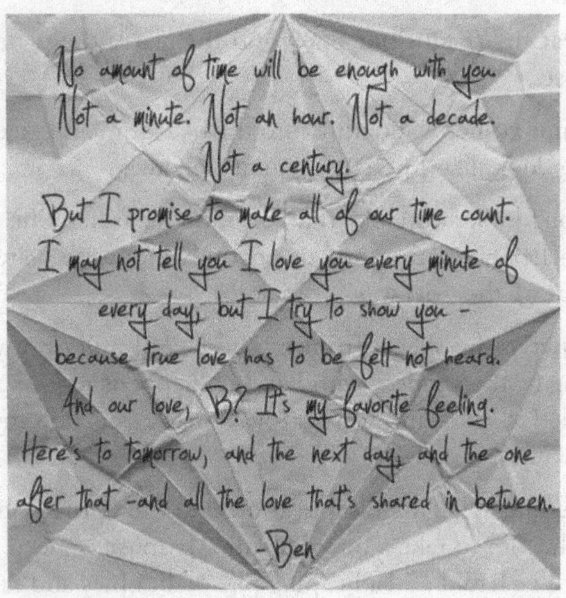
No amount of time will be enough with you.
Not a minute. Not an hour. Not a decade.
Not a century.
But I promise to make all of our time count.
I may not tell you I love you every minute of
every day, but I try to show you -
because true love has to be felt not heard.
And our love, B? It's my favorite feeling.
Here's to tomorrow, and the next day, and the one
after that -and all the love that's shared in between.
-Ben

My phone rings from the bedside table and my brows furrow. It's nearly midnight. Why would anyone be calling me?

I pick up the phone and shake my head at the name. It's one of the nurses that works with Ben—her name's Laura and we went out to dinner with her and her husband a few times.

"Hello?" I answer. "Laura?"

"Hey, have you seen Ben?" she asks, sounding frazzled. "He was supposed to be here an hour ago. I tried calling him but his phone keeps going straight to voicemail."

I sit straight up in bed, white-knuckling my phone. "He left for work on time. What do you mean he's not there?" My voice spikes with fear.

I hear a sudden ruckus in the background—Laura and Ben work in the ER.

Laura's quiet and I hear shouting. Orders for meds and IVs and other things I can't understand.

Suddenly, Laura mutters, "Oh, shit."

"Laura—?"

"I have to go."

The line goes dead.

My stomach sinks, full of dread. I feel my heart stutter and race, trying to pump blood to my starving brain—starving because I'm holding my breath.

My phone has fallen to the bed but I pick it up and call Ben.

Like Laura said, it goes straight to voicemail and all I hear is Ben's cheery voicemail. "Hey, it's me. Ben. I'm not able to answer my phone right now, but don't worry, I'm a doctor so I'm probably just saving lives. I'll call you back later."

I try again.

And again.

And again.

I've never been so desperate in my life.

I know, logically, it's probably nothing. Laura probably had a critical come in and it was bad, and she had to go. It means nothing.

Nothing.

Nothing.

Nothing.

Then why am I freaking out so bad?

My phone rings again, and it's Laura. I breathe out a sigh of relief. She probably realized what it sounded like and she's calling to tell me not to be crazy.

"Laura?" She sniffles in response. "Laura?" I say again, the unease creeping back in me.

"It's Ben." Her voice cracks. "They brought Ben in."

"W-What do you mean?" I stutter, even though I do. I have to hear her say it, though.

"It's bad, Blaire. He got hit by a drunk driver or something, I don't know the details yet. They rushed him back to emergency surgery, but ..."

"But?" I can barely utter the word. I'm holding on so tight to my phone that I'm surprised it doesn't shatter in my hand. I think I'm unconsciously using it to hold myself together.

"I'm not going to lie, it's bad, Blaire. Really bad. You should get here."

At her words, I crumble and the sobs break through. "I don't know if I can drive," I tell her with honesty.

"I'll call a cab for you," she says, and her own distress is palpable. "And Blaire?"

"Yeah?"

"I know this means shit, but I'm so sorry."

"Thanks," I mumble and hang up the phone. I immediately run to my closet and pull on a pair of jeans and a sweatshirt. I slip my feet into a pair of flats when I hear a horn honk outside. That was fast.

I grab my phone and purse and dash outside into the waiting car. They already know to take me to the hospital so I don't have to say a word.

I know I have to call Ben's mom, so I force my frozen fingers to move over my phone and find her information.

I'm surprised by how quickly she answers, but I guess most people assume a late night call is an emergency.

"Blaire?" she asks. "Is everything okay?"

Another sob breaks through my lips. I keep seeing Ben lying broken and bloody on the side of a road, waiting for someone to help him and it's killing me. I know he's at the hospital now, but what about before.

"Blaire?" she says again and I realize I haven't spoken.

"It's Ben," I say, and my voice is almost unrecognizable to myself. "You need to come to the hospital. Now."

"I'll be there as soon as I can," she says, and I can already hear her bustling around her room. "Hang in there, Blaire."

I close my eyes and pinch the bridge of my nose. "I don't know if I can," I say, but she's already gone.

The cab lets me off at the emergency room doors. I throw a wad of cash at him. I don't know how much it is or if I even have enough to cover the cost. I don't care. All I can think about is Ben.

Ben.

I feel like there's a hole in my heart and someone's tearing at the edges, damaging it beyond recognition. I've never been more scared in all my life.

He'll be okay, I tell myself.

What if he's not? I ask.

I don't know.

I rush into the hospital and the glass doors whoosh open and closed behind me. I run up to the counter and the women working there look up.

"Can I help you?" one says in a pleasant, calm tone.

"M-My fiancé," I stutter, out of breath, "h-he was brought in. I think he's in surgery."

"Name?" She blinks up at me, no urgency in her tone.

I know she's trying to be helpful, but I want to bash her head in. "Benjamin Carter."

"Let me look." She taps her fingers against the lacquered table and scans the computer. "It looks like he's still in surgery, but you're welcome to wait in the waiting room." She points to the plastic blue and green chairs.

I take a deep breath. "That's it? That's all you can tell me."

"I'm sorry. I'm not at liberty—"

I hold up a hand. "Got it."

I take a seat in the corner by the double doors. I want to be there, ready and waiting, for any doctor or nurse that comes out.

A short time later, one does, and it's Laura. It's clear she's looking for me. When she spots me, almost immediately, she rushes toward me in a determined gait.

"Blaire," she breathes out a sigh of relief, "do you know anything?"

"Me? No. I was hoping you knew something." She shakes

her head, nibbling on her bottom lip. "I was on the team treating him when he first came in, but he was rushed into surgery. It's not likely any of us will get any updates on him."

My chest seizes. "How bad was it?" I ask her, wiping at the snot running out of my nose. "Be honest with me, Laura. I need to know. I need to …"

To what? Prepare myself. That's absurd. He's going to be fine.

She winces. "Blaire—"

I grab her hand and hold on tight. "Don't lie to me. Is it really as bad as you said when you called?

She makes a face. "Worse," she whispers.

I close my eyes and a lone tear leaks out of the corner of my eye. I don't even have the energy to wipe it away. My breath passes between my lips and I count to three before opening my eyes.

"I'm going to lose him, aren't I?" The words feel like knives clawing at my throat.

Tears pool in her eyes. "I don't know."

I lean my head back and look up at the ceiling. "Fuck."

She laughs softly. "Yeah, fuck," she echoes.

"This sucks."

She takes my hands in both of hers and I lower my head to look at her. "Don't give up hope," she tells me. "Whatever you do, don't stop hoping. We don't know anything yet."

I nod. "I won't," I promise her.

She presses her lips together. "I have to get back to work.

I snuck away to see you."

"I understand. Thanks, Laura."

She gives me one last sad smile and leaves me alone in the too-bright waiting room.

God, I hate everything about this room. The uncomfortable plastic chairs with their stupid wood arms. The pathetic coffee table covered in a blanket of magazines pretending to be cheerful and uplifting. I especially hate the wall of windows that reflects all the halogen lights and the people inside.

Sometime later, Ben's mom comes running into the waiting room.

She sees me and slows to a walk. "Do you know anything?" she asks, sitting down on the chair beside me.

I shake my head. "No. He must still be in surgery."

"That's a good thing, right?" she asks, sounding hopeful.

"I don't know." I shrug. I hate feeling this helpless. I know nothing, and it's killing me.

Loraine tightens her hands around her purse strap where it rests in her lap. "I guess we wait and see then."

"I guess so."

I rub my hands up and down my face.

Remain hopeful, Blaire. Do not give up hope. He's going to be okay. You'll see. They're going to walk out of those double doors any minute and tell you that he's fine. You have to hope. Just believe.

And then there is a doctor walking through the doors. I sit up straight.

I know. Somehow, I already know.

"Mr. Carter's family?"

"Over here," I call and begin to stand.

He waves his hand for me to sit down.

No.

He makes his way toward us, head downcast staring at his clipboard.

No.

"Are you Mr. Carter's mom and . . . ?"

"Fiancé," I say. My voice sounds soft. Distant. Like I'm speaking through a tunnel. There's a roar in my ears, like my mind is trying to drown out the words I know are coming.

He nods. He presses his lips into a thin line and fiddles with his thick-framed glasses. "I'm sorry to say he didn't make it. He died on the table."

I close my eyes. I latch onto those two words.

He died.

He's dead.

Ben's gone.

The man who's made me smile and laugh every day for the last seven years of my life doesn't exist anymore.

Poof.

Gone.

Game over.

"I'm so sorry for your loss," he says. "We did everything we could, and unfortunately, it wasn't enough."

I lose it. Completely and utterly lose it. A sound that can't even be described as a sob leaves my throat. I'm drowning in tears. My whole face is wet.

"H-He's really gone?" I find myself saying. I don't know how I find the strength to say the words. They feel like gasoline on my throat and my tears are the fucking match.

The doctor nods once. Solemn. Resolute.

I crumble to the floor.

"Ma'am," he says, bending down to me.

"No, no, no." I cry and beat my fists against the floor. I'm causing a scene, I know, but I can't stop. I need to let this out. I need to do something. I can't just sit there and listen to this man tell me the love of my life is gone. Dead.

Dead. He's dead.

"Ma'am?" he says again.

"No!" I scream. Scream from the very depths of my soul. "He can't be dead." I pull at my hair. "This is all a bad dream. Wake up. Wake up." I slap my face, but I'm still here, firmly rooted in reality. "No, no, no, no, no," I whisper to myself. "No." I stand and make a run for the doors. "Ben!" I scream, like he can hear me. The doctor grabs me around the waist and holds me back, keeping me from the doors. "Ben! Please! Ben." I tug and yank on his arms, trying to get him to let me go, but he doesn't budge. I sink into his arms and scream. I cry. I pour it all out from my very soul. "Why?" I sob into the doctor's coat. "Why?"

The doctor surprises me by wrapping his arms around me. "Shh," he soothes, trying to coax me back into my chair. I let him. My legs can't hold me up anymore—the muscles have given out.

Loraine sobs quietly beside me. I wish I could be like her. Quiet in my grief.

"Let me get you some water." The doctor's speaking to me, but I can no longer look at him. I refuse to look at the man that has just told me that my love, my heart, my soul is gone. If I don't look at him then I don't have to face the truth.

He returns with a paper cup full of water and holds it out to me. I don't take it. I can't move. Frozen. I am frozen.

He bends down in front of me and taps my knee with an index finger. "Hey," he says in a soft tone. I stare at my lap. "It'll be okay," he whispers. "I know you don't want to hear that, but it's the truth."

He sets the water cup on the chair beside me and leaves.

The waiting room is quiet. I feel the stares. I hear the whispers.

I don't care.

How can I care when Ben is gone?

"Blaire?" Loraine says my name around a sob.

I squish my eyes closed and more tears leak out. I never knew it was possible to cry this much. It's like they're seeping from my pores. I know I need to answer her, but I don't want to open my mouth again. I'm scared if I do I'll start screaming and not want to stop. I've already caused enough of a scene.

"We should go," she says. "We don't need to be here anymore."

I shake my head.

I'm not leaving.

What if the doctor goes back there and finds that he was

wrong? What if Ben is really alive?

Don't give up hope.

"Blaire," Loraine says, "he's not going to walk out those doors. Stop it."

I grip the thin wooden arms of the cheap chair and hold on so tight that my knuckles turn white. I shake my head roughly once. Twice. Three times. I think I'm trying to shake some sense into myself.

"Blaire. We have to go."

"I can't," I whisper, staring at the shiny white floor. "I can't leave him."

I know I should be strong for her right now, Ben's her son, but I'm too lost in my own grief. I'm pathetic.

She stands and somehow gets ahold of me, hauling my leaden body up. "I'll drive you home. Can I stay in your guest room?"

I nod. "Of course," I whisper.

She guides me out of the hospital and to her car. How she has the capability to drive is beyond me. But I guess she's a mom. She's used to having to take charge in the face of meltdowns.

She starts the car and turns down the radio; I don't think either of us wants to listen to music right now.

I'm not sure I'll ever smile again.

The lights from the hospital parking lot shine through the windows. I lean my head against the cool glass of the car window beside me and close my eyes.

"We were trying to have a baby," I say the words softly.

Loraine gasps and hiccups on a cry.

"We were so excited," I continue, "about the future. The wedding. A baby. Life. It's all gone now."

Loraine is quiet and I don't open my eyes to see her. Finally, she says, "It's not gone now. It's just different."

"It's not the same without Ben."

She's quiet again, and then with what must be a lot of effort, she says, "You're young. You'll move on."

My hands clench into fists and my eyes fly open. "How can you say that? He's your son. Was. Was your son." I lean my head against the headrest and bang my fists against my thighs. It isn't fair.

Her lower lip trembles and the red from the stoplight reflects over her face. "It kills me to say that, Blaire, but it's true. You will move on."

I shake my head. "Shut up."

She turns to me. "We have to stay strong. For ourselves. For each other. Can you do that?"

"I don't know."

"Come on, Blaire. That's not the fighter I know you to be."

I wipe at the tears that have continued to fall. "I need to scream," I tell her.

"Then scream."

I do. And she does too.

We both sit there at that stoplight, even as it changes to green, and scream.

I scream until my throat is raw and aching and sore. I

scream until I can't scream anymore and then I collapse back against the seat.

Loraine drives us back to the house and we don't say a word. Not as she parks the car and not even once we're inside. We both head into separate bedrooms.

I sob as soon as I see my bed. The bed Ben and I had been rolling around in only hours ago and now he's dead.

I've never had to deal with death head-on before.

My dad's parents were dead when I was born and my mom lost her dad shortly after. The only death I was around for was my grandma when I was five and I didn't know her well so it didn't hurt. Yeah, I was upset, especially because my mom was but my five-year-old brain couldn't process grief. Not this soul-crushing, suffocating feeling.

I strip out of my clothes and stay in my underwear and bra. I don't have time for pajamas. I climb beneath the covers, burrowing myself over to Ben's side. I wrap my arms around his pillow and inhale his scent.

How long until that smell fades?

I cry. I let the tears soak my hair and the pillow. I cry until I'm too tired to cry and can't keep my eyes open anymore. I let my dreams take me away. To a heaven where Ben still exists and life doesn't suck so much.

8

My eyes feel like they're taped shut. I try to open them and I can't. I rub at them and sit up in bed. I look around me at the mess of covers and daylight shining through the windows. The clocks says it's nearly noon. I narrow my eyes.

Last night …

Oh God.

"No, no, no, no, no." I start up with the chanting again and rush out of my bed. I hurry down the hall and peek in the guest room. My heart sinks at the ruffled bed.

It's not dream—not some dastardly nightmare. It's real. It's so fucking real.

I clutch at my chest, like there's a visible wound there and slide down the wall as sobs overtake my body again. In my sleep I'd been able to delude myself into believing it hadn't really happened. Dreams are liars. They show you what you want to see, what you hope for, and it's nothing but a lie.

I draw my knees up to my stomach and sob into my hands. How I have any tears left to cry is beyond me.

I feel so lost, so scared, so alone.

What am I going to do?

I wipe at my face and pick myself up off the floor. I have

to find Loraine.

I make my way downstairs and find her standing by the front window, clutching a mug of tea. She glances over her shoulder at me with red-rimmed eyes. My lip trembles. I'm trying so hard to hold it together, but I can't. I don't want to.

She takes a seat and sets her cup of tea on the coffee table there. Her drink is practically untouched. I take a seat in the chair across from her. I know I should say something, but words evade me.

She crosses and uncrosses her legs. She's restless and I am too. Neither of us knows what to do. I don't know if there's anything we can do.

"I don't know where to go from here," I say. I wrap my arms around my body like the gesture alone can hold together the crumbling pieces of my life.

Her lips press together in a thin line. "As cliché as it sounds, I guess you take it one day at a time."

I nod. I don't know what else to do. I feel like an imposter in my own body going through the motions. I don't want to eat, or drink, or even talk.

"I'm going back to bed," I finally say.

She nods and doesn't fight me on it. In fact, she even says, "Me too."

Neither one of us wants to deal.

For now, we don't have to.

9

I stare at the closed casket as one of Ben's high school friend's, Tyler, drones on and on about what a great guy he was. I want to yell at the guy because he hasn't even talked to Ben in recent years. But he's here sharing in a grief I don't feel like he has a right to claim.

The flowers overflow the casket in colors of purple and yellow. I think his mom chose those colors. I can't remember. I've been too checked out the last few days—only mumbling responses when spoken to. I left all the funeral planning up to Loraine. I can barely stomach the word funeral. It's so final.

My parents are here. I didn't call them and tell them. I should have, but I didn't. I'm not sure who told them. I guess it doesn't matter. All I know is one morning my mom climbed into bed beside me and held me as I cried.

"It'll be okay, baby girl," she whispered like she used to when I was little. "Mom's here."

Only, unlike when I was a small child, her presence didn't make this any easier. She couldn't wave a magic wand and heal me. My grief would have to take its own course, and I was scared it might destroy me in the process. The sad part was I couldn't bring myself to care if it did.

My mom sits beside me and she takes my hand, like she is silently aware of my thoughts. She gives my hand a squeeze, and I wish I could take some small comfort in the gesture, but I feel nothing.

Tyler finishes speaking and takes a seat.

Ben's mom gets up and stands near the casket. Ben's brother, Jacob, stands beside her, offering support.

She holds a tissue to the corner of her eye, dabbing away the moisture. Everyone sits quiet and rapt, waiting for her to speak.

I swallow past the lump in my throat. Getting through this is killing me.

She clears her throat and taps the microphone. A pitched noise whizzes around everyone and I wince.

"Benjamin," she says, "he was a good boy. He was always so sweet and thoughtful—putting others needs above his. I wasn't surprised when he told me he wanted to be a doctor. Saving lives … it was just ingrained in him. Once, when he was little, probably six or so, he tried to save the life of a dying mouse he found in our backyard. A cat had gotten it, and let me tell you this mouse was in bad shape. But Ben …" She shakes her head. "He didn't give up on it. And even when it died in his hands he said to me, 'Next time, mommy, I'll know what to do. I'll save the next one.'"

I squish my eyes closed and tears dampen my cheeks.

So many tears.

"And, Ben," she continues, "he grew up to live his dream. He met the love of his life. He was to get married in less than a month and I know he would've been the best husband he could be to Blaire. I'm sorry that he'll never get to prove that to you."

I lift my head and find her looking at me.

"We were all robbed of a future with Ben in it. As a parent, you never want to outlive your child. I've had a hard life and a lot of bad days, but I'd relive those bad days a thousand times over if it meant I never had to live one of today. Thank you." She hiccups on a cry and Jacob helps her back to her chair.

This is the part where I know I'm supposed to speak—to shed some enlightening words on my time with Ben. I can't. To say the words is to accept that he's dead and I don't want to. I don't want the finality.

"Blaire," my mom whispers, nudging me with her shoulder.

I don't move. I don't even breathe.

I feel the weight of everyone's eyes—waiting, hoping, for me to do or say something.

After a long stretch of awkward silence, the preacher, or whoever he is, gets up and says a few final words.

I don't even hear them. Everything becomes a dull roar in my ears.

I feel a drop of water hit my cheek and it's not my own tears—although those are still falling too. I look up and see that the sky has turned a dark stormy gray. Thunder rumbles in the sky. The sky—the heavens—they're echoing my pain. I know it. It's like Ben's up there and he's sad and angry because this is happening and it's all so unfair.

People begin to stand, and I know it's time to leave, but my butt is glued to the seat. I can't go. To leave is the final good-bye and I need one more minute. One more second.

"Blaire?" My mom stands and waits for me to do the same.

I shake my head.

"Blaire," she says again, this time in a harsher tone.

"No." I stare at his casket and the waterfall of flowers. "Give me a minute."

She shakes her head. "Your father and I will be in the car."

I sit there until everyone's gone. I need one last moment alone with him. This is all I'm going to get for the rest of my life.

Make it count.

I stand and touch my fingers to the cool dark wood of the casket. I pluck one of the flowers from the overflowing bunch with my free hand and twirl it between my fingers.

There are so many things I want to say. My mind is overflowing with an overabundance of words and I can't seem to grasp any of them. I don't think there's any way to try to convey my thoughts and feelings.

"Oh, Ben." I choke on a sob and wipe at my tears. "What has become of us?" My fingers tremble against the wood. "How did things end up like this? We're good people, right? What did we do to deserve this?" I cry. "It hasn't even been a week yet and I miss you so much. My heart aches, Ben. I never thought heartache was a real thing, but it is and it sucks." I wipe at my face and groan, trying to hold myself together. "You are the love of my life—dead or alive that hasn't changed. Your mom says I'll move on, but she's wrong. Most people are lucky if they find one ever-lasting love. I don't think you can find two." I can feel the anger building inside me once again, but I stamp it down. I don't want to be angry right now. Not in my last moments with Ben. I shove my fingers through my hair. It's neatly curled, but that's not my doing. My mom forced me to let her do my hair this morning. I think she was afraid I'd show up at the funeral in my pajamas and bed-head if she didn't help me.

"I hope, that up there in heaven—because I know that's where you are—that you can hear me, and you know that I love you. I love you so damn much." I shake my head. "That love isn't going to fade because of death. You're going to live on forever, right here." I touch my fingers to my heart like he's there to see. "I love you, Ben. Now and forever and always."

I open my purse—some small clutch-type thing—and pull out a paper crane.

I laugh a little—it's the first time I've laughed since the accident. "I finally made one of my own." I set the bird amidst the flowers. I kiss my fingers and touch them to the casket. "I love you," I say one last time.

And then the sky opens up and it pours.

I believe that the rain stinging my cheeks is kisses from Ben. He's here. He'll always be here.

10

Stage One: Denial

It's been three days since Ben's funeral, and I still don't believe it actually happened. It's like I've shut down—gone into zombie mode or something.

My mom sets a plate of food in front of me. I stare at the rubbery eggs and greasy bacon.

Ben.

Ben's going to walk in the door any minute from work and tell me this is all a big joke. Ha, ha! Got you! I'm not really dead but now I know how much you really love me!

On some logical level I know that's not going to happen, but denial has set in and I'm holding onto it with a strong-handled grip.

"You need to eat, Blaire." My mom pulls out the seat beside me and crosses her arms on the table. She leans her head down, looking at me with eyes the same color as my own, only hers are now lined with wrinkles in the corners from laughing so much. "Please, B. Eat something. You're getting too thin."

I shake my head. I know I should eat, I know my body needs it, but I don't feel any sort of hunger, and the thought of eating makes me feel like vomiting.

She sighs.

From the family room, my dad says, "Leave the girl alone, Maureen. She needs time."

I can tell he's watching a football game and I cringe. If Ben was here Ben would be watching it with him.

Ben loves football.

Loved. Ben loved football.

Because he's dead and can't love things anymore.

I can feel my throat closing in.

No, no. I refuse to believe he's gone. I can't imagine a world without Ben in it. It doesn't seem right that the world lost someone as kind and bright as him, while the drunk driver who murdered him gets to walk free. That's how I look at it—murder. Cold-blooded murder. That person drank, knew they shouldn't drive, and got behind the wheel anyway. They didn't care who they hurt. The man's tried to talk to me, to apologize—I guess—but I never even want to see his face. If I did I'm pretty sure I'd try to claw it off. I have no sympathy for that man, and he can carry the guilt of this for the rest of his life because he deserves that. He deserves to be punished just like me.

"Blaire?" my mom says. "Just one bite." I shake my head. She sighs and forks some eggs onto the spoon. "Open up."

I bat her hand away and the eggs fall on the floor. "I'm not a baby, mom. I don't want to eat."

"And now she talks." My mom throws her hands in the air. It's not lost on me that she uses the word she like I'm not sitting right there—because in a way I'm not there. We all know it. I've checked out. I haven't even worked since the night I got the call. I can't bring myself to continue on with my life without Ben—I'm so afraid that if I pick up the pieces and go on with my life that … that … I don't know. I don't even know what I'm thinking anymore. My thoughts are a jumbled mess.

"Is there anything you can eat?" my mom asks. "Seriously, Blaire, I will drive an hour away if it means I can get something you'll eat."

I sigh. I know I'm scaring my mom, and I feel awful, but I can't seem to snap out of this ... this… whatever this is.

"I could have a milkshake from Chick-fil-A," I tell her. "Vanilla."

She breathes a sigh of relief. "Good, that's good. I'll go get that." She hurries up and grabs her purse, probably trying to get out of there before I change my mind. "Anything else?"

"No."

She nods. "Okay. I'll be right back."

"Kid," my dad says gruffly from the couch, "you're gonna dump that shake in a plant, aren't ya?"

I laugh. "Possibly. I'll take a sip or two for her benefit."

He grunts. "Come join your old man over here." He glances at me from the back of the couch.

I shake my head. "Nah, I'm okay over here."

He turns off the TV. "It's the football, isn't it? We don't have to watch that. We can talk. Or not. I don't care. Just get out of that chair, kid."

I sigh. It's impossible not to listen to my dad. He worked a lot while I was growing up, but he always made sure I knew I could come to him with anything.

I get up from the chair and push it in, stalling for time.

"Kid," he says in warning.

I want to smile at the familiar childhood nickname, but frankly I don't feel like smiling.

I sit down beside him and he wiggles a bit. "Here, you want the blanket?" he asks gruffly, reaching for the blue throw blanket.

"Sure," I say, even though I don't really want it. I know my dad wants to feel useful in some way so I give him that.

He hands me the blanket, and I wrap it around me. It still smells like Ben. I close my eyes, and it's like he's right there. With me.

"When are you going back to work?" my dad asks. He never goes easy on me.

I shrug and glance toward the ceiling where my office lays upstairs waiting for me with several hundred emails. "When I feel like it."

He grunts and wiggles some more. "When will that be?"

Never. "Soon," I say, because I know it's what he wants to hear. I pick at the frayed edge of the blanket. "When are you and Mom going home?"

He stares at me for a moment. His eyes are a kind brown, and he has short lashes. Like my mom, he's wrinkled now from years of laughter and hard work. "We're staying as long as we need to."

"I don't need you to stay here. I'm fine."

He snorts. "Kid, if that's what you call fine I don't want

your definition of bad. You're barely eating and you smell like a sweaty gym sock. You've been wearing those pajamas for three days straight." He points at the dirty sweat-jacket and striped pajama pants I wear. "You're not foolin' me, and you're not foolin' your momma, either," he tells me. "Don't go into the acting business, because you suck."

"Thanks, Dad."

"Hey, just tellin' it to ya straight." He raises his hands innocently. "You're my little girl, Blaire, and I love you more than you know, so don't lie to me. You're not doing well, but let me let you in on a little secret." He leans toward my ear and lowers his voice. "That's okay." Pulling away, he says, "There will be good days and bad days in everyone's life, it's how we deal with those bad days that determines how we live every day. You have every right to be angry, Blaire. To be sad and hurt. But you also have to get up, and go on about your life. Time doesn't wait for anyone. You can't forget to live your life—Ben might've lost his, but you're still here."

My cheeks are wet. I hadn't even realized I was crying.

"I didn't mean to make you cry, Kid."

"It's okay. I do that a lot lately." I grab a tissue and dry my damp face. Since the accident I've set tissue boxes on almost every available surface. I never know when a thought or a sight might strike a meltdown. I lost it this morning when I came downstairs and saw Ben's shoes sitting beside the door. My mom had promptly tried to hide them in the hall closet, but I wouldn't let her. I didn't want to hide his existence.

"I know I haven't said it, but I'm sorry, Blaire. I'm so sorry this happened."

I nod once. "Sorry doesn't bring Ben back," I whisper,

"but I wish it did."

"I know," he agrees. "I wish I could make this better for you. Do you want me to put a movie on?"

I shake my head. Ben and I used to watch movies all the time.

"Okay," my dad says and grows quiet. He soon fills the silence with stories from his working days. I know most of them are funny and I should laugh, but I can't. I don't know if I'll ever laugh again.

My mom returns a short time later with my milkshake. I take a reluctant sip, and I'm surprised to find that it actually tastes pretty good. Lately, nothing has had any taste. I end up drinking the whole thing, and my mom literally claps her hands together because she's so happy. I hate that the simple act of me drinking a milkshake makes her happy. It's further proof that I've completely checked out.

"I'm going to bed," I say a short while later.

They both nod and watch me head upstairs.

I burrow beneath the sheets—sheets I've refused to wash—and close my eyes. If I think hard enough I can feel Ben's arms wrap around me and his lips press to my neck. I smile. I love you, he murmurs. When I open my eyes, though, I'm alone.

He's gone and he's not coming back.

Denial is a bitch.

11

Stage Two: Anger

Two weeks. It's been two fucking weeks since I sat in front of Ben's casket. Two weeks since he was lowered into the ground. Two weeks that have passed at a snail's pace—thanks in part to my refusal to work. I know I eventually have to. I have a car payment and a mortgage and bills to thinks about. I just need time, though.

I close the bathroom door and slip the box from beneath my shirt. I never thought I'd be an adult sneaking in a pregnancy test around my mom, but here I am.

I hold the box in my hands and take a deep breath. "Please," I whisper. "Please."

I lift my gaze to my haunted and hallowed reflection in the mirror. I've lost weight. Too much weight. My cheekbones are shallow and sharp enough to cut glass now. Dark circles rim my eyes all the way around and my skin has turned a sickly gray color. I don't look good, not at all. Grief has this way of sucking the life out of you.

I open the box and hold the slender white stick in my hand.

I'd give anything to have Ben here, fighting to be in the

bathroom with me. Hell, this time I'd even let him watch me pee. But he's not here and he never will be. If I am pregnant he'll never know and our child will never know its father. Maybe it's selfish of me, but I want to be pregnant. I want to know his child is growing inside me—that I have some physical piece of him left.

I say one last silent prayer and don't stall a moment longer.

Waiting for the results to come back is some of the most stress-filled minutes of my life. I keep eyeing the timer on my phone, and when the alarm vibrates I lift the directions off the pregnancy test.

Not pregnant.

The words glare up at me. Mocking me.

I inhale a breath, then another, and then I lose my fucking mind.

I scream—a blood-curdling kind of scream. I shove everything off the bathroom counter. Towels, makeup, toothbrushes, lotion—everything, goes tumbling to the floor. I scream and I keep screaming. I can't stop. I have to let it out.

Knocking starts on the door and the knob rattles. "Blaire? Blaire?" my mom calls, sounding concerned. "What's wrong? Let me in." I don't know whether she's asking me to let her in the room or to just let her in.

I tear at my hair and I kick the bathroom cabinet.

I'm crying again. I'm so sick and fucking tired of crying and now I'm angry. I never understood the term 'seeing red' until now. I seem to see everything through a red-tinged, anger-filled rage. I clench my fists and lean my head back, screaming at the ceiling.

"Blaire?" My mom sounds more urgent now. "You're scaring me."

"Let me scream," I yell through the door.

I hear my dad say, "Let her be, Maureen."

I wish there were more things for me to shove off the counter, but since there's not I settle for throwing anything I can get my hands on. I throw a shampoo bottle at the wall and then my makeup bag. I stupidly throw a bottle of foundation at the wall and the glass shatters and makeup splatters everywhere. I can't bring myself to care. Ben's gone and I'm not even pregnant. My body failed me again. Or maybe I failed me, because I haven't been taking care of myself the last few weeks. Maybe this is my fault.

I slide down the wall, sobbing, and wrap my arms around my legs. I'm falling apart at the seams and I don't know what to do. Ben's always been the strong one. He always knows—knew—what to do in any situation. I'm not like that. I'm more of a follower, and he's a leader.

"Kid?"

I can't answer my dad around my choking sobs. I can't tell him I'm okay anymore, because I'm not. I'm sad. I'm angry. I'm hurt. I'm confused. I'm tired. I'm feeling a million things and none of them are good. There's no happiness inside me and that scares me. What if I never feel happy again? What if it will always be this way? Ben was my sun— What do you do when the sun doesn't shine anymore?

I wipe my tears on the sleeve of my shirt. I'm a fucking mess and now so is the bathroom. It looks like a hurricane hit it.

"Kid?" my dad says again, rapping his knuckles against the

door. "Just tap the door or somethin'."

My breath leaves me in a shaky breath and I lean over and flick the lock on the door. He hears it and slowly eases the door open. He takes one look at me and the mess around me and clucks his tongue.

"Well, Kid, that's one way to go about it."

My lips tremble with more tears.

"I take it the anger set in?" I nod. "'Bout time. I couldn't take your mopin' a moment longer."

I know he's trying to make me smile, but I can't. I try, and I'm pretty sure it looks more like a grimace.

"Let's get this cleaned up," he says. I don't move. "I'll clean up. You just sit there and look pretty."

Surprisingly, a small laugh bubbles up my throat. His lips twitch with a smile, and I know he's pleased to have caused such a reaction.

He begins to pick things up and put them on the counter, and he refolds the towels, putting them under the sink like I should have earlier.

"Hey, what's this," he says suddenly. "Oh. Never mind."

It's too late. I've already seen it. A paper crane. The first one anyone's found in the last two weeks—that I know of. I think they've been hiding them from me when they find them, afraid that I'll break down yet again.

"Give it to me," I plead, ready to fight my dad for it if he doesn't give it to me.

He reluctantly hands me the paper bird. I sit it on my lap and run my fingers around the worn edges. It looks like Ben had lodged it in-between the cracks in the cabinet wall. I lift it to my nose and smell it. It doesn't smell like him, only ink and paper, but it's still a familiar smell, and one I love.

"Kid, you sure you should open that?" My dad watches me like I'm a bomb that might detonate in front of his face at any second.

I nod. I have to open it.

I slowly unfold the edges, peeling back the folds Ben previously made to reveal the message hidden inside.

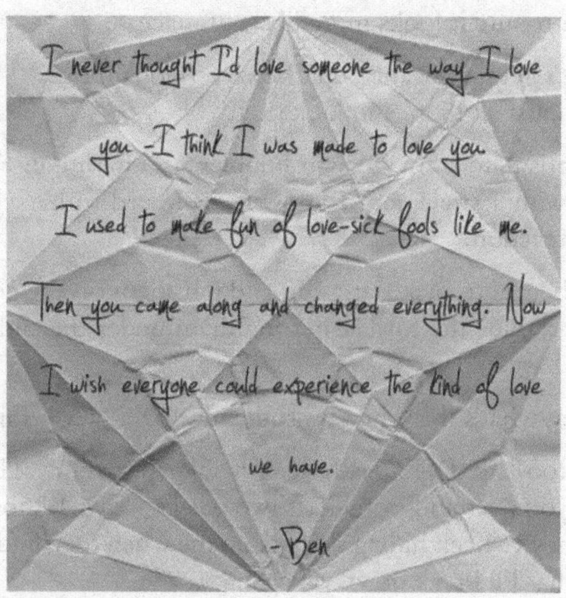

I never thought I'd love someone the way I love you—I think I was made to love you. I used to make fun of love-sick fools like me. Then you came along and changed everything. Now I wish everyone could experience the kind of love we have.

-Ben

I know I'm crying—because it's all I do anymore—but I fold the paper crane back up and hold it to my chest.

"Blaire? You okay?" my dad prompts.

I nod. I'm okay. For the moment, at least, because right

now Ben's here with me. I can feel him even if I can't see him.

12

"You need to go back to work." My mom glares at me across the kitchen table.

"You need to get out of my house."

"Blaire," my mom scoffs, "don't be ridiculous."

I eye her over my bowl of cereal. "I didn't know I was."

She huffs out a breath and her bangs brush her forehead. "We're not going home until we know you're okay."

"I am okay," I tell her. It's a lie, and we both know it. I don't know why I bother even saying the words. She can see right through me.

"You are so far from okay." She rests her arms on the table. "Dan, come talk some sense into your daughter." She calls to my dad where he sits in the family room. He's taken up residence on the couch and claimed it as his own. That's fine with me since I'd rather lie in bed all day.

"Why does she suddenly become my daughter when you're mad?" he calls back.

"You both are exactly the same," she grunts. "Stubborn to a fault." She points a finger at me. "Go take a shower. At least do that."

I resist the urge to roll my eyes. I'm irritated by the fact that my mom thinks she can come to my house and boss me around.

"I honestly don't know what's been wrong with you the last two days." She shakes her head. "You're even worse than you had been."

She doesn't know about the pregnancy test. My dad does, though. He found it when he was cleaning the bathroom. He looked at it, then me, then tossed it in the trash and hasn't said a word since. He's probably afraid I'll bite his head off if he says something. He might be right.

"I'll go shower," I mumble. I'll do pretty much anything to get out of my mom's sight. I know she's trying to help, but I just want to be left alone. I'm sad and angry—I lost Ben and then the news that I'm not pregnant has been devastating. I know I should tell her that, she'd understand, but voicing the words out loud—I'm not pregnant—makes it real.

My mom nods as I leave. I think she's as happy to see me leave as I am to do the leaving.

I take a long shower—washing my body more than once. I even wash my hair which I haven't been doing much of. I haven't had the energy. Something I learned is that crying non-stop makes you exhausted. I feel drained even when I wake up. It sucks, but I'm learning to live with it.

I change into jeans and a t-shirt. It's the first time I've worn real clothes in too long. I've been living in sweatpants and pajamas. Ben wouldn't be happy with me. I know he's probably up there, watching over me, cursing me for being such a bum. I keep telling myself one more day, but one more day has turned into three weeks. What if three weeks turns into three months? I know I can't keep going like this, but my argument is: it's easier than dealing.

I dry my hair, but I don't bother styling it. This is better than I've been doing so I figure it'll make my mom happy.

When I pad downstairs she's sitting in the chair in the front room reading a book. Her jaw drops. "Are those jeans?"

I look down, pretending I didn't already know. "Yeah."

"I feel like I should take a picture," she mutters to herself.

"Don't even think about it," I warn her, coming the rest of the way downstairs.

"Since you're dressed, why don't we go somewhere?" she suggests. "Target? Wal-Mart?"

I stare at her, a bit shocked. My mom considers Wal-Mart the tenth ring of hell. Seriously, she hates the place, so she must be desperate to get me out of house if she's suggesting Wal-Mart.

"Nah, I don't feel like it," I say automatically, starting for the kitchen.

"Dan, grab your daughter and the car keys, we're going to Target."

I stop in my tracks. I know that tone of voice. She's going to kill us if we don't get in the car.

My dad looks over at me from the couch. "You gone and done it now, Kid. You awakened the Kraken."

"Car. Now."

My dad and I get moving. You do not mess with my mom when she sounds like that.

I grab a coat while my dad shoves his feet into his shoes and shrugs on his own coat. My mom is already waiting by the door with her coat on and her giant purse—seriously, the thing is so huge you could smuggle a puppy and a couple of hamsters in there.

We pile into my parents' rental car and Dad drives us to Target. He grumbles the whole way. I would too if I wasn't afraid my mom would beat me over the head with her giant ass purse. The woman can be crazy.

We arrive at Target twenty minutes later.

"Out," my mom says in a clipped tone. If she was a bad guy she'd have a gun held to my middle right about now. I half-expect her to demand, "Walk," when I get out, but she doesn't.

She grabs a shopping cart and sets her purse in the child's seat.

"Let's go." She gestures with her hand for us to follow—almost like she's herding cattle or something.

My dad shoves his hands in his pockets and barrels forward. "I'm getting popcorn."

My mom huffs, "Like hell you are. You don't need any popcorn." She points to his round middle.

He makes a face. "If you expect me to get through this, I'm gettin' me some damn popcorn." He heads off before she can protest further.

She looks to me and sighs. "He's like trying to raise a big kid. He never listens. Ooh, look at this stuff," she says, distracted by the dollar section. "I need these." She grabs a handful of cheap notepads.

I don't bother explaining the difference between need and want to her.

"Kid, you want anything?" my dad calls from across the

way.

My mom makes a face and hisses, "Could he not make a scene?"

"Yeah, get me a Dr. Pepper," I yell back, just to spite my mom. She looks like she's about ready to lose it between my dad and me. It's pretty funny—serves her right for dragging us out of the house.

"You two will be the end of me," she groans. "The end, I tell you."

Normally, I'd make a joke right about now, but I don't feel like it. Instead, I stand there mute.

"Come on, let's look at the clothes," my mom says, ushering me over to the left. "This would be nice on you," she points at a flowery summer dress—and please, someone explain to me why companies put out summer clothes in the middle of winter; no one's thinking about hot days when there's a foot of snow on the ground.

I make a face and move on down the aisle. Not even retail therapy can pull me out of this funk. I commend my mom for trying, though. God, she's trying so hard. Bless her heart.

"How about this?" She holds up another dress, this one a little more weather-appropriate. It's cobalt blue with long sleeves. I actually like it, but I only shrug in response. She sighs and puts it in the cart anyway. That almost plucks a smile from me.

"Here, Kid," my dad says, appearing with a large bag of popcorn and two drinks.

I take mine and mutter, "Thanks."

My mom throws her hands in the air. "Why do you talk to

him and not me?"

My dad looks over his shoulder at her. "Because Maureen, I don't irritate the girl like you do."

She sighs for probably the fiftieth time that day. "I'm not irritating," she argues.

"Yes, you are."

"No—"

"Guys," I interject, "please stop. And Mom, you are irritating—" her face falls "—but I know you mean well." She brightens at this. "Thank you for trying."

She smiles, and I know I've said the right thing.

We walk around the rest of the store and checkout. On the way home, my dad veers off course.

"Dan?" my mom questions, but he doesn't answer her. He continues driving like the two of us aren't staring a hole into his head.

When he stops in front of the café, I nearly have a heart attack.

"Get out of the car, Kid."

All the blood drains for my body. At least it feels that way. "No."

"Kid," he warns, "get out of the car before I drag your ass out. Your friends are waiting."

My eyes flit from the front of the café to my dad. "How?" I ask.

"You left your phone on the couch and you got a text—I'm a sneaky bastard, so I read it. Your friends miss you and want to see you, so I pretended to be you and said you'd meet them for lunch."

I glare at my dad. "You're worse than Mom. You're like the sneaky snake that waits in the grass to get you when you least expect it."

He smirks. "Yeah, that's me. Sneaky Snake. Has a nice ring to it, don't you think?" he asks my mom.

"It's perfect," she agrees.

"I don't want to go," I argue. "I can't see them."

My dad sighs. "Five minutes, Kid. That's all I ask. We'll wait right here for you."

My lips press together in distaste. I haven't seen my friends since the funeral, and I barely spoke five words to them then.

"Out of the car." My dad points to the car door. "You do this thing where you wrap your hand around the handle there and push. Then the door does this magical thing called open. Try it."

I roll my eyes. "You're ridiculous." I put my hand on the knob. "I'm going. See? Bye."

"Good girl." My dad winks. "I'll give ya a sticker later."

I crack a small smile. When I was a little girl, my dad used to give me stickers for every little accomplishment. Get an A on a paper? Here's a sticker, Kid. Win the Spelling Bee? Here's a sticker, Kid.

I head inside the café and find Casey, Chloe, and Hannah waiting for me.

They all flash me a small smile as I approach. My favorite sandwich and coffee is already waiting for me. I take a seat and wave awkwardly.

"How have you been?" Casey asks me.

"Not good." I frown. My hands are shaking so I press them in-between my legs.

"Stupid question, huh?" Casey says.

I shrug.

"I brought by some food; your mom answered the door and said you were sleeping. I hope it was okay. You know I'm not the best cook," Casey says.

I didn't even know she brought food. I'm sure my mom told me, and I probably ignored her. I don't even know if I ate any since I've barely been able to stomach anything. When I do eat, I tend to throw it up. I'm too upset to keep anything down.

"Yeah, it was good," I lie.

"Great." Casey breathes out a sigh of relief.

We all sort of stare at each other and then Chloe loses it. She begins to cry. "I'm so sorry, Blaire. This is all so tragic and sad."

Her tears signal all the rest of us and we all sit at the table in the café bawling our eyes out. Somehow, we end up in a group huddle, holding each other as we cry.

As much as I hate breaking down in public, I need this. I need it so much. I need to cry. I need to be angry. I need to let it out.

"I'm so mad," I say through my tears. "Why Ben? He didn't deserve this. He's so good."

"I know," Hannah says. "It's not right."

"It's not fair," I sob into my friends' shoulders.

I've never been one to use those words before. It's not fair. But that's the way I feel. It's not fair that Ben's time on Earth got cut short. It's not fair that I'm not walking down the aisle to him next week like I should be. It's not fair that I'll never have his baby. It's not fair that I'll never grow old with him. It all fucking sucks.

"It's okay to be mad," Chloe says. "You have every right."

I sniffle. Sometimes I feel like it's wrong that I'm so angry. Angry at myself. At the world. At Ben. I hate myself for being angry at him. It's not like he chose to die, but I'm angry anyway. I know it's part of grief, but I don't like it. I'd rather feel sad than angry.

"You'll be okay," Hannah sniffles. "We're here for you."

I nod. I know they are even if I haven't let them be. "I love you guys," I tell them. I'm lucky to have such amazing friends. I've ignored their calls and texts the last few weeks but they still wanted to have lunch, and if it wasn't for my dad I wouldn't be here. I'll have to remember to thank him later. I needed this.

We separate and sit back. I won't lie, it hurts seeing the empty chair that Ben used to sit in, but for now I ignore the pain in my chest.

"Tell me something, anything," I plead.

"I'm all moved into my new place," Hannah says with a semi-happy smile. I wince, but she doesn't notice. Ben was supposed to help her move. "You should come by and see it, I think you'd love it. My neighbor is a bit … annoying, though." She shudders. "Cyrus. He's constantly throwing parties and he's kind of a jerk, but a hot jerk."

Chloe perks up with interest. "How hot? Like on a scale of one to ten."

"Twelve," she says. "Maybe more."

Chloe fans herself. "Oh, girl, please tell me you're going to try to get under him."

Hannah's eyes widen. "Um, no, I hadn't really thought about that."

Chloe shakes her head. "I will never understand you. You're hot, Hannah, in that nerdy-cute kind of way. Guys dig that. Embrace it. Get some lovin'."

Hannah wiggles uncomfortably in her seat. "Yeah, no thanks."

Casey wraps her hands around her coffee mug. The dark liquid is probably cold by now, but she sips at it anyway. "I broke up with James." We all grow quiet. "What?" She looks at each of us and waves a hand. "You guys knew it was bound to happen. Sooner's better than later, right?"

"Well, yeah," I say slowly, "but how are you feeling about it?"

"Fine." She shrugs like it's no big deal. "It's not important." When we all continue to stare at each other, she huffs. "You all knew it wasn't going anywhere with us—in fact, you've all on more than one occasion urged me to break up with him, so what's the big deal?"

"You didn't say anything," Chloe says softly.

"I didn't think I should, not with . . ." she trails off, but I already know what she was going to say.

Not with Ben gone.

"It's okay," I tell her. "My life is on pause, but I know no one else's is. Please don't treat me like broken glass. It only makes this harder for me."

Casey nods. "I'm sorry, I should have said something, but it only happened a week ago and it's not like we've all been able to get together."

I know her excuse is a feeble one, but I don't bother calling her on it. I don't have the energy. I take a few bites of my sandwich for manners sake, and push away from the table.

"Well, it was good seeing you guys, but I need to go." I stand up from the table.

They take turns hugging me and say goodbye.

As promised, my mom and dad are still waiting outside in the car.

"How'd it go, Kid?" my dad asks when I slide into the back and begin buckling my seatbelt.

"Surprisingly well," I answer.

He smiles in the rearview mirror. "Good. Here's that sticker."

I actually laugh when he passes back a gold star sticker. "Thanks, Dad," I say and stick it on my shirt.

He smiles and nods. He's pleased, and I'm happy that he's happy. My mom looks happy too. I know I've scared her the last few weeks. It's been hard adjusting to life without Ben and I know this isn't even the half of it. The storm is only beginning.

13

"I can't find my pen," I shout at no one in particular. I'm in my office trying to catch up on work and my mountain of emails is out of control. I'm so overwhelmed, and this is just adding to my stress. I can't take much more. I'm losing my mind.

"What's wrong?" my mom asks, standing in the doorway of my office.

"I can't find my mother-fucking pen," I yell, slamming my hands on my desk.

"Blaire—" I begin to sob. "Blaire," she says again, taking a hesitant step into my office. "What's really going on?"

I cover my face with my hands and wail. I'm pretty sure this is my soul crying. I never knew that was a thing until today. I can't believe my mom hasn't figured out what today is.

I wipe at my face. I know it's bound to be red and splotchy. I point to my desk calendar even though she can't see it from where she stands. "We were supposed to get married today," I croak.

Her mouth parts in a surprised O shape. She forgot. Ben hasn't even been gone a month yet and she already forgot our wedding day. He's gone, so suddenly today doesn't mean anything to anyone else.

"I'm so sorry, B," she says, coming around my desk to hug me. I don't want her hug, but I do at the same time. It's a weird feeling—feeling like you want someone to hold you together, but wanting to fall apart at the same time. "I'm sorry," she says again as she holds me. "God, I wish you didn't have to go through this."

"I wish no one ever had to feel this kind of pain." My voice cracks when I speak. My throat is raw and sore from so much crying and screaming.

"Me too, sweetie." She lets me go and looks me over. "I'm going to make you some homemade soup. How about that? Your favorite—broccoli and cheese?"

I'm not hungry, and the thought of food makes me want to throw up, but I nod anyway. I know she wants something to do besides sit around while my dad watches sports. "Sure, yeah, that'd be great."

She smiles. "I'll go to the grocery store, is there anything else you want?"

I think. "Fruit roll-ups," I say. I don't know why I ask for that, of all things. I haven't eaten any in years, but right now it sounds like the best thing ever.

"Okay. Anything else?"

"I don't think so."

She starts for the door, but turns back. "Is that the pen?" She points at one lying five inches to my right.

I look at the pen—studying the slender barrel. "Yeah, that's the one." I sigh.

She leaves me alone then and I breathe a sigh of relief.

I force myself to focus on replying to emails—there's over

two hundred so it's going to take awhile. I'm grateful that so many people are interested in working with me—and city people, at that—but it's a bit overwhelming. After answering close to thirty emails, I decide to take a break. It's probably not a good idea, because the chances of me going back to work are slim, but I can't take another second of staring at my computer. I go to shove my keyboard back under the desk when my pen goes flying through the air.

"Stupid pen," I mumble to myself and climb under my desk to retrieve it.

While I'm under there, I happen to look up at the underside of my desk. Taped beneath it is a paper crane. I gasp, and my heart momentarily stops before restarting and picking up speed.

Ben.

It's like he's speaking to me from beyond the grave.

I carefully peel away the tape and the paper crane comes loose. I want to open it and read it immediately, but at the same time I want to savor the moment.

I opt for savoring.

I slowly peel open the wings of the bird to find what he's written.

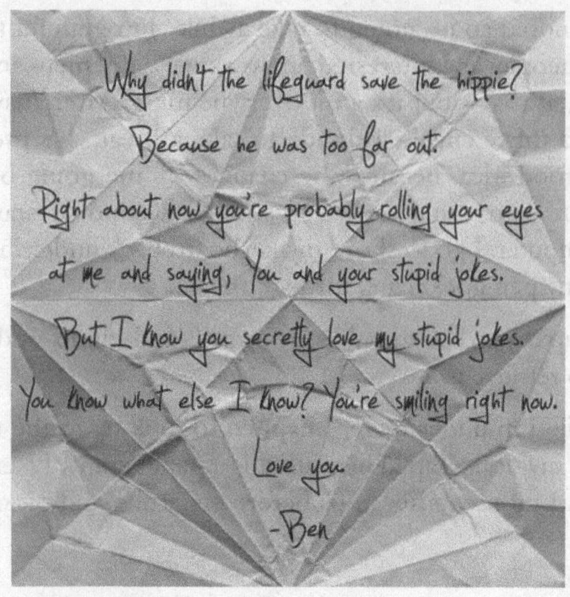
Why didn't the lifeguard save the hippie?

Because he was too far out.

Right about now you're probably rolling your eyes at me and saying, You and your stupid jokes.

But I know you secretly love my stupid jokes.

You know what else I know? You're smiling right now.

Love you.

-Ben

He's right. I'm smiling. Not a little smile, but a full-blown grin. Despite my smile, I feel tears creep into my eyes.

"Oh, Ben," I whisper. "What has become of us. When did our love story become a tragedy?"

I take a deep, shaky breath and refold the bird. I climb out from under my desk and let out a scream when I find my dad standing in the doorway.

"Any particular reason why you're under your desk?" He raises a brow, holding his hands behind his back.

"I dropped my pen and then I found this." I hold up the paper crane for him to see.

"Ah." He nods.

"What are you hiding?" I ask, nodding at his still hidden

hands.

He smiles sheepishly and holds out a plate. "I made you lunch—I figured you'd use lunch as an excuse to stop working." My dad knew me way too well. "So here." He sets the plate on my desk. I eye the sandwich. It's a mess—seriously, it looks like a bear mauled it. Before I can say anything, he says, "I know it looks bad, but I tried. Give your old man some credit."

"It's great. Thanks, Dad."

He stands by my desk. "Aren't you going to take a bite?"

I stare at the ham and mustard sandwich and my stomach rolls. "Um…"

"Come on, Kid, one bite?" he pleads.

"I'm not hungry," I say. "I promise it has nothing to do with your sandwich making skills." He frowns. "Fine," I groan. "I'll take one bite."

He brightens immediately. "I made one for myself too," he says. "It was good, I promise."

I lift the sandwich and nearly gag from the smell, but I swallow back the bile and take a bite. I chew slowly and the texture of the meat and bread is too much.

"I'm gonna be sick," I cry, and launch out of my desk chair. I run into the hall bathroom and fall to the floor, throwing up all the contents in my stomach—which isn't much.

My dad appears in the bathroom and grabs my hair, holding it back while I'm sick.

"Jeez, I'm sorry, Kid." He rubs my back, trying to soothe me. "I guess I shouldn't have pushed you—was it really that bad?"

I finish retching and he lets go of my hair. I stand and rinse out my mouth.

"No, Dad, I think I'm getting sick." I lean against the counter, suddenly feeling weak. I bend down and grab a cloth from the cabinet and dampen it with cool water. I press it to my forehead and take deep breaths through my mouth.

"Blaire . . ." He hesitates in the doorway, seeming unsure if he wants to continue what he has to say.

"What?" I prompt.

"Nothing." He waves a hand dismissively.

"Dad?" I raise a brow. "Spit it out."

He sways slightly—something he only does when he's super nervous. "Do you think maybe you're pregnant?"

Shutters come down over my eyes, and I give him the most withering glare I can muster. "We both know that's not possible."

He shrugs. "Those things are wrong all the time. Maybe it was too early or somethin'. I don't know."

"I'm not pregnant, dad," I say harshly. The last thing I need right now is false hope. My heart can only handle so much heartbreak. "I just have a bug or something, that's all."

He nods. "Fine. Sure." He doesn't look convinced.

"Seriously," I say, moving past him and back into my office. I gag at the smell of the sandwich. I pick up the plate and turn around, practically shoving it at him. "Thanks for trying, Dad, but get this out of here."

"Is there somethin' else I can make you?"

My stomach rolls. "Nope, I'm good."

He looks crestfallen. I feel bad, because I know he tried—there's nothing wrong with the sandwich, just me.

He leaves me alone and I return to my emails. I set up a few meetings with potential clients. As I work, I bite my nails—a habit I gave up long ago, but it's suddenly returned with the amount of stress I feel. I hope my extended absence hasn't ruined my business. I know there's nothing I can do about it now, so I have to take everything in stride.

When I'm all caught up I shut down my computer and turn off the desk light. The chandelier in the center of the room still shines, though. I close my eyes, smiling lightly at the memory.

"Are you sure you want that gaudy thing?" Ben asked, reaching up to touch one of the dangling clear jewels.

"Yes," I laughed. "It's perfect."

He made a face. "It doesn't seem very you."

"I want it for my office," I said defensively. "I want that space to be different."

He shrugged. "Okay, it's your office. We'll get it if that's what you want."

"It is."

He wrapped his arms around me and kissed my forehead. "You're awfully sure about that chandelier—how do you know it's the one?"

I raised my brows. I knew he wasn't talking about the chandelier anymore.

"I just know," I whispered. "When it's right, it's right. Why question it?"

He nodded. "Good answer."

I open my eyes, and they're now clouded with tears. That memory feels like it happened a lifetime ago, when it was really only two years ago. That girl, the one who was so happy and in love, she's gone.

I don't think she's coming back.

14

Stage Three: Bargaining

I lie in bed, staring at the smooth white ceilings. There's not a blemish on the surface. Not a crack or speck. Nothing to look at it. Nothing but whiteness. It's after one in the morning, and I've been in bed for hours, sleeping off and on, but now I'm wide awake and sleep is elusive.

I've been crying off and on. I've grown used to the random bouts of tears that overtake me every day. It's something I'm going to have to live with.

"Please," I beg, staring at the ceiling, "I'll do anything, just bring him back. Anything, I mean it." A tear slides down the side of my face and gets lost in the sheets. Sheets that no longer smell like Ben. When I want to smell him I have to sneak into our closet and smell his shirts. My mom is urging me to donate his stuff, but I don't want to. Not yet. It's too soon.

"I love him," I continue, "so much. I'm lost without him. Bring him back to me." I choke on a sob. "I'm a good person, right?" I question. "Why would you do this to me? What did I do to deserve this? Whatever it was, I take it back. I'll be a better person. Please. If someone had to die, it should've been me, not Ben. He was good. A better person than I'll ever be. He didn't deserve this."

I cover my face with my hands and sob. My hands grow wet with my tears, and my eyes begin to feel puffy. I roll over and clutch the pillow Ben used to sleep on. His head hasn't touched that pillow in over a month.

He's been dead for five weeks.

Even thinking the word makes me want to throw up. It still doesn't feel real. I feel like I'm trapped in a nightmare that's never going to end. I guess in a way I am.

I push off the covers and head downstairs to the kitchen. I know there's no chance of me sleeping. Once in the kitchen, I turn on one set of lights and rifle through the cabinets. I find the packet of hot chocolate and set about making it. I grab a mug and dump in the packet and hot water. I stir the mixture around, the spoon clinking against the side of the mug. I add whip cream, a little bit of chocolate syrup and some chocolate shavings. Extravagant? Yes, but it helps quiet my mind.

I pull out one of the barstools and take a seat. I take a tentative sip. It sucks. Seriously, it tastes like dirty dishwater—not that I know what that tastes like. I drink it anyway, though.

I hear footsteps and I look up to see my dad shuffling into the room in his robe and slippers. His thin hair is mussed around his head, and his eyes are tired.

"I thought I heard ya, Kid." His voice is thick with sleep. "What are you doing up?"

I shrug. "Couldn't sleep."

"What's that?" He nods at my mug.

"Hot chocolate. It tastes awful, but . . ."

He laughs and shakes his head. "But you wanted it anyway," he finishes for me.

I nod. "Yep." I take another sip and wince.

"Give me that, Kid." He swipes the mug from me. "If there's anything your old man can make it's hot chocolate, or have you forgotten?"

I smile and shake my head. "No, of course not."

Hot chocolate late at night—granted, not at one in the morning—was something my dad and I cherished. We didn't do it often, maybe once a month, but it was our time. He'd ask me about school, and I'd ask him about work. Then we'd usually end up talking about my friends. He'd listen with rapt attention, even though he was probably bored out of his mind.

He dumps my pathetic attempt at hot chocolate out in the sink and grabs a pan. He places it on the stove, adding milk, cocoa powder, and a little bit of sugar. He stirs the mixture as it heats.

"Talk to me, Kid. No one's up at this hour unless their mind's full."

I trace the pattern in the granite countertop. "I was wondering what I did wrong," I whisper. "To deserve this," I add.

He continues to stir, but turns to look at me. "You didn't do nothin'. You're a good girl, Blaire. Things like this … they just happen."

"It's my fault," I cry. "I know it is." I inhale a shaky breath and look away. I don't want my dad to see me break down—I mean, he already has about a million times, but I don't want to add another one to the list.

He finishes stirring and adds the mixture to two mugs. He tops it with whipped cream and marshmallows. He hands me my cup and then sits down beside me.

"You've got to stop this, Kid. You're goin' down a slippery path. You can't blame yourself for this. The only person at fault is the guy that was drinkin' and drivin'. He did this, not you. But you can't blame him, either. Blame gets you nowhere in life. You have to move on, Blaire."

I shake my head. "It's too soon."

He shrugs. "Maybe so, but you have to move on eventually. I hate to burst your bubble, Kid, but he ain't comin' back. He's gone. But you, you're still here. You have to live your life—he'd want that for you. You don't need to feel guilty for that."

"I need more time," I whisper.

"You keep sayin' that—" he shrugs "—but I don't see you doin' anything to get better." He wraps his weathered hands around the mug. "I think you should talk to someone. A therapist."

I roll my eyes. "You sound like Mom."

"Your momma's a wise woman. You should listen to her more often—but you're stubborn like me." He bumps my shoulder with his. "Sorry about that, Kid. She's right when she says we're exactly alike."

I soften. "That's not a bad thing, Dad."

"Sometimes it is." He stands and empties his mug. "Goodnight, Kid." He kisses my forehead as he passes. "Get some sleep."

"I'll try," I whisper, but he's gone.

15

Stage Four: Depression

I dress robotically.

Slacks.

Blouse.

Sweater.

Heels.

Necklace.

Watch.

Bracelets.

I stare at my reflection in the mirror. My hair has grown longer, and it's now past my shoulders, but the once lustrous brown locks are now dull and lifeless. My eyes are much the same. My cheeks are still hollowed, and my lips have thinned. I look like I've aged ten years in a month and a half. Stress and grief will do that to you.

I grab my purse and walk out of my closet. I'm meeting a

client at a local hotel so we can check it out before booking any space for an event.

When I step into the kitchen, my parents are both sitting at the kitchen table with a spread of breakfast food. My dad has a pair of reading glasses perched on the end of his nose and a newspaper held between his hands. He must've gone out to get it because Ben and I don't get one.

I mean I don't get one.

"I made you breakfast," my mom smiles cheerily. She's ecstatic to see me up and dressed, ready for work. It's all a façade, though. My insides are gray and stormy and the effort to get ready has nearly drained me. I only hope that I can make it through this meeting before I give up.

My nose wrinkles. "I'm not hungry."

"Blaire—"

"I'll grab a bagel from the coffee shop or something." I wave a hand dismissively. I'd say just about anything right now to get her off my back. I'm horrible, I know. She's only doing what any concerned mother would do in her situation. I'm just testier than normal—I think I have that right.

I grab a bottle of water from the refrigerator and stick it in my purse.

"I'll be back soon," I say.

"Good luck," my mom says, giving me a thumbs up.

"Bye, love you guys." I wave and head out the door.

My mom might be driving me up a wall, but I am thankful that they're here. A few weeks ago I wanted nothing more for them to leave, and now I'm dreading the day they fly back to Florida. The last thing I want is to be alone in this big house.

I get in my car and drive over to the local coffee shop. I end up ordering a caramel latte and a croissant, then I park my car in the lot so I can eat in relative peace. I still have thirty minutes before I have to meet my client.

I take a bite of the chocolate croissant and moan. It's the best thing I've eaten in weeks—completely unhealthy but wholly delicious. I eat the whole thing in a matter of bites. I should probably be embarrassed by that fact, but I'm so happy that something actually tasted good that I can't bring myself to care.

I take a sip of my latte and—oh no.

I throw open my car door and spit up the coffee.

That was awful. I take off the lid and eye the amber-colored liquid. It looks normal, and I've had this drink plenty of times, but man it was strong today. I end up dumping it out, tossing the cup on the floor of my car to throw away later.

I drive over to the hotel and park across the street in the parking garage. The hotel is fairly new in a busy part of town. I've never been here before. The outside is nice, in a minimalistic modern way. It's gray on the outside, four levels, with long glass windows everywhere. The name of the hotel is spelled out in blue neon cursive letters on the outside of the building. I grab my purse and sling it over my shoulder before I head inside.

The inside has concrete floors and long gray couches with no backs. The front desk is directly in front of you when you walk in, and the front of it shimmers with blue light that matches the sign on the outside of the building.

My client isn't here yet, so I take a seat on one of the uncomfortable couches and wait. I grab my compact mirror from my purse and check my makeup. I haven't worn any in so long that applying it this morning took some effort. Luckily, it doesn't look cakey, but my lipstick is fading so I reapply it.

A few minutes later, a tall woman dressed in a business suit with long red hair comes into the lobby.

"Jessica?" I call.

"Blaire?" she responds. "It's nice to meet you."

I stand and offer her my hand. She gives it a quick shake and lets go.

"Have you checked out the space yet?" she inquires.

I shake my head. "I was waiting for you."

"Do you know which way it is?" she asks.

I frown. I should've asked the receptionist that before Jessica arrived. In fact, that's what I normally would've done. My brain isn't working right.

"No, sorry. Let me ask. Wait here." I leave her by the couches and go to ask. Once I have directions, I lead her through the hotel the event room.

The room boasts large, glass, double doors that are tinted so you can't see inside. I open the door and motion her in first.

The space is large and currently empty since they don't have any events happening today. One wall is lined with windows while the others are solid. Three modern chandeliers hang from the ceiling.

"We could hang some draperies around the windows," I say. "To soften it," I add.

"I think this space will be perfect. It's large enough to section space off into rooms, right?" she asks.

"Yes." I nod. "We can do that."

"I think this will be perfect for the reception." She smiles and looks around some more. "You don't plan weddings too, do you?"

I flinch, but she doesn't notice. "It's not really my thing," I say. "I prefer parties."

"I understand," she nods. "I think my wedding planner was disappointed I didn't use her for the reception, but I love your style." She shrugs. "I'll admit to stalking your website."

I laugh. "Well, I'm glad I could help make your day special. We'll get the place booked and then we can meet again to discuss your ideas. Or you can email me, whichever is easier."

"I think I'd prefer to meet. Lunch next Friday?" she asks.

"I'll check my schedule, but that should be perfect." I pull my planner from my purse and check the date. "Yes, that's fine. I'm writing you in now. You can email me where you want to meet."

She smiles. "Great, I'll see you then. I hate to run out, but I'm missing work for this so I have to go."

"Oh, of course." I wave my hand. "Go on, I'll take care of this."

"Thanks so much." She smiles gratefully and leaves.

I walk around the space, taking measurements and allowing myself to visualize what can be done with the space. Unfortunately, I'm not getting many ideas like I normally would. It's like I'm all tapped out.

I head to the front desk and let them know when we need the space. I give them Jessica's contact information so they can get ahold of her for the deposit and then I leave to head home.

I'm exhausted by the time I walk through the door and it's not like I did anything. I hate feeling like this—like I'm walking through sludge.

"Hey, sweetie," my mom says before I can close the door.

"Hey," I reply, kicking off my heels and shrugging out of my coat. I drop my coat on the chair instead of hanging it up and putting it away in the closet.

"How'd it go?" she asks.

"Good."

"Good?" She raises a brow from where she sits on the couch in the front room. "That's all I get?"

"We saw the space, she decided to book it, and left because she had to get to work. There isn't much to tell, Mom." I collapse on the chair in front of her.

She sets the book she'd been reading on the coffee table. "So I was talking to this woman at the grocery store today about your situation, and she told me about this group—"

"Mom," I groan, "why do you have to talk about my business with strangers?"

My mom has always been that way—telling everyone everything. When I was twelve she told the neighbors I'd started my period. I couldn't look them in the eyes for six months.

"Because you never know what you might learn when you talk to people, Blaire," she admonishes. "Anyway, she told me about this grief group. I guess it's sort of like alcoholics anonymous only for sad people."

"For sad people? Really, Mom?"

She shrugs and smiles. "I didn't know how else to say it."

"So what do they call it? Sad Saps Share?"

She laughs. "No. It's just called Group."

"Sounds like an illness."

"That's croup." She shakes her head. "I think you should go. At least once. It might help you to cope, and it might be better than seeing a therapist. These people have lost someone too."

I shake my head and push up from the chair. "The last thing I need is to be surrounded by more people like me." I head for the kitchen and she follows. I grab the orange juice from the refrigerator and pour a small glass. "I'm fine … Okay, I'm not fine," I add when she glares at me, "but I'll get there."

"Not on your own," she whispers and tears pool in her eyes. "You need help, Blaire."

I lay my hands flat on the counter. "Mom, Ben died." I choke on the word. "I don't know how you can expect me to be okay so soon. It doesn't work like that."

"I know," she agrees, "but you're not even trying."

I close my eyes. We have this argument practically every day.

"Here," she says, and I open my eyes. She's pulling a scrap of paper from her pocket and she slides it across the counter to me. It has a phone number scrawled across it in unfamiliar handwriting. "That's the number of the guy who leads the group. Call him. Please. But don't do it for me. Do it for you."

I take the piece of paper and hold it in my palm. I stare at the ten numbers. I want to throw the paper away, but for some reason I don't.

I close my fist around it and hold on.

16

"Here, Kid." My dad holds out a plastic bag from Walgreens.

"What is this?" I raise a brow and take it from him. I peek in the bag and pale. "Dad. No." I shake my head back and forth rapidly and shove the bag back in his hands. "I'm not pregnant. I got my period this morning." I sniffle and look away. I hadn't wanted to tell him, or anyone. I'd been holding onto one last ounce of hope that I was pregnant. When I saw the pink stain in my underwear it was like a kick to the gut. Now, I think my illness was normal and probably a result of not eating much and not being able to eat much. Grief, I've learned, is crippling.

His shoulders sag dejectedly. "I really thought …"

"Me too, Dad," I whisper. I wipe away a tear. I think a part of me believed a baby would fix this. Fix me. But I realize now it would've only made things worse—how on Earth would I raise a baby by myself?

He tosses the bag in the trashcan and covers it with stuff so my mom won't find it. I have to smile to myself over the thought of my dad going to a drugstore and buying a pregnancy test. I mean, he dresses like a lumberjack—jeans, flannels, and heavy boots—and he just has the aura of being a tough guy.

I'm sitting at the kitchen table with my laptop, working on

ordering decorations for a corporate party.

"How you feelin', Kid?" He pulls out the chair across from me and peers at me from over the top of my laptop.

I shrug. "Better than I thought I would. This is … It's for the best," I say. He raises a brow like he highly doubts that. "Look at me," I add. "I'm a mess. I can't raise a baby right now."

"Your momma and I would help you."

"Dad …" I shake my head. "you guys have your own life." I sigh and look away.

"You are our life," he says. "We'd do anything for you."

"I know that." I nod. "But you don't have to."

"There's no have to about it—we want to."

"Thanks, Dad." I pick up the cup of hot tea beside me and take a sip. I instantly cringe. So much for hot tea, it's cold now. "I've got work to do," I tell him.

He nods. "All right, I'll leave you alone." He raises his hands innocently.

He leaves me to go watch TV.

I finish what I'm doing and close my laptop. I rub my hands over my face and groan. It's not even lunchtime, and I'm exhausted. All I want to do is go to bed and sleep. I don't seem to have the energy anymore to make it through the day.

I glance to my right at the refrigerator. The stupid phone number for the grief group. I'd ended up throwing the number away, but my mom found it and stuck it there. I haven't moved it. It's taunting me. My gut tells me to call, but my heart says it's not ready to move on. Besides, I don't know if I can handle being around other grieving people—hearing their stories, sharing their pain. I'm scared it'll push me over the edge I'm dangling precariously from, but on the other hand, I think it might actually help.

"Call the number, Kid."

I jump at the sound of my dad's voice and turn to find him watching me from the family room—the TV now muted.

"How'd you know?" I ask.

"I know everything." He taps his forehead. "Dad powers." I look back at the phone number but make no move to grab my phone. "Look at it this way," he begins, "if you go to one and hate it you don't have to go back. But if you like it, this might be exactly what you need."

I give him a small smile. "Dad, has anyone ever told you that you're really smart?"

His dismisses my words with a wave of his hand. "That's your momma, not me."

"She's smart," I agree, "but you are too."

As if conjured by our words, she arrives home at that moment, bumbling through the door with bags of groceries. She goes to the grocery store almost every day. I know it's an excuse for her to get out of the house. She usually buys ingredients to make some recipe she finds on Pinterest. Seriously, the woman is a Pinterest addict. I'm expecting her to start crafting any day now.

"Hey," she says, closing the front door, "what are you guys up to?"

"Blaire was just about to make a phone call," my dad answers. I'm thankful that he doesn't make a big deal out of this.

If he told my mom was going to call the group she'd probably start dancing and singing, which would only embarrass me and make me not call. "Did you get me any beer?" he asks her, distracting her from me.

She answers him, but I've already tuned them out.

I have the number memorized, so I don't even have to look at the paper when I enter the numbers into my phone. "I'll be in my office," I say, holding up my phone.

My mom nods, thinking it's a work call.

I head upstairs and into my office, closing the door behind me.

I take a seat on the swing and make the call.

It rings. And rings. And rings. Just when I'm about to hang up, a man answers.

"Hey, hello? Sorry—hold on a second," he says. "Cole, don't do that. I told you not to color on the walls. Give me that." I hear some shuffling and then, "Sorry about that, my son was trying to color on the walls. You take your eyes off him for five seconds and suddenly your walls are covered in blue scribbles."

"Uh … sure."

"So, what can I help you with?" he asks. His voice is deep and pleasant.

"I think I might have the wrong number," I hedge. This certainly doesn't sound like someone who'd be in charge of a group about grief. "I'm looking for the person in charge of … of Group," I whisper the word like it's something dirty.

The man chuckles. "You got the right number. I'm Ryder, and I'm the head of the group. We have a meeting tomorrow if you want to join?" he suggests.

I bite my lip, thinking it over. I know if I don't go tomorrow I never will. "Yeah, I'll be there," I say. "Where do you meet?"

"We meet at the high school in the gym. Do you know where that is?"

I nod and then realize he can't see me. "Yes," I say.

"Cool, we'll see you there …" he pauses, waiting for my name.

"Blaire. I'm Blaire." I clear my throat awkwardly.

"See you tomorrow, Blaire. Bye."

"Bye." The phone clicks off, and I stare down at the screen. I know this is what's best for me. What's right. But I'm scared. I'm learning that I'm scared a lot lately. It's not something I'm used to, and I don't like it.

17

I park outside the double door entrance to the school's gymnasium. I'd had to call Ryder back to get the time to meet—he'd apologized profusely for the slipup, but I promised him it was okay. There are a few other cars here, but otherwise the lot is empty. It's seven in the evening and already pitch-black out. I hate that about the winter.

I turn the car off but make no move to get out. I know I need to. The group is starting any minute. But I need a moment to gather myself.

I lean my head against the back of the seat and close my eyes. I startle a moment later when someone knocks on the glass, screaming and jumping straight up in my seat.

The guy raises his hands innocently. He looks to be around thirty years old with thick black hair and almond-shaped eyes hidden behind a pair of glasses. He's wearing a gray sweater with the sleeves rolled up to the elbows. How is he not freezing?

He motions for me to roll down the window, but since I turned the car off, I can't. I'm not afraid of him—there's nothing scary about him—so I step out of the car.

"I'm Ryder," he says, holding out a hand. "I'm going to assume you're Blaire?"

I nod, my dark hair blowing around my face when I put my hand in his. His hand is warm despite the cold air.

"I usually check the lot for first-timers." He shrugs, and we head toward the building, out of the cold. "I've been leading Group for a year now, and I've learned that people tend to hide in their car the first time they come. I know I did my first time."

My eyes widen in surprise. "You've lost someone?"

"Yes—" he chuckles "—why else would I be leading Group?" He opens the door for me and waves me inside.

I step into the warmth of the school, and the door clicks shut behind us. "I don't know." I lift my shoulders. "I guess I figured you were a therapist or something. You're not?"

He laughs. "No, I'm a teacher." I lean against the cinder-block wall and he stands across from me. "Group isn't a therapy session. It's a place for people who've been through similar things to just … talk. It helps being around people that understand and don't constantly say, 'I'm sorry for your loss,'" he mimes with a sneer. "If I could have a dollar for every time I've heard that," he mutters. "Are you ready to go in?" He points to the doors leading into the gym.

I nod. "I don't really know what to expect?" I let my question hang in the air.

"You'll see." He winks. He opens the gym door, and like before, he holds it open for me. I step inside and find ten or so people sitting in chairs positioned in a circle. There's a table set up near the wall with coffee, water, and donuts.

"Hey, Donny." Ryder waves to an older balding man. "Thanks for bringing the donuts." Under his breath, Ryder whispers to me, "He usually forgets when it's his turn."

I laugh lightly and it feels good. For the moment, at least, I've forgotten where I am.

"Amy, can you grab another chair for Blaire?" Ryder asks.

"Sure thing." A woman a little older than me with shiny blond hair stands and heads into a closet.

"Do you want some coffee? Donuts?" Ryder leads me to the table.

"I think I'll have some coffee," I say, reaching for a white Styrofoam cup. I pour a little coffee in and Ryder hands me a thing of creamer.

"You look like a creamer kind of girl." He grins. He has a nice smile and his dark eyes light up. He doesn't look sad, or grieving, but maybe he's not anymore and that's why he's in charge of the group.

"Thanks." I take the creamer from him and pour it in.

Ryder nods and waits for me to take a seat—the empty chair now beside Amy.

Ryder takes the other empty chair, which is almost directly across from me.

"How are you guys?" he asks, taking a sip of his coffee. "Christopher, did you get that promotion?" he questions a man to my right.

"Sure did." The man nods, smiling from ear to ear. "It's the first good thing that's happened to me since my Beth died."

"Good, good. I'm happy for you, man." Ryder sets his cup of coffee on the floor near his feet. He leans forward and claps his hands together. "As you all can see, we have a new member. Blaire, this is everyone. Everyone, Blaire."

"Hi." I wave awkwardly.

"Hello," they all echo.

"Shall we go around and introduce ourselves?" Ryder asks. They all nod. "Please say your name and one thing about yourself. Anything you choose. I'm Ryder, and I hate the color orange."

"I'm Donny, and I love the color orange."

Ryder laughs and says to me, "Donny likes to spite me."

The next person speaks up. "I'm Debra, and I love to knit." She proudly points to a gray scarf wrapped around her neck.

The next eight people introduce themselves and then Ryder looks at me. "Your turn, Blaire."

I nibble on my bottom lip as I think. "I'm Blaire," I begin, "and I'm happy I decided to come here."

Ryder grins. "Good, Blaire. You see, here we're not defined by our grief. We're just people like anyone else."

My lips lift and spread. I'm smiling, and it's real.

This … this is going to be good for me. I feel it.

We all chat for the remainder of the hour. I find out that Amy has two little boys and she's newly married. Peter, the man to my left, is in college and studying astronomy. I've never met anyone like him before, and I find his stories about the stars to be amazing. By the time we leave, I feel happy and not once, through the whole hour, did I think about Ben. I was normal.

I'm walking to my car when Ryder jogs up beside me.

I pause outside my car and tilt my head up at him. "I just wanted to say goodbye," he says. "And see if you're coming back next week."

"Yeah, I am. I … This was nice. It was nothing like what I expected."

"That's the point." He grins, and his eyes crinkle at the corners. I'm finding that Ryder is an upbeat, always-looking-on-the-brightside, kind of person. I wonder who he lost, though, and if he was always like this. "I'll see you next week."

"Bye," I say and lift my hand to wave. "Whoa," I cry suddenly when I feel dizzy. I sway unsteadily and hold a hand to my forehead.

"Hey, are you okay?" Suddenly Ryder is right there and he wraps his hand around my arm, like he's ready to hold me up if I begin to crumble. His touch is electric and I feel it even through my thick coat.

"Yeah, yeah, I'm fine," I mumble, waving away his concern. "Just got a little dizzy, that's all."

He lets me go and looks me over. "You should've had a donut," he jokes. "The sugar would've kept this from happening."

I laugh. "You're probably right." I unlock my car. "Bye … again."

"Bye." He laughs and walks away, toward a white Nissan Murano.

I head straight home.

My mom is waiting right by the door for me. It's like she has spidey-senses or something.

"How was it?" she asks before I can even close the door.

I lock the door and lean against it. "Good," I answer. "I

enjoyed it."

She's positively beaming at my words. "I made dinner. Lasagna."

I can smell it from here. "I'm not very hungry." Now that I'm home, all I want to do is crash. It's been a long day.

She frowns. "Blaire—"

"I'll eat later," I promise her. "I just need to lie down for a while. This was exhausting." Even though I actually liked Group, it was pretty draining. I spent so much time worrying about what it would be like that I think I used up all my energy.

"All right." She sighs. "If you want some in bed, just text me."

"Thanks, Mom." She brightens at my words, and I frown. Is this the first time I've told her thank you? I hope not. She's been doing so much. Feeding me. Keeping the house clean. Heck, she even got my checkbook and paid the bills when it was obvious I wasn't going to do it. "I love you," I tell her, and lean over to kiss her cheek before I head upstairs.

If there's one thing Ben's … death … has taught me, it's to love and appreciate everyone you care about. Young or old, they can be gone too soon.

Once in my room, I kick off my shoes and head into the bathroom.

I pull out my tampon and wipe. Nothing. Not a drop of blood now. My period has been non-existent since two days ago when I thought I'd started. Now, I'm not so sure that what I saw was actually my period.

I finish up and wash my hands but I can't get it off my

mind. I shower and change into my pajamas. I grab my laptop off the chair in my bedroom, where I'd left it last night, and get fixed in my bed. I Google spotting. I bite my lip nervously. According to the almighty Google gods, spotting can be normal during the first trimester of pregnancy but it's not a sign of pregnancy.

I close the laptop and set it aside.

My heart is racing, but I don't want to get too excited. I'm so afraid of being disappointed again and I don't know if I can handle the crushing pain I felt after the last pregnancy test I took.

I turn on the TV and try to distract myself.

It's futile, though. I can't get it off my mind. I need to know.

I slip out bed and downstairs. My dad is parked in front of the TV like usual but my mom is nowhere to be seen.

"Where's Mom?" I ask, tiptoeing into the kitchen. I don't know why I'm sneaking around. It's not like I'm doing anything wrong.

"She said she was going to take a bath," he answers.

I nod and open the trashcan. I don't have to rifle through it very much, because we're not messy people. I pull out the pregnancy test, still wrapped in the plastic bag from Walgreens.

"Whatcha' doin', Kid?" he asks. I pull the box out of the bag and drop the plastic bag back in the trash. He raises a brow. "Thought you didn't need that?"

"I didn't think I did, either," I whisper, turning the box over in my hands. I open the box and pull out the white stick. Rip it off like a Band-Aid, Blaire. I tell myself.

It's better to know now.

I head into the hall powder room and pee. I put the cap back on the test and head out to the family room, sitting down beside my dad.

"I didn't want to be alone," I tell him. My throat is thick with unshed tears. I'm scared. I still want this even though I shouldn't. I'm not in a good place mentally.

"It'll be okay, Kid." He pats my shoulder. "Breathe," he adds.

I exhale. I hadn't even realized I'd been holding my breath. "How long has it been?" I ask.

"Twenty-seconds. Cool your jets."

I sigh and set the timer on my phone. I place the pregnancy test on the table so that I'm not looking down at it every few seconds.

"It'll be okay, Blaire. Either way." I know he's picked up on my tension.

I nod once woodenly. There's nothing else I can do right now but wait.

When the timer on my phone goes off in my lap, I jump. I press the button to stop it and then I sit there. I'm completely frozen, terrified to move.

"Do you want me to look first?" he asks me.

I shake my head. I know I have to be the one to do this, but I need one more second—one last moment to hope.

I exhale and reach forward, picking up the test. I don't look right away, still clinging to a fraying shred of rope. I let go of that rope and look down.

It's positive.

I choke on a sob and cover my mouth with my hand. I'm having a baby. Ben's baby. It's actually happening, and I hold the proof in the palm of my hand.

"Is that a good cry or a bad cry?" he questions. "Shit, Blaire. You're scarin' me."

"What's going on?" I look up to find my mom walking into the room. The ends of her hair are damp, and she's wrapped in a pink robe.

I hold out the test to her and she takes it. She squints down at the small screen. Her mouth slowly parts in surprise. "You're pregnant?" She grins.

I nod and tears—tears of happiness—roll down my cheeks. "I'm having a baby," I whisper. It's really happening. It's the first good thing to happen to me since Ben died. I'm still scared shitless, and I know I have a long way to go before I'm okay, but this … this makes me happy.

My mom sets the test down on the coffee table and sits down beside me on the couch.

"Oh, Blaire, I'm so happy for you." She hugs me.

"Thank you." I hug her back, crying into her shoulder. She doesn't complain, though, she lets me hold on and cry. I finally pull away and my dad holds a tissue out for me. "Thanks," I say and take it, dabbing at my eyes.

"I'll make you a doctor's appointment," my mom tells me, clapping her hands together. "You want to make sure everything's okay before you tell anyone," she warns.

I nod in agreement.

"Well, Kid," my dad speaks up, "you ready to raise your

own kid?"

I laugh. "I guess I have to be." I look down. More tears form in my eyes. I take my mom's hand in mine and squeeze. "We were trying to have a baby before … before …" I can't say the words out loud. Thinking them is bad enough.

My mom nods and brushes a few errant hairs off my forehead. "This baby is special," she says, tears pooling in her eyes. "This is a little piece of Ben left on this Earth. Not everyone gets that, B."

"I know," I whisper and wet my lips with my tongue.

Suddenly, I feel a slight bit of cool air brush against my cheek. I close my eyes.

Ben's here—I know he is.

We're having a baby, I tell him.

The cold air brushes against me again.

I take that to mean, I know.

18

My leg bounces nervously as I sit in the doctor's office, waiting for them to call my name. My mom wanted to come with me, but I insisted on going by myself. I probably should've let her join me, but I was afraid she'd make me more nervous than I already am.

"Blaire Kessler?" a nurse calls my name.

I grab my purse and stand. "That's me," I say unnecessarily.

She smiles pleasantly. "Hi, how are you?"

"Good," I mumble, wiping my sweaty palms on my jeans as I follow her down the hall.

The walls are painted a horrid tan color with brown trim. I'll never understand why doctors' offices are always painted such dull colors. She leads me into a room, and I take a seat on the crinkly white paper covered bed.

"So, Blaire you think you're pregnant?" she asks.

I nod. "That's what the test said."

She smiles. "About how far long are you, do you think?"

My nose crinkles in thought. "Probably around six almost seven weeks." I feel a crushing weight on my chest. That would mean I might've gotten pregnant the last night Ben was alive. I suddenly feel sick.

"Okay, so newly pregnant then." She writes something down.

"Well, I don't think I'm about to give birth in a toilet, if that's what you mean." I laugh awkwardly.

"Change into this gown," she says, pulling one from a drawer. "The doctor will have to do a vaginal ultrasound."

I pale. "That sounds painful." I take the gown from her hands.

"It's not too bad," she says and stands. "The doctor will be in soon."

I nod and with one last smile she leaves me alone.

"Breathe, Blaire," I whisper-hiss to myself. I exhale a long breath and change into the gown. I sit back down and let my now bare legs dangle beneath me. The paper is scratchy beneath me, and I find myself wringing the cotton gown between my fingers. My eyes flicker to the clock above the door. It ticks endlessly as I wait for the doctor arrive.

When the door finally opens I mutter, "Oh thank God," under my breath. I'd been about to lose my mind.

"Hello, Blaire." Dr. Hershel smiles pleasantly and washes his hands in the sink. He's been my doctor for years now. He's probably in his fifties, with brown hair only beginning to gray at the temples. He has kind green eyes that are always full of laughter.

"Hi," I squeak. My nerves are through the roof.

"Don't be nervous," Dr. Hershel says, drying his hands and tossing the paper towel in the trashcan. The nurse comes in behind him and hands him my folder. "Let's take a look here," he mutters, laying the folder aside. He sits down on the stool and begins fiddling with some items hooked up to a monitor.

I'm pretty sure I'm about to throw up.

I wish Ben was here.

He should be here.

This moment belongs to him as much as it does me, and yet here I am, alone. So, fucking alone.

I should've let my mom come with me, but it's not the same.

"Let's see your baby," he says.

"Wait," I hold out my hands, "shouldn't you do a blood test or something first?"

His lips quirk. "Pregnancy tests rarely lie. We see a lot of false negatives, but they're usually pretty accurate when it comes to positive."

I nod. "O-Okay. Proceed."

He chuckles. "You're funny, Blaire." I wasn't trying to be funny. "Put your legs in the stirrups."

I cringe. Stirrups. I don't know why, but I hate that word the way some people hate the word moist. I do as I'm told and lie back with my legs up. Such a flattering position. I close my eyes and cover my face with my hands. I do better if I don't see what's happening. I jolt when I feel something slide inside me. Oh, Jesus.

And then a moment later …

I lower my hands and my mouth parts. "Is that?"

"Your baby's heartbeat?" Dr. Hershel asks for me. "It is. It's a bit early to hear the heartbeat, but it's a strong one. It looks like you're almost seven weeks pregnant, like you predicted. You see that?" He points to a tiny dark blob that flickers on the screen. "That's your baby. Congratulations." He smiles up at me.

I immediately burst into tears.

Happy tears.

Sad tears.

Angry tears.

Basically, they're every sort of tear rolled into one. I'm excited and relieved to know there's a baby inside me, but sad and pissed off at the same time because Ben's not here to experience this with me. He'll never hear the sound of our baby's heartbeat. He'll never press his hand to my stomach and feel our child moving inside me. So many nevers when I thought I had a life full of forevers.

"I'll print off some ultrasound photos for you," Dr. Hershel says. Neither he nor the nurse comments on my tears. I'm sure they get them a lot.

"Thank you," I croak, wiping my eyes with the backs of my hands.

This is really happening, I think to myself.

I leave the doctor's office and sit in my car staring at the grainy black and white photos. I touch the tiny blob reverently. That's my baby.

My phone rings from the depths of my purse, and I rifle through it to find the slender silver phone. It's my mom.

"Hello?" My voice is thick with emotion.

"How'd it go?" she asks. "Is everything okay?"

"Yeah, I'm definitely pregnant," I say. "I got to see the baby and hear the heartbeat. The doctor said it was early, but it was so strong, Mom. It's like the baby knew I needed to hear it." I sniffle and look for the small pack of tissues I keep in my purse. I pull one out and wipe the dampness from beneath my eyes.

"Oh, sweetie," my mom breathes in relief. "I'm so happy for you."

"Thanks," I reply. "I'm happy too, but …"

"But what?" she prompts.

My lower lips trembles, and my knuckles turn white where I grip my phone. "But I wish Ben was here."

I can hear her intake of breath over the phone. "I know, sweetie. I know."

I lean my head back, and my throat bobs when I swallow past the lump in my throat. "It's all so unfair."

"Blaire," she says sharply. "Stop it. You can't do this to yourself."

I hear her words, but they don't make much impact. "I'm going to see Loraine," I tell her. "I want to tell her in person."

"When will you be home?" she asks me.

"I don't know. It'll be a few hours. It'll take me at least one hour each way depending on traffic, not including the time I spend with her."

"Just call me when you leave her house," she says. "I worry about you."

"I know, Mom," I whisper. "I will."

"I love you," she says.

"Love you too." I end the call and toss my phone on the seat beside me.

I look at the ultrasound photos one last time before sliding them into the envelope the nurse gave me. I run my fingers through my hair. I know I look like a mess, but there's not much I can do to make myself look presentable at this point.

I turn the radio up, hoping to drown out my thoughts as I drive to Loraine's.

When I get there, Jacob's shiny silver Lexus is in the driveway. My throat catches at the sight. Poor Loraine. I haven't reached out to her at all. I've been so consumed by my own grief that I've forgotten about hers.

I go to pull down my sun visor, in the hopes of fixing my makeup since I know mascara is smeared beneath my eyes, and I jolt in surprise when a paper crane begins to fall. My eyes seem to watch it in slow motion as the white piece of paper flutters to my lap. Ben. He always knows when I need him most. Even in death he's still here when I need him.

My fingers shake when I pick up the paper crane and unfold it.

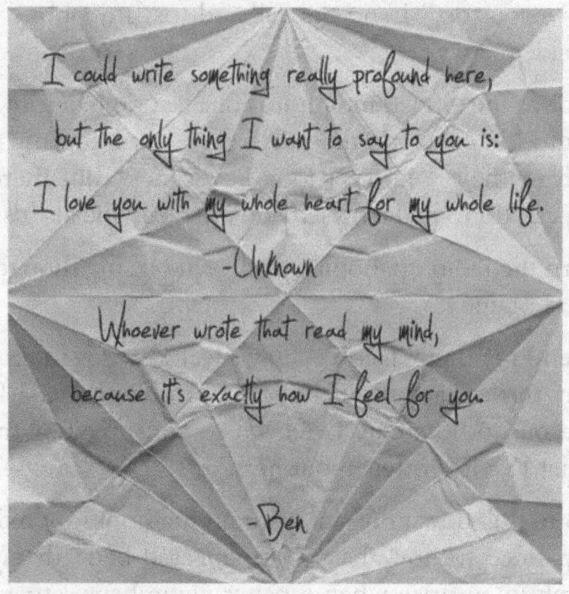

I hold the paper to my heart and close my eyes as tears leak out. "Me too, Ben," I whisper. "Me too."

I grab a tissue and clean up my ruined makeup before refolding the paper crane and sticking it in my purse.

I cradle the ultrasound photos protectively in my hand and heft the heavy purse onto my shoulder.

When I reach the door, I hesitate a moment before knocking, but I finally raise my hand to the door and do just that. My feet shuffle against the porch as I wait.

The door opens and Jacob stands there in a pair of jeans and a t-shirt. Seeing Jacob is like a kick to the gut. He looks so much like Ben, only a little older. His hair is a similar golden shade, only a little bit darker. His face is more carved, whereas Ben's is—was—more boyish. Jacob's eyes are nearly the same color blue, but his now boast small wrinkles at the corners.

Whereas Ben had the dimples in his cheeks, Jacob has one in his chin.

"Hey, Blaire." He holds the door open for me. "How are you?"

I shrug. "I have good days and bad days." I don't tell him that there are more bad than good. "How are you? Why aren't you working?"

"I'm doing okay." He ruffles his hair before closing the door. The inside of the house is dark, like there aren't any lights on. Normally, the house is so warm and cozy. Not today, though. Today, it feels empty and lifeless. "Mom was having a bad day so I decided to work from here."

I nod and bite my lip, looking up at him through my lashes. "I should have called her or something …" I trail off.

"She could've called you too," he reasons, crossing his arms over his chest. "You've both been through a lot. Don't beat yourself up over this too." He reaches for my shoulder and gives it a reassuring squeeze. "She's this way," he says, and leads me through the house to the kitchen.

"Whoa," I mutter under my breath.

"Mom bakes when she's sad." He shrugs.

The kitchen is covered in flour, sugar, and all kinds of other baking things. There are finished pies lined up on the table, cupcakes, cookies, and what looks like fudge.

"Jacob, can you take one of those pies to Maryann? I think she'd appreciate it."

"Sure thing, Mom," he says. "You have a visitor."

"A visitor?" She turns away from whatever she's working on now. "Oh, hi, Blaire." Her lips turn down in a frown like she's not happy to see me.

"I'm sorry I haven't called or been by." It seems like the right thing to say.

"Oh, that's fine." She waves a hand dismissively. She wipes her flour-covered hands on her apron. "Let's sit in the family room." She motions us out of the kitchen. "Too much clutter in here." She turns to wash her hands in the sink and removes her apron, getting flour on her hands again in the process. She curses—in all the time I've known her, I've never heard her say one bad word—and washes her hands again. She runs her fingers over her frizzy hair that's trying to escape the confines of a clip. "Want a cookie?" she asks suddenly. "I have chocolate chip, raisin, oatmeal, sugar—"

"A sugar cookie would be great," I say, not wanting to turn down her offer.

"Here, take the whole plate," Jacob says. "She's already made more."

"Um, thanks." I take the plate from him when he hands it to me.

"I'll get you a baggy," Loraine says, opening a cabinet drawer. I can tell she's just trying to busy herself. "Here you go." She brings me a gallon-size Ziploc bag.

I dump the cookies inside and hand Jacob back the plate. Loraine promptly takes it from him and starts for the sink to wash it. Jacob wraps his hand around her upper arm to stop her. "Mom, we should go sit down. You can wash that later."

She nods. "Right. Yes. I'll wash it later," she says in short, clipped sentences. I've never seen Loraine so unhinged, and I don't like it. She's always been such a strong woman—someone I've looked up to—and to see her come undone like this hurts. If Loraine is still doing this badly, it doesn't bode well for me.

We all move into the family room, and I immediately hate the choice of venue. The beige walls are covered in family photos. Pictures of Ben from a tiny infant to a grown man cover the walls. It's like looking at a timeline laid out of his life—one that ends abruptly and all too soon.

I take a seat on the dark-brown chair that matches the couch Jacob and Loraine sit on.

I clear my throat and clutch the envelope the photos are in. "I'm sorry for just showing up," I say, my hands shaking, "but I got some news I wanted to share with the both of you." They stare at me, waiting for me to go on, but I flounder unable to find words. "I ... um ... I," I stutter. I didn't expect this to be so awkward. "Loraine," I begin, "I ... Do you remember when I told you that Ben and I ... we were ... we were trying to have a baby before ... well, before ... and well, I'm pregnant." Tears fill my eyes once more.

Loraine chokes on a sob. "Ben's ... Ben's baby?"

"Of course," I snap in anger. "Who else's would it be?"

"I'm sorry." She rubs her eyes. "I'm just surprised. That's all."

"Me too," I whisper, the anger leaving me. "The first test was negative, but when I took another a while later it was positive. I guess I took it too soon," I muse. "The doctor confirmed it this morning. Here—" I hand her the envelope, which I forgot I was holding "—that's our baby."

She opens the envelope flap slowly and pulls out the photos even slower. There's only three of them and they're hooked together.

"Oh wow," she murmurs, lifting a hand to her mouth. Jacob sits beside her staring at the photos with an open mouth. Jacob, speechless—that's a first. "What a miracle," she breathes. "A complete and utter miracle. Come here, hun. I need to hug you." She stands and crosses the small space to me.

I stand too, and she wraps her arms tightly around me. I sob into her shoulder. My emotions are all over the place today.

"He should be here," I cry against her. "We should be telling you together."

"I know." She runs her fingers through my hair, trying to soothe me. "I miss him too." She pulls away and takes my face between her hands. "You're a brave, strong, woman, Blaire. Don't ever forget that. Even when the bad days seem endless, remember that. Promise me?"

"I promise."

"And remember, you have me. You have Jacob. Just because Ben's gone it doesn't mean we are too."

I nod and hug her again. I then go to hug Jacob.

"Congratulations," he whispers in my ear and hugs me tight.

"Thank you." I step back and wipe at my eyes. I let out a little laugh and point at my face. "All I do is cry."

"Me too." Loraine points at her own tear-stained cheeks. "Do you want to stay for lunch?" she asks.

I bite my lip, torn. I know my mom's probably waiting for me to get home and worrying herself endlessly, but I haven't seen Loraine since the funeral. Finally, I nod. "Yeah, I'll stay."

"Great." She claps her hands together. "I don't feel like

cooking. Jacob, why don't you go pick up Chinese and bring it back here?"

Jacob chuckles under his breath and bumps my shoulder with his. "The irony," he mutters.

"I heard that." Loraine swats him playfully.

"I'll call it in and be back," he says, pulling his car keys and phone from his pocket. "Don't burn the house down while I'm gone."

Loraine rolls her eyes, but he doesn't see. To me she says, "He's a worry-wart."

"I heard that," he yells before the front door closes behind him.

While he's gone, Loraine and I chat about all the random things we can think of. Neither of us really wants to talk about Ben; it's too painful.

Jacob returns with enough food to feed ten people.

I'd worried about being here, but in the end, I enjoy myself, and I promise to come back soon. I can't shut Ben's family out just because it hurts. They're in as much pain as I am.

19

I stand in line waiting to order a cup of hot tea. I'm meeting a potential client in an hour for breakfast, but I needed out of the house and away from my mom. Now that I'm pregnant, she's become even more of a clinger than normal. "B, are you hungry? Blaire, you should really eat something. Here, let me clean that." I'm trying to work on not snapping at her, so I decided to leave this morning.

I finally reach the register and place my order for a hot tea and muffin. I pull out my wallet and search for my debit card.

"Here, I got it," a voice calls before I can hand over my card. I look up and see Ryder walking over with a ten-dollar bill extended to the cashier. I'm too shocked to stop him. "Blaire, right?" he says with a crooked smile.

"Um, yeah." I nod. "Thanks," I say, when the cashier hands over the receipt and change.

"No problem." He shoves the coins in his pocket. "I thought that was you, and I thought I'd do something nice." He flashes another smile. He's dressed for work in a pair of gray dress pants and a white, button-down shirt.

"Well, thank you," I say again. "It's … uh … nice to see you." The words come out stiff and awkward.

He chuckles and grabs my tea and muffin bag. "I'm sitting

over here, if you'd like to join me?" he asks, tilting his head toward a table where a cup of coffee and a breakfast sandwich waits. He holds my items out to me, though, giving me the option to take them and leave.

A big part of me wants to do just that—leave—but it feels rude. So instead, I nod and tuck a piece of hair behind my ear. "Um, yeah, sure," I say. "I'll join you."

"Great." He smiles widely and carries my things over to the table. He sets them down across from his stuff and pulls out a chair for me.

"Thanks," I say with a grateful smile. Thanks and thank you seem to be all I can say to him.

Ryder sits down across from me and his knee bumps mine. "Sorry," he says immediately and scoots back a bit. He picks up his coffee and takes a sip. "How are you?" he asks and then cringes. "Stupid question, don't answer that. It was my least favorite question when I lost my wife." He takes a bite of his sandwich, not missing a beat.

"So, you lost your wife?" I question and then I'm the one cringing. "Sorry, that was rude of me to ask."

"Nah—" he waves a hand dismissively "—it doesn't bother me now. But I remember when it was fresh every little thing someone said could set me off." He shrugs. "But yes, my wife died."

I bite my lip. I want to ask how, but I don't want to bring up the topic of my loss so I let it go. "Are you on your way to work?" I ask instead.

He nods and wipes his hands on a napkin. "Yeah, I forgot to eat breakfast. Don't worry, I fed my son before I dropped him off at daycare," he jokes.

"How old is your son?" I ask. That seems like a safe enough question.

"Two," he answers. "And let me tell you, they don't lie about the Terrible Twos. They're the worst." He takes another bite of his sandwich. "Not complaining, though. I love that kid."

I laugh. "I didn't doubt that."

"So where are you headed?" he asks.

"Breakfast meeting with a client." I pull out my muffin and break off a piece. It's chocolate chip and warm inside so the chocolate is a gooey melted perfection.

"What do you do?" he asks.

"I'm an event planner. I have my own business."

His dark almond-shaped eyes widen in surprise. "That's awesome. Good for you."

"Thanks." I fiddle with the paper that once surrounded my muffin. Oh God, I said thanks again. Kill me now. I take another bite of muffin before I can say thanks yet again.

"What got you into event planning?" Ryder asks, flicking a dark piece of hair from his eyes.

I shrug. "I don't know. I've always liked planning parties, so I decided to see if I could make a go of it. It helps that we live so close to D.C. Lots of business," I answer.

Ryder clears his throat suddenly. "I wanted to clarify something. I know I said that in Group we don't really talk about our loss, but it's not forbidden. If you need to talk about it, you can. I just like group to be more … relaxed, you know? I want people to get to know each other and be comfortable. I think that comfort makes it easier to talk about it, but I knew I made it sound like it was forbidden or something so, I wanted to clear that up," he rambles, his tanned cheeks turning slightly red. It's kind of adorable.

I laugh. "I understand, and I think the way you run things is great. I'm not … I'm not ready to really talk about things."

He nods. "I was like that, too, but once I opened up, I felt a lot better. And Blaire?" He waits for me to nod. "If you want to talk about it to me, or any of the other Group members individually, that's fine too. You don't have to share with the whole group."

"I'll keep that in mind." I finish my muffin and dust the crumbs off the table.

Ryder glances down at his watch. "I have to go if I'm going to make it to school on time."

"What grade do you teach?" I ask him.

"Fifth," he says, finishing his sandwich and gathering up his trash. "I'm glad I saw you, Blaire. Have a nice day." He smiles and picks up his coffee cup before heading out the door. I watch him leave, and it's not until his car disappears that I realize I'm smiling.

20

It's been three days since I saw Ryder, and in those three days I have not been able to stop thinking about how he made me smile. Sure, I've forced a few now and then since Ben died, but never has one come so readily to my lips in the last few weeks. My frozen cheeks damn near cracked from the pressure of it.

I park outside the school gym, and unlike last week, I don't linger in the car. I head inside the building and find that I'm early. Only four other people are here, including Ryder.

He smiles and waves when I enter.

I lift my hand and wave back before grabbing a bottle of water from the table and a cupcake. These people like their sweets, but I guess when you're grieving, you usually do.

I take a seat and drop my purse at my feet.

Ryder excuses himself from his conversation with Bill, another member of Group, and sits down beside me. He's dressed casually today in a pair of dark wash jeans and white t-shirt and an open navy cardigan. His glasses are perched on his nose again, completing the nerd-chic look.

"Hey, Blaire." He smiles. "How are you?"

I ponder over his words. Normally I would answer with an ambiguous fine, but the fact of the matter is I'm not fine. I see no point in lying to him or anyone else here for that matter. We wouldn't be here if we were okay. We're here to work on our demons.

"It's been a rough few days," I answer honestly.

His lips turn down in a frown. "I'm sorry to hear that, but thanks for being honest. We'll talk more about it once everyone's here." He taps my knee lightly with his fingers before standing. He moves his attention on to the next member to arrive at Group. I admire the way Ryder goes out of his way to make us all feel comfortable.

When everyone's arrived and grabbed a cupcake and drink, we begin.

Ryder takes his time addressing each and every person—asking them about children, parents, their dog, and job, basically anything not related to death.

When he gets to me, he says, "Blaire, you said you'd had a rough few days, tell us about it." He crosses his foot over his knee and waits for me to speak.

With all the eyes suddenly pinned to me, I find myself closing up. These people, they're nice, but I don't really know them. I look around, from one face to the next. My heart begins to pump faster, like a runner about to cross the finish line, and sweat beads on my upper lip.

Suddenly, I find myself standing and running from the room. There's a bathroom across from the gym and I burst inside. I grip the white porcelain sink in my hands and breathe in and out through my mouth. My head is lowered, staring into the depths of the sink because I'm too scared to look up and see my frazzled reflection in the mirror.

The door opens behind me, and I swing my head in that

direction, expecting to find Ryder, but instead it's Amy. The woman who got the extra chair for me last week. Her blond hair is pulled back in a ponytail and her eyes look tired, much like mine. She's dressed in a black pencil skirt, pink blouse, and black heels like she came from work to here.

"Hey." She approaches me slowly like I'm a wounded animal that might rear-back and pounce on her if she gets too close. "Ryder asked me to check on you."

I turn away from the sink completely and face her. "I'm . . ." I don't know what I am.

"Please come back, Blaire," she pleads. "You don't have to talk if you don't want to. Sometimes listening to other people helps distract your mind. At least, it works for me." She shrugs and her heels clack against the tile as she comes a bit closer.

I don't realize it until she grabs both my hands and forces me to loosen them that I was digging my fingernails into the palms of my hands. She releases me and tilts her head, studying me.

"I was you, once. Still am, I suppose. Every little thing made me jumpy. I would overthink everything instead of allowing myself to be in the moment. This group . . . it's really helped me—all of us. Trust me, you'll feel better if you go back in there and stick it out."

I nod. "I don't even know why I freaked out," I tell her, my lower lip trembling with the threat of tears.

"Overthinking," she repeats, and taps her index finger against the side of her head. "We've all done it."

"Even Ryder?" I find myself asking. He's so calm, cool, and collected that I find it hard to see him ever losing it like me.

She raises a brow. "Especially Ryder. He might be the head of Group now, but he still has his moments where it gets to be too much."

"Just give me another minute," I tell her. "Please?" I add when she doesn't move.

"I'll be waiting outside the door," she says. I hear her warning loud and clear—she's not going to let me sneak out of the building. I wasn't planning to anyway.

Once she leaves, I turn back to the sink and twist the knob for the cold water. I splash some on my face and pat the back of my neck. I turn the water off and grab a paper towel to dry my hands.

As promised, Amy is waiting outside the door. Together, we head back inside the room and take our seats. No one looks at us. They go on with what they're saying, and I breathe a sigh of relief that I'm allowed to fade into the background.

But when I look up, my eyes connect with the dark-brown of Ryder's, and I know he wants to speak to me. I quickly look away, hoping to avoid him calling me out.

When the hour is up and Ryder launches into his "goodbyes" and "see you next weeks", I grab my purse and get out of there as quickly as I can without running away … again.

I'm almost to my car when I hear footsteps pounding behind me.

I know it's him, but I don't stop or turn around. He jogs in front of me and stops, forcing me to stop as well.

"What do you want?" I ask, my tone sharper than normal.

Ryder's tall, like really tall, so he bends down a bit so he can look into my eyes better. I think he's looking for something in them. "To make sure you're okay," he answers me.

"I'm fine."

He shakes his head. "You're not fine or you wouldn't have run out. It's okay to get scared and not want to talk. What I want to know is, would you have told me if it was just the two of us?"

"I don't know," I answer honestly, adjusting my purse strap on my shoulder.

"Try it now," he says, tapping his chest. "Tell me why you've had a rough few days, Blaire."

I look away. I don't want to talk even though the words are right there, bubbling at the surface.

"Come on, Blaire," he says again, getting right in my face. He's not mean about it, just persistent. "Talk about it."

The words burst forth from me like water breaking free from a dam. "My life sucks right now," I shout into the empty parking lot—since everyone has either left or is still inside the building. "I'm having a baby and Ben's dead. I miss him so damn much and I'm going to have to raise our child all by myself," I cry. "How can I teach my baby to love someone they'll never know?" I choke on the last part.

Ryder stands there, seeming to think carefully about what he's going to say.

"I know it seems impossible," his voice is soft, "but you'll find a way."

"I won't." I shake my head.

"You will." He touches his hand to my arm.

I bite my lip and look up at him through my damp lashes.

"How can you be so sure?"

"Because I did. Granted, my son's only two, but I make sure he knows who his mom is and that she loves him even though she can't be here. I know he loves her too, because he's always asking for her. Her picture, at least." He shrugs and shoves his hands into the pockets of his jeans. "And as he gets older, I'll continue to tell him stories about her and what a wonderful person she was. It's not the same as her being there, but it's enough."

I inhale a shaky breath and choke on a sob. "How do you do it?" I ask him. "All on your own?"

He nods. "It's just me and Cole. My parents help some, and Angela's parents too. They all love Cole to pieces, even if he's a little hellion most of the time." Ryder smiles fondly. "I know things probably seem impossible right now, but trust me, once that baby is in your arms all that goes away. Heck, maybe even sooner for you," he says. "As a dad, I don't think it really hits you until the baby's here."

"I'm scared," I confess. I don't know why, but I find it easy to talk to Ryder. Maybe because our situations are similar, or maybe it's just him. He has this sweet, easy way about him that instantly puts me at ease without him even trying.

"I'd be more worried about you if you weren't scared," he says. "I was scared shitless when Cole was born and knowing that Angela wasn't going to be around much longer. I didn't even know how to change a diaper. I'm pretty sure the nurse in the hospital rolled her eyes at me fifty billion times before we left. I bet you at least know how to change a diaper."

I giggle and he grins, having had his intended effect. "I do," I say.

He touches my arm again briefly. "You'll be okay, Blaire. Not today, or tomorrow, or even the next day, but I promise you this: one day you'll wake up and say I'm okay. After a time, you'll even wake up and say I'm good. And then, I'm great. But healing doesn't happen overnight. It takes time and you have to allow yourself to do it. Let yourself feel the pain; your heart will mend itself." He looks down at his watch and cringes. "I have to go. I'm late to pick up Cole. You have my phone number, though. If you need to talk, call me. You won't bother me."

"Do other people call you?" I ask quickly. I don't know why, but I need to know. I want to make sure he isn't offering me special treatment.

He shrugs and his t-shirt stretches over his firm, muscular chest. "Sure. Sometimes."

I nod and tuck a piece of hair behind my ear so that it's not blowing in the wind.

"Bye," I call after him. When he turns and smiles at me over his shoulder I add, "Thank you. I … I needed that."

His smile grows. "You're welcome." He tips his head at me and then ducks into his SUV.

I shiver from the cold air and get in my car, cranking up the heat.

I sit there a moment, marveling at how one conversation made me feel a thousand times lighter, before I finally drive away and head home.

21

Morning sickness is the worst, but I refuse to complain. Okay, maybe a little bit.

I stand and wipe my mouth on a damp washcloth before washing my hands and brushing my teeth.

I'm silently thankful that I work from home and don't have to endure this while at a job.

I pull my hair back in a sloppy bun and a few strands fall forward to frame my face. My hair has gotten pretty long, longer than I've worn it in a while. I should probably schedule an appointment and get it cut, but I don't feel like parting with it.

I turn off the bathroom light and step into my closet. I change into a pair of jeans and a loose purple sweater that falls over my shoulder. It's comfy and one of my favorite outfits.

When I get downstairs, my mom is already waiting with a steaming cup of hot tea. Since I'm not allowed to drink coffee, hot tea has become my go-to drink.

"Thanks, Mom." I kiss her cheek.

"You look nice," she says, rummaging through the refrigerator and pulling out a carton of eggs.

"Thanks." I look down at my plain outfit. There's nothing

that nice about it, but I quickly realize this is one of the first mornings I've come down dressed in regular clothes and not my pajamas. I'm sure my mom is about ready to burn all of my pajamas so she never has to see them again.

"Morning, Kid," my dad says from the kitchen table. "Sleep good?" he asks, looking at me over the top of the newspaper he's reading.

"I did, actually." It's one of the first nights I haven't fretted before falling into a fitful sleep. Talking to Ryder yesterday has really helped.

"Good." My mom positively beams as she cracks an egg into the pan. "Your dad wants an egg sandwich; do you want one?" she asks.

"Sure." I shrug and take a seat next to my dad.

Her smile widens in surprise. "You want it the same way you used to like them?"

I nod. "Yeah, cheese, tomato, and mayonnaise," I tell her. My stomach rolls. "You know what, scratch the tomato."

She laughs. "Okay, then."

My phone vibrates in my pocket, and I pull it out to see a text from Casey.

Casey: Can u do lunch 2morrow with the girls?

Me: Yes.

Casey: :) Great! You know the place. ;)

I set my phone aside. "I'm having lunch with the girls tomorrow," I announce. My parents exchange a look from across the kitchen. "What?" I ask.

"Glad to see you acting normal, Kid. You might not need

us around much longer."

Panic seizes me. Not too long ago I would've been thrilled for my parents to head back home to Florida, but now I need them here.

"Don't get any ideas," I say.

They exchange another look. I don't want to know what that one means, so I don't ask.

My mom finishes making our breakfast sandwiches and sets the plates in front of us. She even brings over the carton of orange juice and glasses. I make a mental note to get her something nice like a gift card to her favorite store. She deserves it. She's kept this house running while I've fallen apart.

I thank her and dig into my sandwich. For the first time in weeks I actually have an appetite. I'm not sure if my lack of one has been due to being pregnant or a part of the grieving process. Maybe it's a bit of both.

I eat every morsel, and my mom grins at my empty plate. "Want another one?" she asks, all too eager to hop up and make it.

"No." I wave her down before she can jump out of her seat. "I'm full, but that tasted great."

"If you change your mind and want another one, all you have to do is ask," she assures me.

"Thanks, Mom." I stand and pick up my plate, rinsing it off in the sink before sticking it in the dishwasher. "I'm going to go work for a bit."

"But it's Saturday," my mom says, a wrinkle forming in her brow.

"I know, but I haven't exactly been working consistently

and I need to make up for it."

"Oh, that makes sense." Her frown leaves, replaced once more with a smile.

I hug my dad as I pass and kiss my mom's cheek before heading up to my office.

Today, so far, is a good day. I haven't had many of those in the last two months.

I lose myself in my work for a few hours, and I'm amazed by how much I'm able to get done. By the time I finish up for the day, I've made a decent dent in planning two events and I'm all caught up on emails with clients and potential ones. It's nice to feel on top of things for a change. I don't know how much longer it might last, but I take this as a small victory, because that's what it is. One small win in a battle to heal.

22

Today is not going to be a good day. I wake up and immediately want to go back to sleep. I don't want to have to get out of bed and deal. The empty space beside me in bed suddenly feels ice cold and as vast as the ocean. I stretch my fingers across the cool expanse, reaching, searching, hoping. But Ben's not there and he'll never be there again.

I'll never get to wake up to his smiling face while he says, "Morning, beautiful," and I complain about my stinky breath when he tries to kiss me. He always said, "I don't care," and kissed me anyway.

I swallow thickly, and a tear leaks from the corner of my eye, falling onto the sheet. I roll to my side and close my eyes. If I think hard enough, I can picture him in my mind. Tousled blond hair, soft but firm lips, wide grin, and bright-blue eyes. But his voice … I'm forgetting what his voice sounded like, and that scares me more than anything. I don't want to forget anything about Ben. Not ever.

"I miss you," I whisper. "So fucking much. It still doesn't feel real," I admit. "I keep feeling like someone's going to jump out from behind a wall and say, 'Haha, got you.'"

My eyes are still closed, and the Ben I see in my mind laughs at me.

I unconsciously scoot closer, but instead of being met with

warm, inviting arms, there's just sheets and blankets. I slowly peel open my eyes and take in the emptiness of the bed once more.

No amount of imagining is going to bring him back. I wish it was that simple.

I roll back over onto my back and cover my face with the crook of my arm. I don't want to get out of bed. I don't want to go about my day like everything's okay when it's not.

And then, like a swift kick in the stomach, I feel like I'm going to throw up.

I throw the covers off my body and run to the bathroom, collapsing in front of the toilet.

Morning sickness. Lovely.

I have to laugh, though, at the irony of it. All I wanted was to stay in bed and mope and my unborn baby is having none of it. Their dad was the same way—always pushing me. I feel like this is my baby's silent way to encourage me to get up and deal.

"You're already bossing Mommy around," I say when I stand up and flush the toilet. "Your daddy would be proud."

I brush my teeth and wipe my face off.

When I look in the mirror, I want to cringe. I look exhausted despite getting a full night's sleep. I look haggard and I'm not even thirty-years-old. I know I'm supposed to meet the girls for lunch, but I find myself coming up with every excuse possible in my mind—they all sound ridiculous.

I glance longingly through the doorway at my unmade bed. It calls my name, but I don't allow myself to succumb to the temptation.

Instead, I do something completely out of character and call Ryder.

As the phone's ringing, I realize that it's probably way too early to call on a weekend. It's barely seven in the morning. Before I can hang up, though, he answers.

"Hello?"

I pause. "Um, hi … It's Blaire."

"Hey, Blaire," his tone of voice brightens, "are you okay?" Before I can respond, he says, "Dumb question, you wouldn't be calling me if you were okay. What's up?"

I hop up on my bathroom counter and let my feet dangle. "Today's a bad day," I say simply.

"Ah, I see."

"I was wondering if maybe we could meet for coffee or breakfast or something," I ramble.

He hisses between his teeth. "I can't, sorry. I have Cole today."

I wince. "Oh, right. I forgot."

"You could come by my house, if you don't mind?" he asks. "I'd suggest meeting at a park so Cole can burn off some energy but it's too cold."

"Um …" I pause, nervously wringing the fabric of my pajama shirt in my hands. It feels awkward and like I'm crossing boundaries to go to his house, but then again, that's silly. We're two adults having a conversation, that's it. "I can do that," I finally say after a lengthy pause. "Can you text me your address?"

"Yeah," he says. "And, Blaire?"

"Yes?"

"Bring coffee."

I smile. "I can do that."

"Good. See you soon."

I hang up with Ryder and I already feel lighter. I change into a pair of jeans, a long-sleeved t-shirt, and a sweatshirt. I don't feel like dressing nice, and I think Ryder will understand.

I slip my feet into a pair of flats and grab my purse, stuffing my phone inside.

Downstairs, my mom's already awake, sitting on the couch reading a book.

She closes it immediately when she sees me and launches into a million questions, not even giving me a chance to answer. "How are you feeling? Did you sleep well? Are you hungry? Do you want juice? Tea? Is there anything I can do? Blaire?"

"I'm fine," I tell her. "I'm … meeting a friend for breakfast."

Her brows furrow. "I thought you were seeing the girls for lunch."

I sigh. "I'm meeting someone from Group, okay, Mom?"

Her eyes widen in surprise, and her mouth parts slightly. "Oh."

"Yeah." I hedge toward the door. "So, I'll see you later."

"Okay," she says. "Is there anything you want in particular for dinner?"

My mom, always concerned about what I'm going to eat. I

think, for her, she feels like it's one of the only things she can control in the chaos that is my life now.

"No," I say, picking up my keys from the side table. "Whatever you want is fine with me."

I can feel her frustration from across the room, but she only says, "Okay," and goes back to reading her book.

I dash out the door before she can decide to ask me anything else.

Ryder has already texted me his address, so I put it into my navigation system and listen to the monotone British lady try to guide me to his house—she keeps telling me to turn around since I'm going to the coffee shop first. I've always wondered why the voices on navigation systems are British when we live in America. Is it some kind of conspiracy or something? Is it someone's way of trying to tell us the British are coming? I frown when a memory prickles at my mind.

"Ben, I'm telling you, someone's trying to warn us. A modern day Paul Revere. But instead of just saying, 'The British are coming,' they've used a British person for our navigation systems. Someone's trying to communicate something to us. I know it." He laughed at me. "Don't laugh." I glared at him.

He only laughed harder. "What?" he asked innocently. "Telling me not to laugh is only going to make me laugh harder. I think it's pretty adorable that you've given this so much thought."

I crossed my arms over my chest and looked out the window. "It'll be really adorable when I shove my foot up your ass," I mumbled under my breath.

"What's that?" he asked, grinning from ear to ear. I knew he heard me, so I didn't repeat myself. "I know you're trying to be menacing right now, but you look too cute for me to be afraid of."

I frowned. With my puffy coat and pom-pom beanie, he was probably right. There was nothing frightening about me. "I'm not cute," I said anyway.

"Beautiful?" he supplied. "Magnificent. Breathtaking. I can keep going." I cracked a smile. "Ah, there it is."

"What?"

"Your smile. Anytime you lose it, it's my job to find it."

The memory fades, and I fight against the tears that want to fall.

I miss him. So much I ache inside. There's this vast emptiness that now lives inside my chest without Ben. He was my sun—and what am I supposed to do now that my world has fallen into complete darkness? Ben once called me his flower, but a flower cannot live without sun.

My hands tighten around the steering wheel as I turn into the lot of the coffee shop I saw Ryder at earlier in the week. It doesn't have a drive-thru, so I park and head inside. I order him their regular coffee, since he didn't specify, and also get him the sandwich he was eating the other day. Since I'm already here, I get myself a hot tea and a muffin. I ponder the menu a little longer and end up getting another muffin for his son. It doesn't seem right to come in with food and not bring anything for his kid.

I take a seat on the velvet couch and wait for my name to be called. I have to wait a little longer than normal because of the sandwich. When my name's finally called, I grab the bag with the sandwich and muffins, plus the cardboard drink carrier. Someone's nice enough to hold the door open as I head out. I set everything on the floor of my car and I'm pretty sure my navigation system breathes a sigh of relief when I finally listen to her.

Ryder's house turns out to be only a few neighborhoods over from mine.

It's a small two-story bungalow. Three steps lead up the front door and a small porch with two white rocking chairs. There's a large window on the second floor with a balcony. It's cute and homey, definitely still boasting small touches left behind from Ryder's wife—like the navy and white striped pillows on the rocking chairs.

I open my car door before reaching over to grab the bag and cup holder. I balance everything carefully so I can get out of the car without spilling coffee all over the inside of my car.

I walk up to the front door, and since my hands are full, I bump my shoulder against the doorbell. It's only after it rings loudly that I realize I shouldn't have done that in case his son is still sleeping.

The door swings open and Ryder stands there in a pair of sweatpants and a waffle-knit Henley. Behind him, a little boy runs across the hall, yelling, "Weeeee," as he goes. The boy is completely naked and Ryder looks exhausted.

"Sorry about that," Ryder says, pushing his glasses up his nose before ushering me inside.

The little boy comes running back by. "Weeeee," he cries again.

"Don't have kids," Ryder jokes.

"Bit late for that." I laugh.

He chuckles and closes the door. "Right. Here, let me take

that." He reaches for the items in my hand.

I start to hand them over, but then his son comes running back to us and crashes into Ryder's legs, making him stumble. I quickly move so that the drinks don't spill.

"Cole," he admonishes, "where's your diaper? And your clothes?" To me, he says, "The kid won't leave his clothes on. I'm going to start duct taping them on." He picks up Cole, and the little boy smiles bashfully before ducking his head against his dad's shoulder. He looks a lot like Ryder with a mop of dark hair and dark eyes framed by thick black lashes. He points to my right. "Kitchen is that way. You can't miss it. I'm going to get this one dressed … again." He sighs and starts up the steps.

I head in the direction he indicated and through a dining room into the kitchen. It's bright and cheery with white cabinets, gray countertops, and yellow walls. I set the drinks and paper bag on the oak wood table and pull out one of the chairs, taking a seat while I wait.

I hear the steps creak a few minutes later and Ryder steps around the corner into the kitchen with a fully-dressed Cole.

"He'll be naked in twenty minutes, tops." Ryder shakes his head as he puts Cole in his highchair.

"I got you breakfast," I tell Ryder. "And I got Cole a muffin; it's blueberry, so hopefully he likes that."

Ryder grins. "Thank you, you didn't have to do that. Cole loves blueberry muffins, but only because he thinks it's dessert." He shrugs.

I smile and open the bag, handing Ryder his sandwich and Cole's muffin.

"I'm starving," he says, staring at the Saran-wrapped sandwich with longing. "When it's just Cole and me it's hard to find time to feed myself. He's at a stage where I can't let him out of my sight." He picks up the muffin and goes to get a plate. He cuts it into small bite-size pieces for Cole and puts it on an animal-shaped plate. It looks like a tiger.

Ryder puts the plate on Cole's highchair and the little boy's face lights up.

I take my own muffin and peel the wrapper off.

"So, what did you want to talk about?" Ryder asks, already on his second bite of sandwich.

I shrug and sip at my tea to stall for time. I have no idea what to say.

"Blaire," Ryder says in a stern tone, "you can talk to me."

"I know, otherwise I wouldn't be here. Talking to you makes me feel better."

He grins. "Good. I take it our talk the other day helped?" He raises a single dark brow and waits for my answer.

"It did." I wrap my hands around my cup. "Yesterday, I was good … not great, but more normal than I have been since I lost … since I lost Ben." I swallow around the lump in my throat. I hate saying his name out loud now, and I, in turn, hate myself for hating it. Ben was the love of my life and it feels like an injustice to his memory to not be able to say his name, which is why I'm forcing myself to use it. "But today," I pause, searching for the best way to explain, "… today I woke up and as soon as I opened my eyes I knew it wasn't going to be a good day. All I wanted to do was lie in bed and not do anything."

Ryder is quiet and he seems to be mulling over what I said. "But you did get out of bed," he comments, peering at me over the top of his glasses, "and you called me. Look, Blaire, you even went by the coffee shop and got drinks and food."

"What does that have to do with anything?" I ask, my nose crinkling with my confusion.

"Everything." He gives me a look like he can't understand why I don't see what he's saying. "You didn't let your grief conquer you, you conquered it. You saw where your day was going and you stopped it. You should be proud of that, Blaire."

"How can I be proud when all I want to do is scream?" I confess.

Ryder's lips twitch. "Then scream if that's what you want to do. Stand on the chair, lean your head back, and scream, Blaire."

I pale. "Are you serious?"

"Yes." He stands up and scoots his chair back before standing on it. "Come on, Blaire," he coaxes, "you want to scream? You scream. You want to cry? Then cry. And guess what? If you want to laugh, or smile, or be happy, you can do that too. Don't hold yourself back from feeling whatever it is you need to feel." He speaks with so much emotion, like he's giving a speech to a room full of people and not me and a toddler. "Up," he says, pointing at me. "I'll stand here all day if I have to." He sticks his hands on his hips and tips his head down at me.

After one more second of hesitation, I push my chair back and stand on it.

"Hey, Cole?" Ryder says, and the little boy angles his head up to his dad. "Wanna scream with us?"

"Yes!" The little boy smacks his fist against the highchair

tray. "Scream!"

Ryder looks at me. "We're ready when you are."

"This is silly," I say, still nervous.

"No, it's not." He shakes his head. "It'll make you feel better and there's nothing silly about that."

I nod. He's right. It will make me feel better.

I close my eyes, tilt my head back, and scream.

And it's the greatest feeling in the world, like I'm emptying all the sadness and anger out of me. I scream and scream and scream. I'm aware of Ryder and Cole screaming with me, but it suddenly doesn't matter. I no longer feel silly for screaming. It's what I needed to do. When I finally stop, I lower my head and I smile—no, I grin—at Ryder. He smiles back.

Since we've stopped screaming, Cole does too, and he looks disgruntled, like he wants to keep going.

"Feel better?" Ryder asks me.

I smile and bite my lip. "Much better." I step down off the chair and so does he. We both take a seat once more and it's like the previous moments never happened. Ryder resumes eating his sandwich, I take a sip of my tea, and Cole throws a piece of muffin at Ryder. The chunk of muffin lands in Ryder's hair.

Ryder's dark eyes flit to me and with a straight face he says, "I want to laugh so bad right now, but if I do it'll only encourage the demon."

"Demon?" I laugh.

He shrugs with a grin. "I mean that with the utmost of fondness." He reaches over and ruffles Cole's dark hair.

"How long did it take you?" I ask him suddenly. "To … move on?"

He winces and presses his lips together so they're nothing but a thin straight line. "I don't know that I've ever truly moved on. I still miss Angela every day, but there's not this aching, gaping wound in my chest anymore. I think I'll always miss her and think about her, but maybe it'll get to the point that it's not every day and only occasionally—but I hope that's not the case. I'm good now, great most days, but I don't want to ever forget her."

"How … Never mind." I shake my head and look away.

"How'd she die?" he asks for me. He flicks a dark piece of hair away from his eyes, waiting for me to answer.

"You don't have to tell me." My words are no more than a whisper.

"That question doesn't bother me, not anymore, at least." He shrugs and takes a sip of coffee before clearing his throat. "It was breast cancer," he answers. "She was young to get such an aggressive form and she didn't find out until she was four months pregnant." He looks to Cole with a forlorn smile. "Her doctors wanted her to get an abortion, but she refused. She wouldn't have given up this little guy for anything." His smile grows and he reaches over, poking Cole's cheek lightly. The little boy giggles in response and then looks at me shyly.

"And what about you?" I ask. "Did you … agree with her decision?"

"Honestly? No, not at first. It's different for guys. We don't have a child growing inside us, so we don't feel that immediate bond. We argued a lot about it. We both knew she was giving up her life for our child's by not undergoing treatment, and

I constantly reminded her that she could get better and we'd have other children." He sighs. "But Angela was stubborn, and she refused to do it. She wanted him no matter what. Watching her grow weaker and weaker through her pregnancy was hard. It was even harder watching her prepare the nursery and knowing she wasn't going to be here to use it." His eyes fill with unshed tears. "And then Cole was born and they placed him in my arms and I got it. I finally got it. I never questioned her decision after that. She died two weeks later, and even though she was so tired and weak, I think those were the happiest two weeks of her life."

Ryder's story crushes my already aching heart. He surprises me by not asking about how I lost Ben, but I'm even more surprised by the fact that I want to tell him. He understands the kind of heartache I feel and it's nice to be able to talk to someone who gets it. I'm sick of being looked at with pity and being told, "I'm so sorry," or "It'll be okay." Neither are things I want to hear right now.

"It was a car crash," I say, looking down at the worn table and then up at Ryder. "Ben was a doctor, and he was on his way to start a late shift and . . ." I feel the tears come and slide down my cheeks, and I look away hastily so he can't see me cry.

I startle a moment later when warm fingers grip my chin and turn me back. Ryder looks at me intensely, like he sees me—not the physical me, but the pain and suffering and heartache I feel underneath.

"Don't hide from me," he whispers, his own tears still threatening to fall from his eyes. "Don't ever be ashamed of what you feel. You're allowed to cry, Blaire, and no one will judge you for it. Definitely not me."

"Why does this kind of stuff happen?" I ask him. "It's not fair."

He lets go of my chin and sits back. "No, it's not fair," he agrees, "but it's life and life is rarely fair. I used to stay up every night and ask myself what I did wrong in my life to deserve losing Angela, and then on one of those nights I realized there wasn't anything I did or didn't do. These things just happen. It's not a personal attack on you or me. It was a freak thing, and that's it."

"I've been doing that," I admit. "Asking myself what I did to deserve this," I confess, wiping my tears on the sleeve of my sweatshirt.

"It's normal," he tells me, glancing toward Cole. "I think we all go through that when we lose someone tragically."

"Getting that call ..." I begin. "I've never felt so panicked and helpless before."

He winces. "Death is never easy, but at least I had some preparation with Angela."

I think over his words. "I think in some ways that would be worse. Every moment you'd wonder if it was your last."

"True," he agrees. "It just sucks all the way around."

I nod. "We were engaged," I tell him.

His eyes flit to my finger. "And you're still wearing the ring."

"I am. You're not." I nod at his fist resting on the table.

He opens his hand and lays his palm flat on the table. "I used to. I only took it off recently. I think you know when it's time."

"Two months ago I thought I had my whole life ahead of me, and now I see nothing."

He shakes his head rapidly. "No, no, that's completely wrong. You have a life, you have everything. Especially now." He waves his hands toward my stomach. "Not everyone gets to hold onto their love that way." His eyes flit to Cole. "But it's really special when you do."

"Right now I'm still too sad and scared to see that. What if I never do?" I worry my bottom lip between my teeth.

He reaches across the table and wraps his hand around mine, giving it a small squeeze. "You will, I promise."

"Thank you," I tell him. "For letting me come over and talking. I ... I feel a lot better."

He smiles widely. "Good, I'm glad I could help. I'm here for you anytime you need it."

I stand and pick up my tea and muffin wrapper. "Well I better get going."

"Yeah, of course." He stands and picks up Cole before leading me to the door.

"Bye," I say, and wave at him over my shoulder.

"Bye." He smiles and waves back.

"Bye-bye." Cole grins and buries his face in the crook of Ryder's neck.

I smile at the little boy before the door closes. Cole doesn't know it, but he just gave me even more hope, because suddenly I see what I'll have with my baby.

23

I drive around for a while after I leave Ryder's. I don't feel like going home or shopping, so that leaves driving. I turn the radio up and let my thoughts leave me. I feel better, a lot better, since talking to Ryder; there's something about him that's like a balm to a wound. Maybe because our experiences are somewhat similar I feel more connected to him. I trust him, without really knowing him. There are not many people I've ever had that kind of connection with. Only Ben and him.

After a while of driving around, it's finally time to meet the girls at the café. I still don't feel like going, but I no longer dread it like I did this morning.

I park my car and head inside. I'm the first one there, so I order a hot chocolate and take a seat in my usual spot.

Chloe arrives first and waves before heading over to the register to place her order. She grabs her own drink and sits down, unwinding her plum-colored scarf from around her neck. Her nose is pink from the cold and her cheeks are flushed. "Hi," she says.

"Hey," I say back.

"How are you?" she asks, wrapping her hands around her mug of coffee.

I shrug. "Same old, same old."

Her lips twist together and she looks away. She doesn't know what to say and neither do I, so I pick at an invisible stain on the sleeve of my sweatshirt.

Hannah and Casey arrive at the same time, saying a quick hello before placing their orders and coming to sit down. They both got a sandwich while Chloe and I stick to our drinks.

Casey pulls out a chair and sits down. I look up at her slowly, wondering if she's really doing what I think she's doing. I keep expecting her to move, but she doesn't. She's chatting with Chloe—she might even be speaking to me, but I can't hear her if she is.

"What are you doing?" I ask. My voice is unrecognizable, distorted by anger.

"What?" Her gaze swings to me and her blond curls bounce.

"You're. Sitting. In. Ben's. Seat." I bite out each word through gritted teeth.

She looks at me like I've lost my mind. "It's a seat."

"It's Ben's seat," I shriek, turning more than a few heads in our direction.

"Blaire," she hisses, "you're making a scene."

"And you're still in Ben's seat," I snap at her. I shake my head and laugh under my breath. "You know, you tried to hide, it but it was always obvious how much you wanted him for yourself," I say in the nastiest tone I can muster. I don't know what's come over me, but I suddenly want to hurt her. I want someone else to hurt the way I do, even if it's for a different reason. "We both knew it. Ben made fun of you for it," I lie. Ben would've never made fun of Casey for any reason.

Tears fill her eyes. "Blaire, what the hell is wrong with you? It's a fucking chair. If you want me to move that badly, I will. All you had to do was ask."

She's visibly upset as she moves chairs, and I feel better, but only for a second. Then the reality of what I said and how I acted hits me, and I'm horrified. My mouth drops open and I shake my head.

"Casey," I begin, "I'm sorry, I don't know what came over me. I'm sorry. I . . . I have to go."

I dash out of the café, even as they call my name. I get in my car and speed out of the lot before any of them can stop me.

I head straight home, and once I'm inside, I slam the door and drop my keys on the side table before running upstairs.

"Blaire?" my mom calls from the bottom of the stairs. "What's wrong?"

I don't answer her. I don't know what's wrong with me. I close my bedroom door behind me and peel off the sweatshirt I'm wearing, tossing it haphazardly toward the laundry bin. I undo my jeans button and slide down the zipper, kicking them to the floor. I run to the dresser and pull the third drawer open to find Ben's t-shirts. I haven't allowed myself to indulge in this since his death, but right now I need this. I pick up a shirt and slide it over my body before climbing into bed.

I cry into the pillows. I'm confused and still slightly angry. I don't know what came over me. Maybe it's a normal part of grief, or maybe I'm just crazy. Being crazy seems like the more plausible explanation. I hate feeling this way—where my emotions are one way one second, and another the next. I'm giving myself whiplash, so I can only begin to imagine the way the people around me feel. I hate that I'm doing this to them, but I can't seem to control my emotions.

"Ben," I sob. "I need you."

I reach across the pillows.

Reaching.

Searching.

Hoping.

But he's not there. My heart breaks over and over again each time I realize that I'm never going to see him again. Never hear him say my name. Hold me in his arms. I guess I thought we were invincible, but I never imagined losing him or anyone I loved this soon. Death was something that happened to old people, but that's not always true. There are babies that die. It can happen to anyone, at any time, for any reason, and what I understand now is that no matter the circumstances, you're never truly prepared to have someone die.

My bedroom door creaks open, but I don't rise up to see who's there. More than likely it's my mom coming to check on me.

The person creeps to the side of the bed and then the bed dips with their added weight. Arms wrap around me and I smell familiar floral perfume.

"What are you doing here?" I ask, my voice thick from tears.

"My best friend needed me," Casey whispers. "I don't know why you can never trust me to hold you together when you're falling apart. You'd let Ben do it, but I was around long before him. I'm your best friend, Blaire, but sometimes you treat me like a stranger."

"I'm sorry." My body shakes. "I'm falling apart," I admit, staring at the wall, "and I don't know how to stop it. I feel like I'm watching a train speed into a car. I don't know whether I'm the train or the car … maybe both," I muse.

"Everyone falls apart now and then," Casey assures me. "But something I've noticed, even in my profession, is that people are like puzzles. You may break apart, but there's always someone that can put you back together."

I roll over to face her and she lets me go. She cups her hands under her head and blinks, waiting for me to speak.

"I really am sorry for what I said," I tell her, my gaze lowering in shame. "It was wrong of me, and also a lie. Ben never made fun of you. We never even talked about you having a crush."

She winces. "I'm sorry if you ever picked up on anything. I mean, I guess I had a little crush on him, but I think everyone that met him did. He was such a nice person, and the way he loved you … I wanted that, but not with him. Never with him," she vows. "You two were perfect for each other."

A tear slides down my cheek. "I'm pregnant," I tell her—saying it out loud fills me with so much joy. "Ben and I were trying to have a baby before … before he died," I force the words out of my mouth.

Her face breaks into a grin, and tears shimmer in her eyes. "You're having a baby?"

I nod. "I'm scared," I admit, afraid she might judge me for being afraid.

"Don't be," she says. "You'll be a great mom, and you'll have all of us to help you. Not to mention your parents and Ben's mom."

"I'm still going to be on my own," I tell her. "People can't help me forever."

"No," she agrees, "but by that point, you'll be sick of us." She winks. "Don't stress so much, Blaire. I know how you overthink things. Take it one day at a time. Right now, the future is just that—the future; the last unknown territory to conquer." She gestures wildly with my hand and I giggle. I actually giggle.

"Thank you." I scoot closer to her and wrap my arms around her neck. "I love you."

"Love you too, Blaire," she says into my hair. "You'll get through this. I know it."

I'm glad someone believes I will, because most days, I believe I'll never make it out of this hell.

24

I lead Jessica around the ballroom, telling her what I have in mind for the reception.

"I was thinking swaths of white fabric here, or in the color of your bridesmaids' dresses if you prefer." I motion with my hand to a length of the wall. "This room is pretty modern, so I feel like it should be softened. What do you think?"

She nods, mulling over my words. Her long red hair is pulled back into a sleek ponytail, and she's dressed in a pair of gray slacks and a pale pink blouse. She has a "take charge" persona, but she's actually been very nice to me and willing to let me take over with the planning. I've grown used to people telling me exactly what they want, so it's nice when someone allows me to plan an event entirely.

"I like that idea a lot." She continues to nod. "I agree on white too."

"Good." I smile and take notes. I lead her to another part of the room and begin to go over more of my plans. She nods some more and approves everything I say, which makes my job a lot easier. We finish and head out to the parking lot together. "Bye," I call cheerily.

"Bye." She waves and gets into a sleek white BMW sports

car.

I slide into my car and start the engine. Before I can pull out, I get a text.

Unknown number: Danielle is sick and can't make it. Can you pick up coffee and donuts? Or cupcakes? Or cookies? Anything? I'm desperate here.

Even if the contents of the message didn't give it away, I already had the number memorized.

Ryder.

Me: Sure

Ryder: You're a life saver. Thanks. I would've done it myself, but I have to get Cole from daycare and home to the sitter.

Me: You don't have to explain.

Ryder: I wanted to. See you at Group.

I set my phone in the cup holder and head over to a local cupcake shop. I get a random assortment of two dozen and then go across the road to Dunkin Donuts to get the coffee. I also beg them to let me buy some cups too, just in case. I haven't been responsible for bringing the food and drink before, so I'm not sure if I'm supposed to bring the cups too. I snag a mountain of napkins from there too and receive glares from the staff. I ignore it, though. I have more important things to worry about than grumpy Dunkin Donuts workers.

I head straight to the high school after leaving Dunkin Donuts. I'll be early, but since I have the stuff, I figure I should get there to set it up.

I get to the stoplight to turn onto the road that leads back to the high school and I end up behind Ryder. I follow him down the road and we park side by side. He hops out of his car and hurries over to mine to help me with everything.

He opens my door and I can't help but look him over.

He's dressed in a pair of khaki pants and a light-blue sweater that makes his olive-toned skin look even darker than normal. He's not wearing his glasses today, and I find myself missing them.

"Hey," he says, and it's then that I realize I've been staring at him like a psycho.

My cheeks turn pink and I look away hastily, embarrassment clinging to me like a second, slimy skin. "Hi," I mutter, reaching over for the coffee.

"Let me take that," Ryder says, and grabs it from me. Our fingers touch and fireworks ignite across my skin. I jump back and my eyes widen in surprise. "Stupid static electricity," he mutters, and I pale. That's a much more plausible explanation for what I felt instead of … of … I can't even describe what I thought it was.

I grab my purse and the cupcake boxes. Ryder waits patiently while I get out of the car and then closes the door for me.

We head inside the building together.

"How have you been?" he asks me as our feet squeak across the gym floor.

"Okay, I guess." I keep ahold of the cupcake boxes while Ryder unlocks a door so he can grab the table. Still holding onto the carafe, he carries the folded up table out one handed. The muscles in his shoulders bunch, and his sweater stretches tight across them. I may or may not lick my lips at the sight. Almost as soon as I do it I'm horrified. Am I attracted to Ryder? No. Hell no. I can't be.

Ryder sets the table and coffee carafe down so he can unfold the legs and stand it up. I stand there like a complete numbskull, mulling over my previous revelation. I don't have a crush on Ryder, do I? I'm not even over Ben yet? How could I possibly have feelings for another man? One I barely even know?

"You okay?" Ryder asks, his dark brows furrowing together as he takes the cupcake boxes from my outstretched hands.

"Me?" I ask, and my voice is several pitches higher than normal. "Fine." I wave a hand dismissively and scurry into the closet to begin setting up the chairs. Before I flee, I see the look of confusion flash over his face. I'm being a freak, I know, but there's no way I can explain to him that I think I might have a crush on him. There has to be some rational explanation for this. Like the warm and fuzzy feeling inside me is from gas or something. Yep, I'm totally blaming this on gas.

I carry two chairs out and set them up. I'm not paying attention, and have my head down, and when I turn to head into the closet, I bump into Ryder's very hard, very muscular chest. I freeze, with my palms splayed across his stomach, holding onto the fabric of his shirt so I don't fall.

"Whoa," he says and the chairs fall from his hands so that he can grip my waist. I'm pressed right up against him and I can feel his heart racing beneath his sweater. I'm positive mine's beating just as fast, and I wonder idly if he can feel it. My eyes flit up to his and he stares down at me with warm brown eyes. His tongue slides out to wet his lips and time seems to stand still. I don't let go and neither does he. It might only be seconds, or minutes for all I know. Regardless, I know we're both holding on longer than what's appropriate. His arms feel wrong around me, but right at the same time. I'm so conflicted and that confliction makes me feel sick to my stomach. I jerk away and he lets me go immediately.

"I … I'm sorry. I have to go," I mutter, looking down. I grab my purse and head for the door.

"Blaire?" I hear him call after me, but members of Group are already beginning to arrive. "Blaire?" he calls again. I don't look back to see if he's following me. I want to, but I can't let myself.

I hurry down the hall and out the double doors into the crisp, early, April air. I inhale a breath before running to my car. I drop my keys before I can unlock the door and let out a loud string of curses. A guy from Group glares at me for my foul language before he heads off toward the building. I'm tempted to give him the finger, just to spite him, but I don't have time. I swipe up the keys and get in my car.

When I back out, I see Ryder come out of the building. His black hair is blown away from his forehead by the wind and he waves his arms, begging me to stop, but I don't.

I leave. I have to. Before I do something I'll regret. Or worse, something I won't regret.

25

The day after running out on Group I'm mopeyer than usual. I'm so angry with myself for my irrational feelings. It was a fluke, I tell myself. Nothing and you made it into something.

I stir my cereal around and around the bowl, my spoon clanking against the side of the glass bowl.

"Kid," my dad speaks from behind his newspaper, "if you don't stop that I'm going to steal the spoon from your hand and throw it across the room."

"You're so nice," I tell him, but I stop stirring. "I'm not very hungry."

"You're growing a human. You're starving. Eat."

"You're bossy." I glare at him, but he can't see since he's behind the newspaper. He laughs, but quickly turns it into a cough like he can feel the heat from my stare.

"So your mom tells me." He reaches over and grabs his cup of coffee. It disappears behind the newspaper before being placed back on the table. "You need to eat, you're growing a human and that has to be exhausting. Your mom was a bitch the whole time she was pregnant with you."

"I heard that," my mom says, coming out of the downstairs bedroom. Her hair is damp from a shower. "Your dad's right, though. You need to eat."

"What is it with you and food?" I mutter, staring down into the milky depths of my cereal bowl, like I'm waiting for a fortune to appear or something equally as ridiculous.

"Food equals life, Kid. Therefore, you must eat to live." My dad lowers the paper slightly so I see his eyes.

I make a face and he quickly raises the pages back up.

"Maybe you'd like a sandwich?" my mom asks. "Oatmeal? Toast?"

"Eh." I shrug and lift the spoon of soggy cereal to my mouth. "I'll stick with this."

"That's hardly enough for the baby," she argues.

I lift my eyes to hers as she leans a hip against the table. "This is good," I tell her.

She sighs and moves away. "Suit yourself," she says.

"Hey, Mom?" I call after her while she pours herself a cup of coffee.

"Yes?" She turns back around, raising a brow.

"I was thinking we could go to the mall today. Look at some baby things. It's too early to buy anything—" I shrug "—but I thought it'd be fun to look."

She instantly brightens and nods eagerly. "Sounds like fun. I'll get ready. Dan, do you want to go?" she asks my dad. He grunts. My mom smiles at me and squeezes my shoulder as she passes. "I'm going to take that as a yes."

I take a shower and blow-dry my hair before curling it. This is the first time I've styled my hair for myself and not because I'm meeting a client. I even put on more than a minimal amount of makeup. I swipe some red lipstick on and I automatically feel like I can conquer the world. I dress nicely too, in a pair of slim-fitting jeans and a plum-colored turtle-neck sweater. I even add some jewelry. It's the most effort I've put into myself since I lost Ben. Since he died I haven't seen the point in dressing up and looking nice. It seemed trivial. But today, I wanted to, and I actually feel better.

I grab my purse and head downstairs where my parents are already waiting.

"Oh, Blaire," my mom breathes and begins to cry. "You look so pretty."

It says a lot that the sight of me dressed nicely, with hair done and makeup on, makes my mom cry.

"Mom." I drop my purse to the floor and go to hug her. "Please don't cry."

"I'm just so happy to see you looking like yourself." She sniffles against my shirt.

My dad grabs her arm and tugs her away. "Maureen, don't sob all over the poor girl's sweater. It's not likely we'll be able to get her to change if you ruin it," he jokes.

I roll my eyes at his pathetic attempt to lighten the mood, but I am smiling, so I guess it worked.

We all pile into their rental car and head to the mall. There's a kid's furniture store there, and I want to see what they have so I can get an idea in my head for what I want for the nursery.

Since it's the weekend, the mall is packed and we have trouble finding a place to park. My dad ends up parking about as far away as you can get from the entrance, but it was the only place he could find.

My mom chats excitedly as we head inside, but I'm not listening.

Instead, I'm thinking—thinking about what it would be like if Ben was still here and we were shopping for our baby together. It would be a lot more exciting, that's for sure. I hate so much that I feel like I can't even enjoy being pregnant because I miss him so much. I wish he was here to touch my still-flat stomach, and kiss it, and talk to it. I wish he was here to feel the baby move when the time comes, find out the gender, and pick out names together. Instead, I'm all on my own. It's my baby, not ours. Okay, so that's not exactly true, but it feels like it. I don't have him to ask questions and share every little moment with. It's not the same as it would be if he was here.

We walk past the food court on our way to the store and I hear someone call out, "Blaire?" I ignore it and keep going. There are plenty of other Blaire's in the world besides me, so it doesn't even faze me. "Blaire?" they call again, closer this time. "Blaire?" This time I recognize the voice, even above the cacophony of the mall.

I stop dead in my tracks and my parents keep walking. They stop and turn around when they realize I'm not with them. My head swivels from side to side, and finally, I see Ryder hurrying toward me, wrangling an uncooperative Cole.

"Blaire," he calls in relief this time when he sees that I've stopped. It looks like he's just run out of Chick-fil-A in the middle of placing his order. He scoops Cole into his arms and holds on tight to the wiggling boy. "We'll get your chicken nuggets in a minute," he tells him when Cole begins to cry. He stops in front of me, and motions to a table with the flick of his head. "Can we sit down and talk for a minute?" he asks.

"Um … I … I'm here with my parents." I point over my shoulder in their general direction.

My mom comes forward and asks, "Who's this?"

Before I can answer, Ryder holds out his free hand. "Ryder, ma'am. Nice to meet you."

"Mhm," she hums, looking him over and giving me side-eye. She clearly wants to know what's up here.

"He's the leader of Group, Mom," I say, deflating her love bubble she's created. She's probably already planned my wedding to Ryder and named our children.

"Oh," she mutters, crestfallen.

I sigh and look back at Ryder. "I only have a minute." To my parents I say, "You guys go on without me. I'll find you in a bit."

My dad takes my mom by the elbow and drags her away, because there's no way she's going on her own.

I take a seat, the legs of the chair squeaking loudly across the gray tile. Ryder sits too and plops Cole in his lap. He promptly hands Cole his phone and the little boy becomes occupied pressing buttons.

"I wanted to talk to you about yesterday," Ryder begins, then clears his throat and looks away awkwardly.

"There's nothing to talk about," I say and go to get up.

"Wait," he cries, and I stop. "This is so much more awkward than I imagined." He glances up at the glass ceiling. "Yesterday, I think … I think we had a moment, or maybe more than one moment." He shakes his head and his dark hair brushes against his forehead. On most men it would look like a shaggy mess, but on Ryder it just works. "I don't really know what happened." His Adam's apple bobs. "But I think you felt it too, and that's why you left." I look away. He's right, so I don't refute what he says. He continues when it becomes obvious I'm not going to say anything, "But I wanted you to know that I would never act on anything. I know you're still getting over Ben and despite what I think we might feel for each other, it's too soon for you, and that's okay. Please don't stop coming to Group because of me, though. It can really help you and I promise to leave you alone."

"I don't want you to leave me alone." My voice is soft when I speak and I look down at the table. I don't miss the flash of his pearly white teeth, though. I force myself to look up. "But you're right, I'm not ready for anything between us." I motion from me to him, like that's somehow necessary for him to understand what I'm saying.

He nods. "I can live with that. I'm glad I ran into you, Blaire. I wanted to call you, but I didn't think you'd answer."

"I probably wouldn't have," I admit.

He grins and stands. "I better go feed this monster." He tickles Cole's stomach, and the boy giggles.

We say our goodbyes and I watch him head back into Chick-Fil-A with Cole. He looks back at me once he's in line, and I quickly avert my gaze, walking in the direction my dad pulled my mom.

I end up finding them sitting on a couch in one of the sitting areas in the mall. When they see me, they stand and head toward me.

"He was cute," my mom cries, grabbing onto my arm.

"He's okay, I guess." I shrug.

"Are you kidding me?" she asks. "He's a looker." She then proceeds to glance behind us like he might be there. "Is he married?"

"His wife is gone," I tell her, heading toward the furniture store. "Can we let this conversation drop?" I say it rather rudely and hurt flashes in her eyes. "I'm sorry, Mom," I say quickly.

Her eyes widen and her mouth parts in surprise. "You like him, don't you?"

"I'm not allowed to like him," I counter.

Her brows furrow. "Why? Because of Ben?"

"It's wrong to like someone so soon after he's gone," I argue.

"I don't think so." She shakes her head. "With Ben, once you guys started hanging out, how long was it before you knew you liked him?"

I look away and my dark hair falls forward to frame my face. "Pretty immediate," I admit.

"Exactly." She snaps her fingers together. "I'm not saying you're in love with the guy, but it's okay that you like him. Normal even."

I look at the floor and sigh. Her words make sense but I still feel conflicted. It doesn't feel right to think that I might one day move on from Ben and love someone else. He was my everything, it doesn't seem possible that someone else might take on that role someday.

I say no more and head inside the store. It's an explosion of everything baby. Most of the bedding items are done in pale shades of yellows, greens, blues, pinks, and purples, but I do see the occasional brighter pop of color. I gravitate toward a white crib with tufted gray fabric on the side. It's soft and pretty, but definitely on the feminine side. I then move over to a bassinet with a ruffled white skirt. I run my fingers over the soft fabric of the bedding and smile, imagining a wiggling baby inside.

"Do you think it's a boy or girl?" I ask my parents.

"No clue, Kid, but you've got a fifty-fifty shot," my dad jokes.

My mom smiles and shrugs. "I don't have any guesses yet. Are you going to be surprised or find out the sex?" she asks.

I shrug and move over to another crib, this one black and more modern in style. "I don't know," I answer. "I haven't really thought about it, but I'll probably find out. I'll want to decorate the room accordingly."

"I figured." She laughs. "Sometimes I think you should've been an interior designer instead of an event planner."

"I would've loved it," I agree. "But I love my job now too, so …" I trail off and pick up a stuffed duck. I set the duck down and take a seat in one of the many gliders. "Oh," I say, putting my feet up on the ottoman, "this is nice. I could take a nap here."

My dad laughs. "Me too, Kid. Maybe I'll find one of my own."

"Dan—" my mom grabs his arm before he can move away "—if you fall asleep in the store I'm leaving your ass here."

My dad turns to me. "Marriage summed up in one sentence."

I laugh and stand. "This is cute for a boy," I say, pointing to a navy and white bedding set with pops of orange. It's decorated with cute little giraffes.

"Do you have a theme in mind?" my mom asks.

"Not yet. This is nice too." I point at a gender-neutral option in shades of beige and gray. "Ooh, and this." I pick up a pale pink set with little gray stars. Tears well in my eyes, and I inhale a deep breath. "I wish Ben was here."

"I know," my mom says, resting her hand on my shoulder. "We all do."

And then I turn to my left and Ben is here. Not in the physical sense, of course, but he's here. I move toward the crib, my tears falling freely now as I gaze at the mobile above it. Paper cranes.

I reach up and touch one of the folded white birds. "I want this," I say. "I'm getting it." I look around hastily for someone to come help me, like as if someone's going to snatch the mobile down from the ceiling and run away with it.

When my eyes meet my mom's I see that she has tears in her eyes too. "It's perfect," she breathes. "I think you found your nursery theme."

A clerk must see my desperation because one soon appears. "I want this," I tell her, pointing at the mobile. I don't ask her how much it costs or anything like that. It doesn't matter to me. I have to have it.

"Of course." She smiles. "Let me check in the back for that. The last time I looked there was only one left and it's being retired so we won't get any more."

"I'll take the display if I have to," I tell her, desperation lacing my tone.

She winces. "I'm sorry, we're not allowed to sell displays. Let me go look in the back, though." She all but runs away from me before I can grab her arm and beg and plead for the mobile.

I look to my mom with panic in my eyes. "Mom—" I begin.

"Don't worry about it," she tells me, holding up a hand. "We'll figure something out." She's already on her phone, probably Googling paper crane mobiles.

I want this one, though. With the different colored paper cranes—white, cream, and gray—and waterfall style it's beautiful and I want it to be mine. It feels like a sign it, being here. I haven't found a note from Ben in a while, and I feel like he guided me to this because he knew I needed him.

Before I can have a full-blown panic attack the clerk returns with a large cardboard box. "It's still here," she cries with joy. She was probably afraid I'd hit her or something if they didn't have it.

I take the box from her and hug it to my chest like it's a person. I feel a single tear wet the box.

"Thank you," I tell her. "You have no idea how much this means to me. No idea," I repeat.

She looks from me to my parents and there seems to be some sort of understanding passed through all of us.

"Come on, let's get you checked out." She smiles and leads me over to the register. "If you like the paper crane theme," she begins, "I can look around and see if we can find some bedding for you." she suggests.

I nod eagerly. "That'd be amazing. Thank you."

She rings up the mobile and I hand over my card.

"Do you want it in a bag?" she asks, giving me back my credit card.

"If you have one big enough," I say. "It's no trouble if you don't."

"There should be some right here." She clucks her tongue as she searches. "Aha, here you go." She stands up from behind the counter with a large bag and slips it over the box. "I'm Stephanie, ask for me if you come back."

"I will." I take my bag and meet my parents at the front of the store. They start to head back the way we came, presumably to leave, but I point in the opposite direction. "Why don't we look around for a little while?"

They both stare at me in surprise and then my mom breaks out into a grin. "Of course, you lead the way."

There's a clothing store I love in the mall, but I haven't been there in months. I head inside and straight to a jean jacket with fraying edges. "Ooh, I like this," I say more to myself than them.

I see them exchange a look, but I ignore it. I know I haven't been this exuberant about anything in months. I pick up a few shirts in a larger size—preparing for the belly I'll soon have, and get some dresses since summer will be here in no time and all the good stuff gets picked over.

"We can go home now," I announce when I'm done.

"Maybe we should go out to eat?" my mom suggests. "Get some lunch?"

I have to laugh to myself. Her main concern is always

whether or not I'm eating. "Sure," I say.

They both look surprised that I agreed so quickly.

"Where would you like to eat?" she asks me. "Any preferences."

"Um … Red Lobster?" I ask. "I could really go for some biscuits right about now."

My mom nods eagerly. "That sounds like a great idea."

"Cool," I say for lack of anything else to say.

We head toward the exit and I don't look for Ryder as we go. I definitely don't, so why am I disappointed when I don't see him?

26

Spring was officially in bloom as we reached the end of April. Flowers began to blossom, and the weather turned from chilly to warm. I no longer had to wear a jacket and could get by with a thin sweater and sometimes even a t-shirt depending on the day. May was fast approaching and it marked four months since Ben had been gone. Four whole months since he held me in his arms and whispered I love you.

"What are you doing, Kid?" my dad asks when he steps into the kitchen. I can't blame him for his question—it's two AM and I'm baking a cake.

"I couldn't sleep." I blow out a breath and a piece of hair goes flying with it.

"So you decided to bake a cake?" he asks, his slippers shuffling across the floor. "Makes sense." He shrugs and takes a seat on a barstool. "Your mom won't let me eat cake anymore, but you'll slip your old man a piece, right?"

"Of course." I laugh lightly and stir the batter.

"You have some kind of powder on your nose," he tells me. I rub it away, but I think I actually just smear it more. "Got a lot on your mind?" he prompts, playing with the pepper shaker.

"I guess you could say that." I stir the batter like I'm trying to beat it into submission.

"Talk to me, Kid." He looks up at me from beneath his fuzzy eyebrows. "I only seem to find you in the kitchen at the ass crack of dawn when you really need to talk," he continues. "So talk."

I set the bowl down with the batter and stick my hands on my hips. "It's going to have been four months, dad. Four months without Ben. It feels like an eternity." I put my hand over the slight roundness of my stomach. "I keep thinking about all the things he's going to miss out on."

"No, Kid." He shakes his head rapidly. "Don't focus on that. Instead, think about all the things he did get to do."

"You don't understand," I mumble. "He won't be here to see our child grow up. When they learn to walk and talk. Birthdays. Christmases. He'll always be missing. I want this baby to love him the way he deserves to be loved, but you can't love a ghost," I whisper and look away, overcome with emotion.

"Blaire," my dad says, his voice full of sadness. He gets up and comes around to hold me. I hold onto his robe and cry into his chest.

"I'm in love with a ghost, dad," I whimper. "He's never coming back, but I can't let go."

"B," he says softly, worry clouding his voice, "you don't have to let go. Moving on is different than letting go."

"I miss him s-so much," I sob, my words disjointed. I feel like I've said those words a million times but they're not any less true now. I do miss him. All the time. Every minute. Every hour. Some part of me is always thinking of him.

"Sit here." My dad guides me to a chair at the kitchen table. "I'll be right back," he says, holding his hands out in front of him. My knee bounces restlessly as I wait for him to return. When he does, he has something small clasped in his hands. "I found this a few weeks ago in the closet and I held onto it until you needed it. I haven't read it, I promise." He opens his hands, revealing the paper crane.

My breath catches in my throat. I haven't found one in so long. So long. That I began to think there were no more. I take it gingerly from his hand and hold it in my palms.

My dad bends and kisses my forehead before leaving me alone with the paper crane.

I sit it on the table, just staring at it. A part of me doesn't want to open it. What if it's the last one? But I know I could never not open it.

I take my time unfolding the carefully-constructed origami bird.

I close my eyes when I see the thin black lines that form the words he wrote. I'm not ready to look yet. I need a moment.

I inhale a deep breath and exhale slowly.

When I open my eyes, his messy handwriting appears before me.

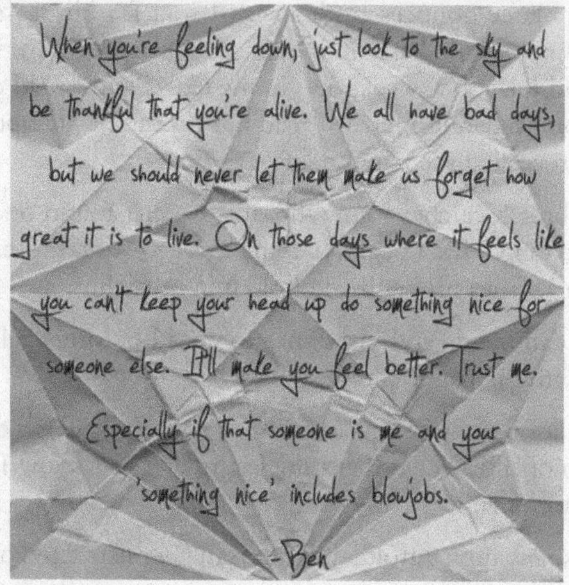

I can't help it, I laugh. That's my Ben. Sweet and romantic one second a complete wise ass the next.

I fold the note back up so that it's a paper crane once more.

"Thanks, Ben," I say out loud. "I needed that, and I know exactly what to do."

27

I walk into Group with my shoulders back and my chin held high. I'm armed with sheets of paper and sharpies. There are a few people already there when I step into the gym, but I'm early so it still gives me a chance to speak with Ryder. He looks up when I walk into the room, his eyes instantly drawn to me. I'm not sure he even notices but his lips lift into a crooked smile and his eyes sparkle. I walk up to him and he excuses himself from speaking to Amy.

"What's that you've got there?" He points at the sheets of paper I clasp to my chest and the markers in my other hand.

"My something nice," I say with a shrug. His brows furrow in confusion. "It's my way of healing," I whisper softly. "If you don't mind, I'd like to explain to everyone and see if they'd like to help."

"Of course." He smiles widely. "But you're not going to tell me first?"

I shake my head. "Where's the fun in that?"

He laughs at my pathetic attempt at a joke. "Okay," he agrees, "the floor is yours when you want."

"Thank you." I stand there a second longer before taking my seat. I feel nervous but excited about my idea. I have Ben to thank for it, though. It was his words in the last note that gave me the idea. I just hope I can execute it right.

I wait nervously for everyone to arrive and take their seats. Ryder speaks for a few minutes, but I don't really hear what he says because the blood's rushing so loud in my ears. When he finishes speaking, he looks across at me and tilts his head, giving me a significant look.

I take a deep breath and stand. I clasp my hands together, my thumbs rotating around each other with nerves.

"Hi, guys," I say awkwardly. "I … I know Group isn't really talking about our losses, but in order to explain what I want you to do I need to tell you about Ben." I take a deep breath and look to the lofted ceiling, giving myself a moment to compose myself. "I'd known Ben while we were in school, but we never really knew each other. Not until college, anyway. From the moment we started hanging out I knew he was different, that what we had was special. We soon began dating and years later became engaged. I put off the wedding because Ben was studying to be a doctor and completing his residency, working crazy hours, and I was starting an event planning business. We finally set a date for this past February, but Ben died in January. A drunk driver t-boned his car." I clear my throat, trying to get control of my emotions. "He hung on long enough to make it to the hospital and for the doctors to attempt surgery, but he died on the table." My eyes meet Ryder's, and he watches me with an encouraging smile. He doesn't judge me, and for that I'm grateful. "He was such a good person and for months I've been so angry at myself, the world, at everything because he died. I'm still angry," I admit, "but not as much as I was, so I guess that's progress. Anyway, I'm getting side-tracked. Ben always left me these notes on paper cranes he made. He was making a thousand before our wedding. In Japanese custom, a thousand paper cranes being made by one person before a wedding gives that person one wish to be carried to the heavens—usually the wish for a happy and prosperous marriage." I press my lips together. "I guess it's ironic that he's in heaven now." I sniffle and pick up the sheets of paper in all different colors. "In one of the notes Ben left for me, he told me that on the days where I feel like I can't keep my head up to do something nice for someone else. In his memory, I want to start something and I want you guys to help. I'm calling it The Paper Crane project. Like Ben did, I want us all to write notes on them. Positive things. And then make the paper cranes. If you don't know how to make them, that's fine. It's easy and I'll teach you. This means a lot to me, and I hope you guys will help." I take a deep breath and sit down, my cheeks suddenly heating with embarrassment as everyone stares at me.

Ryder brings his hands together and begins to clap, his lips quirking into a closed mouth smile.

Everyone else begins to clap too and my face breaks out into a grin. Tears fill my eyes, but for once they're tears of happiness.

"That's an excellent idea, Blaire," Ryder says, standing and walking toward me. He bends down in front of me and reaches for a piece of paper, choosing a green piece. "Green's my favorite color." He winks and stands back up, holding out his hand. "Marker me."

I laugh and hand him one. The others get up and come to me too, selecting a piece of paper and grabbing a Sharpie. My heart feels full and happy looking at them write their notes. I feel like I'm honoring Ben and his memory in some small way, and it makes me feel good. He might be gone, but he'll live on in the paper cranes, and hopefully I can spread around the kindness he extended to everyone he met.

I begin writing my own notes. Most are simple, like: You're beautiful or You are appreciated, but something I've learned is that sometimes only a few words can make someone's whole day better.

One other person in Group, a woman named Ivy, knows how to make paper cranes, so the two of us take the time to go around and help everyone learn how to do it.

When I get to Ryder, he smiles up at me from where he sits on the floor with his legs spread out and sheets of paper scattered between them. "This was a great idea," he tells me. "Seriously. I think we should do this every class from now on." He laughs lightly.

I warm at his words. "Really?" He nods. "Thanks," I say and sit down beside him on the gym floor. "I'm happy I can get everyone involved in something that means so much to me. I thought it might help us all to heal if we focus on the positive and putting a smile on someone else's face." I shrug and cross my legs.

"Mhm." His tongue sticks out between his lips as he writes. He lifts his eyes to mine as he recaps the marker. "Okay, show me what I need to do. Origami was never my forte." He chuckles.

"It's easy," I tell him, reaching for one of his pieces of paper.

"Not that one." He quickly snatches it back.

My brows furrow. "Why?"

"Because it's special."

I shake my head. "Okay then." I pick another one, and this time, he doesn't object. I show him what he needs to do and he follows along, step by step. He gives it a decent shot but the neck of his crane is a bit limp.

"Show me again." He hands me another piece of paper and I go over the instructions once more. This time, he makes it perfect. He holds it up proudly in his palm, looking at it from each angle.

He lowers his eyes to mine and says, "Beautiful."

I duck my head shyly, letting my dark hair fall around my face like a curtain. The look in his eyes told me he wasn't talking about the paper crane.

"I think you've got it," I say and move on to help someone else, but I still feel the weight of his gaze. It settles over me like a warm cozy blanket, one I want to wrap myself in, but I can't let that happen. I pretend not to notice him watching me and stand in the center of the circle we formed on the floor to say, "I thought we could each take our paper cranes with us and leave them in random places. On a restaurant table, a parked car, you get the idea." I clasp my hands together and emotion clogs my throat. "It means a lot for you guys to participate in this."

Murmurs go around the group and I go back to helping people finish before we have to go.

When group ends, I gather up the paper cranes I made and go to stuff them in my purse, but there's already one in there.

For a moment, my heart stops and cries Ben, but I know there's no way that's possible. I take out the paper crane and lift it up.

It's green.

I unfold it, revealing the words written on it.

In elegant handwriting, it says:

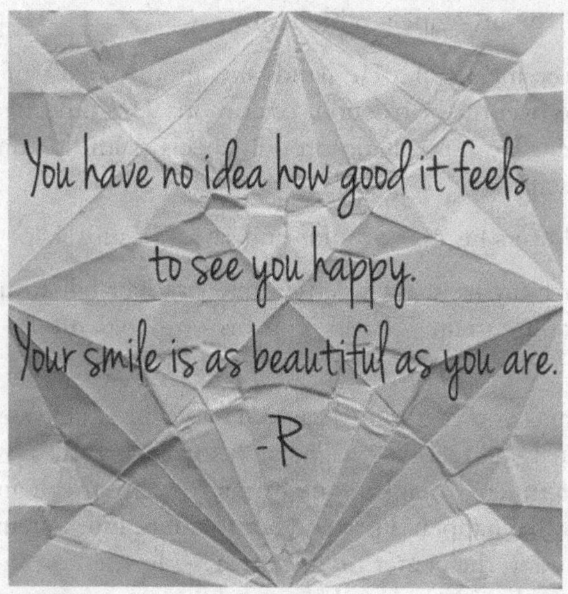

My throat catches and I lift my head, looking around. When my gaze collides with Ryder's, everything else seems to stop and it just becomes the two of us. So much is communicated in that one look. Stuff we'd never say out loud.

I refold the note and put it back in my purse along with the others.

I find him again as I go to leave and I lift my hand to wave. He tips his head at me, and it's enough, enough for now, because it's all I can have.

28

A mysterious number flashes on my phone. I glance at my computer and the emails I've been answering. It's more than likely a client calling to discuss an event more in depth, so I answer.

"Hello?"

"Hi, is this Blaire?"

"Yes, may I ask who's calling?"

"Hi," she says again, "it's Ivy from Group. I got your number from Ryder. I hope that's okay."

"Yeah, yeah, of course." I wave my hand dismissively as if she can see me. "What can I help you with?"

"I don't really know." She laughs nervously. "Maybe it was the crane thing or I don't know ..." she trails off. "I thought maybe we could get coffee and talk?" she asks. "I completely understand if you don't want to. I'm practically a stranger to you, but we have similar situations and I ... I need someone to talk to. Someone that won't treat me like broken glass." She grows quiet then.

"Um, sure," I say, flabbergasted by her request. "When are you thinking?"

"I'm busy with work all week," she says, "but I was thinking Friday before Group?"

"Uh … let me check my schedule." I flip through my planner, making sure I don't have a meeting that day. "Yeah, I'm free. Does four o' clock sound okay?" I ask, poising a pen above my planner pages.

"That'll be perfect." She breathes a sigh of relief. "Thank you, Blaire. See you then."

"Mhm, bye." I hang up and set my phone on my desk. I make a note in my planner so I don't forget.

My mom knocks on my office door and I look up. "I hope I'm not disturbing you."

"I'm working," I say, motioning to my computer and suppressing a laugh.

"Right," she says, and looks a bit ashamed. "Anyway, I wanted to let you know that your dad and I are going out to dinner. We can bring you back something, if you like."

I raise a brow and look at her over the top of my computer. "Do you spend ninety percent of your day thinking about what and when I'm going to eat?"

"Yes, and I spend the other ten percent wondering when you'll shower," she quips.

"Ha, ha, ha," I intone, trying not to smile. "You know what I like so just get me whatever." I wave a hand dismissively.

"Okay." She eases out the door. "And Blaire?" She pauses, looking unsure.

"What?" I lean around my computer to see her better.

"You look better," she says softly, like she's afraid those words might set me off. "Happier." She shrugs. "It's nice to see that."

"Thanks." I nod. "When you guys get back I'll have to tell you about something I'm starting."

She leans forward curiously, but doesn't press me to answer. After a moment, she turns to leave, and I hear them head out a few minutes later.

I finish up with my emails and then grab a book, settling onto the couch to read for a while. It's nice to have a moment home by myself where I'm actually comfortable alone. I don't feel worried about anything or overcome by the fact that Ben's gone. I still have a long way to go, but I'm getting there, and that counts for something.

I'm almost finished with the book when my parents arrive home. I set the book down as they come inside. My dad holds a takeout box in his hand and shoves it at me.

"Here you go, Kid," he says before taking a seat beside me. He lets out a groan. "I ate too much," he complains as he rubs a hand over his stomach.

I open the box and nearly moan out loud when I open the box and see the chicken tenders, fries, and honey mustard sauce.

"You know me well," I say to my mom when she comes into the room.

She laughs and sits on my other side. "I know you love your chicken tenders, but I'm pretty sure it's the honey mustard you love more."

"You're right." I shrug, already dunking a chicken tender into the sauce. I take a bite and moan again. "So good."

"So what's this mysterious news of yours?" my mom asks, vibrating with barely-contained energy.

"I … um … I'm starting a charity in memory of Ben. Maybe not a charity, per se, but a movement." I take another bite of chicken tender—I'm pretty sure nothing has ever tasted this good before.

"And?" she prompts when I'm too busy stuffing my face to continue.

"Oh, right," I say, wiping my hands on my pants. Very lady-like, I know. "I call it The Paper Crane Project. Basically, the goal is to spread the love and happiness Ben gave me in the notes. A random act of kindness sort of thing," I explain. "Like Ben did, I'm going to have people write short notes and make them into paper cranes to leave around at random places. Hopefully someone will find them and it'll make their day." I go back to stuffing my face. When my mom begins to cry, my eyes widen in surprise. "What? Why are you crying? I'm usually the one crying," I muse.

She laughs through her tears. "It's just … I'm so proud of you, Blaire. You've been through so much and I think this is an excellent way to honor Ben. There's no better way, honestly."

I smile. "You think?"

"I know." She nods and reaches over to rub her fingers over my cheek. "You're so strong, Blaire. So much stronger than you think you are."

I shake my head. "You're wrong."

"A mother's never wrong." She kisses my forehead and stands. "I'm proud of you."

"Thanks." Emotion clogs my throat as she and my dad leave the room to get ready for bed.

I feel like I've barely been getting by, but maybe she's right. Maybe I am stronger than I think. I haven't given up, and that has to count for something.

29

Ivy and I end up meeting to get an early dinner instead of coffee. I told her I couldn't stomach any more hot tea this week and she agreed to the change in plans.

I park in front of the restaurant and head inside to wait to meet her. I've only spoken to her briefly in Group and pretty much the only thing I know about her is that she knew how to make the paper cranes.

I tell the hostess that I'm waiting for someone, and she nods as I take a seat on the bench.

Ivy arrives a few minutes later and cries, "I'm sorry I'm late."

I dismiss her words with a shake of my head. "You're not late, I was early," I tell her.

The hostess takes us to our seats and we both look over the menus. I'm only looking at mine to be polite. I know exactly what I want. Chicken tenders. I think this might be my first official pregnancy craving. Since the night my mom brought me home the takeout I've wanted them every night since.

We place our drink order when the waiter stops by and then Ivy goes back to looking at the menu. I slide mine to the edge of the table.

She must finally make her decision because a few seconds

later she slides hers over as well.

The waiter returns with our drinks and takes our order before leaving again.

I take a sip of my water. "So," I begin, "how are you?" I don't really know what to say to her so that seems like a safe enough option.

"As good as I can be." She plays with the paper from her straw. She's a beautiful woman, older than me—probably in her late thirties—with dark skin and eyes. Her hair is short and she's dressed stylishly in a pair of skinny jeans, heels, a billowy white top, and a gray jacket. "Grief is strange, isn't it?" she muses. "I didn't want to talk about that with you, and yet I find that it's the only thing on my mind—missing him, I mean."

"Your husband?" I ask.

"Yes," she answers sadly, twisting the wedding band on her finger. "I lost him in a car crash like you lost your Ben." She gives me a sympathetic look. "Maybe that's why I felt like I wanted to talk to you. Someone that actually knows what it feels like. My friends and family … they try, but they don't know how I feel."

I nod my head in understanding. "I know what you mean," I agree. "It's hard to lose someone that close to you and people … They feel bad about it, but they don't get it because they're not experiencing it. Humans are inherently selfish creatures, and unless it's happening to them directly then it's not real."

She nods and snaps her fingers together. "Exactly." She takes a sip of water. "Being in Group helps. It's nice being around people who've been through the same thing."

"Yeah," I agree, "I think it's helping me. I like it." I shrug.

She smiles knowingly. “Is it Group that you like or a certain Group leader?” She waggles her brows.

I look away and my cheeks heat. I don’t know what to say because I don’t even know what I think.

“It’s okay,” she says, “you don’t have to say anything. The chemistry between the two of you is enough to start a fire.”

I pale slightly. If Ivy’s noticed, how many other people have? I was naïve enough to believe it was something only the two of us felt.

“We don’t have chemistry,” I mumble, stirring the ice around in my water with the straw. “Ben and I … we had chemistry.”

Ivy tilts her head to the side. “So you think you can’t have chemistry with anyone else?”

My lips purse. “I don’t know,” I whisper.

“It’s a complicated feeling and I understand completely,” she tells me. “There’s a man at my work that I really like, but there’s all these doubts and hang-ups because I’m afraid it’s too soon, or he won’t measure up to Gregory, my husband. And the fact of the matter is, no one will measure up to him. You can’t compare people. We’re all different and that’s a beautiful thing. You can never replace someone for that very reason. There’s only one Gregory and one Ben” she waves her hand at me “—but that doesn’t mean there’s not a new person out there, waiting for the both of us.”

I ponder over her words. I don’t really know what to say, but they make sense. The problem is I’m still grieving, and as much as my feelings for Ryder are growing, it doesn’t seem fair to give him a chance until I’m over this hurdle.

I need to accept Ben’s death, and I’m just not there yet.

"I'm sorry," Ivy says with a wince. "I didn't mean to go off on a tangent like that or to sound preachy. I think I was saying that to myself more than you," she rambles.

"It's okay," I tell her. "I understand where you're coming from. You should ask that guy out at your work. And maybe one day I'll ask Ryder out, but I need more time."

"They say time heals all wounds," she muses over the saying, "but I think it only stitches the wound and we do the rest of the work ourselves. You can't heal until you're ready."

The waiter brings our food and we move on to safer topics. I find out that Ivy is a social worker and I tell her about my job. We have a surprising amount in common and I think I might've found a new friend in her.

We don't bother saying goodbye since we're both heading to Group. I end up behind her and follow her the whole way to the school.

We head inside together, chatting about the surprisingly hot weather. There are already a few people there, either sitting or grabbing a snack.

Of their own accord, my eyes seek out Ryder.

When I find him, he looks up from the piece of paper he's reading and smiles widely.

I feel it. The sparks and tingles in my body. Something I thought only one person would ever give me. This feeling both scares and excites me.

We both look away and then, like we can't help it, our eyes connect again. It's like we're dancing but only with our eyes and the electricity crackling through the air.

I swallow thickly and duck my head, hurrying quickly to

my seat.

My mind is a jumble of incoherent thoughts. I've never been more confused in all of my life.

My heart still yearns for Ben, but there's this small piece that yearns for Ryder too. And that small piece … it's growing, and I'm unable to stop it.

30

I stand in front of the mirror in my bathroom. There's color in my skin now, I've gained a little weight, and my hair has been trimmed. My eyes, though, my eyes still look sad and tired. Haunted. I guess it's baby steps.

I turn away and flick off the light.

Sunlight streams into my bedroom through the open blinds.

I'm eighteen weeks pregnant today.

Twenty weeks since Ben took his last breath.

My chest feels heavy with the thought. I don't want to dwell on his death on today of all days. The day when I find out the sex of our baby. At my last appointment, Dr. Hershel couldn't get a clear shot. He thought he knew but I wouldn't let him tell me. I wanted to wait until he could be one-hundred percent sure.

"Blaire, are you ready?" my mom yells up the steps.

I asked her last night if she'd take me to the appointment and somewhere else afterward. I didn't want to be alone either place.

"Yeah, I'm ready," I call back, looking around my bedroom.

Despite the fact that it's still decorated exactly the same, there's an emptiness in the space. In the whole house, really. I miss hearing Ben laugh from the family room at something on TV. Or the smell of bacon in the morning when he'd make breakfast. I miss so many little things—things that never seemed that important before.

I find my mom waiting by the front door downstairs. She might be even more excited than I am.

She ushers me into the car and we're quiet on the drive to the doctor's office. I think she knows that even as happy as I am about today there's a part of me that's incredibly sad too. Ben should be here, holding my hand, and waiting with bated breath for the news of whether or not we're having a baby boy or girl. At least my mom can be here with me but it's not the same. It never will be.

She parks and we head inside the building. I sign in and sit down to wait.

"Are you nervous?" my mom asks me when she picks up a magazine with a cover of a smiling mom and baby.

"No," I answer honestly. "I'll be happy either way."

She smiles and pats my knee. "I know that." She laughs lightly. "I meant are you nervous about being here without Ben?"

I don't wince at his name like I would have even a month ago. "Not nervous, but sad." I twist my lips in thought. "He should be here for this, but he can't be and that sucks. It really freaking sucks." My hand falls to my growing bump. It suddenly popped out more in the last week. I was slow in showing, probably due to the weight I lost after Ben died.

She takes my hand and holds it in hers. "You're doing so much better, though, Blaire. Focus on that."

I nod. "I am."

I'm doing better. I really am. I still have my moments, where I feel sad or the grief becomes too much, but I don't feel like that all the time the way I did initially. Now those moments come briefly throughout the day and then I'm better until they come along again.

When it becomes apparent I'm not going to be called back any time soon, I pick up a magazine and flick through the pages.

"Man, babies need a lot of things," I comment, glancing horrified at the pages. "Expensive things," I add.

My mom laughs and takes the magazine from my hand and puts it back on the table. "They do," she agrees, "but don't stress about that. Your dad and I will help you."

I shake my head back and forth rapidly. "No," I say sternly, "you will not."

"We were talking about moving back up here," she admits.

"Mom." My eyes widen in surprise. "You guys love it in Florida. Please don't move back here because of me."

"We're only talking about it." She shrugs. "It might not happen."

"Mom," I say sternly and she looks over at me, "you guys wouldn't be happy back here. Not permanently, anyway."

"We'd be happier than you think."

"I don't need you to take care of me forever. I've been so incredibly thankful that you guys dropped everything to stay with me." Tears pool in my eyes. "I know it might not seem that way with how bitchy I can be, but it really has meant a lot. And I'll miss you so much when you're gone, but I'll be fine.

I can do this." I look down at my bump and smile. "I know I can."

She wraps her arms around me and hugs me tight. "I know you can too, B."

When she pulls away, there are tears in her eyes too. Before I can say anything else, a nurse calls my name. "Blaire Kessler?" I stand and my mom does too. We follow the nurse down the hall into the room. She goes over her usual series of questions and I answer them as best as I can. "The doctor will be in with you shortly," she says cheerily before closing the door.

I lie back and the paper sheet crinkles underneath me.

Today I find out if I'm having a son or a daughter. The little being inside me stirs, as if it too knows that big news is coming.

When the doctor comes into the room, I breathe out a sigh of relief. One minute closer to knowing.

He takes a seat and talks over things and then it's time.

He squirts the jelly-like substance on my stomach and swirls the wand around.

"Oh my," my mom breathes out when the baby appears on the screen and the heartbeat rings through the room. Tears well in her eyes and she looks at me in awe.

"That's a good profile shot," the doctor says, pointing at the screen. "Cute nose."

I laugh around my tears—tears I didn't know I was crying. "That's Ben's nose."

"Do you still want me to write down the gender and put it in an envelope?" He asks. "Or do you want to know right now?"

"No, no, write it down," I plead.

He nods. "Okay. I'll give you another minute with your little one." He chuckles as I watch the wiggling baby on the screen.

"You're one-hundred percent sure what it is?" I ask him.

He laughs again. "Yes, Blaire. No doubts this time—and so you know, I was right then too. All right," he says, removing the wand and wiping up the goop, "I'll see you next time." He slides in his chair over to the counter set up as a desk. He grabs a sticky note and pen and scribbles something across it before stuffing the paper in the envelope. He also slips the new sonograms in there. "Here you go." He hands me the envelope. "Bye." He stands and heads for the door.

"Bye, and thanks, Dr. Hershel."

He smiles over his shoulder before the door closes.

"Ready?" my mom asks me.

"As I'll ever be."

My mom parks the car and looks over at me. I can see the worry in her eyes, but I don't comment on it. I know she probably thinks I'm crazy for doing this. Torturing myself, really, but I have to.

"I'll be back soon," I tell her.

"I'll come look for you if you're not," she warns.

I pick up the envelope and get out of the car.

It's a sweltering hot day in June, and while the grass is brown and brittle everywhere else, here it's bright green and lush—clearly well taken care of.

The grass is cushiony beneath my feet, propelling me forward.

I don't look around at my surroundings. Instead, I hold my head high and stride forward with a purpose. When I reach the grave, I sink down to my knees.

"Ben," I breathe, touching my fingers to the cool stone. His name is engraved into the surface along with his birthday and the day of his death. Beneath that it says: Loving son and devoted husband. He never got the chance to be my husband, but Loraine had said that it wasn't fair for that to be left out. I hadn't cared at the time, too overcome with my grief, but now I was glad it was there. That our love wasn't cast aside like it was unimportant.

I haven't visited his grave until now. I couldn't bring myself to do it. To come here felt like I had to finally face his death head-on. I guess that's what I'm doing.

"I miss you," I say, my voice thick with emotion. "I miss the sound of your voice, and your laugh, and the way your eyes lit up when you saw me. I miss everything about you." I inhale a shaky breath. "I'm sorry I haven't visited. I … I couldn't," I admit. "But I'm here now and I have something special to share with you." I reach for the envelope. "You probably know by now that we're having a baby. I wanted us to find out its gender together, so I hope you're ready." I speak into the air and I feel a gust of wind brush my cheek. I smile and I know that it's Ben's way of saying he's here and he's ready. The envelope is still clasped in my hand so I lift it up and open the flap. I close my eyes and pull out the piece of paper. I want to prolong this moment for as long as possible. Finally, I can't stand it any longer and open my eyes. Only, of course the side of the paper I'm looking at is blank. I turn it over and gasp, my hand flying to my lips. Tears cascade down my cheeks. "Ben," I can barely say his name, "we're having a little girl. We're going to have a daughter."

My tears fall onto the stone of his grave, disappearing into the porous material. My throat is thick with emotion. I'm going to have a daughter. A precious little girl.

"I wish you were here," I breathe. "I miss you so much."

I close my eyes and I feel the wind again. It seems to whisper, I miss you too.

At least, that's what I tell myself.

31

"You're smiling," Ryder says, sitting down beside me on the gym floor the following Friday.

"I am," I agree, finishing the paper crane I'm making.

"You're glowing too," he notes.

"I hear pregnancy does that to you," I joke.

He grins. "It's more than that. Are you going to make me beg?"

I laugh and add the finished crane to my growing pile. "I found out I'm having a girl and I'm really, really happy. For the first time through this whole pregnancy I can say I'm happy. Not that I wasn't happy to be pregnant," I add quickly, "but I was so sad over Ben's death that I just … couldn't grasp that it was actually happening I guess." I shrug and pick up another piece of paper I've already written on. "My sadness overshadowed my joy," I elaborate.

Ryder nods. "I can see how that would happen. It was hard when Angela passed. There's a lot I can't remember about Cole's first few months. It's like you're there, but not."

"Exactly," I agree.

"So, I was thinking," he begins, "why don't we go out together this weekend to set our paper cranes around?" I look at him like he's grown another head. "Not like a date or anything," he explains quickly.

"Why would I think it was a date?" I ask, fighting a smile.

He looks away and says, "No reason."

"I think that would be fun." I put the poor guy out of his misery. I normally do it by myself, but it would be nice to have someone to go with me.

His face splits into a grin, and I'd be lying if I didn't say that butterflies took flight in my stomach. "Good. It'll be fun. My parents are watching Cole this weekend, and I normally just chill at home by myself, but I didn't want to do that this time." His eyes roam over my face, like he's drinking in every feature of mine and filing it away so he can remember it when I'm no longer in front of him.

"Just text me," I tell him, setting aside the newly finished paper crane. "I can meet you whenever." It wasn't like I had any plans.

He nods. "I will." He clears his throat and stands. "I'll see you sometime tomorrow then?" he asks one last time, like he's afraid I've changed my mind in the last two seconds.

"Yeah," I say, fighting a smile at his awkwardness. I find it endearing, honestly, how nervous he gets.

He walks off to speak to someone else and beside me Ivy makes a noise. "He's got it bad for you." She laughs under her breath, scribbling words across the page in her lap.

"No, he doesn't," is my automatic rebuttal.

She eyes me. We both know I'm lying through my teeth. I look in the direction that Ryder went.

He's smart.

Good-looking.

Kind.

And he sets my heart aflame.

But I'm scared. Terrified of loving someone else the way I loved Ben and losing them.

My breath catches. Is that the real reason I'm holding myself back? Not because it's too soon, but because I'm scared I might love him and lose him too?

I lower my head and go back to work on the paper cranes. I try to dismiss my thoughts from my mind, but they hang around like a pesky fly, and I don't think they're going to go away easily. If at all.

32

Ryder asks me to meet him at the coffee shop—the one we ran into each other at several months ago—at eleven.

I had planned to dress simply and not bother doing much to my hair or messing with makeup. After all, it's not a date. But once I receive his text, I end up shutting myself in the bathroom and doing everything I vowed not to do. I curl my hair and apply more than the bare minimum of makeup. Since it's blazing hot out I dress in a cute floral dress that rests over my bump. I slip on a pair of flats and gather my purse and the envelope full of paper cranes.

My mom eyes me with a knowing look when I come downstairs.

"Where are you off to?" she asks, glancing up from the book she's reading. Her purple reading glasses slide down the edge of her nose.

"Going with a friend from Group to set our paper cranes around," I say, hedging toward the door. It's so close, but so far away.

"Ivy," she asks and then with a knowing smile, she adds, "or Ryder?"

I can't lie to my mom—I mean, it's my mom. "Ryder," I mumble. Her face breaks out into an ear-splitting grin. "It's not a date." I point a finger at her in warning. Her smile never falters, though.

"Mhm," she says.

"It's n-o-o-o-t," I sing-song.

Before she can make a comeback, I bolt for the door and I'm out of there. I'm pretty sure I can hear her laughing through the door.

I get to the coffee shop a few minutes late and Ryder's already there waiting. He sits outside on a bench, one leg crossed over the other with two clear cups filled with something iced and delicious looking. He dressed casually in a pair of khaki shorts, a white t-shirt that stretches across his muscular chest and leaves little to the imagination, and a pair of black tennis shoes. A pair of sunglasses hides his eyes but I know he's spotted my car.

I get out and head toward him.

"Hi," I say shyly. I don't know why I feel so nervous all of a sudden. I mean it's Ryder. He's my friend, despite the fact that we both might kinda-sorta have feelings for each other.

"Hey," he holds out a drink for me, "I got this for you. You like iced tea, right?"

I smile and take it from him, immediately taking a sip. "I love it," I say, as if that wasn't obvious by the way I slurped it down. "Thank you."

He smiles up at me and even though I can't see them I know his eyes are crinkling at the corners. "You're welcome." He stands and nods to his right. "Shall we?" There's a strip mall that way, with lots of parking, and also several restaurants. It's an excellent place to lay around our paper cranes.

"Where are yours?" I ask, holding up my envelope as we walk along the sidewalk in front of the coffee shop.

Ryder grins and pulls out the white envelope stuffed in his back pocket. "Got it right here. You didn't think I'd forget them did you?" He jokes and pulls out one of the folded birds.

I duck my head so he can't see my smile. Being with Ryder, it's easy. As easy as breathing—normal and completely natural. It's something I could get used to and I think that's another reason why it scares me so much.

Ryder opens his envelope and lays one of the origami birds on a car we pass by. I smile at the sight of it and my heart … It feels happy.

"So," I ask him, squinting from the brightness of the sun even though I'm wearing sunglasses, "your parents watch Cole some weekends?"

"Yeah—" he looks down at the ground when we step off the sidewalk onto the parking lot "—they do it maybe once every other month or so. It gives me a break and they love spending time with him. He loves it too. They spoil him rotten and give him too many cookies."

I laugh at that and pull one of my own paper cranes from the envelope and leave it on the bench we pass. "It's nice that you have them."

"It's nice that you have your parents too," he comments. He hasn't asked me anything about them since that day at the mall. It kind of surprised me, but then again it didn't. Ryder has made it obvious he wants to know me, but he's not pushy about it.

"They're great," I agree, my throat closing with emotion.

"They … uh … they live in Florida now, but they dropped everything to come back here and be with me after Ben died. I didn't always make it easy on them to stay, especially my poor mom, but they persevered and I'm so incredibly thankful that they're here. I'll be sad when they leave."

"That was nice of them." He sets a paper crane on one of those large planters that hold small trees and people tend to sit on.

"They're good people," I say. I take a sip of my iced tea and look around for a place to lay a crane. I end up running into the parking lot and sticking one on a random car. Ryder and I continue through the strip-mall, now beneath a covered awning. The shade feels nice and is much needed. It's hot enough to fry an egg out there. "What do you normally do on your off weekends?" I look up at him, waiting for his answer.

He shrugs. "Most of the time I just hang out at home—catch up on laundry, grade papers, that sort of thing. If I'm really feeling adventurous I might go see a movie. I love movie theater popcorn; the stuff you get at the store isn't the same." He smiles boyishly.

I laugh lightly. "That's kind of boring."

"Maybe so," he says, "but I enjoy the peace and quiet of being at home."

"So…" I begin and then pause, unsure if I should ask what I want, but I finally decide what the hell. "Have you dated any since…?"

"No." He shakes his head adamantly. "I haven't wanted to and I've been too busy with Cole, but I … I think I'm ready," he admits. He looks me over, and even through his dark sunglasses the intensity in his stare burns.

Since I don't know what to say, I end up exclaiming, "Ooh. Look. Bookstore!" It's a horrible segue, and Ryder's laughter tells me he knows so, but he's nice enough not to comment.

He holds the door open for me and I step inside the cool shop. The air-conditioned air feels good to my heated skin. There's already a slight sheen of sweat on my forehead from our trek outside.

I inhale the scent of books and I can't help but smile.

The bell above the door jingles as Ryder comes in behind me. The store is small, but every surface is covered in books. I've never been in this particular store before. I usually order my books or get them from the local chain store, but the quirkiness of this place immediately speaks to my soul.

"You love popcorn," I say to Ryder, "and I love books."

He chuckles behind me and his fingers lightly graze my waist as he squeezes in beside me. "I do too. Mysteries are my favorite and the occasional thriller." He removes his sunglasses now that we're inside and hooks it onto the collar of his shirt. I take mine off too, but slide them into my hair.

"Romances," I say, "especially historical romances."

He sucks his bottom lip into his mouth and I know he's fighting a grin. "Those books with the covers of the women with big boobs draped around some shirtless guy and they both look like they're seconds away from having an orgasm?"

I snort. I hadn't expected all of that. "Yep, those are the ones," I say.

"And I'm sure they're highly historically accurate?" He raises a brow, his eyes sparkling with laughter.

"Absolutely." I fight a smile.

Is this flirting? Are we flirting? I've been out of the game so long that I have no clue. What I do know is, if we are I like it entirely too much.

"I have an idea," Ryder begins, leaning his back against one of the many shelves and crossing his arms over his chest. "Why don't you pick out a mystery for me and I'll pick out a historical romance for you—and even if it's one we've already read we have to get it and re-read it."

My lips lift into a smile. "I like that idea. And—" I look around "—while we're at it maybe we could slip some of these into the books?" I hold up my envelope of paper cranes.

"That's a good idea," he agrees and hedges toward the romance section. "Meet you at the checkout in fifteen minutes?"

I nod and he turns around fully, quickly disappearing amongst the shelves.

I find the mystery section and scan the titles. I want to pick out something he isn't likely to have read, but it's impossible to know. While I browse, I slip some paper cranes inside books and stick some others on the shelves.

I glance down at my phone and see that my time is almost up.

I end up closing my eyes and picking a book at random. It seems fitting considering they're all mysteries. Armed with the book, I head to the checkout. Ryder is waiting, a black plastic bag hanging from his fingertips. He sports a wry grin and my heart pounds inside my chest.

"No peeking," I tell him, using my back as a shield when I hand the clerk the book I chose.

Ryder turns away, playing along. I pay and accept my own black bag.

The two of us head back out into the blazing sun. We take a seat on one of the planters and swap bags.

"One, two, three," Ryder counts and we both pull out our books.

I immediately burst into laughter at the one he chose for me. It's called The Highlander's Love Kilt. It features a shirtless man wearing a green kilt that's blowing slightly in the wind. There's a woman behind him with her arms wrapped around his neck, looking at him in adoration.

"You like it?" he asks with a pleased smile.

"It's perfect," I say and lean over to kiss his cheek.

The action comes so easily that I don't even realize what I've done until I pull away.

Ryder's mouth parts in shock and he looks at me with this stunned expression. Neither of us seeming to know what to do or say.

"I-I … Forget that happened," I stutter, looking away.

His fingers brush my chin and he turns my head back to him, angling my face up to his. "I don't want to," he says, his eyes flicking down to my lips.

My heart jumps to my throat. The air grows thick between us and it's not from the humidity. "Ryder—" I begin.

"Shh," he murmurs, lowering his head toward mine. "Don't think." His breath brushes against my lips and then it's his own lips I feel pillowed against mine. I freeze and my heart stutters in my chest. His hand cups my cheek, and when I don't pull away, he deepens the kiss. I still don't pull away. I don't want to. I like the feel of his lips on mine. His tongue brushes my lips and my mouth parts for him. Electricity seems to spark beneath the surface of my skin. I kiss him back, pressing closer to his body. He groans lowly and my mouth swallows the sound. I'm pretty sure I whimper too. I'm so lost in the feel of him that my thoughts completely disappear. This isn't something I imagined happening between us, but I don't want to stop it, either. We break apart and we both swallow thickly. "Whoa," he murmurs.

I look at him with wide eyes. I have no words. I liked that. Way more than I should have and that scares me. My hands shake and I look away. I feel dirty for enjoying kissing Ryder—for kissing anyone that's not Ben. I shouldn't have liked it, but I did. Oh, God, I did. I don't know how to sort my racing thoughts and I jolt upright.

"I have to go." My words slur together in my haste, and I nearly stumble over my own two feet as I try to get away.

"Blaire," Ryder calls after me and starts to follow.

I turn around and hold up my hands. "No," I say. "No."

He pauses and hurt flashes in his eyes but he must see the pain in my eyes too because he doesn't push. I turn and leave, the shattered pieces of my heart pulsing and aching in my chest, yearning for the man I leave behind me.

33

I arrive home and sit in my parked car for longer than necessary. I can't seem to wrap my head around that kiss. My lips still tingle from the feel of Ryder's. I want to hate the kiss, but I can't. It doesn't make it any easier to accept that I kissed a man that's not Ben. My feelings for Ryder have been something I've downplayed not only to everyone else, but to myself as well. I didn't want to believe that they were real or that they carried any weight. But what I feel for Ryder, it's very real and it scares the crap out of me. I've been hurt so deeply by Ben's death. I lost the love of my life—the man I thought would be the one I'd love until I died. I'm scared to love someone that much again and my brain screams that it's too soon while my heart … my heart just wants Ryder.

Tears pour from my eyes. I don't know what to do.

Ben's gone.

I'm pregnant.

And I might be falling for another man only six months after losing the one I believed to be my everything.

I'm a fucking mess.

And on top of my messed up love life, the bills are piling up—something I've pushed to farthest recesses of my mind. I could barely deal with everything else, let alone the reality that

I need to sell my house too. The house I bought with Ben. The house we were going to raise our family in.

I lean my head back into the headrest and let out a groan, pent-up anger that needs to come out before I explode.

My life is a complete cluster-fuck at the moment and I really don't need my feelings for Ryder complicating it at the moment.

My phone buzzes in my purse and I reach over and grab it.

Ryder: I'm not sorry for kissing you. Maybe I should be but I'm not. If you want an apology I won't give it to you. You're the first woman I've kissed in nearly two years. It meant something to me. You mean something to me.

I place the phone on the seat beside me and clutch the steering wheel. I need to hold on to something. My eyes close and I breathe out through my mouth.

My feelings are all over the place. I—

The baby kicks and my breath stutters.

I haven't felt the baby kick before now. I've felt little flutters I thought might be something, but not this. Not a full-blown kick where it's like the baby is saying hello. I press my hand to the spot, hoping to feel it again.

"Hi, Little Girl," I say, my voice thick with tears. "Mommy loves you." And I do, so much. Even if I feel like my life is falling apart around me, this baby is everything that I want. She's keeping me going—keeping the hope alive. I rub my hand against my stomach, trying to coax her to kick again, but she doesn't. It doesn't matter, though. That one kick filled me with so much joy. The joy is fleeting, however, because like always the sadness soon accompanies it. The sadness that Ben's not here to experience this.

He's not here.

Our baby is growing inside me.

And I'm kissing someone else—and liking it.

What the hell is wrong with me?

I press the heels of my hands to my eyes. I can't escape these complicated thoughts. Maybe I never will because there's nothing easy about my situation.

Finally, I know I can't sit in the car any longer.

I head inside and my mom's working on a crochet project—she said she wanted to learn so she could make things for the baby—and my dad is parked in front of the TV per usual.

"Hey," I say, trying to act normal.

"How'd it go?" my mom asks, lowering the … whatever it is she's making. It looks like a knotted mess to me, but what do I know? "You're back early."

"It was fine," I say, trying to sound normal. I fail. Epically. I can't keep it together and I begin to cry.

"Oh, honey." My mom cries and jumps up. She hurries over to me and pulls me into her warm, comforting arms. How I ever thought I didn't need her here is beyond me. I do need her. Every single day—and selfishly, I don't want them to go back to Florida, but I know they need to even if my mom still insists on looking into moving back here. "What happened?" she asks. "You'll feel better if you talk about it." She guides me to the couch in the front living area so we're away from the raucous of the TV.

"H-He kissed me," I admit, my lower lip trembling. "And I didn't stop him. I liked it," I confess on a whisper. I sink down on the couch and place my head in her lap. She runs her fingers through my hair. The gesture both comforting and familiar.

She's quiet, and I know she's thinking over what she wants to say. Finally, she speaks. "It's okay that you liked it," she whispers.

I shake my head in her lap, my tears soaking into her soft jeans. "But Ben—"

"Blaire," she says sternly, "he's gone. He's not coming back. But you … You're here. Living and breathing with a life. One you have to live. You're allowed to move on. To love."

"It feels wrong," I reason.

"You can't end your life because he's gone, B. He wouldn't want that for you, and I think on a deeper level you know that. Ben never held you back from your dreams or what you wanted while he was alive and he wouldn't want to do it dead, either." I swallow thickly at her words. She continues, "I'm not saying that you need to ride off into the sunset with Ryder. You still need time, I know that, but it doesn't mean you shouldn't give him a chance."

I understand where she's coming from, but it's hard for me to let go. I think this small part of my brain still believes one morning I'm going to wake up beside Ben and all of this will have been a bad dream. What's different now, though, when I have that thought is I automatically think of Ryder and how much I do care about him. I don't want to live in a world where I don't know him.

I'm torn between two men.

One a ghost, and one very real.

"I'm scared.

"I know you're scared," she says softly, still combing her fingers through my hair, "but don't miss out on something great because of that. The greatest things in life are usually the scariest—but that doesn't mean we shouldn't do them."

I close my eyes, absorbing her words. "Are you saying I should go talk to him?"

She laughs. "I don't know. That's up to you. What does your heart say?"

"That I should go talk to him." I laugh lightly. "I just ran away from him. I want him to know that I liked it, but I … I don't know."

"Then go." She urges me up and I move to a sitting position.

"Right now? What if he's not home?"

"Then wait for him," she reasons.

I nod. "Okay, I will."

I don't hesitate. I know if I do I'll talk myself out of it.

She smiles as I grab my purse again and leave. I know the way to his house now so I don't take the time to enter it into the navigation system.

When I arrive at his house I'm surprised to find his car in the driveway. I honestly expected him to still be out.

I park, take a deep breath, and head to his front door before I can talk myself out of it.

I ring the doorbell and wait, nervously wringing my hands together. I'm afraid I've ruined things between us with my constant need to flee uncomfortable situations. I know that I have every right to be cautious and nervous when it comes to our relationship—I've suffered so much already—but that doesn't mean Ryder has to deal with it.

I hear his footsteps on the other side and then the door swings open. "Blaire?" He gasps, clearly surprised to see me. "What are you doing here?"

"I . . . I . . ." I look around, feeling shaky. "Can I come in?" I finally ask.

"Sure." He holds the door open wider and I step inside. He closes the door behind us and places his hand on the small of my back—not low enough to be suggestive but almost protectively—and leads me into an open family room.

It has high ceilings with wood beams crisscrossing it. The walls are painted a cheerful yellow—not school bus yellow—and the two couches are beige in color with yellow throw pillows. There's a large, fluffy, white rug with several stains that look like they're from markers. A TV resides above the fireplace and there are several photos of Cole and some with Cole and Ryder. I don't see any photos of his wife, and I figure he's packed them away.

I take a seat on the couch and he sits on the other one, purposely putting space between us, I'm sure.

I take a deep breath and smooth my hands down the front of my dress. I don't know what to say, let alone where to begin. I let out the breath I'm holding and raise my eyes to his. His brown eyes reflect hurt and confusion.

"Ryder," I breathe out his name and my voice cracks slightly. "I feel so conflicted right now. I . . . I liked kissing you. I might've even loved it. I definitely kissed you back," I say, not wanting him to think I blame him for the kiss. "But I'm dealing with so much right now. I lost the love of my life, I'm pregnant with his baby, I'm probably going to lose my house if I don't move soon, and I … I have feelings for you. Strong feelings. But how soon is too soon to move on and let go? I don't want to rush into anything. I want us to take our time, if that's what you want, and just get to know each other. See where things go," I explain. I sit against the pillows and wait for him to speak.

"I'm sorry if I've ever made you feel like I want to rush into something with you, that's not the case at all. You're the first woman I've felt a spark of anything with since Angela so maybe I was a little pushy—"

"No," I interrupt him, "not at all. From the moment I met you I felt this … connection. Spark. Whatever you want to call it." I probably sound cheesy as all get out, but it's the truth.

"So I'm not the only one that felt it?" he asks with a small grin.

"No, definitely not." I breathe out a sigh of relief.

He chuckles and claps his hands together, leaning forward. "I don't know where we'll go from here," he says and my heart clenches, "but I do know I want us to see where it goes." My heart releases and I exhale. "I'm here for you, Blaire. As a friend, whatever you need me to be." He shrugs. "I want you to know you can come to me. The feelings of confliction you have about me; I have them too. Probably not as bad, but there is a part of me that feels like I might be trying to replace Angela. I know that isn't the case, though. When I think of you, it's you I see. Not a version of her." He moistens his lips with his tongue. "I think it's human nature to fear we're replacing something with something else. We don't like to let go of the past, so sometimes moving forward is a hard concept to grasp."

"Yeah." I nod in understanding. "I can see that." I stand up then. "I better go. I don't want to keep you."

He shrugs and stands too. "I was just going to put a movie on. You can stay if you want."

I shake my head even though a part of me yearns to stay. "I need to go."

"Okay." He nods and leads me to the door. He follows me outside and stands on his front porch, leaning against a column while I walk to my car. I open my car door, and I'm about to slip inside when he calls, "Blaire?" I turn back and see his lips lifted in a crooked smile. "The next time we kiss you won't run away."

"You're sure there will be a next time?" I'm fighting a smile.

His grin widens. "Definitely."

34

I stare at the pile of bills. This is a reality I haven't wanted to face. In the midst of losing Ben, I couldn't bear the thought of losing my home too. The fact of the matter is I don't make enough money on my own to cover the costs of a house this size. I've been scraping by for months and my savings is dwindling. With the baby coming I can't go into debt.

I push the bills off the table. "I'm moving," I announce.

My mom looks up from the book she's reading. "What?"

"I'm moving," I say again. "I have to."

She's suggested that I move in the past, but not because of the bills—although she probably assumed those were bad too. She thought I should move because this place holds so much of Ben in it. I guess that's true too. Several months ago I would've thrown a fit about moving for that very reason, but now I only feel a very mild sting.

"You're moving?" she repeats. "Where?"

"I don't know yet," I exhale, standing up from the kitchen table. "I'll figure it out. All I know is I can't keep paying this." I point to the envelopes and papers on the floor.

"Your dad and I can help you with the bills if that's an issue—" she begins.

I shake my head. "No. I won't let you guys do that. I'm a big girl, this is my mess, and I'll clean it up. I have to think about my daughter." My hand falls to the swell of my belly. I'm nearing the seventh-month mark of pregnancy. It's hard for me to believe she'll be here so soon. There's so much left I have to do.

My mom's face softens. "I understand. Do you want me to help you look?" She perks up.

"Sure," I say. "I'd like to be out of here in a month," I admit. "It's a short time frame but I can't keep doing this, I really can't," I emphasize. "Plus, I need to get moved in somewhere and everything set up for the baby."

She nods her head in understanding. "I'll contact a realtor and see about selling the house."

My stomach clenches at her words. I love this house. I love that Ben and I bought it together. I wanted to raise our children here. But things … Things change and I have to change with them. I can't hold on to this house any longer and it's only a house. I'll make a new place my home too. A new start. A clean slate.

"Thanks," I tell her. "I'm heading up to my office to do a little work."

She nods and says, "Okay." I wonder if she even really hears me because she's already on her phone, busily getting to work on selling my house.

As I go upstairs, I'm hit with a memory.

Ben parked on the street in front of the house, and I smiled giddily at the SOLD sign.

It was our house.

It was large for two people, but we both knew we wanted a family in the future and didn't see the point in having to move.

"Do you still love it?" Ben asked, his blond hair glowing in the sunlight shining in the car window.

"Of course," I said excitedly.

He held up the keys and jingled them. "Ready?"

"Absolutely." I swiped the keys from his hand and bolted out of the car.

He caught me before I made it very far and swept me up into his arms.

"What are you doing?" I laughed, wrapping my arms around his neck.

"Carrying my bride over the threshold," he joked, starting up the stairs to the front door.

"I'm not your bride yet," I told him.

He chuckled. "Only because you refuse to set a date."

"We're busy," I reasoned. "It takes a lot of time to plan a wedding."

He kissed my forehead. "I know. Don't worry. I'm willing to wait for however long it takes you to plan the perfect wedding. Okay, do the honors." He lowered with me in his arms so I could slip the key in the lock.

I stuck it inside and twisted the knob. Ben stepped inside with me in his arms.

"Wow," I said, my voice echoing around the empty space.

He set me down and kissed me squarely on the lips. "Welcome home, baby."

I open my eyes and find that I'm leaning against the wall for support. I don't want to leave this house. I don't want to leave behind the memories and happy memories I had here, but I have to. Not just because of the money, but because I know deep down, being here, sleeping in that bed every night, it's holding me back.

I have to move on.

35

I meet the girls at the coffee shop. We've met a few times since that disastrous day where I was so rude to Casey. I'm so much better now than I was then. Day by day I'm getting back to normal. When Ben first died, I didn't believe that normalcy was possible for me. I'm happy to have been proven wrong.

I wave at the girls, already seated at our usual table, and head to the counter to place my order. Once I have a drink and sandwich I sit down at the table.

"Hey, how are you guys?" I ask, taking a sip of my iced tea. It's blistering hot outside, but thankfully it's cool in the café.

"Good," Chloe says, looking at her freshly manicured nails. "I got promoted to management." She grins with this news. Chloe works at a high-end retail store in our mall.

"That's awesome," I say, digging into my sandwich. Lately, I'm hungry all the time. My dad says I'm trying to make up for all the weeks I barely ate. I nearly moan with how good it tastes.

"Same old, same old over here," Casey sighs. "My life is so uneventful."

"Ugh, I wish I could say the same," Hannah groans, flipping her hair over her shoulder. "You know that hot neighbor I told you about?"

"Yes," we all chime.

She makes a face. "So, um, one morning I went over to tell him exactly what I thought about his parties, and … and … I mean, he's so hot. So hot, you guys. And … I fucked him," she cries. "I'm talking, against the wall, hair pulling, slam-me-down-on-the-bed-and-ride-me-hard, kind of fucked him." We all sit open-mouthed staring at her. Sweet little Hannah whom I've never even heard use the word fucked before. "Stop looking at me like that," she mumbles, squirming in her seat.

We're all too stunned to say anything. Chloe recovers first.

"So, you mean to tell me, that shy, quiet, little you banged the bad boy neighbor?"

"Yes," Hannah squeaks.

Chloe dives over to hug Hannah. "My baby's growing up," she jokes.

"Let me go." Hannah pushes her away. "You're embarrassing me."

"I can't help it," Chloe says. "I'm just so proud of you."

"So, is this going to be a regular occurrence?" I ask her.

Her cheeks color. "I don't know. I kind of liked it, though, but I don't know if that's just because he's good in bed or it made me feel good to be so bold." She shrugs.

"I'm betting both." Casey points her finger at Hannah.

Hannah makes a face. "Regardless, I doubt it'll happen again."

"Why not?" I ask.

"Cyrus seems like the kind of guy to only have one-night stands," she reasons. "We'll see." She turns her attention to her B.L.T., signaling that she's done talking about this.

"I'm moving," I announce, further changing the subject.

"Wait, what?" Casey asks, a piece of lettuce stuck to her lip. "When did you decide this?"

"A few days ago." I shrug.

"You're moving and you haven't even seen my new place." Hannah gives me a look.

"I know, I'm so sorry. I've been … Well, you know how I've been." I give her a sympathetic smile. "How about I come over Friday evening? We could all have a girls' night if that's okay with you?"

Hannah nods and bites into a fry. "Yeah, that's fine with me."

"I'm in." Chloe raises her hand.

"Me too," Casey chimes.

"Good." I nod. "It'll be fun to all hang out somewhere besides here." I laugh, looking around at the café.

"There's actually an upper-level apartment available in my building," Hannah says. "I'm pretty sure it's the whole top floor so it's bigger than mine. You'd probably have a separate room for you and the baby."

"Oh, really?" My eyes light. "That might be perfect. I don't know about walking all the way to a top floor, but you do what you have to do, I guess."

"It's a small building so it's the third floor that's available."

"That's not too bad." I shrug and take a bite of my sandwich. "So far I haven't found much of anything. It's either too expensive or too small." I sigh.

"When's your house going up for sale?" Casey asks.

I wince. This news still bothers me. I know it was my idea, and it's truly what's best, but it's hard to let go.

"Probably Thursday or Friday. The realtor was talking about doing an open house this weekend. She's already come by and taken photos."

Things are moving fast, too fast, but I knew it had to be that way. The sooner I could sell the house, the better. But that didn't make it any easier to accept.

"Wow," Casey says, looking at me with worry. "I'm sorry, Blaire."

I know what she's thinking. Poor Blaire. First she loses Ben and then she loses her house. What's next?

My hand falls protectively to the swell of my stomach.

"It's okay," I say. "I'm okay," I add, and for the first time in nearly seven months, I'm not lying.

36

I leave Group Friday evening and head straight to Hannah's apartment. It's in the center of Old Town as it's affectionately called. Old Town is filled with older buildings dating back to the town's founding. Most have been renovated, but they managed to keep the vintage style of the buildings by keeping the exteriors true to their original charm.

I park on the side street and head to the front and inside. There's no buzzer or anything like that. I know Hannah is on the second floor, and if I remember correctly, she said she was the first door on the left.

I knock and wait patiently for her to open the door. The hallway is dark with only one lone light. There are doors for two apartments on the other side of the hall and the one beside Hannah's that belongs to Cyrus.

I look around and find that the floors are surprisingly clean and the walls look freshly painted.

The door in front of me swings open and Hannah stands there in a pair of cotton shorts and a tank top damp with sweat. Her strawberry blond hair is pulled back in a messy ponytail and she looks ready to pass out.

"Um," I hesitate. "Should I come back? Is Cyrus here?" I whisper-hiss the last part.

Her brows furrow in confusion and then her eyes light in understand. "Oh, God no, my air conditioner broke." She waves me inside. "And of course it's hot as hell today." She fans herself with her shirt, and I get an eyeful of her lacy pale pink bra.

"Casey and Chloe aren't here yet?" I ask unnecessarily. The place is small enough that I can see everything from where I stand. It's cute, though. The wall with windows is exposed brick and the rest of the walls are white. Her couch is a light gray color and mismatched rugs add color to the wood floors. The kitchen is barely big enough for one person but it's clean with new black cabinets and shiny white countertops. It's a studio apartment so her bedroom can be seen from here. Her headboard is a tufted gray fabric that matches the couch and her bedding is white. It's currently rumpled—but as much as I'd like to think it's because Cyrus was here I know Hannah hates making her bed.

"Casey says she's running late from work and Chloe's picking up the Chinese. Do you want anything to drink?" Hannah asks, opening the refrigerator door.

"Water." I kick off my shoes and sit down on the couch. The TV is on and I laugh. "Family Feud?"

"Diss it all you want, but I love that show."

She sits down and hands me a glass of ice water. It's already dripping condensation onto my lap. "You weren't kidding," I say. "It's hot in here."

The breeze from the open window is doing little to help with the heat and she only has one fan blowing.

"My brother said he'd bring another fan over for me, but the loser probably forgot. I better go text him," she mumbles the last to herself.

While she does that, I sip the water. It doesn't do much to help cool me down though. Hannah returns and sits cross-legged on the couch. "So, what's new with you?" She asks.

"The FOR SALE sign went up in my yard today." I sigh. "So many changes."

She frowns. "I'm really sorry, Blaire, and I know that's the last thing you want to hear, but I am. It's unfair that you have to shoulder so much right now. This should be the happiest time of your life."

I look away. I refuse to cry or feel sad tonight. I want to have fun with my friends like we used to. "It's for the best," I say, and it's true. "This place is really nice," I tell her. "Are you liking it?"

"Oh yeah. That upstairs apartment is still for sale," she says with a coaxing tone.

I make a face. "I'm not sure … I'm going to have a newborn in a few months."

"I understand," she agrees. "But I'll be here, so I could help out."

My lips twist. "Good point."

"Come on." She grabs my hand and tugs me towards the door. "Justin—he owns the building—should be downstairs." I let her take me downstairs where she knocks on a door. It opens up a minute later to reveal a younger-looking guy—probably in his early forties when I was expecting someone much older—sitting at a desk in a closet-sized room. "Hey, Justin," Hannah greets him. "Blaire here is looking for a new place. Would you mind showing her the upstairs apartment?"

"Sure." He stands and grabs a ring of keys off a hook. "Hi, nice to meet you Blaire, I'm Justin." He holds his hand out to me.

I shake it. "Hello."

"The upstairs apartment is a little pricier than the others, but it has two separate bedrooms, one full bath, and a half-bath."

"Sounds like it's exactly what I need." I try to sound cheery, but I'm anything but. My stomach is knotted into a tight ball. This … this feels too real. I take a deep breath and remind myself that it has to be done. Justin leads us upstairs to the third floor. "You seem a little young to own a building," I comment, then cringe. "Sorry," I say quickly. "I didn't mean to sound rude."

He chuckles and opens the door. "It's okay. I inherited the building from my Uncle; he didn't have any kids and when he passed he left it to me. I've been fixing up the empty units." He shrugs.

"Oh, cool," I say.

Hannah and I step inside. The apartment is much larger than hers, probably double the size. Like her apartment, there's an exposed brick wall, but this one extends into the kitchen. The kitchen is L-shaped with an island that sits against the wall on one side with a butcher-block countertop. The other countertops are the same white stone as Hannah's with black cabinets. There's a sink in front of a window that overlooks an old-fashioned bank.

I step into the empty living area. It's large enough for my sectional, a few bookshelves, and the TV. The space is also large enough that I could add a small table for a dining area other than the island. When I move over toward the half-bath—also newly redone with shiny white tile—there's a nook that would be perfect for my desk.

Hannah trails behind me as I enter the first room. It's small, but cute, perfect for my baby girl. I can see it now. Cream walls, pale- pink curtains, and the paper crane mobile above an antique-style crib. Tears swim in my eyes.

"It feels like home," I confess, turning to Hannah. "This … It feels right."

I take a deep breath and warmth floods my belly. I feel like that warmth is Ben telling me it's okay, that this is what I need to do. I have to let him go.

Letting go is never an easy thing, but I've taken the necessary steps to do it, and now it's time to commit.

I know I don't need to see the rest of the apartment to know I want this place, but I look anyway and it only cements my decision.

As Justin locks up I say, "I'll take it."

His eyes widen in surprise and he smiles. "Really?"

"Yeah." I nod, resolute. "It's perfect."

Hannah claps her hands together giddily and throws her arms around my neck. "We'll practically be roommates." She laughs as she pulls away.

"Great," Justin says as we start down the stairs. "I'll get started on the paperwork. Are you okay with a three-month deposit?"

"That's fine."

When we reach the second level, Casey and Chloe are waiting outside the door.

"There you are," Chloe groans. "We've been banging on the door for an hour."

"It has not been an hour." Hannah moves past me to unlock the door while Justin heads back to the office.

"Who's that?" Casey asks, watching Justin go downstairs.

"Yeah," Chloe chimes in. "Who is he? And why were you both up there? Was there some kind of weird threesome going down?"

Hannah pales, and I burst out laughing. "God, no," Hannah cries. "He's my landlord. He was showing Blaire the apartment upstairs. Remember me talking about that?"

"I like my theory better." Chloe shrugs as we all file into Hannah's apartment. "It's more interesting."

"So what'd you think?" Casey asks me, plopping on the couch.

"About what?"

She shakes her head. "The apartment?"

"Oh, right. It was perfect." I tuck a piece of hair behind my ear and sit down. "I told him I'd take it."

"Good," Casey chimes. "Things are working out for you, aren't they?" She's trying not to show it but I can see the worry in her eyes.

"Yeah, I guess so." My face twitches.

"Honey." She clucks her tongue in sympathy and takes my hand. "Talk to us."

"Yeah, that's what we're here for," Hannah says, carrying

over the food while Chloe brings plates.

I look at my three friends and see they don't understand. "I don't want to burden you with my problems," I explain. "Not when I can't shoulder yours too."

Hannah's face crumples. "Blaire, that's what friendship is. Being there for each other no matter what. We understand you're hurting, we get it, and you can talk to us. Whatever you need to say, we're here for you."

"I just … I don't want anyone's sympathy," I explain. "In the beginning, when Ben died, people were constantly saying I'm sorry and tiptoeing around my feelings, and I know that's normal, but I don't need that anymore. I'm not broken glass—I promise I won't cut you if you step on me. In fact, I think I need to be stepped on." I hold up my hands. "Metaphorically speaking, of course."

Chloe laughs. "You're so weird, B."

I shrug. "I know."

Casey nudges my shoulder with her arm so I'll look at her. "Since you're not broken glass," she winks, "I want to say that you're not the only one that lost Ben. He was our friend too. Did you think we haven't mourned him? That we buried him and that was that? Because it wasn't, Blaire. We all still miss him." She motions to the three of them. "I know it's so much worse for you. I'm not denying that, but for so long you acted like no one else was allowed to be sad but you."

I wince. She's right; I know she's right, but it doesn't make the words hurt any less.

I take a deep breath, preparing my thoughts before I speak. "Wow," I begin, "I … I didn't know I was like that, but now that you say that, I can see how I was and it wasn't right.

I pushed you guys away. I let my grief override everything else—"

"Blaire," she interrupts me with a soft look and shake of her head, "don't go down that road. Focus on the positive. It's been almost seven months since he died and you're more and more like yourself every day. You're coming back, and much sooner than I thought you would. Grief is a deep dark hole, and some people never climb back out of it. But you've always been stronger than you give yourself credit for. You are a fighter. And Blaire?" She waits for me to nod. "You're my hero."

I hug her, holding on tight. "Thank you," I whisper in her ear.

She nods against my shoulder as I let go.

Hannah reaches over, from where she sits on the coffee table and grabs my hand. "We love you and we're here for you. Never think that you're alone in this."

"Yeah," Chloe pipes in. "We're a team."

I smile at each of them. "I love you guys." Chloe and Hannah take turns hugging me. "Look at us," I say with a laugh, "we're all a bunch of saps."

They laugh too and I smile even bigger. This feels good, being here with them. I'm not shutting myself away anymore. Day by day I'm getting back to normal … Well, not normal, but a new normal.

Life will never be the same after losing Ben, I accept that, but I believe now that in time everything will be okay. Maybe even better than okay.

37

My phone rings beside me on the couch, flashing Ryder's name on the screen. I stare at in confusion, wondering why he's calling me.

"You gonna answer that, Kid, or look at it all day?"

I look up from the phone to my dad. He turns down the volume on the TV and nods at my phone, urging me to answer.

I sigh and answer, "Hello?"

"Hey, Blaire, it's Ryder."

"I know."

"Oh, right. Of course," he says awkwardly. "Anyway, I wanted to call you to see if you wanted to come over for the Fourth of July? I'm having a cookout. My parents are coming over, a few friends, and some of the people from Group. Ivy will be there," he adds, knowing I talk to her frequently. When I don't say anything immediately he continues, "I know it's super last minute and I promise my feelings won't be hurt if you say no. And your parents can come too if they want." He's rambling now, and I find it endearing.

"Sure," I say. "Sounds fun."

He breathes out a sigh of relief. "Really?"

I laugh. "Yeah."

"Okay, see you tomorrow then. It starts at two o' clock."

"I'll be there."

"Great, bye."

"Bye."

I hang up the phone and plop it in my lap.

My dad gives me a knowing look. "You're grinning, Kid."

"Stop it," I say, turning my head away so he can't see my smile.

"Someone's got a crush."

"Dad," I cry, and hit his arm lightly.

"It's true." He chuckles.

I shake my head. "He invited me to his house tomorrow for a Fourth of July party. He said you and mom could come too."

"Oh, we're going," my mom calls from the kitchen. I think she's baking cookies. The woman is always up to something in the kitchen.

My dad chuckles. "Looks like we're going, Kid."

"Yeah, only because Mom wants to spy on me," I joke, smiling at her over my shoulder.

She winks and stirs some sort of batter.

"I better figure out what I'm going to wear," I mumble, spreading my fingers over my belly. My stomach is now large enough that there's no hiding the fact that I'm pregnant.

I hop up from the couch and start up the stairs. I hear my

mom say to my dad, "She's doing good. So much better. She smiles all the time now."

My dad grunts in response.

My heart clenches for my mom, though. When I think of my daughter, and her going through something like this, it breaks my heart. I understand now that this has been difficult for my mom—worse than she's let on. I know there's no way I can ever thank her enough for the last seven months, but I hope somehow, someway, I can show her that it's meant the world to me.

"Stop fidgeting," my mom scolds as we walk up to Ryder's front door. "You look nice," she adds in a softer tone. "You don't need to worry." She smiles up at me, tightening her hold on the bowl of macaroni salad she holds.

I ring the doorbell and wait. My nerves are all over the place. Coming here, to Ryder's party where his parents and friends are in attendance, feels pretty personal. Then again, I guess kissing the guy is pretty personal too.

The door swings open and an older gentleman stands there. He's tall, with salt and pepper hair, and kind brown eyes. I know instantly that he's Ryder's dad; the resemblance is uncanny.

"You must be Blaire," he says to me, pulling me into an immediate hug.

"Oh, uh, hi," I mumble, hugging him back.

"I'm sorry." He releases me. "It's just that I feel like I know you. Ryder's told us so much about you."

"Oh, of course. It's okay," I say awkwardly. It appears that even at twenty-seven years old, I still haven't learned how to handle uncomfortable situations. "These are my parents: Maureen and Dan."

"Hi," Ryder's dad says and shakes each of their hands. "I'm Kenneth. Most everyone's in the back. I'll show you guys the way."

He gestures with his hand and we follow him down the hall and out the back door.

There's a small deck that leads out into a fenced-in yard. The grass is green and well taken care of with a few trees. A few tables and chairs are set up for people to sit at. There's a game of horseshoes going on—a few guys standing around with beers partaking with that while I assume their wives or girlfriends watch. Ryder's standing with them, laughing at something. I study the side of his face. The elegant slope of his chiseled cheekbones and the slight crinkles by his eyes from laughing so much. His skin was always darker in tone, but the summer sun has deepened it even further to a russet color.

He must feel me staring because he turns slightly away from the guy he's speaking to and looks toward the deck where I stand.

Our eyes connect and I feel butterflies fill my stomach. A part of me wants to believe that what I feel is simply the baby moving, but no, those are definitely butterflies.

He excuses himself from the guy he's speaking to and starts towards me.

I laugh when Cole jumps from the lap of a woman—whom I'm assuming is Ryder's mom—and bounds into Ryder's legs. Ryder scoops up the little boy, not missing a beat, and taps him on his nose. He smiles at his son with so much love that I can't help but think of the feeling I'll have with my own daughter.

"Hey," Ryder says, bounding up the steps. "I was worried you wouldn't show."

I start to answer him, but my mom beats me to it.

"We would've been here on time if this one hadn't changed her outfit five times." She bumps my arm with hers.

"Mom," I hiss.

Ryder laughs. "Trying to impress me?"

My dad clears his throat. "The only person here who needs to be impressed is me." He gives Ryder the look. The dreaded look that every father gives his daughter's potential boyfriend.

Ryder chuckles. "I understand, sir."

I look to the heavens. Have I been transported back in time? Am I seventeen again and this is the prom debacle with Joey Stevenson? Because it sure as hell feels like it—although, that involved my dad polishing his shotgun in the dining room and saying, "I'm watching." Suffice to say, I was certainly still a virgin after that particular night.

"I'm hungry," I say, and clap my hands together, trying to divert the attention.

"Food's this way." Ryder nods, and I gladly join him, leaving behind my parents.

"I'm so sorry about that," I say to Ryder once we're out of earshot.

He laughs. "It's okay. I find it entertaining. I feel like I'm seventeen again."

I breathe out a sigh of relief. "Oh good, so I'm not the only one who feels like they've been transported back in time?"

He shakes his head and his dark hair falls into his eyes. "No, definitely not." He adjusts his hold on Cole and points. "Plates, utensils, and napkins are all right there, and the food's obviously there. Take as much as you want. We have more burgers and hot dogs to grill."

I grab a plate and immediately start making a burger. I'd asked about the food as a distraction, but now that I was in front of it I was hungry.

We weren't alone for long when my mom wandered over to the table to set down the macaroni salad she made.

"So, Ryder," she began, "what is it you do exactly?"

"I'm a teacher," he answers.

My mom looks to me. "Wow, that's nice. How long have you lived here?"

"In this area?"

"Yeah." She crosses her arms over her chest. I quickly look away and continue adding food to my plate. I know nothing I do or say is going to stop the inquisition.

Ryder's brow furrows as he thinks. "Six years."

"Where are you originally from?"

He chuckles and sets Cole down when the boy begins to wiggle too much. I watch Cole run off to his grandma. She swoops him up into her lap.

"Bethesda," he answers.

"Hmm," my mom hums, "well-rounded. Why'd you move out here? This is practically the country to you."

"I like the quiet."

"Have you ever killed anyone?"

I pinch the bridge of my nose at her newest question and balance my plate in the other hand. I haven't even been here thirty minutes and I can already feel a headache coming on.

"No, ma'am, I haven't." Ryder bites his lip to keep from laughing.

My mom shrugs and announces, "I'm done. He's a keeper," and walks off.

I stare after her, horrified. Ryder clutches his stomach as the laughter overtakes him. Cole sees him laughing and joins in with his own over-exaggerated laughter.

"I love your parents," Ryder says when he can speak; there are tears of laughter on his cheeks.

"Good," I say, moving to an empty table. "You can adopt them then."

Ryder clucks his tongue and follows me. "I don't think it works like that." He pulls out a chair when I set my plate on the table. I take the seat and he sits down beside me.

"I'm so embarrassed," I mumble, picking up a chip and crunching on the end of it.

He laughs. "That's our parents' job. I'm sure my dad probably said something to you I would've rather he didn't." I shrug. I can't argue with him there. "I feel like I haven't seen you in forever. Is it moving too fast if I say I missed you?" he asks, looking at me beneath his thick dark lashes. I feel my throat catch and I shake my head. I missed him too but I don't say the words out loud. "So, I was thinking," he says. "I'm taking Cole to the pool tomorrow. You should come."

I twist my lips in thought. "I don't know …"

"Just as friends," he assures me. "We can talk about the weather." He laughs. "But I think we'd both have fun and Cole likes you."

"Cole barely knows me," I counter.

"Okay, so Cole likes everybody, but it'll still be fun."

I find myself nodding. "Okay, sure," I say and take a bite of my burger. I then point to my belly. "Just don't expect to see me getting into a skimpy bikini."

Ryder laughs. "You can wear whatever the hell you want. I don't care as long as you're there." There's a vulnerability in his eyes, like he fears he's revealed too much.

I look at him and I see the promise of a future full of laughter and happiness. He's everything I ever wanted before I met Ben. But I did meet Ben. I lived and I loved Ben, and I also lost him. I'm scared I'll lose Ryder too—but where I did fear losing him to death, I now fear losing him to my own inability to move on. I know he won't wait forever for me, but I still don't know how long it'll really take for me to be ready to take that next step with him or anyone for that matter.

"What are you thinking about?" he asks me.

"N-Nothing," I stutter and drop my gaze from his face to the plate.

He chuckles and reaches over the tap my forehead. "Really? Because those creases suggest otherwise."

I shrug. "Just the future."

"You look worried," he comments.

I bite my lip. "There are a lot of changes coming and . . ." I pause, searching for the right words. "I'm not sure I'm changing with them."

He shakes his head. "Blaire, if you could see how much you've changed since I first met you, you wouldn't be saying that. You've done remarkably well given your circumstances. I don't know many people that wouldn't have cracked under the pressure."

"I'm pretty sure I did." I try to laugh, but there's no humor in the sound.

"You didn't, trust me. You're one of the most resilient people I've ever met, and I admire that about you. Remember, we all grieve differently and we all heal differently. No two stories are ever the same." He pauses and inhales a breath. "You were so sad when I first met you. There was no light in your eyes. You didn't smile or laugh. You were simply on auto-pilot, like most people who are grieving. But you didn't stay that way. Yes, it's taken months for you to get to this point and it'll take more months for you to get to a different point, but you're doing it and that's what matters. You're not letting grief beat you, you're beating it."

I stare at him for one second, two, three, and then I burst out laughing, clutching my stomach. "You sound like a drug coach or an AA advisor or something." I laugh so hard tears fall from my eyes.

Ryder begins to laugh too. "Oh, shit, you're right." We both dissolve into a fit of laughter. I bury my face in my hands, trying to stifle the sound. "I really need to work on my speeches," he chortles.

When I'm no longer dissolving into a fit of giggles, I say, "I understand what you're saying."

He sobers. "And I also should add that I'm not saying that one day you'll wake up and forget him. That the pain will cease to exist, but in my own personal experience it does dull—but there are times where I wake up and it's like there's this crushing weight on my chest and it kills me that I'll never see Angela smile again or hear her laugh."

"Yeah." I sigh. "That's what bothers me the most," I agree. I look away and inhale a breath. I let it out slowly and with it I exhale all my sadness—at least, that's what I tell myself. I refuse to think about the fact that today should've been my first Fourth of July as Ben's wife.

Some of the guys shout Ryder's name and he cringes. "They're starting another game and want me to join."

"I'm okay here," I assure him. "Go," I urge. He looks torn. "I'm okay," I say again. "No tears and no breakdowns from me, I promise."

He laughs and taps his hand against the table. "Okay, but I'll be back, and we're not talking about Angela or Ben anymore. Instead, we're just Blaire and Ryder—a guy and a girl enjoying the Fourth with friends and family."

I nod my head in agreement as he leaves. He's gone no more than thirty seconds until my mom slides into his empty chair. "So what was that about?" she asks, looking back at him where he stands with his friends. "It looked serious. Are you okay?" She brushes my hair away from my forehead like she used to when I was a little girl and she was trying to comfort me.

"He was just giving me a pep talk," I explain.

She starts to speak, but someone says, "Hey," behind us. I turn and find Ivy heading toward us.

"Hi!" I say much more cheerily than normal for me. I stand up to hug her. "I'm so happy you're here."

She hugs me back and sits down in the chair to my left. "I wasn't sure I was going to come. I told Ryder I would, but then I woke up and didn't feel like it, so that's why I'm so late. I didn't decide until an hour ago that I was actually going to come."

"Don't feel bad," my mom says. "We were late because of this one." She points at me.

"This is my mom," I tell Ivy. "Mom, this is Ivy. From Group."

"Nice to meet you," my mom says with a smile. "I'm Maureen. I'll leave you two to talk. I need to go find your dad. The man's probably stopped up the toilet or something." She laughs.

"Mom," I scold, laughing too.

"It's the truth," she sighs and stands. "Seriously, where is that man?" she mutters to herself as she leaves.

"So what's new with you?" Ivy asks.

I rub my stomach. "This little lady is giving me hell." I sigh. "I think she's preparing me for the sleepless nights because she's wide awake all night rolling around in there. Other than that, I'm moving."

Her eyes widen in surprise. "You're moving?"

I nod. "Yeah, it's for the best. I mean, I'm not thrilled, but I know this is what I need to do."

Ivy shakes her head. "I wish I was that spunky. I'd probably be better off if I moved. There are too many reminders of my husband at my house."

"I know what you mean." I sigh, lovingly stroking my stomach when my daughter gives a kick. "I still haven't gotten rid of any of Ben's things. His clothes are still in the closet, but I keep telling myself that when I move I have to get rid of them."

"It's hard," she agrees. "Moving on … It takes guts."

"Yeah, I agree."

I fear that I'm not moving on. I'm scared I'm running away from my problems out of desperation. Who knows? I still feel so lost. Sometimes I'm worried I'll never find my way.

"I'll be right back," she says. "I'm going to get something to eat."

I nod as she leaves and my attention is drawn to Cole. He's now running through a sprinkler, his laughter echoing through the yard. He's happy, not a care in the world. He's too young to truly understand that his mommy isn't around. I don't know how you explain to a child that their mom or dad is gone. How can you show them that the person loved them as much as you do when they're not here? It's one of my biggest fears with my daughter.

I quickly dismiss those thoughts from my mind. I came here to have fun and that's what I'm going to do.

I finish eating as Ivy returns and we chat about the baby and my move. I talk about how I plan to decorate the nursery and already I can feel myself getting back into a better headspace.

Soon, music begins to play and people dance. Cole jumps

around, doing his own interpretation of dancing, and it's the cutest thing I've ever seen. He jumps and flails his arms, even wagging his tongue. Ryder scoops him up and the little boy cackles in happiness. I'm surprised when Ryder comes over to me.

"Dance with us?" He holds out his hand, urging me up.

"I don't know," I hedge, shaking my head.

"Come on," he coaxes. "You don't want to make us sad, right, Cole?"

The little boy nods and pouts his bottom lip. Ryder laughs at him and then does the same, curling his bottom lip under.

"Well—" my lips quirk "—I can't refuse those faces, can I?" I stand and take Ryder's hand.

The three of us make our way over to where everyone else is dancing. Ryder spins me around and I laugh.

I let my fear and worries fade away and I'm simply Blaire—spending the Fourth with the guy she likes, friends, and family.

Ryder pulls me against his chest, and of course, my belly gets in the way. He laughs and looks down, bouncing Cole in his other arm. "It's like there's a person between us." He winks.

I laugh at his corniness. "Something like that."

We sway to the music awkwardly—thanks to my stomach and Cole. I don't mind, though, it feels right.

Ryder lowers his head and presses his forehead to mine. "I want to go on a date with you so bad." There's so much longing in his voice. "I know you're not ready, but I'm putting that out there." His lips brush my forehead before he pulls back.

I adjust my arms around his neck and purse my lips. "A date might not be so bad," I whisper.

His eyes widen in surprise. "Really?"

I shrug. "I'd … I'd like to get to know you better. Just something casual—no fancy dinners, please. That's not my thing."

His lips crook up in a lopsided smile. "Next Saturday good for you?"

I nod. "Yeah."

His smile widens further. "Thank you," he says.

I laugh. "Don't thank me yet. I still might run away," I joke. "But I'm trying. I like you." I swallow thickly and gaze up at him. I've gotten to know Ryder a lot over the last few months, and he's honestly one of the nicest guys I've ever known. And I know my mom's right when she says Ben would want me to move on—he'd want me to do whatever made me happy. But trusting my heart—especially one that's been so broken is no easy feat.

Ryder brushes his nose against mine. "If you run, I'll run too, this time. Not away, but I'll be right there beside you. You're not alone, Blaire. You have so many people that love and care about you."

I hold on tighter to his shoulders. "I know."

That's what scares me most.

38

I'm going on a date with Ryder.

I believe if I keep repeating the words to myself I'll somehow become desensitized to them. So far, my theory isn't working. Ryder is the first man, besides Ben, that I've gone on a date with in years. Seven, almost eight, if I remember correctly. That's insane to me. I've been out of the game for nearly a decade.

I take extra time curling my hair and putting on my makeup. It's not really for Ryder's benefit—okay, maybe a little bit—but it's the only thing I've found to completely silence my mind. It's a bit impossible to think about anything but lining your lips when you're yielding a lip pencil and your mouth is gaping like a fish.

Ryder didn't give me much information on what we were doing, except to say that we'd be outside most of the day. That could mean a million different things and I had no idea what to prepare for. A large part of me wanted to freak out and completely overthink things, but I was trying to go with the flow.

I finished my makeup, fluffed my curled hair, and headed into my closet.

I didn't look at Ben's side. I never did. I couldn't bring myself to notice his shirts and jeans stacked neatly on shelves and his shoes scattered on the floor. It especially seemed wrong that they were still there on a day like today when I was going on a date with another man. I felt like I was cheating in a way. Logically, I knew that wasn't the case, but it didn't stop me from feeling that way.

I scanned my closet for something to wear. I felt like a whale so everything my fingers touched I immediately vetoed. I stood with my hands on my hips, frowning at my wardrobe.

What to wear? What to wear?

I figured a dress was a safe bet so I'd narrowed it down that much. But I wasn't in the mood to wear something floral, white seemed … wrong, and stripes would only add to the whale affect. I end up settling on a long black dress with thicker tank top straps. I add some jewelry to dress it up a bit and a hat.

I check my phone for the time and then begin to panic. Ryder will be here any minute.

It's not that I don't want to go on a date with him—I do, but it's a big step for me among a bunch of other big steps I've been taking lately. I'm worried it might be too much, but I keep pushing forward.

I don't linger upstairs any longer. My parents are conveniently gone—thanks to the movie tickets I got them—so I don't have to worry about them making me feel uncomfortable about the situation. Not that they would purposely, but since I'm already nervous it wouldn't take much to completely set me off.

I busy myself by wiping the counters clean. It looks like my dad ate a cookie or something and crumbled it everywhere.

Men.

The doorbell rings a few minutes later.

My heart promptly stops and restarts five times faster.

I pause and take a deep breath before heading for the door. I open it to find Ryder standing there with a cluster of white tulips.

"Oh, they're beautiful," I say, taking them from him. "Thank you."

"I wasn't sure what your favorite flower was." He shrugs shyly.

"These are perfect." I smile at him. "Would you like to come in?" I ask, motioning over my shoulder. "I need to put these in water before we leave."

"Yeah, sure." He clears his throat and steps inside. I close the door behind him. I can tell from the tightness in his shoulders that he's as nervous about today as I am, which instantly makes me feel better. I like knowing that I'm not alone in my worries.

I head into the kitchen, and he follows, stuffing his hands in the pockets of his shorts. I set the bouquet down on the counter and stretch up on my tiptoes to grab a clear vase from the cabinet.

"This is a nice place," Ryder comments, looking around.

"Thanks," I say, filling the vase with water. "I'm moving, though."

His eyes widen. "Why?" He winces. "You don't have to answer that. I didn't mean to sound like I was prying."

I laugh and empty the packet of stuff that came with the flowers into the water. "It's okay. I can't afford this place on my own, and frankly it's too big. It … it doesn't feel like home anymore," I confess. I haven't said those words out loud before now, but it's something I've been thinking for a while.

Ryder crosses his arms over his chest and leans his hip against the counter. "I've been meaning to move for a while too. I'm usually so busy with work and Cole that I'm too exhausted to bother." He chuckles.

"Maybe you should move before school starts back up?" I suggest.

"Doesn't leave me much time, but maybe," he muses.

I put the flowers in the vase and move them around a bit so they're not so squished together. I carry the vase over to the table and set them in the center.

"Thanks," I say again. "They really are pretty."

He grins and steps a little closer to me. "For future reference, what is your favorite flower?"

"Sunflowers," I answer with a smile. "They make me happy."

"Sunflowers," he repeats. "I'll remember that."

"Tulips are beautiful too, though," I add, not wanting to hurt his feelings.

He chuckles. "Shall we get going then?"

"Oh, yeah." I jump away from the table and grab my purse.

Outside, I lock up while Ryder goes to his car and holds the door open for me.

As I slide into the car, he says, "A gentleman should hold every door open on a date," and winks before the door closes.

"Where are we headed?" I ask as he backs out of the driveway.

His lips quirk into a smile. "A park."

"Is that all I get?" I ask. I can't really base his agenda off of an answer as ambiguous as a park.

"Yep." He nods. "I have a few quick stops to make first," he tells me. "So sit back and enjoy the ride."

I laugh and look out the window at the passing scenery. I've always found my hometown to be quite pretty with the many green trees and blue shadow of the mountains in the distance. Ben and I talked about moving away once. Maybe to Colorado, but this place will always be home and I'm glad we stayed. Especially now. I can't imagine losing him and being away from my friends and family. I don't think I would've made it.

After about twenty minutes, Ryder pulls into a convenience store lot. "I'll be right back," he says, undoing his seatbelt.

"You mean I can't come in?" I joke.

"No." He shakes his head. "Super-secret plans are about to go down, and I can't have you witnessing anything."

I watch curiously as he leaves and goes inside the building. Shelves block me from seeing anything so I end up watching people in the parking lot. It's far more entertaining.

Ryder comes back a few minutes later and puts the bag in the trunk.

"Why do I have a feeling there aren't any gummy worms in there?" I laugh as he gets in the car.

He taps his finger against the steering wheel. "There might be something kinda like that in there."

He pulls out of the lot and drives out of town.

There's a park close to us but he's clearly not going to that one, which only adds to my bafflement.

"So," Ryder says as he drives, "tell me something about you I don't know."

"Um ..." My lips twist in thought. "I was a bit of a nerd in high school."

He glances at me. "I figured you were a cheerleader or something."

I laugh. "Yeah, that'd be a definite no. I was a major dork and super clumsy. What about you? What were you like in high school?"

"Band geek." He chuckles.

I smile at this bit of information. "What did you play?"

"Saxophone."

"What's your favorite food?" I ask, loosening up. I've gotten to know Ryder pretty well over the last few months but not specific details like this.

"Hmm," he thinks. "Probably these chicken dumpling things my mom makes. What about you?"

"Pasta, and now I'm hungry." I laugh.

He smiles over at me and his brown eyes are light with happiness. "It's a good thing I plan to feed you then." He adjusts the volume on the radio and it prompts him to ask the question, "What kind of music do you like?"

I cringe. "I'm a pop music kind of girl," I admit.

He pretends to wince and presses a hand to his heart. "You

wound my poor rock 'n roll heart."

I laugh. "Sorry."

"It's okay. I forgive you for your horrendous taste in music." Before I can ask him another question, he says, "We're here."

I'd been so busy talking to him that I hadn't even noticed where we were going. He's turned onto a dirt road that I know leads down to a trail that ends up at the river.

He parks by a few other cars and hops out. I follow him to the trunk. There's a cooler and the bag from the convenience store. I peer closer at it.

"Are those live worms?" I gag and scuttle a few feet back like the worms are going to grow wings and fly at my face.

He laughs at my reaction. "Yeah," he answers. "I'm sorry they're not gummy."

"Why do you have worms?" I nearly shriek at him.

"To go fishing, of course." He grabs the cooler and bag, then goes around to the back passenger side to grab two fishing pools that were lying on the floor of the car.

"Here, let me get that," I say, reaching for the cooler. There's no way in hell I'm holding the bag with the worms.

"I got it," he says, side-stepping me.

"You're going to drop something," I warn him as we head down the path.

"You better hope I don't or worms might end up all over your feet."

I look down at my open-toe wedges and gag. "I think I might throw up if that happens."

It doesn't take us long to get to the shore. The water is a little choppy, but there are people in it kayaking. We walk aways down and Ryder sets everything down. There's not a picnic table or anything like that so we sit on the ground.

"I should've brought a blanket." He frowns. "I'm sorry."

"It's okay. I like this."

I'm not just saying that, I really do. This is so much better than anything I could've imagined.

Ryder smiles sheepishly and opens the cooler. "I got subs on my way to your house and chips. It seemed fitting for this kind of setting." He shrugs. "I also brought water and iced tea. Which do you want?"

"Water," I say and take a bottle from him when he holds it out. He hands me one of the wrapped subs from a local place and a bag of chips. I unwrap the sandwich and wait for Ryder to do the same before taking a bite. "I didn't realize how hungry I was," I tell him.

"Me either," he agrees.

"Is Cole with your parents this weekend?" I ask.

He nods. "Yeah, it wasn't their weekend to do it but I asked if they'd mind. They were cool with it, of course. They've told me they'd like to do it more often but usually weekends are the only times I can do something fun with him."

"Maybe next time Cole can come with us? We could go to the movies or something?"

His eyes shine as he grins. "Already planning on a next time then?" I duck my head, embarrassed. His fingers touch my chin, lifting my head up. "I like that you're already thinking ahead." His voice grows deep. Husky. "Why are you embarrassed?" he asks and lets go

I want to look away but it's impossible. "This is all so new and different," I say.

"Yeah, I know what you mean," he agrees. "But new and different isn't always a bad thing."

"No, it's not." I smile up at him. "I like being with you," I tell him. It's a bold statement for me but I don't cower. I want him to know I mean it.

His smile is so large and bright it rivals the sun. In fact, I think he might be the sun. My own personal sun, that is. He came into my life when I was in the darkest of places and immediately filled it with light. He hasn't healed me, but he's given me the strength to do it on my own.

"I like being with you too, Blaire." He tilts his head towards the sun. "I feel like I'm living again," he whispers so low I'm not sure I heard him right.

We finish eating and stuff our trash back in the cooler.

Ryder then picks up the two poles and the bag of worms and we head closer to the shore. I kick off my shoes and chide myself for wearing a long dress. The end of it will have to get wet.

We step into the water and Ryder hands me a pole. I immediately say, "Don't even think about handing me a worm to put on the end of this thing."

"Aw, don't be so skittish, Blaire," he jokes, rifling through the bag. He pulls out a worm and throws it at me.

I scream, like the little girl that I am, and flail. I lose my balance on a rock and slip into the water.

"Oh. My. God," I say. Ryder is laughing uproariously at me.

I can't really blame him. It is pretty funny even if I can't see the humor at the moment.

"I didn't even throw it," he chortles, holding out the worm.

"I hate you so much right now," I say. I haven't bothered getting up. What's the point? I'm already soaking wet. Instead, I kick out at Ryder and splash him with water. He holds out his hands against the spray and drops the stupid worm in the water.

"Oh, you've done it now." He laughs and splashes me with water. He ends up slipping in the process—seriously, those rocks are slippery—and goes down in front of me.

I bust out laughing. Now this is funny.

"Oh, so it's funny when I fall?" he jokes.

I can't answer because I'm too busy laughing. He splashes me, just a light spray, and I send a whole wall of water at him.

I can't stop laughing and neither can he. I haven't had this much fun in a long time.

We both completely forget about the objective of fishing. This, living in the moment, is too much fun.

Minutes later, and out of breath, I gasp, "We're a mess."

We're both completely soaked. My hair drips onto my shoulders and I'm sure my mascara is streaked across my cheeks. I can't bring myself to care, though. Not when I'm having this much fun.

Ryder sits beside me in the water—it's not very deep where we are—and neither of us makes a move to get out.

He shakes his wet hair like a dog and droplets of water spray across me.

"Hey." I laugh and hold up my hands to protect against the onslaught.

He laughs and glances over at me. A droplet of water drips from the end of his nose, to his chin, where it gets lost in other sluices of water.

"Some date, huh?" He chuckles and stands up, holding his hand down for me. I slip a bit on the rocks as he pulls me up and he holds me tight against his chest. Despite the cool temperature of the water, his body is warm and I'm instantly heated.

"This is the most fun I've had in a long time," I tell him.

"So much for fishing, though." He holds my hands and we cross the few feet back to the grassy shore. "We better change our clothes."

I look down at my soaking wet dress and shiver. "Yeah, good idea," I agree.

We grab everything and head back to his car. While he loads everything inside I try to squeeze as much water as I can from my dress so I don't completely soak his car. When he has the trunk packed he hooks his thumbs in the back of his shirt and pulls it over his head.

Time slows and I stare as his stomach is exposed. It's smooth and tan with dark hair disappearing into the band of his boxer-briefs that peek out of the top of his shorts. He's muscled, but not overly so. It's clear he works out and stays in shape, but he's not the body builder type. He's real, and I like that.

He tosses the shirt in the trunk before closing it. The sound of it slamming closed snaps me out of my reverie.

"Ready?" he asks, hands settling on his narrow hips.

"Mhm." I nod, trying not to stare. My skin prickles with awareness, tightening all over. I hurry into the car before I do something stupid.

Inside the car, Ryder turns the heat on despite the fact that it's nearly ninety degrees today. We need it, though, thanks to the chill from the water.

"I'm sorry we have to cut our date short," he says a few minutes later.

I look away from the window. "I don't want it to be over," I admit.

He looks surprised. "Really?" I nod. "We could hang out at my house? Dry our clothes? I have a ton of movies, or we could just talk, or—" he rambles endearingly.

I reach over and touch the tips of my fingers to his forearm. His muscle tightens at my touch. "That sounds great."

Ryder looks nervous, but happy. I can understand his nervousness. I'm not normally so forward so he's probably afraid that it might end up being too much for me and I'll get scared again. Maybe I will, but I don't know if I don't try, and I want to spend more time with him. I'm not ready for today to end. For the first time in seven months, I feel like a normal woman again, and that's not a feeling I'm ready to give up.

We both grow quiet the rest of the drive. I think we're both too lost in our thoughts to speak, but there's no awkwardness in the silence, which is nice—it reminds me of what my mom used to say to me.

"Find a man that even in silence you're comfortable with. That's a telling factor, B. If someone makes you nervous to the point that you have to chatter endlessly, then they're not the person for you. You need to be able to communicate without saying a word."

Those words came back to me many times over the years as I was dating and would inevitably encounter the wall of awkward silence. Until I met Ben. There was no awkward silence with him, only comfort, and now I felt the same with Ryder.

"We're here," Ryder says, snapping me out of my thoughts.

I look up to see that we're parked in his driveway.

My dress is still damp and sticks to my body. I slide off the leather seat and it makes this horrible squishing sound.

"I feel gross," I announce, meeting Ryder at the trunk where he grabs his shirt and the cooler.

"Me too," he agrees. I follow him up the front porch and inside the house. He drops the cooler in the sink and turns around, bracing his hands behind him. He's still shirtless and the movement flexes all of his muscles. I swallow thickly and force my eyes up. "I don't know about you, but I want to shower."

I nod in agreement. "Y-Yeah, a shower would be nice," I stutter, completely distracted by him. He's beautiful in a different sort of way—and being a guy, he'd probably hate that I think he's beautiful, but he is, not just in his appearance but who he is as a person is beautiful.

"Okay." He claps his hands together. "Showers are upstairs. Come on. I'm sure I have a shirt you can borrow."

I follow him upstairs and I can't help but glance into the rooms. There's a guest room that also appears to double as an office space, a bathroom, Cole's room, and at the end of the hall: Ryder's room.

It's obvious to me that he must've redecorated the room after his wife died. Unlike the rest of the house, it looks like a bachelor pad. The bed is unmade and there's stuff cluttered everywhere—papers, coffee mugs, and laundry. It's not dirty, more lived in, and it gives me a bit of insight into who Ryder is. He keeps the rest of his house spick and span, but this room—his space—is a mess, and I wonder how much of a reflection it is of him. Is he calm, cool, and collected on the outside and a mess on the inside? I don't mean that in a bad way. I, personally, find that there's beauty in chaos—if it's the right kind of chaos.

"Sorry for the mess," he says, smiling sheepishly. "I would've cleaned up if I would've known you were coming over."

"It's okay." I dismiss his concern with a wave of my hand.

He rifles through a dresser drawer and pulls out a shirt and holds it up. It's navy with a faded logo on the front.

"This should work," he says, handing it to me. "I have some old basketball shorts in here somewhere that are too small," he muses, moving to another drawer. "I meant to throw them away and never bothered. A-ha," he exclaims and holds them up proudly. "Here they are."

"Thanks." I take those from him too.

"Wait here," he says. "I have some extra soap in my bathroom. You'll either smell like a man or a toddler, though …" he trails off.

I laugh and clutch the clothes against my chest. "That's okay."

I watch as he goes into the attached bathroom and rifles through the bottom cabinet. He comes back with body wash and shampoo. "I wasn't sure if you'd want to wash your hair," he says, clearing his throat.

I hold my arms out so he can pile the bottles on top of the clothes. "I probably should. Who knows what's in that river water."

"Shower's down the hall," he says. "I'll show you."

"That's okay." I edge toward the door. "I saw it on the way up."

"Oh, okay." He stands there nervously. We're both on edge, not knowing what the right thing to do or say is. Maybe if we were both normal—not tainted by losing ones we love—we wouldn't feel that way. Maybe things wouldn't feel so … foreign.

I can feel him watching me as I go down the hall. I look back before I close the bathroom door and my gaze seems to break him from whatever trance he's in. I smile at him and he smiles back, his Adam's apple bobbing. The door clicks shut and I lock it. I lean my head against the cool wood and breathe in and out. Ryder does strange things to me. His presence shakes me up until I can't think straight. It's not an unpleasant feeling, though.

I turn around and set everything on the counter. I turn the shower on, waiting for steam to fill the room before I undress.

Beneath the spray of the water, I close my eyes as I scrub my body—pretending it's Ryder's hands on my body and not my own. My breaths pick up speed, coming out in short, sharp pants. I pretend to feel his lips on my neck, ghosting over my collarbone, sucking on my breasts. My legs grow weak from my fantasy and my body shakes. I picture his hands sliding down my sides, pulling me against his slick hard body. He kisses me long and deep, drawing a moan from my throat. His fingers dig into my thighs as he lifts me up and presses my back to the tiled wall. My fingers clasp around his neck as I lower onto his cock—

My eyes shoot open.

What the hell am I doing?

I swallow thickly and slap my hands against my face.

"Snap out of it, Blaire," I say to myself. "It's too soon. Too soon."

My words have no effect on my body, though. I'm still incredibly turned on, my core pulsing, and my nipples pebbled. I've never had a fantasy quite that detailed and with Ryder.

Tears leak out of my eyes, lost in the water. I feel like I'm cheating on Ben, even though that's not true. He's gone, and I have every right to move on, but I can't seem to let go. I guess it's easier to hold on.

"Fuck," I curse, slapping my hand against the tiled wall. "Dammit, Ben, why did this have to happen," I scream, still beating my hands against the wall. "It's not fair! I hate you! I fucking hate you for leaving me! I hate you so much! I hate this!" I sob and sink down onto the floor of the shower. I feel like I'm going to throw up. I draw my legs up and wrap my arms around them. "I hate you, I hate you, I hate you," I repeat over and over again, but what I really mean is I hate myself.

"Blaire?" I hear pounding against the door. I cover my ears with my hands. I don't know what's happening to me. Is this a mental break? "Blaire?"

I can still hear the pounding even through my covered ears and the roar of the water.

When the shower curtain is torn back, I jolt away, covering my body.

"Oh, Blaire," Ryder breathes. He grabs a towel and bends down to me in the bottom of the tub, cowering away like a wounded animal. He's the last person I want to see right now after my fantasy or whatever you want to call it.

He turns the water off and wraps the towel around me. His strong arms wind around me and he lifts me up, cradling me against his chest. I hang there like a limp rag doll. I'm scared to touch him—scared of what I'll do.

Ryder carries me down the hall to the guest room and lays me on the bed.

"I'll be right back," he tells me. The worry is evident in his eyes and his boxers hang loosely on his hips like he heard me screaming and put on the first thing he could get his hands on.

I'm so mad at myself, for breaking down like this, especially after such a good day, but I guess moments like this are unavoidable.

Ryder returns with the clothes he'd given me and helps me to sit up since I don't have the energy to do it myself. He directs me to lift my arms and he slides the shirt down over the towel. When my body is covered he whips the towel away and it drops to the floor. He helps me into the shorts next and then stays bent in front of me while I sit on the bed. My hands find their way to his shoulders, needing the support to stay upright. Droplets from my wet hair drip onto his naked chest but he doesn't move away.

He swallows thickly, his eyes flitting over every exposed piece of me. He's looking for an injury—some sign to explain this.

"What happened?" he asks when the answer to his question isn't obvious. I stay immobile. There's no way I can tell him I had a fantasy about him and it set me off. "Blaire," he says, "I can't help you if you don't talk to me. I thought everything was okay today. What changed? Is this too much for you?"

I cover my face with my hands. "I don't know," I cry. "I'm so confused."

"Hey, hey," he soothes, tucking a piece of damp hair behind my ear. "It's okay to be confused."

"I want you in my life," I tell him, biting my lip. It's more of a confession than I meant to give.

"I'm here for you," he says, his dark eyes flickering over my face with so much care. His fingers ghost over my cheek. "In whatever way you need, I'm here."

I clutch at his chest and break down, falling off the bed and into his arms.

Maybe it's wrong to seek comfort in his arms—he's the reason for my breakdown after all—but I need to be held and I need him to be the one to do it. Yeah, it's definitely wrong, but everything about this is wrong. Us, being together, it's all because we lost the loves of our lives. What does that mean for us? Do we even have a chance for a future? A chance to love each other completely and as we are, without comparing the person to the one we lost? Right now, every time I get close to Ryder I have Ben creep into my mind and it confuses me.

My fingers shake against his skin and I murmur, "I'm sorry."

"Don't apologize," he breathes.

"I ruined today," I whine, pressing my forehead to his chest.

He lifts my head up. "No, you didn't," he assures me. "I've enjoyed every second."

"Did you break the door?" I ask him.

"What door?" His brows furrow.

"The one to the bathroom?" My fingers curl into the hair at the nape of his neck.

"Probably," he says with a slight shrug. "I wasn't paying attention in the moment."

I lean my head against his chest, my ear over his heart, and close my eyes. His hands rub up and down my back, soothing and relaxing me.

After a little while, I pull back and say, "I should probably go home."

"Okay," he says, brushing stray hairs away from my forehead. "I'll get dressed and meet you downstairs."

I climb off his lap and watch him go.

I head down the hall and gather up my clothes then go downstairs and wait by the door. Ryder jogs down the steps a minute later, dressed in a t-shirt and shorts similar to the ones he let me borrow.

"Ready?" he asks, opening the door.

"Yeah," I say.

He holds the car door open for me and I climb inside. It doesn't take long for him to reach my house. I don't make any move to get out of the car, though.

"Thank you for today," I say. "I really did have fun."

"Good." He smiles and leans over, pressing his lips to my forehead. "And maybe one day you'll tell me exactly what goes on in that pretty head of yours."

"Maybe," I echo.

I slip out of the car and he watches until I'm in the house. I close and lock the door, then turn around, exhaling a heavy breath.

My eyes land on the vase full of paper cranes from Ben and my heart clenches. It's been too long since I found a new one and I need to hear from him. Compelled by some unknown force I stride across to the vase and pluck out one of the carefully folded birds.

He left this paper crane for me on our bed shortly after the first negative pregnancy test. Those words, though, I need them now just as much a needed them back then.

Maybe it was fate that made me pick this particular crane, or maybe it was just random, but whatever the reason, I'm supremely thankful for it.

I fold the paper crane back up and put it back in the vase with the others.

"Until next time," I whisper.

39

I sit in bed snacking on chips with the baby name book propped on my belly. I crunch down on the chip and Winnie glares at me from the windowsill. The silly cat is finally coming around more. She's mostly hidden under the bed the last few months, only coming out to eat in the middle of the night. At one point I thought she'd died, but when I crouched on the floor and lifted the bed skirt, mean blue eyes glared back at me.

Animals, they know things we can't comprehend, and I believe she understood that Ben was gone and never coming back. I think in her crazy cat brain she thought I'd done something to him and it gave her more ammunition to hate me.

"What are you looking at?" I ask her, chomping on a chip.

Her dark brown tail swishes and her eyes blink lazily. The disdain in her expression is almost hysterical. I should probably find her a new home, but she's been with us for so long that I can't fathom her not being there. With the baby coming it's something I have to seriously contemplate. I can't imagine Winnie doing well with a baby.

I flip to the next page in the baby name book. I never realized there were so many names before.

I glance at the empty space beside me in bed and my heart aches. This should be something that Ben is a part of. I feel wrong picking our child's name on my own, but it's not something we ever talked about.

"Bernadette," I say, cringing. "No way." I skim through the B names and find nothing. "Carly. Hmmm, maybe." I scribble it down on my piece of paper. It joins a very short list of names. Granted, I'm only on the C's so it's bound to grow.

I make it to the H names before I have to set aside the book. I end up picking up What to Expect When You're Expecting. It seems to be the go-to pregnancy book but most of the passages scare the crap out of me.

After reading a few pages, I yawn and decide to call it a night. I pile the books on my nightstand and flick off the light.

The boxes in the corner cast strange shadows across the walls and I find myself childishly imagining the bogeyman emerging from behind them. It's a silly thought, I know, but it's weird seeing the boxes there.

The last two weeks have been spent packing up my belongings. Some things will go to the new apartment with me, others will be donated, and I'll try to sell some. The house is slowly but surely emptying out. It's a sad process and it kills me a little bit each time I pack something away. I keep reminding myself it's for the best.

I cross my hands beneath my head and close my eyes, willing sleep to come.

After a few minutes, I drift away.

"What about this?" my mom asks, holding up a wooden spoon. It's stained and old, hardly anything anyone would want.

"Toss it," I say, sorting silverware into a box. I just got the call that there's been an offer on the house. It's a good one, great, even, so I accepted it.

This is really happening now.

My dad and Ryder are painting the apartment today. Ryder was kind enough to ask if I needed any help so I gladly accepted. Plus, I didn't like the idea of my dad there painting by himself. I was afraid of him falling off a ladder or something. The man isn't exactly the most coordinated.

I finish with the silverware and move on to wrapping the plates and setting them in the box.

The kitchen and master bathroom are the last rooms I have to pack. Everything else is pretty well taken care of apart from the closet. My clothes have already been moved to the apartment—aside from a few outfits—but Ben's clothes still hang inside. I know I can't take them with me, but I'm having a hard time letting go. I know I've kept much more important things that belonged to him, but getting rid of his clothes seems monumental. Maybe I'm just overthinking it. I tend to do that.

I finish with the plates and tape the box shut before carrying it over to the front door.

The house that was once so full—full of love, laughter, and happiness—now echoes with emptiness. It's a shell of what it once was. Sort of like me. It's sad, really, how much this place doesn't feel like home anymore.

I go back to the kitchen and begin sorting the pans. I'm

trying not to think about the fact that tonight will be my first night sleeping in the apartment. My parents will in a hotel for the next two days before they head back to Florida. My mom is still talking about moving back here. I told her I don't care if they do, as long as it's what they want, but not to move because of me. So, we'll see.

"You're quiet," she comments as we work. I sit on the floor, going through the bottom cabinets while she works on the top ones, sorting glasses.

"I have a lot on my mind," I say with a sigh. It's not a lie. I'm all torn up inside.

Life is a confusing melody and right now I can't hear the music.

Nothing makes sense and I only hope that one day I hear the music again.

"That's understandable," she says, wrapping a glass. I tuck a piece of hair behind my ear and lay a pan on the donate pile. I don't know if the hospice will even take pans but it's barely used so I figure it's worth a try. If not, I'll just toss it. "Why don't you let me finish this and you can go do your bathroom?"

I know what she's really suggesting—clear out Ben's things.

I set a pot in the keep pile. "It'll go faster if it's both of us," I reason.

She clangs a glass against the countertop and I look up at her. "B," she says sternly, "you're avoiding."

I look away. She's right. Moms are always right. It's like they're gifted special magical powers or something.

"Fine," I grump. "I'll go do it."

I wobble as I stand, still not used to the growing belly in front of me.

Boxes litter the downstairs, labeled with either room names or the word donate. I tiptoe around them and up the steps.

The master bedroom is empty, the furniture already gone. I sold it online—I hadn't wanted to take it with me. The new stuff was delivered yesterday to the apartment. It's slightly more feminine in style since it's just me. I figured since this was a new start I might as well get new stuff. Besides, a lot of the things Ben and I bought together would never fit in the apartment.

I grab an empty box off the floor and head into the bathroom. Things like towels and washcloths have already been packed—except for one set while I stayed here—but all the toiletries are still there. I pile them into the box. There's no rhyme or reason to my method. I just want to get this done and face the last obstacle.

It doesn't take me long to fill the box with hairspray, shampoo and conditioner, and various body washes and deodorants. Ben always made fun of me for hoarding deodorant, but it's one of those things I never like to run out of.

I carry the full box to the doorway and grab two more empty ones.

I fill one with things from the medicine cabinet and that ends up being all that's left in the bathroom. My heart races as I pick up the other empty box.

I pad into the closet and flick on the light. It's empty except for the one side. My breath catches at the sight of all of Ben's clothes. They hang there, waiting for him to return, only he's never coming back. I have to accept that fact.

I step forward with determined strides. I drop the box on the floor and then grab a handful of button-down shirts still on the hangers and shove them in the box. My breath catches when I look down at them but I keep going. I shove everything that's left of his—jeans, socks, boxers, shirts, all of it—into that one box. The box overflows, unable to hold that much stuff, but I don't care. My throat catches and I choke on a sob. There's a sweatshirt on top of the pile. One from our high school with his last name spelled out across the back. He got it for playing football. I pick it up and cradle it to my chest. The baby kicks my stomach, like she feels my turmoil.

I sink to the floor on my knees and sob into his sweatshirt. I remember his sweet smile and kind blue eyes. I feel the whisper of his lips against my cheek and the stroke of his fingers through my hair.

"I miss you," I whisper, and the baby kicks. I think she's saying she misses her daddy too. I press a hand to my stomach and feel her little foot press against my skin. "It's just me and you baby girl," I choke. "I hope that's enough for you. I hope I'm enough."

I wipe my tears on my arm. I'm not wearing any makeup so there's no smear of mascara, thankfully.

I hold onto the sweatshirt. This … This I refuse to let go.

I leave the box in the closet and turn off the light. Someone else can sort everything into separate boxes.

I did my part. I made the decision to get rid of it all.

40

Later that evening, my mom and I arrive at the apartment. The walls of the main living area are painted a beige color. It's not much of a color change but it warms up the space from the stark white. I'm thankful that Justin was willing to let me change the paint colors—as long as he approved them first.

For the bedroom, I chose a color that was in-between brown and gray. It was an odd color, but I liked it, and it made the light upholstered headboard even more of a statement piece.

Ryder and my dad sit on the couch—a gray colored tufted design—drinking a beer. They're both covered in paint. Ryder even has some sprinkled in his hair.

"Hey," he says, turning to smile at me as we enter the apartment. "Let me get that." He jumps up immediately to grab the box from my hands.

"I'm surprised you're still here," I say. "What about Cole?"

"My mom insists he's fine." Ryder waves away my concern. "I'll pick him up as soon as I leave here. There was something I wanted to show you first." He checks the label on the box and sets it in front of the bathroom.

"Oh," I say, surprised. "What's that?"

"Come here." He nods towards the door that leads into

what will be the nursery.

My brows furrow in confusion. He takes my hand and leads me to the door before swinging it open.

"Oh my God," I gasp. An antique chandelier has been installed in the middle of the room, and as impressive as that is, that's not what takes my breath away. The walls are painted in horizontal stripes of a cream color and a pale pink. It's perfect, and exactly what I wanted without even saying anything. "Ryder," I breathe. "It's gorgeous. Why? How? This must have taken forever."

He shrugs. "I know you've been having a hard time and I'd hoped this would make you happy. I'm glad I was right."

I throw my arms around his neck. "Thank you." My voice muffles against his skin.

He hugs me back—his hands solid and strong against me. "You're welcome," he whispers. "I'm happy you like it."

"Like it?" I repeat, letting him go. "I love it. It's like you read my mind. This is perfect for what I have in mind for the baby." My hand falls to my stomach where she kicks. I laugh. "I think she approves."

He smiles adorably.

My mom finally steps into the room, and she gasps the same way I did. "This is gorgeous." She turns around, looking at each wall before pointing at the ceiling. "That's beautiful, where'd you find it?"

"Flea market," Ryder answers. "I had to fix it up a bit, but it was a good find."

"You go to flea markets?" I ask, fighting laughter.

He chuckles and ducks his head so that his paint spackled hair falls into his eyes. "Yes," he says. "You should come sometime."

"Maybe I will."

He grins and quickly sobers. "I better go."

"Oh, right," I say, shaking my head. "Thank you so much for spending your day doing this."

"There's nothing I'd rather do." He strides toward the door. "Besides, your dad is a pretty cool guy."

"He didn't grill you anymore, did he?" I whisper-hiss, opening the door for him.

"Only a little bit." I groan at his answer. "Don't worry," he adds, "I didn't mind."

"Thank you," I tell him again.

He nods. "I'll see you." He waves before starting down the steps.

I close the door and find my mom already going to work organizing the kitchen. "We better order pizza," she says. "I don't think there will be time to make dinner." She's right. It's already after five, and right now, everything we need is in a box somewhere.

"Yes," my dad cries from the couch. "Pizza." He rubs his stomach and licks his lips.

My mom rolls her eyes. "You're ridiculous. But since we're busy you can order."

"What do you want, Kid?" he asks me.

"Sausage and green peppers," I say.

"You hate sausage." My mom laughs, pulling a skillet out

of a box.

I shrug. "Must be a pregnancy craving."

She shakes her head. "Better ask for extra sausage then, Dan."

While my dad places the order and my mom's busy in the kitchen I decide to unpack the bathroom things. I have almost everything completely in order. My closet needs some work, and my desk needs to be better organized, but at least this place actually looks livable.

I scoot the box into the bathroom and sit on the floor. I organize things into drawers and trash a few things I should've gotten rid of before.

By the time the pizza arrives I'm almost done and starving.

My dad pays for the pizza before I can get off the floor.

"Geez, you're speedy," I say, making my way over to the small table. It has a stainless steel tabletop with acrylic chairs. I liked the fact that the chairs were clear, considering how small the space is. They seem to just disappear into the background.

"I didn't want you payin'," he says, clearing his throat. He sets the box down on the middle of the table.

I gasp. "You got breadsticks too?" He nods. I pat his arm. "Good man."

He laughs and grabs glasses and fills them with water. As he scoots around my mom, he bends and kisses the side of her forehead. She closes her eyes and smiles. Their love is a special one. It's the kind of love I had with Ben. It's rare and beautiful.

I pull out a chair and sit down. They join me a minute later.

"Thanks for being here," I tell them. "Not just tonight, but through all of this. I'm going to miss you." Tears fill my eyes.

"We're not leaving yet, Kid." My dad chortles. "Save the tears for Friday."

"I'm sorry," I say, wiping away my tears. "I can't help it."

"I'm glad we could be here for you." My mom reaches over, pressing her hand to my cheek. I place my hand over hers, holding it there.

"I'm so sorry I was such a bitch to you early on," I tell her.

She laughs. "Oh, Blaire. I hardly batted an eye at it. You were going through so much of course you were going to be testy, but someone had to push you and I knew it had to be me."

"Thank you," I say again. "I love you." I lean over to hug her.

My dad chuckles.

"Dan," my mom scolds, even though he didn't say anything.

I let her go and sit back. "You guys are going to come back when the baby is born, right? At least for a week?"

"Of course," my mom says, shock in her tone. "We can't wait to see this beautiful grandbaby." She points to my stomach.

"Not much longer now," I say. I'm fast approaching the eight-months mark. "Casey and the girls want to throw me a baby shower."

"You should let them," my mom says, picking out a slice of pizza.

I grab a slice too, my stomach rumbling. "But it would only be us," I say. "It's not like I know many other people."

She levels me with the look. "Blaire, what about the people from Group?"

I wrinkle my nose. "I doubt they'd want to come to my baby shower."

"Who knows?" She shrugs. "Maybe you should ask. What better way to forget about death than to celebrate life?"

"She has a point," my dad says around a mouthful of pizza.

I breathe out, "Okay." I nod. "I'll see."

"Good." She smiles and reaches over to squeeze my hand where it rests on the table.

We finish eating and clean up. They stay for another hour, helping me unpack the last of things, before they head to their hotel for the night.

The cable guy hasn't been by yet so the TVs aren't hooked up and my internet isn't set up, either. It leads to an eerily quiet apartment. I'm only surrounded by the sounds of my breaths and the beating of my heart. I haven't been by myself like this in years and I don't like it.

I get in bed and will sleep to come, but instead I toss and turn.

I cover my eyes with the crook of my arm and groan. I'm never going to get any sleep feeling like this.

I grab my cellphone off the nightstand and text Ryder.

Me: Are you up?

I hold my breath, waiting for his response. I jump when the phone rings in my hand, flashing his name on the screen.

I swipe my finger across the screen. "Hello?"

"Hey," he says, and I hear rustling in the background like he's rolling over in bed. "What's up?"

I swallow thickly. "I'm sorry I called—"

"It's okay that you called," he says quickly.

"It's weird being here … by myself," I say, drawing the sheets up to my chin. The ceiling fan whips around above me. "It's too quiet." I glance to my right where Winnie sits in the window. Apparently, windows are her favorite spot. Even so, she glares at me. First I took Ben from her and then I took her away from her home. If she didn't hate me before she definitely hates me now.

Ryder's breath echoes across the phone. "We'll talk until you fall asleep then. That way you won't be alone."

I roll to my side. "Thank you. I know this is silly, I've been sleeping by myself for a while now, but there were always other people in the house. Now it's a new place and it's so … empty." I shake my head even though he can't see. "Not empty like there's nothing here—but empty of memories."

"You'll fill it with memories," he says. "One day at a time."

"Will you help me?" I ask. "To fill it."

I can't see him but I know instinctively that he's smiling. "Absolutely."

I close my eyes then, feeling better already. "Don't hang up yet," I tell him.

"I won't." I yawn and he chuckles. "Finally getting sleepy? I'm not boring you, am I?"

I laugh. "No, but you are making me feel better."

"You make me feel better too," he says.

We both grow quiet and only the sounds of our breaths fill the phone. I don't feel so alone now. I eventually drift off to sleep, and it's one of the best nights of sleep I've had in a long time. I know it's because it felt like Ryder was there with me.

41

Goodbyes suck.

My lower lip wobbles as I look between my mom and dad. I met them for lunch before they have to leave to catch their flight. I don't want them to go, but I know they have to. It's such a turnaround of thought compared to when they first arrived. I couldn't wait for them to leave—practically begging them to go—but they've both been there for me through this whole tragic process and I don't know how am I going to make it without them. I feel like they've been my crutch, and now I have to learn to stand on my own two feet.

"Blaire, we'll visit soon. The baby will be here in no time. Speaking of the baby," my mom says, crossing her hands under her chin with her elbows on the table, "have you decided on a name?"

I dam my tears back and take a sip of my iced tea. I'll have to pee in five minutes from drinking the stuff, but it's so good I can't seem to stop. "No," I say, sliding the drink cup away. "I've narrowed it down to five."

"And they are?" she prompts, batting her eyes, practically begging me to spill the beans.

I shake my head. "Not telling."

She groans and sits back against the booth. "Dan, talk to

your daughter."

My dad raises his hands innocently. "It's her decision not to tell anyone and you have to respect that."

"Thanks, Dad." I flash him a grateful smile.

He tips his head at me. "You two are always conspiring against me," my mom huffs.

The waitress stops back by our table and gathers up the dirty dishes. "Can I get you anything else?"

"Uh, yeah," I say. "I want a chocolate shake to go."

"Whipped cream and cherry?"

"Yes, please."

"Anything for you guys?" she asks my parents. They shake their heads. "I'll be right back with that milkshake," she says with a kind smile.

"So, you're really going to miss us then, Kid?" My dad asks.

I nod, pulling my hair back into a messy bun and securing it with a hairband. "Yeah, I am," I say—there goes my lip wobbling again.

My mom reaches across the table. "We're only a phone call away if you need us," she assures me.

I nod. "I know." My mom exchanges a look with my dad. She's worried about me. She's worried them leaving will set me back and I've been doing so much better. I don't want her to feel like she has to stay because of me, though, and I know that the best thing for me is for them to go. Then I'll have to rely solely on myself again. "Don't worry about me," I tell her. "I don't want you to go but I'll be okay."

"You're a fighter, Kid." My dad tips his drink glass up and

crunches on a piece of ice.

"Thanks, dad," I say.

The waitress returns with my milkshake and the check. I try to pay but my dad insists it's his treat.

I slide out of the booth and we head outside. The sun blazes above us and the humidity is thick in the air.

"Well," my mom begins, "we have to go."

I wrap my arms around her neck and squeeze her so tight she squeaks. I loosen my grip. "I love you."

"I love you too, B." She lets me go and there are tears in her eyes. She hurries to get in the rental car before she completely breaks down.

"Well, Kid—" my dad ruffles the hair on top of my head, destroying my bun "—we'll see you soon."

I open my arms wide. "Come here," I say. "There's no way you're leaving without giving me a hug." He chuckles and wraps me up in the biggest bear hug ever. A tear leaks out of my eye, absorbed by the material of his shirt. "Bye, Dad. I love you."

"Love you too, Kid." He ruffles my hair again and then gets in the car.

I stand in the lot and watch them pull away. My mom looks back and I wave. She lifts her hand too, and keeps it there until they completely disappear from sight.

I exhale a heavy breath I didn't realize I was holding.

I get in my car and drink my milkshake. I don't have any meetings with clients this afternoon so I have nothing to do until it's time for Group. I decide to call Ryder.

"Hey?" he answers on almost the last ring.

"I just said goodbye to my parents," I say, the sadness echoing in my voice.

"Oh. How are you feeling?"

"Sad," I answer honestly. "What are you doing?"

"Just hanging out here at the house with Cole. Do you want to come over? It's pretty boring here but you'll be with us."

"Yeah." I nod. "I'd like that."

"I'll see you soon then."

"Yep." I hang up and drop the phone on the seat beside me.

I finish my milkshake and get out and toss it in the trashcan in front of the diner. I then decide to stop by Target and pick up a few toys for Cole. I get an assortment of things—like puzzle piece alphabet letters and a talking dinosaur thing—since I don't really know what he likes.

When I get to Ryder's house, he answers the door with Cole clinging to his leg screaming bloody murder.

"The Terrible Twos," Ryder sighs, stepping back so I can come inside.

"What's he upset about?" I ask.

"I told him he couldn't hold the fish."

I snort. "Interesting."

"Yeah." Ryder chuckles. "Being a parent is weird sometimes."

"Maybe this will make it better." I hold out the bag from

Target.

Ryder peeks in the bag and grins at what he finds. He looks back up at me and the look in his eyes makes my stomach clench in anticipation. He looks like he's about to kiss me, but he quickly shakes his head and the look disappears.

"You got these for Cole?" he asks, even though he already knows.

I nod.

"Me! Me!" Cole cries, having heard his name. He lets go of Ryder's leg and makes a grabbing motion with his hands.

Ryder pulls out the large size racecar I got. "Here you go, bud." He hands it to Cole after pulling off the price sticker.

Cole starts driving it around on the floor making car noises. "Vroom, vrooooom."

"Enjoy the playtime," Ryder says. "It's naptime in…" He looks at his watch. "Ten minutes."

Cole frowns. "No. No nap."

"Yes, nap." Ryder bends down and tickles his stomach. The little boy's laughter fills the room. I can't help but smile at the father and son. "Bring your car into the family room, Cole." Ryder says and the little boy toddles along, following him.

I linger behind, just watching them. When I take a seat on the couch I say, "How did you feel when he first started walking and talking? You know, without Angela being here to see and hear it too."

He shrugs. "I tried not to think about it. I can't change the fact that she's gone so I choose not to dwell on it. I don't want to feel saddened by milestones in his life just because she's not here, you know?"

"That makes sense," I say, resting my hand on my stomach.

"You're thinking about your baby," he surmises.

I nod. "Ben's the one that wanted to have a baby—not that I didn't want a baby," I hasten to add, "but I probably would've waited if he hadn't brought it up. Once we made up our minds that we were going to try we both wanted this baby so bad," I say, my throat growing thick with emotion. "I feel like I took a hundred negative pregnancy tests. I know that's not true, but all the negatives seemed endless. And then, when it finally happened, Ben wasn't even here to know." I lean my head back against the pillows on the couch and rub my stomach. "She's a gift, that's for sure."

Ryder picks up Cole from the floor and sits him in his lap. "You'll be a good mom."

I quirk a brow. "Really? I wonder sometimes," I sigh.

"You will be," he assures me. "All right," he says, "naptime."

"No!" Cole cries, kicking his legs.

Ryder laughs and looks over at me. "Want to help with naptime?"

I eye the squirming child. "Um …"

Ryder stands and holds his hand down to me. "Come on," he coaxes. I reluctantly put my hand in his and follow him upstairs to Cole's room. He sets Cole on the floor and says, "Go pick out your pajamas, Coley."

Cole runs over to a chest and tugs on the bottom drawer. He struggles so I bend down to help him.

The little boy smiles gratefully at me and pulls out a pair of pajamas with various Disney characters on them. He shoves them at me and tries to close the drawer, making the cutest grunting noise.

"You dwess me." Cole points at me and then him.

"Me?" I ask in surprise.

The little boy nods and starts stripping off his clothes.

"Whoa, whoa, whoa," Ryder chants and scoops up the little boy. "Diaper change first."

"Ugh." Cole grunts in irritation.

Ryder carries him over to the changing table and changes his diaper. He then sets the little boy on the bed in only his diaper.

"He's all yours." He winks and stands back, crossing his arms over his chest to watch me.

I stand up and dress Cole in the pajamas he picked out.

"Ook! Ook!" He chants, jumping on the bed.

"Look? Look where?" I look up at the ceiling and all around.

Ryder laughs. "Not look. Book. He wants you to read him a story."

"Oh," I say, stifling my own laugh. Cole holds out his arms for me to pick him up. I hesitantly pick him up and he holds on tight to me. I carry him over to his bookshelf and let him pick. He points and I pick up the book. "To Give a Mouse a Cookie," I read the title. "Good choice." I carry him back over to his toddler bed and put him down. "You have to lay down under the covers if I'm going to read to you," I tell him.

He nods so I pull back the covers and he scoots under them, giggling when I draw them up to his chin. I lie down beside him and crack open the book. I begin to read and he snuggles against me. I stiffen at first and then relax. He giggles when I make funny voices for the characters and points at the pictures, naming various objects in them. By the time I make it to the end, he's fast asleep and I close the book, easing out of the bed. Ryder's gone and I hadn't even noticed he left.

I ease out of the little boy's room and close the door.

I find Ryder downstairs in the kitchen making a cup of coffee.

"You left," I say. "Why?"

He shrugs and grabs a mug from a cabinet. "You didn't need me. You're a natural. I told you that you'd be a good mom." He gives me a significant look as he pours his coffee.

I swallow thickly. "But that was only for a moment," I argue. "This will be all the time." I touch my stomach.

Ryder steps around the counter and pulls out a kitchen chair, taking a seat. I do the same. "I know it seems overwhelming, but trust me, once the baby is here you'll forget all that."

"I'll be all alone," I say, my voice cracking. "How can I do this by myself?"

"I did." His voice is soft. "And look at Cole. He's happy and healthy, and me? I'm good too." He leans back in the chair and takes a sip of his coffee. "You will be too."

The baby kicks and I smile, pressing my hand against the spot. "I think she's telling me you're right." I laugh. Ryder smiles, looking at my stomach. "Do you … want to feel?" I ask hesitantly.

He looks surprised but his lips crook up into a smile.

"Sure." He holds out his hand and I take it, pressing against my stomach. She wiggles around so I move his hand to a different spot.

"Just wait," I whisper, holding my hand over his.

She gives a good solid kick and Ryder's breath catches. "Nothing else in the world compares to that feeling," he says, looking up at me. She kicks again and he laughs. "She's a strong one."

"She is," I agree and release his hand. He sits back and his hand falls away. "My friends want to throw me a baby shower." I sigh.

He raises a brow. "And that's a bad thing?"

I shrug. "I don't really know anyone except the three of them. My mom said I should invite the people from Group. Do you think they'd be into that sort of thing?"

He shrugs and takes another sip of coffee. "I think some might."

"Hmm," I hum. "Maybe I should let them do it then. I'm the first one in our group of friends to have a baby."

"You should definitely let them. Plus, a baby shower means diapers—and trust me, you're going to need diapers. I'll never understand how something so small can poop so much."

I laugh. "I've always wondered that myself. There's something else I wanted to ask you …" I hedge.

"Yes?" he prompts, lifting a brow.

"I need to start ordering the furniture for the nursery …" I wiggle around, uncomfortable in this conversation. "… and I was wondering if maybe you'd help put it together."

"I can do that."

He didn't pause, or hesitate for even a millisecond when answering me.

"Are you sure?" I ask.

"Yeah, it's not a big deal. It'll be fun."

"Fun?" I repeat in disbelief.

"You'll be there, right?" he counters.

"Yes," I say slowly, unsure where he's going with this.

"Then it'll be fun." He grins now. "Trust me."

"Thanks," I say.

He narrows his eyes on me. "You should know by now that I'd do just about anything for you." I look away, my cheeks heating. "Why does that embarrass you?" He questions, noticing the flush in my cheeks.

"I'm not embarrassed," I say. "I'm … pleased."

"Pleased?" He smiles and sits back in the chair. "Good to know."

"I better go," I say, standing.

He grabs my hand. "Stay."

"Why?" I ask, my fingers shaking in his grasp.

"I could give you some bullshit answer here, but really it's simple. You should stay because you want to, and I want you to, too."

"How do you know I want to stay?" I ask, my voice soft.

"Because you wanted to go."

"That makes no sense." I shake my head.

"You decided to leave because you were feeling too comfortable. It was fight or flight. Simple as that. I'm asking you to fight. To stay."

I sit back down in the chair and my breath shakes because this man … this man is getting to me. I'm imagining more with him. Kisses and romantic dates. Cooking dinners together and giving the kids baths. I'm beginning to imagine a life with him. It's scary, and the reason I wanted to leave—so he's completely right when he says I wanted to leave because I wanted to stay.

"This whole thing confuses me," I confess.

"It does me too." He shrugs, wrapping his long fingers around the coffee mug. "This isn't easy for me, either, you know?"

I look at him from beneath my lashes. "I never really thought about that."

"I know you haven't, and that's okay. You have enough on your mind. But when you get freaked out by what you're feeling just talk to me, I might be feeling it too and it helps to talk."

I clear my throat. "D-Do you see a future with me in it?"

"Yes," he answers without hesitation. "Do you see a future with me?"

I blink back the tears. "Yes," I confess.

"And that frightens you." I nod. "It does me too," he sighs. "I think something would be wrong with us if it didn't scare us."

I smile a bit at that. "This is normal," I state.

"Completely normal," he agrees. "That's why I keep saying

it's okay to take our time. If it ever gets to be too much for you just tell me and we'll slow down."

"The same goes for you too," I tell him. "You can tell me if it becomes too much."

He nods. "I know." He stands from the table and holds out his hand to me. I place mine in his without a second of thought. "I want to show you something."

He leads me outside and around the side of the house to a shed. He lets go of my hand and twists the round knob on the combination. It comes undone and he swings the doors open.

I eye him. "You're not taking me in here to chop me into a million pieces are you?"

He laughs. "No. This is my workshop."

He flicks on a light and the shed is bathed in brightness. "Oh," I say, stepping inside. Wood shavings litter the floor along with other various debris. There's a work table in the corner with a saw and an island-type counter in the center of the shed covered in metal pieces. My gaze moves to a wrought iron headboard leaning against one wall. "So, you make things?" I ask.

"Yes, and refurbish them, like the chandelier in the baby's room." He shrugs and stuffs his hands in the pockets of his shorts. "It's my hobby. I like taking old things and making them new again."

I brush my fingers through some wood shavings on the table and then blow the dust off my fingers. "Are you good at everything you do?"

He chuckles. "Hardly."

"This is beautiful." I point to a step stool. It has the start of Cole's name carved into it—with letters that can pop out and go back in.

"Thanks," he says. "So," he starts, "what's your hobby?"

My brows furrow. "I'm not sure I have one."

He chuckles and steps around the other side of the counter so we're standing in front of each other. "Of course you do. Everybody has one."

"Um," I think, "I like to read?" It comes out sounding like a question. "But you already knew that."

"That's definitely a hobby, but there must be something else."

"I like to bake. I'm not very good." I laugh. "But I like it." My mind goes back to Thanksgiving, and the ill-fated pie I'd tried to make. Life was so much simpler then.

"Why'd you stop?" he asks.

"Life, I guess." I shrug, picking up a small piece of wood before setting it back down. "I haven't had the time."

"Make the time," he says. "It helps."

"It does?"

He nods. "I stopped making things after Angela and I got married. Like you said, I didn't have the time. But when she died I needed something to quiet my mind and my mom reminded me that I used to love this, so I started up again and haven't stopped since. It takes me a while to finish a project, but that's okay. It quiets my mind and keeps me from dwelling on things."

"Hmm," I hum. "I'll have to try. Maybe I can make Cole and you some cupcakes. What's your favorite?"

"Chocolate." He grins. "Cole's too. We both love chocolate anything."

"I'll remember that," I say.

We leave the shed and Ryder locks it up. I follow him back inside, feeling weird to go first, and he leads me to the family room where he collapses on the couch and pats the space beside him. I take a seat, drawing my legs under me.

"How's it going at the apartment?" he asks. "You haven't called me since that first night."

"It's okay." I shrug. "The cable finally got hooked up and Hannah's come over the last two nights and my parents too. Hannah's my friend that lives in the apartment below me," I explain.

He nods. "It's nice you have someone there that close."

"It is," I agree. I wince and move my legs out from under me. "My feet are killing me," I groan. I lean forward and kick off my flats so I can rub my sore feet.

He moves my hand away. "Here, let me."

I look at him like he's lost my mind. "You want to rub my feet?"

"Sure. They're hurting and I want you to feel better." This man. This man. He will be the end of me. I lie back and stretch my legs out, putting them in his lap. "Here," he says, and hands me a pillow. "I'm sure you want a pillow behind your back."

"You're a mind reader." I take the pillow from him and position it behind me. Once I'm situated, he goes to work massaging his thumb into the arch of my foot. It feels so good that my toes curl. "You have no idea how good that feels," I moan.

He chuckles and moves his thumb to a different spot. "I think I have some idea." I let my eyes drift closed, stifling a yawn. "It's okay if you fall asleep," he assures me. "I'll wake you up when it's time to go."

"Mmm," I say. I'm too relaxed to form words.

I don't really intend to fall asleep but then I do.

When I wake up, there's a blanket spread over me and Cole's up and running around with Ryder chasing after him.

"Hey, you're up." Ryder smiles, scooping up Cole in his arms and spinning him around like an airplane. "The babysitter will be here soon and then we can head over to Group."

I sit up and the blanket pools at my waist. "I'm supposed to get the food this week," I say, looking around for my shoes. I find them on the floor and bend over to put them on.

"Don't worry about it," Ryder says. "I asked Ivy to do it. Next week was her turn so I figured you guys could swap weeks."

"Oh, good. Thanks." I run my fingers through my hair. It's a mess from falling asleep on the couch. "Where's your bathroom?" I ask. "I need to freshen up a bit."

"Down the hall on your left."

I follow his instructions and find it easily enough. I lock the door and stand in front of the pedestal sink. I turn the water on and dampen my hands before patting my face and back of my neck. I dry my hands off on the towel and then run my fingers through my hair, trying to make it look halfway decent after being slept on.

I leave the bathroom just as the babysitter arrives. "Oh,"

she says when she sees me. "Hi, I'm Kenna." She's young, probably early twenties, with brown hair and a sprinkling of freckles across her nose.

"Hi, nice to meet you." I wave awkwardly.

She looks between Ryder and me, clearly trying to figure out what's between us. Good luck to her, because I can't even figure it out.

"Kenna knows what to do so we can head out." Ryder nods at the door.

"Bye, Cole," I say and bend down to the little boy. "Oh," I cry out as he dives into my arms to hug me.

"Bwy," he says, in his cute toddler way.

"I'll see you later, Kenna," Ryder calls back to the sitter as she takes Cole's hand and heads to the family room.

Outside, Ryder and I head to our separate cars and drive to the school. We're the first ones to arrive and I follow him in and help set up.

"What's on the agenda today?" I ask him.

He shrugs and hands me a chair from the closet. "We haven't done the cranes in a few weeks since Jason joined, so maybe we should do some today."

I smile. "Do you think the paper cranes we've made have helped anyone?"

He grabs another chair and holds onto it, clearly thinking. "I don't know, but I hope so, and I guess that's enough."

We finish setting up the chairs and Ivy arrives with the snacks and coffee.

"Hey," I call over to her and wave. She gives me a one-fingered wave, struggling to hold onto everything. "Oh, let me help." I hurry over to her and take the donut boxes from her.

"I should've made two trips." She laughs. "Lesson learned."

I open one of the donut boxes and pull out a glazed. "So," I begin, "my friends want to throw a baby shower for me. Would you want to come?"

She gasps. "Of course. I'd love to."

I can't help but smile. "Really?"

"Yeah, absolutely." She nods. "It'll be fun. Who doesn't love all things baby?"

"See, I told you." Ryder chuckles and opens the donut box I hold, grabbing another glazed. "Mmm, these are good, better grab another."

I laugh when he takes a second and leaves.

"Men." Ivy laughs. "They eat everything."

"Speaking of eating, we need to do lunch again. Maybe we could get take-out and you could come see my apartment."

She smiles. "I'd like that. I'm excited to see your place. How are you liking it?"

"I've only been there a few days, but I really like it. It's … different, and definitely an adjustment, but it feels right. You know?"

She nods. "Maybe once I see your place it'll finally inspire me to move on."

"Aw, Ivy," I say, setting the boxes down on the table so I can grab some coffee. "Don't push yourself before you're ready."

She sighs. "I should've been ready a long time ago."

I shake my head. "That's not true. Everyone grieves at their own pace. You can't push yourself—trust me. That's led to many breakdowns on my part. And maybe moving out of your house isn't the best route for you," I continue. "You have to find your own way."

She sighs. "You're sounding more and more like Ryder every day."

I laugh and glance back at where he stands in the doorway. "Is that such a bad thing?"

"No, it's not." She smiles slyly and starts towards the seats. "You've got it bad, girl," she sing-songs.

This time I don't rebuke her, because she's right. She's always been right and I didn't want to see it. It's easier to remain blind so you don't have to accept the truth, but now my eyes are wide open.

42

There's a knock on my apartment door, but I'm not expecting anyone. I stare at the door like it has insulted me or something.

Another knock.

"Blaire, it's me."

Hannah.

I unlock the door and it swings open. "Oh, hey—" I begin and then see Casey and Chloe behind her. "Hi guys," I say, opening it wider.

"We wanted to bring you a housewarming present," Hannah says. "I mean, I know I've seen the place but these goobers haven't." She motions to our friends behind her.

"You're obligated to show us the place since you won't let us throw you a party." Chloe pouts.

"I'm pregnant," I say by way of explanation. "Who wants to party when they're carrying a basketball around all the time?" I point at my stomach.

"Speaking of that," Casey says as they move into the apartment, "are you still nixing the baby shower thing?"

I haven't gotten a chance to talk to them since I was at Group yesterday. Several people said they were interested in coming, even some of the men, so it doesn't seem so pointless.

"I changed my mind. I want one."

Casey squeals and fist pumps the air. "Yes," she cries. "I knew you'd regret it if you told us no."

"Please don't make people play any of those stupid games," I plead, swishing my hands back in forth in an X motion.

"No promises." Casey grins evilly.

"So," I say, "what's this housewarming present you speak of?" I ask.

"Oh, here." Chloe holds out a carefully wrapped package. "It's from all of us."

I rip off the paper, balling it up and tossing it on the floor. In my hand I hold a picture frame with a picture of us a few years ago on New Year's Eve. I touch my finger to the glass, smiling wistfully. Ben took that photo.

"Squish together," Ben said, bringing his hands together like we didn't know what to do. "Closer, closer. There."

By that point the four of us were a giggling mess, our arms wrapped each other. The flash went off and then someone yelled across the room, "It's almost time!"

"Ten, nine—"

"Ben," I cried, stumbling over my own two feet and collapsing against his chest. "I have to get my New Year's kiss."

He laughed and steadied me.

"Six, five—"

"You think you'll still want to kiss me next year?"

"Abso-fucking-lutely."

"One."

He bent down and pressed his lips firmly against mine. My fingers tangled in his silky strands of blond hair and deepened the kiss. He broke the kiss with a half-grin. Around us people cheered and gold confetti rained down on us.

He picked a piece of confetti off my nose. "I love you."

"I love you too."

The memory leaves me feeling sad, but happy at the same time. It's a strange combination but it's the truth.

"Thanks for this," I say.

"You're welcome," Casey replies, looking at me uneasily. "Are you okay?"

"Yeah, yeah I am." I nod. I don't feel like I'm going to cry, surprisingly.

"Good," Chloe claps, "because there's more." She produces a card from her purse. "Again, from all of us."

I open it up and find a gift card to a local home store. "Thanks guys. You really didn't have to do this."

"We wanted to," Hannah says.

"That's what friends are for." Casey hugs me and takes a seat on the barstool.

"I really do love you guys," I say, clutching the picture frame to my chest. "Thank you, for being there for me, for all you—"

"Please do not go all Ya Ya Sisterhood on my ass." Casey holds up a hand to stop me. I can't help but laugh. "Now please tell me your pregnant ass still has some wine around here somewhere."

I laugh again and point. "I was saving that."

"Well, now you're not." She grabs the bottle and starts rummaging through the drawers for the corkscrew. Casey has never had any problem making herself at home.

I twist my engagement ring around on my finger. I've continued to wear it, because I didn't want to part with it, but now I think I'm ready. I expected to have this huge monumental sort of moment when I finally decided—like doves flying and music playing—but of course it's not like that. It almost seems fitting that my friends are here with me when I finally decide to do it.

They're busy pouring their wine into glasses so they don't see me pull it off and place it on the counter.

Hannah is the first to notice when she turns back around. "Is that . . .?" She pauses, afraid to say it.

I nod.

"Blaire," Casey says, her eyes filling with tears. "Are you sure?"

I nod. "It's time. I'm ready."

We start to cry and they wrap their arms around me. I can't help but think back to the photo where we were holding onto each other. It was for a very different reason, but true friends will be there no matter what. For the good and the bad. I know I'm lucky to have people I can count on and I'll never take them for granted. Not ever again.

43

Stage Five: Acceptance

"Hey, Ben," I whisper. It doesn't feel right to speak at full volume.

Not here. Not in a cemetery.

My dress blows around my legs and my hair whips against my shoulders. It's an unusually cool and windy day for early August. Normally, the weather stays blazing hot until the end of the month.

"I miss you," I continue. "So damn much." I clear my throat, my emotions getting the better of me. I really thought I could do this without crying but it doesn't seem likely. "It's taken me eight long months but I've finally accepted things. I never thought I would, but I did. I know you've probably been up there yelling at me to get my shit together. I'm sorry for disappointing you."

Almost as soon as I say the words, I can hear Ben in my ear whispering, "You never disappoint me."

"I want you to know, that even though I've accepted that you're gone, and I'm ready to move on with my life, it doesn't mean I've forgotten you—or that I will forget you. Our love … you … It's unforgettable." I clasp my fingers together. "I used to think that our story ended in tragedy, but I was wrong." I touch my hand to my stomach. "It ends with life and more love—a new kind of love. I wish you were here to witness it, but I know you're up there, smiling down on us." I look up to the cloudless blue sky. I close my eyes, feeling the sun's rays fan across my skin. I look back down at his grave and the fresh flowers I laid there when I first arrived. "I'm happy," I tell him, "and I'm not ashamed of that. Not anymore. I understand that I do deserve to be happy." I clear my throat. "I met a guy and I like him. I really like him, Ben." Tears fill my eyes. "I think I might be falling in love with him. I know you'd want that for me but it's still hard." I pause and take a deep breath. "You'd like him too. He has a little boy and he's great. Just as sweet as his dad. I didn't mean to move on," I whisper. "I didn't even really realize I had." My brows draw together. "But somewhere along the way I did. I guess that's how it works. It's a gradual thing and one day you sort of realize hey, I'm okay and I've been okay. The bad days disappear and you smile and laugh again. And the memories … The memories don't gut you open anymore. I'd forgotten what your voice sounded like but now I can hear it. Is that part of grief—that you temporarily forget and once you're healed you can remember again?" I ask the air around me. I sigh, my hands falling to my sides. "I have to go, but I'll come back soon."

I kiss my fingers and press them to the cold stone of the grave.

I start to leave and then jolt. "Oh, I almost forgot." I turn back around and pull the paper crane from my purse.

I'd written on it: Until I see you again.

***

I left the cemetery and drove back to my apartment. The

girls had kicked me out so they could set up for the baby shower. When I got in the car there was a text waiting telling me to get my ass there.

I walk up the steps, twirling my keys around my finger.

I don't really know what to expect from today, but I can say I'm excited. Surprisingly enough.

I reach the top of the stairs just as the door to my apartment bursts open.

"There you are," Casey sighs, her blond hair curled around her shoulders. "I thought I was going to have to send out the SWAT team to find you."

"I didn't flee the country, obviously." I laugh as my purse slides off my shoulder to my elbow.

"Everyone's here," she says, waving me inside. "So hurry up."

"You're so demanding." I lightly bump her shoulder with mine as I pass and she laughs.

Inside, I'm surprised to find that the place is packed. It looks like everyone from Group turned out, which I wasn't expecting.

"Hi everyone," I say. "I'd make introductions but I'm sure you've already done that."

"Come here." Casey grabs me by the arm and guides me to a chair in the center of the room. "This is your seat," she says, practically shoving me in it. For someone so small she's awfully strong.

Ryder smiles across from me and waves. Butterflies ignite in my stomach.

Casey bends down and whispers in my ear, "You have a lot of explaining to do."

"I know I should've told you guys about Group—" I start.

She shakes her head. "Oh, please, I'm talking about the gorgeous guy over there. He talks about you like you're … I don't know, a goddess or something." I bite my lip and look away. "Don't even think about lying to us about him. I'm on to you." She grins and stands up straight so she can address the room. "Now that the guest of honor's here let's get this party started!" She pumps her fist like we're at the club—not like it's the middle of the afternoon on a Sunday.

"Loraine," I breathe out, spotting Ben's mom. "Hi."

"Hey, how have you been?" she asks, sitting on the couch between Ivy and a guy from Group.

"Good, and you?"

"Better." She smiles. She still looks tired, but not quite as haunted. There's color in her cheeks and her eyes aren't bloodshot. I guess I'm not the only one doing well.

From somewhere in the room, music starts to play. It's some peppy pop tune they play all the time on the radio, so, of course, I love it.

"Blaire told me she didn't want any games at this baby shower, but it's kind of obligatory," Casey says, playing the hostess. "Since Blaire has elected not to reveal the baby's name I thought we could make a guessing game out of it. Hannah is going to go around with slips of paper and pencils and you can write down what you think the name is and stick it in this bowl. You don't win anything, but I figured Blaire could read them aloud at the end and it might give us all a laugh."

I don't tell them but the reason I haven't revealed the name is because I haven't decided. Nothing feels right.

I sit there quietly while everyone scribbles down their name choices and then stuffs it in the glass bowl.

When that's done, Casey takes the reins once more. "For the next game, we're going to guess how big Blaire's belly is. Hannah, do you have the string?"

"Nope, I do," Chloe chimes.

"Oh, okay." Casey laughs. "Chloe will go around with the string and you cut off how much you think it'll take to go around her belly. The person with the best guess will win a gift card."

"You suck," I tell her.

"You'll thank me later," she says under her breath.

I shake my head.

Luckily, the games don't last long and she moves on to the present opening. I'm shocked by the amount of items I get. Blankets, onesies, diapers, pacifiers, bottles, a bouncer, a bassinet, and so much more. I'm honestly so touched.

Tears of happiness pool in my eyes. "Thank you, guys. Thank you." I can't get over all the stuff around me and the amount of care and love my daughter and I are surrounded by. "The fact that this little one is already so loved means so much to me," I say, damming back the tears.

I will not cry. I will not cry. I won't.

"Aw, Blaire, of course she's loved." Casey hugs me.

Loraine smiles over at me and reaches for my hand. She doesn't say anything. She doesn't have to.

"Cake time!" Hannah cries, eliminating the serious tone in

the room.

She cuts off slices of the pink and white polka dot cake and Casey and Chloe pass it out to everyone.

I take a bite and suppress the moan that wants to escape my throat. "This is so good," I say. "You guys did good. With all of this." I indicate the way they decorated. I might be the party planner but they certainly didn't need my help. Pink and white balloons are tied up throughout the room and they cover the back wall with white curtains to soften the space. There are other dashes of pink and white through the room in the forms of candles, confetti, and even the pillows they put on the couch.

"Thanks." Casey smiles, eating her own slice of cake. "We were happy to do it." I finish my cake and Casey takes my plate before I can get up to throw it away. "Now it's time to read the names." She giggles. I'm a bit afraid to know what she put in there.

She hands me the bowl of names and I take a deep breath before plunging my hand inside.

I pull out the first slip of paper and open it up. "Daisy … cute," I say.

"That's mine." Hannah does a little happy dance where she sits—I think the happy dance has more to do with the frosting she's licking from the fork than the name itself.

"Penelope," I read. "Melina. Julie. Lissa."

"That's mine," Casey says, leaning against the chair I sit in.

I go on reading. "Peter … you do know the baby's a girl, right?" I laugh.

"Peter's an excellent gender neutral name," a guy from

group jokes.

"Uh-huh," I say. "It definitely is." I drop the slip of paper to the floor with the rest. "Amber."

"Mine!" Chloe's hand shoots in the air.

"Isabella, Sarah, Zoey, and …" I pick the last one out of the bowl. "Ava."

I smile. I like that one.

"It means bird."

I look up at Ryder. "What?" I say, stunned.

"Ava. It means bird, that's why I chose it." My breath catches.

I really am going to cry this time.

"It's perfect," I whisper, rubbing my fingers against the piece of paper with the three simple letters.

Around me, I know Casey, Hannah, and Chloe are urging people out the door so they can clean up but I'm oblivious to it. I can't stop staring at the name.

Ava. Bird. My little paper bird. That's her name. I know it.

"So," Casey says, dropping plates into a trash bag, "are you going to tell us about the guy?"

"What guy?" I ask, still focused on the name.

She huffs. "Ryder. It was obvious from the moment he walked in that you guys were close. He said he painted the nursery, and the way he talks about you … There's definitely something going on with you two, so spill."

I shrug and wrap my hand around the piece of paper that holds my daughter's name.

"He's the head of Group. He's really helped me." I shrug. "And yes, I suppose there's something between us, but I'm not really sure what it is. I like him, and he likes me and we're taking our time seeing where things go."

Casey pauses what she's doing, her hand hovering halfway to the trash bag. "Wow, I'm happy for you, Blaire."

"Thanks."

"So," Hannah begins, "does he have three brothers?"

We all laugh.

"Yeah," Chloe pipes in. "How is it fair that you get two great guys and we can't even get one?"

"For starters—" I laugh "—you search for them in bars."

Chloe clucks her tongue. "Good point."

"You'll find guys," I say. "When you stop looking. Besides, I think Hannah's already found her guy."

"Who?" She looks mystified.

"Cyrus," I say, crossing my arms over my chest. "I saw him sneaking out of your apartment on my way to a meeting one morning."

Her mouth opens and closes like a fish. "I-I … Um … no … It's not like that. It's just sex."

I raise my hands innocently. "Say what you want but I think you two are meant to be."

Hannah looks horror-stricken. "Cyrus? There's no way." She shakes her head.

I don't push her, but I know there's more there than she even wants to admit to herself. Hannah's always been more like me. Calmer. Shier. She's not the kind of girl to jump in bed with a guy for the heck of it—and maybe that really is what happened the first time, but I honestly don't think she'd continue to sleep with him if she didn't like him.

Casey ties off the trash bag and drops it in the hall. "I'd say today was a success." She nods to herself, looking around at all the baby things I got.

"Yeah," I agree. "I can't thank you guys enough for doing this."

She smirks. "Is that your way of admitting you would've regretted not having a baby shower?"

I laugh. "Yes, but I still could've done without the games."

"Gotta have the games," Casey says, collapsing on the couch. Hannah and Chloe fall down beside her and I stay where I am in the chair. "You can get me back one day when you throw my baby shower."

"Seriously, though," I say. "Thank you."

There was a time where I thought my grief might push my friends away. I tried to push them away myself, but they wouldn't let me. They've always seen through my bullshit.

"That's what friends are for." Casey shrugs like it's no big deal. "Well—" she sighs, standing "—we better go."

I glance at the time. I hadn't realized it was getting so late. It'll be time for dinner soon.

I hug each of them and follow them to the door. "I'll see you guys soon," I say, leaning against the doorjamb. "Let's do lunch next week."

"Sure, how about Wednesday?" Casey asks.

"That's good for me." Hannah shrugs, starting down the steps.

Chloe checks her phone. "Yeah, me too."

"Mhm," I hum. "I'm free."

"See you guys then," Casey says.

I watch her and Chloe start down the stairs before I close the door.

I still hold the paper in my hand and walk through the apartment, over to my desk, so I can grab a piece of tape. I then go into the nursery and over to the lone piece of furniture—a dresser.

I hold the piece of paper against the wall and then press the tape over it.

I smile. "Ava."

44

"Is this the last of it?" Ryder asks, grabbing the knife off the floor to open the box that holds the crib.

"Yes," I say, looking around the room.

In a short amount of time, he's already assembled the stroller, car seat, and changing table. While he'd done that I'd been busy in the kitchen…baking. But he didn't know that. I wanted it to be a surprise.

"You waited until the last minute, didn't you?" He chuckles, pulling the pieces out of the box. The paper with the directions goes fluttering to the ground and I pick it up, setting it on the dresser.

I shrug. "With the move it didn't make sense to start getting things until now."

He grunts, pulling out one of the side panels. "Makes sense."

"I'll be right back," I say, when I hear the timer ding.

I run out into the kitchen and pull the homemade cinnamon rolls from the oven. I haven't made them in a long time, and they take a while to make, but I know it'll be worth it. I lay them out to cool so I can frost them in a bit with the homemade cream cheese frosting. Ryder was right, the baking helped. It quieted my mind and I needed all the quieting I could get.

When the cinnamon rolls are cooled enough I slather them in icing and put two on a plate.

I pad into the nursery and find that Ryder already has half of the crib together.

"You're fast," I say, sitting down on the floor beside him. He's so focused on tightening the side panel to the headboard that he doesn't notice the cinnamon rolls. "I made you something."

That gets his attention. He looks away and sees the plate in my hands. "You made these?" He grins, his eyes flickering from the cinnamon rolls to my face.

"I did," I say proudly. I haven't made them in so long that I was worried I would totally butcher them, but they turned out pretty good.

He picks one up and takes a big bite before setting it back on the plate. Icing is smeared all over his perfect mouth.

I don't think, I just act on instinct. I lean over and cover his lips with mine, kissing away the icing. He stiffens at first, shocked, and then his hands are on my face, angling my head back so he can kiss me deeper. It doesn't feel wrong and I don't want him to stop. My fingers wrap around his shirt and my lips move against his, licking away the traces of cinnamon and icing. I realize with a sudden clarity that this man is what I want. I can't deny it anymore.

His tongue brushes mine and his mouth swallows my moan. My hands grasp at his shoulders, trying to hold on because I'm pretty sure I'm about to fly away.

When the kiss breaks, I lean my forehead against his solid chest, breathing in and out heavily as I try to catch my breath.

"I wasn't expecting that," Ryder admits, his fingers tangling in my hair.

I tip my head back to look up at him. "I wasn't planning on it." I laugh. He looks wounded so I quickly add, "But I'm glad I did."

He smiles and lights up my whole world. I know, in that moment, that I'm in love with him. I think I have been for a long time and I kept denying it to myself because I felt it was too soon, that it was wrong to love someone else. But love…love is never wrong. If there's anything that's right in the world, it's love.

He kisses me again, only a quick peck, before he grabs the cinnamon roll and takes another bite.

"It's starting to look like a real nursery in here," I tell him. "It's all thanks to you."

He chuckles. "I'm glad I could help." He pauses. "I notice you taped the paper over there with Ava on it."

I bite my lip. "That's her name."

"Whoa, I guessed right?" he asks, taking another bite of cinnamon roll.

I shake my head. "No, I suppose you kind of named her." I shrug. "I hadn't picked a name out yet—I had it narrowed down to a few—but when I saw that one and you said that it meant bird I knew it was the right name."

His eyes sparkle with happiness and he finishes off the cinnamon roll. He jumps up and goes to the kitchen to wash his hands and get a drink before returning.

He goes back to work on the crib while I eat my own cinnamon roll.

I rub my stomach with my free hand and take a deep breath. The baby is sitting low and the pressure is intense. I breathe out.

"Are you okay?" Ryder asks, noticing the pinched look to my face.

"I'm fine. She's just really low and it hurts," I explain, taking another deep breath.

Ryder finishes with the crib and slides it over to where I told him it would go, beneath the paper crane mobile. The crib I bought has an antique look and it's cream colored. The bedding I got is a soft pink and cream combo that matches the walls.

I look around the whole room. The antique armoire takes up almost the whole wall beside the door. There's the dresser on the other with cabinets above for more storage. The crib is against the other wall with a glider and the changing table while the wood floor is covered in a thick white rug. The stroller sits folded up in the corner with the car seat. The room is completely ready; it only needs the baby.

Ryder reaches down to help me up and I'm thankful for it. My large stomach makes getting up and down a major chore.

"What do you think?" he asks.

"I think it's perfect."

He smiles down at me, his hand on my waist. I'm not sure he even realizes it's still there.

"Ryder—" I begin but a sharp hiss of pain slips through my teeth.

"Blaire?" Concern leaks into his tone. My fingernails dig into his arm and I bend over. "Are you in labor?"

"I don't know!" I cry. "I've never had a baby before!" He looks like he wants to laugh at me but knows better. "I can't be in labor," I say. "It's three weeks until my due date. My parents aren't here. I—"

"Blaire." He puts his hands on my shoulders. "I'm here, okay? You're going to be fine, but I think we need to go to the hospital. Where's your bag?"

"My room." I point even though he knows where it is. "It's on the floor of the closet." The pain begins to ease away and I waddle toward the door to wait for Ryder. "The car seat," I tell him when he comes out of my room.

"Oh, right." He dashes back into the nursery.

My heart pangs. All of this is so normal, but it should be Ben here. I don't feel bereft at that fact anymore. I'm just thankful Ryder can be here.

I grab my car keys while he gets the car seat. I'm not thrilled at the idea of walking down three flights of stairs—and I'm mildly terrified that the baby might fall out of my vagina—but I know I have to do it.

Ryder comes out of the nursery holding the carrier with my duffel bag slung crossways over his body. He looks like he's ready to go into battle.

"I'm sorry you're getting dragged into this," I say, hissing through the pain as another—what I assume is—contraction hits me. "You can just drop me off at the hospital. I can call Casey so I'm not alone."

He looks at me like I've grown three heads as he locks up the apartment for me. "I'm not leaving you," he declares. "If you don't want me in the delivery room, that's fine, but I'm not leaving you. I'll sit in the waiting room all day if I have to."

I'm reminded again of what I wanted to tell him before the contractions started. "I love you," I say.

He turns around on the stairs, nearly dropping the carrier. "What did you say?"

"I love you. That's what I was trying to tell—"

He does drop the carrier this time and then his lips are on mine. He kisses me softly but with so much feeling. "I love you too," he breathes against my lips.

"You do?"

"Hell yes," he growls. I wince in pain. "Shit. Right. Hospital. Now," he says disjointedly, picking up the carrier again and starting down the stairs. He goes slow so he can keep an eye on me.

We finally burst outside into the sunlit late August afternoon. My car isn't too far and Ryder helps me into the passenger seat before installing the car seat as fast as humanly possible.

He gets behind the wheel of my car and adjusts the seat so that his long legs can fit. While he drives he calls to tell his parents what's going on since they have Cole. I call Casey and let her know that I think I'm in labor and ask her to let Hannah and Chloe know.

Ryder reaches over and takes my hand, bringing it to his lips he presses a kiss to my knuckles. His eyes flick over to me and he smiles.

My breath catches and my heart speeds up. It feels so good to have my feelings out in the open and know he feels the same.

We finally reach the hospital and in a blur I'm rushed inside and back to a room where they hook me up to all kinds of monitors and determine that I am in labor and dilated five centimeters.

Once it quiets down, it's only Ryder and me left in the room. Casey and the girls haven't arrived yet.

Ryder sits by my bed, holding my hand. "If you want me to leave, just ask, you won't hurt my feelings."

I squeeze his hand, not in pain but in reassurance. "I want you here." I take a deep breath and look around. The beeping of the heart rate monitor fills my ear. "I can't believe this is happening," I admit. "I feel so unprepared."

"You never feel prepared," he tells me, scooting the chair closer to the bed.

"Do you still think I'll be a good mom?" I ask him, thinking back to that day at his house.

"Yes," he answers without a second of thought. "If you saw the way you light up when you talk about her you wouldn't be asking me that."

"I'm still worried I won't be enough."

He brushes the hair away from my forehead, his thumb slowly stroking my skin in a soothing gesture. "You are enough."

"Is there a baby yet?" I turn my head to the door to see Casey and Hannah slipping inside.

"Hey, guys," I greet them. "No baby yet." Hannah holds a vase of pink daisies and sets them on the table. "Where's Chloe?" I ask.

"Still working," Casey explains, setting her purse down on the floor. She comes to stand on the side where Ryder isn't.

"How do you feel?"

"Like I got hit by a truck," I answer. "But I'm hanging in there. I haven't gotten the epidural yet. I'm trying to hold out."

"Girl," she says, "get the drugs."

I laugh. "I'm sure I will, but not yet."

Hannah grabs one of the other chairs and pulls it over. "This is early, right? Or has time gotten away from me?"

"She's coming early," I confirm. "Shit," I curse. "I need to call my mom."

In all the excitement, I forgot about my parents.

"Do you want me to call them?" Ryder asks.

"No, I can do it. But could you go get me some water?"

"Yeah, of course. Anything else?"

"Maybe some ice."

"Sure thing." He grabs my phone and hands it to me before he leaves.

"Please tell me you two are together now, because seriously it's going to happen eventually," Casey says.

I laugh. "We haven't really talked about it, but I think we are. We said I love you, so that counts for something right?"

Her mouth pops open. "What? When did this happen?"

"Today," I answer, scrolling through my phone to find my mom's contact.

"Speaking of today, why were you guys together?"

I press the SEND button and hold the phone to my ear. "He was helping me get the baby's room ready. Speaking of, we didn't finish. Would you guys mind going over to my place and putting the mattress in the crib and the bedding?"

"Yeah, of course, whatever you need," Hannah assures me.

My mom picks up. "Hello?"

"Hey," I greet her, and, of course, a contraction chooses now to show up. I hiss between my teeth and ride it out.

"Blaire?" she says. "Are you okay? What's going on?"

"I'm." Breath. "In." Breath. "Labor."

"Oh my God," she says. "We'll get on a plane as soon as we can. Dan, pack your bags," she yells.

"Mom, I'm still on the phone." I wince from the shrillness of her voice.

"Oh, sorry. Just hang in there, B, we'll be there soon. Flights are only about three hours and there's probably one soon."

"Mom," I cut her off. "Just get here."

"Right. I love you. See you soon."

"Love you too. Bye."

I drop the phone down on the scratchy sheet that covers me and I look at Casey pleadingly. "Get the nurse. I'm ready for that epidural."

She's up and out of her seat before I can blink. Ryder returns almost seconds after she leaves and hands me the water. I gulp it down and then reach for the ice, crunching down on a piece.

"I take it the contractions are worse?" He sits back down and I reach for his hand, squeezing it.

"Oh, yeah," I say, pressing my head back against the pillow

with my eyes squished closed. The pain of the contraction fades and I open my eyes. "Thank you for being here." I smile at Ryder.

"What am I?" Hannah laughs. "Chopped liver?"

I laugh too. "Thank you for being here too."

"That's more like it."

Casey breezes back into the room. "The nurse said she'd let the anesthesiologist know that you're ready."

"Oh, thank God." Sweat dampens my forehead. "They're getting so much worse."

What feels like forever later, but is probably only minutes, the anesthesiologist comes into the room to give the epidural. The drug hits my system and all the pain goes away.

"Feeling better?" Ryder asks, rubbing my shoulder.

"Much," I say, looking at him gratefully.

Casey fake gags. "Oh my God, you guys are so disgustingly in love."

I laugh. "You will be one day too, just you wait."

She makes a face. "Never."

After a little while, she and Hannah head to the food court to get something to eat for dinner.

"You can go too," I tell Ryder. "You must be hungry."

He shakes his head. "I'm not leaving you."

"You know," I begin, rubbing my thumb against his fingers where our hands are twined together, "it should probably be weird having you here, but I honestly don't feel that way. And I'm so sick of worrying about the way I should think or feel instead of owning the way I do feel."

"And how do you feel?" he asks.

I laugh. "Like I'm hopelessly in love with you."

His lips quirk into a smile. "Back at ya." He rises up and kisses my forehead.

I've worried for months that I was trying to replace Ben with Ryder, but that was never the case. I didn't fall in love with what I wanted him to be, I fell in love with who he is. I love him for him. He's not a replacement. He's just the man I love.

I once believed you only had one special love in life—one chance to get it right.

I was wrong.

There are infinite chances. Infinite people to complete you.

I will always love Ben, that hasn't changed, but I've found someone else I can love just as much.

Hours later they check me, and it's time to push.

"Do you want me to leave?" Ryder asks again.

I tighten my hold on his hand and he stands up beside me. "Never," I say.

Everything happens in a rush after that, or so it feels like.

I push and I push while Ryder whispers words of encouragement in my ear.

"You're doing great. Keep pushing. A little more. You're so strong, Blaire. You've got this."

And then, I hear it.

My baby's cry.

I collapse against the pillows sobbing.

My baby. My miracle. My daughter.

"Do you want to cut the umbilical cord?" the doctor asks Ryder.

He looks to me. I'm sweaty, crying mess, but I manage to nod. "Only if you want to."

He takes the scissors from the doctor and cuts. They then lay my daughter on my chest. I'm still crying, shaking with the sobs, and I press my hand to her warm, sticky body. She cries, her lower lip trembling. There's a tuft of hair on her head, but it's so covered in goo I can't tell what color it is. It doesn't matter. She's perfect. Absolutely perfect.

"Hi, Ava," I say touching her tiny hand. "I'm your mommy." She wraps her fingers around mine and holds on.

I look up at Ryder. "She's amazing."

He stares down in wonder. "That she is."

"I loved her so much already while she was inside me that I didn't think it was possible for me to love her any more, but I do," I sob.

Ryder reaches out and rubs the tuft of hair on her head. He looks pretty close to crying himself. I guess the miracle of life gets to everyone.

"So, Mommy, what's her full name?" One of the nurses asks.

I touch my daughter's plump cheek. "Ava Benny Carter."

Her middle name is untraditional, but I wanted Ben's name in there somehow.

"Cute," the nurse says. "I'm going to take her and weigh

her. Clean her up a bit too, but I'll bring her right back," she promises.

I reluctantly let her take Ava from me. "Go with them," I tell Ryder. "Stay with her. Please."

He follows my order and goes to stay with Ava. She just came into this world, and I don't want her to be alone.

They clean her up and wrap her in a blanket. They even put a cute little hat on her head.

"All right, dad, you want her?" the nurse asks.

Ryder looks shocked and he opens his mouth, probably to protest, but I speak up and say, "Hold her."

The nurse hands Ava to Ryder and she busies herself with clearing things out of the room. Ryder slowly makes his way back to me as the room clears of everyone but us.

He rocks Ava in his arms and smiles down at her.

A grin splits my face seeing the man I love love my daughter.

"You, me, Ava, and Cole. We're a family, aren't we?" I ask him.

He glances away from the baby in his arms and down to me. "We're a family," he concurs.

I know we still have so much to talk about, to discuss and figure out, but for now, I'm content to enjoy this little piece of happiness.

45

"Oh, Blaire," my mom breathes as she and my dad rush into the hospital room, luggage towed behind them.

Ryder sits beside me with Cole in his lap while Ava sleeps peacefully in the bassinet.

Ava came into the world nearly twenty-four hours ago, and I still can't believe how much my life has changed in that span of time.

"I'm so sorry it took us so long," my mom sighs, setting her luggage in the corner. "Everything that could go wrong did go wrong."

I'd received several texts explaining their travel woes—from a canceled flight, to a delayed one, to a taxi driver that didn't know his way.

"All that matters is you're here," I say. "Come meet your granddaughter."

My mom immediately scurries over to the clear bassinet and peers down at her. "What's her name?"

"Ava."

She glances over at me and smiles. "Ava," she repeats. "Perfect. She has Ben's mouth."

"His nose too," I tell her. "It looks like she's going to have my dark hair. I hope she gets Ben's eyes too."

She touches her plump cheek. "She's so beautiful." She glances at Ryder. "Thank you for being here with her."

He shrugs off her words. "There's nowhere I'd rather be."

I smile over at him and Cole. "Hey, Cole," I say, patting the space beside me on the bed, "you want to come sit with me?"

Without a word, the little boy scurries off Ryder's lap and climbs onto the bed, snuggling against my side.

Ryder beams. "He's been asking when you're going to come over and read him a story again."

I smile down at the little boy and he looks up at me. "Is that true?"

He nods. "Weed. Weed me stowy!"

I laugh. "Sure thing." I tap his nose.

My dad ventures over then and looks down at Ava. "You did good, Kid."

I smile. "I think so too, but I might be biased." Ava lets out a little cry. "You can pick her up," I tell my mom.

"Oh, thank God," she says, immediately scooping up the squirming bundle. "It was killing me not to hold her." Ava blinks up at her grandma. "When do you get out of here?"

"Tomorrow morning." I glance at Ryder. He's listened all morning to my worries about going home. A baby is hard work and I'm going to be doing it on my own. Ryder and I might be in a relationship now but it doesn't mean we're moving in together tomorrow and riding off into the sunset.

My mom bounces Ava in her arms. "I could stay … sleep on the couch."

My dad chuckles. "And what am I supposed to do?"

She glares at him. "Stay at the hotel, of course."

He shakes his head.

"Mom, that's really sweet of you, but I'll be fine. You're not going to be here forever and I'd rather get a hang of doing things on my own."

She frowns. "But, Blaire—"

"Mom," I say sternly, "I have to do this."

She nods, smiling down at Ava. "I understand."

I ruffle Cole's hair. "Hey, I got you something," I tell him and his eyes light up. I didn't actually get it—I sent Ryder to pick up a toy for him. Since Ryder was bringing Cole to meet the baby I didn't want the little boy to feel left out of all the excitement. I grab the bag off the table and hand it to Cole.

His eyes widen when he pulls out the shiny red fire truck—his latest obsession. His whole body vibrates with excitement as he shakes the fire truck between his hands. "Tank you," he says, in his sweet toddler voice.

"You're welcome." I kiss the top of his head.

I look from the little boy, to Ryder, to my dad, then to my mom and my daughter.

My people.

My family.

My life.

I thought my life was over when Ben died, and maybe that part of it was, but now I know it's only beginning.

46

"New parent fuel," Ryder says, breezing into my apartment with coffee and Cole on his heels. I gave him a key after I came home from the hospital two weeks ago. I kept calling him to bring me various things I needed so it just made sense.

"You're a saint," I say, taking the coffee from him and slurping it down. I hold Ava in my other arm. "She was up all night with her stomach hurting. It was hell. She finally passed out." I indicate her sleeping form in my arms.

"I also brought breakfast." He sets a brown paper bag on the counter and starts pulling out sandwiches.

"I love you," I say, setting down the coffee so I can grab a sandwich. "Hey, Cole." I smile down at the little boy. "I missed you."

He smiles and holds up the book he has grasped in his chubby hands. "Weed! Weed!"

Ryder cringes. "I tried to get him to leave it, telling him that you're tired, but he wouldn't listen."

"That's okay." I shrug, biting into my sandwich. "I can read it to you." I smile at Cole and he jumps up and down with excitement. "I was thinking," I begin, rocking Ava in my arms, "it's probably one of the last nice days we'll have for the summer so maybe we can go for a walk around town? What do you think?" Before Ryder can answer, I look back at Cole. "Want to go for a walk?"

"Walk! Walk!" he chants, still jumping up and down.

Ryder scoops him up and sets him in a chair with his sandwich. "Sure—" he smiles "—that sounds nice."

"I'm going to go put her down right now." I pad down the hall to my bedroom and lay her gently in the bassinet. I pray that she doesn't stir. Thankfully, she doesn't. I might manage to eat in peace and get a shower. I smell like sweat and spit up and it's not a good combination.

I sit down at the table with the boys and finish my sandwich and coffee.

"Do you mind keeping an eye on Ava so I can shower?" I ask Ryder.

"That's not a problem." He wipes his fingers on a napkin.

"If she starts screaming she probably needs her diaper changed," I tell him, starting for the bathroom.

He chuckles. "I can handle it, Blaire."

I know he can, but I still worry.

I grab some clothes from my room and lock myself in the bathroom.

Even a ten-minute shower feels like a luxury at this point.

I turn the water on until it's practically scalding and slip inside.

It feels good to have the hot water beat on my coiled muscles. I wash my hair and soap up my body. I finally smell like a human again.

I get out and dry off my body and ruffle my hair with the towel to help it dry. I get dressed and pull my hair up in a messy bun so it's out of my way. It's been my go-to hairstyle since Ava was born.

I step out of the steaming bathroom and head down the hall to the family room and kitchen area. Cole's sitting on the couch watching a kid's show, but Ryder's not there.

I head back the way I came and peek my head in my room. Not there.

I turn to the opposite side and find him in the nursery, holding Ava against his chest.

My heart lurches and speeds up, pumping blood rapidly through my whole body.

He hasn't noticed me yet.

He stands near the window that overlooks the street below, swaying back and forth. Ava makes a little noise that means she's happy and I smile, leaning my hip against the doorjamb.

It makes me happy to see the two loves of my life together.

Ryder turns then, murmuring something to Ava, and looks up to find me.

"Oh, hey." He smiles, rocking her in his arms. "Someone woke up and needed a diaper change, just like you said."

"She likes you," I comment.

He chuckles and looks at her. "Everyone likes me. I'm irresistible."

I roll my eyes and then bite my lip in thought. "Do you … Do you think Angela and Ben would be happy for us?"

He nods. "Yes," he answers without a second of thought.

"How do you know?" I step further into the room.

"Because we'd be happy for them if the situation was reversed."

I nod, smiling softly. "You're right. You're always right."

"I know." He winks.

I come to stand beside him and lay my head on his shoulder, gazing down at Ava in his arms. "We should get ready for our walk."

He nods. "You're right." He hands Ava to me. "I'll carry the stroller downstairs and you can meet me down there with the kids."

While Ryder wrangles the beast—that's what I call the stroller—out the door, I grab Ava's diaper bag and sling it across my shoulder.

I find Cole still quietly occupied by his show. "You ready to go for a walk?" I ask him. He tears his gaze away from the TV and nods eagerly. I grab my keys and hold my finger out for Cole to grab onto. I close the door behind us and lock it, giving Cole my finger again. With a squirming baby and a toddler to manage it takes me a little while to get downstairs and outside.

We burst outside to see Ryder just finishing with the stroller.

"I forgot how difficult these can be." He stood back to appraise his handiwork. "But I got it done."

I set Ava inside and she makes a happy cooing sound. I adjust the brim so that the sun's not in her eyes. I smile down at her and I swear she smiles back, but it's more likely gas, but I can dream.

Ryder lifts Cole onto his shoulders and the little boy giggles. "Do you like it up there?" I ask him, slipping on my sunglass.

"Yes!" he cries, tugging on Ryder's hair.

"Coley, don't do that," Ryder scolds, holding on tight to Cole in one hand and reaching up to pry his hair from his grasp with the other.

Once we're all situated, we begin our walk. I've discovered living in an apartment in the downtown area has its perks. I'm close to several coffee shops and restaurants, a convenience store, and even some clothing shops. It's nice to be able to get out and have so much within walking distance.

The late summer sun blazes down on us, but there's a slight wind to keep us cool.

"This is nice," Ryder says.

Ava lets out a noise and I laugh. "I think she agrees with you. Don't you?" I say in my overly high-pitched baby talking voice.

That voice has taken over my life.

We walk around without much of an agenda but we end up at the park. Ryder sets Cole down so he can go play on the jungle gym while the two of us take a seat on the bench. I grab Ava from the stroller and she wiggles in my arms.

Ryder stretches one arm behind me, his fingers grazing my shoulder.

"We've come a long way, haven't we?" he asks, shielding his face from the sun.

"We have," I agree.

I think back to those first weeks and months. It was the worst time of my life and I thought I would never get better. I thought it would take a miracle to bring me back to the person I was.

I was wrong.

It didn't take a miracle.

All it took was me.

I brought myself back from the brink of demise.

The people around me, they helped, but I had to do it on my own. I had to accept Ben's death in order to truly move on and accept happiness back into my life. He'll always be with me, though, living on in my heart, in our daughter, and in the paper cranes.

As if conjured by magic, I spot a paper crane on a park bench several yards to our right.

"Is that . . . ?" I begin.

Ryder sees it and stands. "It is." He grins.

My heart skips a beat. I know there's no way it's one from Ben—it has to be from a Group member or some other random person who's picked up on The Paper Crane Project—but it still feels like it's a sign from him.

"Go get it," I tell Ryder as Ava lets out a little cry. Ryder jogs over to the bench and swipes the purple paper crane before returning. He sits back down and I nudge him with my arm. "Open it, please," I beg.

He unfolds it and holds it out so I can read.

My throat catches. The words describe the last few months perfectly—an endless night, but the sun finally rose again and bathed my world in a brilliant light.

EPILOGUE

FIVE YEARS LATER

"Ava, careful! Don't hit your brother!" I scold when Ava whacks Cole over the head with a plastic softball bat.

"Ow!" Cole cries, rubbing the top of his head. "That's not nice!"

"You brokeded my Barbie!" she yells back, drawing the bat back to hit him again.

"Whoa, whoa, what's going on in here?" Ryder asks, breezing into the room with our fussy three-month-old son, Wyatt, in his arms. "What's wrong, birthday girl?" He bends down to Ava's level.

"Coley brokeded my doll!" Crocodile tears coat her face.

"Aw, I'm sure he didn't mean to," Ryder consoles her. "Besides, I'm sure you got lots of new dolls for your birthday." He tweaks her nose.

"Weally?" she asks, looking up at him with wide blue eyes.

"Really." Ryder nods, reaching for her hand. "Why don't we go outside and see your grandparents while mommy finishes your cake?"

I smile gratefully at him and he winks.

"Don't gwive Coley any of my cake," Ava warns me with a pointed finger.

Personality wise, she's my mini-me, but looks wise she's all Ben, except for her dark colored hair.

"I won't. You get the first piece, birthday girl."

"Good." She nods and lets Ryder take her outside where we have everything for her party set up.

My parents flew in for the occasion, plus they've been dying to see Wyatt. Ryder's parents are here too. I've gotten to know them well and they practically feel like my own parents at this point. They even treat Ava like she's really their granddaughter. Loraine drove up for Ava's party too—she tries to see her at least once a week, if not more, and now that Ava's a little older I promised to start letting her keep her overnight sometimes. I like for Ava to spend time with Loraine and learn more about her dad. I talk to her about him too, tell her how we met, and how great he was. Even though Ryder is the only dad she knows, I want her to know that Ben loves her too. His love might not be one we can physically feel, but it's still there.

I finish with the cake and carry it outside.

"Ooh! It's pwetty mommy! Tank you!" Ava jumps up and down eagerly.

"You're welcome, baby girl," I tell her, sticking the five candles in and lighting them. I bend down to whisper in her ear, "Happy Birthday." I kiss her cheek. I lift her up and join everyone in singing "Happy Birthday". When the song finishes, I say, "Make a wish, baby."

She blows out the candles and everyone claps. I lower her and cut her piece first. She takes the plate from me and runs over to sit on my dad's lap. That girl has her grandpa wrapped around her little finger. Talk about spoiled.

I cut everyone a piece and finally take a seat myself between Ryder and Ivy—who's newly married to that guy she liked at work, Jeremy. Casey, Chloe, and Hannah are there too. Cyrus is glued to Hannah's side. I'm pretty sure he thinks she walks on water. Casey has a boyfriend now too, and I have a feeling this is the one but she's too stubborn to admit it.

"Hey, gorgeous, you have some cake just there." Ryder points.

"Where?" I ask, about to frantically wipe at my mouth.

He grasps my face in one hand, holding Wyatt in the other. "Right there." He kisses me. When he pulls away his eyes are lit up with mischief and our son coos in his arms, kicking his legs wildly.

"I love you," I say.

I'm still in love with Ryder Cooper as much today as I was all those years ago. He stole my heart, and I don't want it back. Not ever.

"Mommy?" Ava prompts.

"Yes, baby?" I look over at her, bouncing on her grandpa's knee.

"How twill I know if my wish came twue?"

"You'll know, baby girl."

Her nose wrinkles. "I dwon't tink I twill."

"What'd you wish for?" I ask, my brows drawing in.

She opens her mouth to tell me.

"Wait," Cole cries. "You can't say or it'll never come true."

"Is dat wight, Mommy?"

"It is," I say sadly, "but you can come tell mommy quietly and it'll still come true."

She hops off her grandpa's lap and scurries over to me. I bend down so she can whisper in my ear.

"I wisheded fowr my daddy in hweaven to know I wuv him."

My breath catches. I think I stop breathing altogether.

From the moment I found I was pregnant with Ava that's all I wanted—for my child to love Ben even if he's not here.

I hug Ava to my chest, fighting tears. "He already knows, Ava. I promise you that."

"How dwo you know?" she asks, her blue eyes wide.

I smile. "Because, he's here."

"He wis?" Her eyes brighten.

"Yes," I whisper, poking her stomach lightly. "You see these paper cranes?" I point to the ones on the table and there are even more hanging in the tree. She nods. "Every single one of those is a piece of your daddy's love left here on this Earth."

"Wow," she breathes. "He weft a wotta wuv."

I swallow thickly. "That he did."

Ben may be gone, but his love and heart certainly isn't it. He lives on in The Paper Crane project—which completely took off, becoming a sensation. Now, wherever we go, we always seem to find a paper crane. Each one brings a smile to my face and reminds me to cherish every single day. Life can be cut short in an instant, so make sure to live with no regrets and love with all your heart.

ACKNOWLEDGEMENTS

This book. This book has been ten years in the making. Ten years of starting, stopping it, deleting, and questioning whether or not I'd ever actually tell it. But in that ten years Blaire, Ben, and Ryder stayed with me. They waited patiently until I was ready to tell this story and then they burst forward and demanded that I finally do it—that I take that step out of my comfort zone. I know this book isn't for everyone—in all honesty, as a reader, it's probably not something I'd want to read (is it bad for me to admit it) but it's a story I had to tell. Over the years this story took on many different shapes and forms—in most of them Ben wasn't a main figure early in the story, but in my mind I knew him and it hurt me that readers wouldn't know him. You can't fall in love with a character you've never really met. So I knew that I'd have to build his character up before his demise and I also knew that it was going to crush me. I hope I've done my job right and that the emotions are there, that you feel everything I wanted you to feel as a reader. …And I hope you don't hate me too much.

Regina Bartley, you are my partner in crime. Thank you so much for all the writing sprints and always being there for me to talk to. Your friendship means so much to me—more than you'll ever know.

Hang Le thank you for creating the most beautifully artistic cover I've ever seen. It's exactly what this book needed and

I think it truly speaks to the feel of the story, which is what I wanted.

Wendi, formatter and editor extraordinaire, when I say I don't know what I did before you I mean it. It's such a relief to have someone I can rely on so completely. You're a rock star. Don't forget it.

To the girls in my Facebook group, Micalea's Minions, thank you so much for all your kind words and help whenever I need it. Creating this group was one of the best decisions I've ever made. This group has become my happy place and I'm so thankful for each and every one of you.

To my beta readers (you know who you are!) I can't thank you enough for all your help in making this book, and my others, what they are. I value your opinions and input so much, and I love that you guys love my characters as much as I do.

Haley Douglas I don't know what I'd do without you. I love our talks and how excited you get when I send you chapter. It always puts a smile on my face. And thank you for being my kinda-sorta-assistant since…you know…I suck at giving you things to do. Sorry. Haha!

Emily. Emily. Emily. What is there for me to say that hasn't already been said? You're amazing and I'm so lucky to have a friend like you in my life.

To each and every person that has read this book, and any of my others, thank you. Thank you for allowing me to live my dream. Thank you for your messages, comments, and emails. Thank you for coming to see me at signings. Thank you for everything. I wish I could hug each and every one of you.

COMING THIS SUMMER

The Game That Breaks Us

A standalone New Adult college romance

Hockey's bad boy needs to clean up his reputation…

Bennett James has built his career at being the best, on and off the ice, and now it's come back to bite him. The media has turned against him, and with a near career-ending injury, he needs to clean up his act and prove that he's serious about the game. For Bennett, working with his old coach at his alma mater feels like a step back, but it might be just what he needs.

…and she's going to help him do it.

Grace Wentworth has always been the good girl, and she's tired of that stigma. She wants to prove that she can get down and dirty with the best of them. The problem? She doesn't know how.

Bennett will teach the good girl how to be bad, if she pretends to be his goody two-shoes girlfriend in front of the media.

But what happens when the game becomes real?

Escaping Heartbreak by Regina Bartley

Blurb:

It's time for Sawyer to start living her life. Since she was fifteen she has taken care of everyone but herself, including her older brother Dane. She has been lying to herself to keep from feeling the pain of her parent's death. Now she is twenty and she's ready to start a life of her own. Moving into her parent's lake house would be the perfect escape. Wouldn't it? That's what she thought. Only, it led her right into the emotional place she's been hiding from all this time. All of those years of running from her feelings, she now has to face them. It's too much. She can't deal with it alone. Someone has to help. She'll do anything to escape the heartbreak, but you can only run so far.

Travis can't believe his eyes; his half-opened, blood shot eyes. Sawyer Evans was in the flesh and standing over him. He hadn't seen this girl since he was ten years old. Travis only saw the Evan's during the summer when they moved into the lake house. He and Dane were best friends. When Dane invited him and the old gang to a welcome back party at the Lake House, he couldn't wait to go. It turns out getting wasted was only half the fun. Seeing Sawyer was the other half. She was the sexiest girl he'd ever seen and he was going to make sure that she knew it. Only she shot him down time and time again. He's determined to break down those walls and get inside her head, but he'll have to be sober to do it, and no matter how hard he tries, she'll always run. He can't keep chasing her. He has to figure out a way to make her stay.

It's time to stop running, stop hiding, and start learning where the true escape lies. Everyone will face heartbreak, but not everyone will find love.

Escaping Heartbreak

ONE

Sawyer

"Earth to Sawyer," Uncle Jake snapped his fingers in front of my face. "Where are you at?"

Today marks the six year anniversary of my parent's death. It still feels like it was yesterday. I was fifteen and my brother, Dane, was eighteen when the accident happened. The rain was coming down hard that night. The semi lost control and crossed over the yellow line. The officer said that it was instant and no one felt any pain. There's no way in hell that he could know that. At fifteen, you feel like your life is shattering around you, but when everyone else is crumbling, you have no choice, but to be strong. I'm grateful that I was there to help everybody, keeping busy made things easier for me.

The snapping continued. "I'm here." I shook my head and tried focusing my attention where it was needed. Uncle Jake was a handsome guy. His long brown hair hung down in front of his blue eyes. He had aged so much over the past several years. After mom and dad had died, he stepped in as sole guardian for me. Dane was eighteen and in his first semester of college. He couldn't handle the responsibility. Uncle Jake was only thirty at the time and had absolutely no clue what it meant to raise a daughter, a teenage one at that. He was so young himself. The two of us have practically raised each other. Actually, I'd say I raised him. I did all the cooking and household responsibilities. Someone had to. He worked and made sure that the manly duties were all taken care of. As far as teenage female issues, he had no clue. I learned a lot of things on my own or from my best friend Wren.

"It doesn't look like you're here." He narrowed his eyes at me. "I asked you what you want to do for your birthday."

"It's two weeks away. Do we really have to discuss this now?" I rubbed small circles into my temples. "Besides, I'm sure Dane won't come home. It's been nearly six months since I've seen him." I looked down at my hands. "He barely even calls me anymore. We used to be so close and you'd think that today of all days, he'd call."

"I know pickle, but he'll come around. He's probably busy with finals or something." I love that about Jake. He finds the good in everyone. He has to stop making excuses for Dane though. Dane is a big boy, he needs to start acting like it.

"Uncle Jake," I said taking his hand.

"Yeah," he squeezed mine in return. I gave him one of those overly serious, we-need-to-talk looks. He lifted his brows. "What is it? You're freaking me out."

"How long has it been since you've had a date?"

He looked down at his watch. "What day is it?"

"I'm serious Uncle Jake."

He rolled his eyes. "I don't know maybe a year."

"Or three," I waved my fingers in front of his face. "You have to get out and get yourself a life. You will never be married at this rate. You don't want to end up an old lonely man with nothing but a computer and a dog."

"Sounds like the pot calling the kettle black. You haven't been living much yourself, you know." He tugged on my ponytail.

I set back in my chair and shut my mouth. He was right. Besides my best friend Wren, I have no life. I haven't had a date since my junior year of high school. It went so bad that I refused to do it again, ever. I prefer spending my time taking care of Jake and when Dane's home I take care of him too. Dane's the older of the two of us, but certainly not the wiser. I was supposed to go to college right out of high school. It was what my parents and I had always talked about. I chose to work instead and stay home with Jake. We've always been a team. Only recently have I been thinking that it's time to do my own thing. I've just not found the right time to tell him. Or, maybe I'm just scared of what it will feel like to be on my own.

"I think it's time that you got out more pickle."

"I'm twenty years old. Don't you think it's time you stopped calling me pickle?" I raised my brow and watched him closely.

"Hell no, you'll always be my pickle."

"Whatever," I rolled my eyes. The thought of eating pickles now makes me sick. I used to eat them jars at a time when I was little and the name just stuck.

"What about swimming? It used to be your thing." I took a deep breath. This was not where I wanted this conversation to go. I hoped that it would never be brought up again.

"I don't want to have this conversation." I rolled my eyes and stood up from the table. I poured the left over milk from my cereal into the sink.

"Listen to me Sawyer," Jake walked over and stood next to me in front of the sink. He wasn't much taller than I was so we were nearly eye to eye. "You never want to talk about this, but we need to."

"It's not a big deal." I grasped the frame of the sink in my hands, holding on so tight that my knuckles whitened.

"It is a big deal. Swimming was your life. You can't just give everything up because you feel like the accident was your fault. It was an accident. It was no one's fault. Start living already, you hear me." I heard him alright. This wasn't something that I was prepared to argue about.

"Swimming was my life back then. I'm grown up now. I need to experience new things and find new goals." And I seriously needed a diversion from this conversation.

"Oh yeah, like what? Talk to me." He said.

Good, the diversion worked. It's now or never, Sawyer. "Actually, I was thinking about spending some time at the lake house. No one's been there for a while." He nodded. "I could take care of the place and maybe get a job there, or maybe even take some college classes. I have lots of money saved." I really didn't have to save money the way I did. Mom and dad left us pretty well set. The lake house was our summer home since we were kids. I haven't been there since my parents died. I'm sure the place is a mess and could use some love.

"You know what? That sounds like an awesome idea. I think you should do it. After all, your parents would want you to use that house. There were some amazing memories made there." He nudged my shoulder and grinned.

I shook my head. "I think I will." I replied. He pulled me to him and hugged me. He kissed my temple and whispered how proud he was of me.

"I love you, Uncle Jake."

"I love you too, Pickle." I sighed loudly.

"I'm going to work. We'll work out the details of my trip later tonight." I grabbed my bag and headed for the door. "Oh and Uncle Jake," I yelled back.

"What," I heard him yell from the kitchen.

"I'm going to find you a date. A hot, sexy, blind date," I laughed and ran out the door. I heard him yelling something and running through the house. I was in the car with my doors locked when he came barreling out the front door. The dish towel was still hanging out of the side of his basketball shorts. I smiled and waved and blew him a big kiss. He shook his head and laughed, as I backed out of the driveway. We always have so much fun together; it will be hard being away from him for very long.

The drive to work was a quick one. We only lived about three miles from town and traffic didn't get bad for about another hour. When I pulled in the parking lot of the Printing Shack, it looked empty. I've been working here since my senior year of high school. It screams future potential every time I develop someone's pictures. I'm climbing the corporate ladder one photo dweeb at a time. NOT! Hence the need to get my butt out of town.

I put Sally in park and patted her dash, silently thanking her for another successful trip. She has yet to fail me. I've driven this little Ford truck for so long, I'm wondering when the wheels will fall off. I have the money to buy a new car, but I don't have the heart to part with this one. My dad bought me this truck a few months before my fifteenth birthday. I had begged him for it and couldn't wait to get my license. I swore that I'd never part with it. I think about how petty it was for me to want this truck and about how the bright yellow really stood out now. I would trade it back in a second, if I could get my parents back, but that's only wishful thinking.

I had about twenty minutes before my shift started so I figured I'd call Dane.

Pulling my cell phone from the bag, I dialed his number. After about the fourth ring, his machine picked up. "Figures," I huffed. He was probably avoiding me. "Hey Dane, this is your sister. I'm reminding you in case you forgot about me. I have some big news that I want to talk to you about. I'm going to work right now, but I'll be home around six o'clock. Call me back, please. It's important. Okay, well, I love you. Talk to you later." I pressed the end button and thought no more about it. I had to get inside and go to work. Hopefully, the butthead would call me later.

***

When I got home, I was surprised to see Dane's civic parked in the driveway. The lime green practically glows in the dark. His car is fixed up to race and stands out about as bad as my yellow Ranger.

If Dane is home then that means Wren will be here soon if she isn't already inside. She and I have been best friends forever and she is so in love with my brother. She always has been. She's dated other guys, but swears that she's holding out to marry Dane. Funny I know, right. I'm sure she heard his car pass her house. She's stalkerish in that way. She lives at the end of the street by the stop sign. He had to pass right by her house on the way in. Sometimes I think that he would rather cut off the engine and push his car home than risk her hearing. Dane says she gets on his nerves and that she is too young, but every year Wren's boobs get bigger and so do his eyes. It's only a matter of time. It doesn't bother me. I love them both so I couldn't care less if they get together. As long as I don't have to hear the details, we're good. Honestly, I think Wren is just what he needs to straighten his ass out.

I walked in the front door and set my bag down by the stairs. Our house is big considering it's just me and Jake. It used to seem small when mom, dad, and Dane were all here.

I saw the lamp still on in the living room so I walked in. The television was playing some kind of sports and Uncle Jake was laid back in the recliner napping.

"I didn't wake him up."

"Shit Dane," I said as quietly as possible. I put my hand over my heart. I thought that it might beat out of my chest. "You scared the crap out of me." I whisper yelled. I looked up and saw a shadow of him standing in the doorway of the kitchen. I tiptoed slowly toward the kitchen, trying not to wake up Jake.

"Why haven't you called me?" I started to fuss. "Oh my God Dane! What happened to your eye?" Clearly he'd been in a fight. It was swollen shut and as black as night.

"It's nothing," he waved it off. I went straight to the freezer for some frozen peas. I think we only buy them for injuries because we sure don't eat them.

"Come here and let me look at it." I hoped up on the countertop and pulled him by his shirt over to me. He's a big guy. I stand about five foot three and he's more than a foot taller than I am. Even sitting on the counter, I'll have to reach. "What happened?" I brushed a stray hair from his face. It looked bad, real bad.

"I told you it's nothing. Ouch, damn it Saw," he winced in pain when I put the peas to his eye.

"Quit being a big baby. You took a fist to your eye; all I'm using are peas." He glared at me and I smiled real big. "Are you gonna keep avoiding the question or tell me what happened?"

"Avoiding," he said.

"Fine," we sat there in silence for a moment. "I really wish you would call me more. I've missed you."

"I'm sorry," he wrapped his big arm around my side. Dane and I have always been close, but lately he's been drifting away. When mom and dad passed away, he changed. He became wild and crazy. On weekends that he would come home from college I would nurse his hangovers. He would go on a weekly drinking binge and then sober up at home with us. I would spend both days waiting on him hand and foot. I loved taking care of him. I'm not sure how he managed to complete his courses at school. He took nearly three years off to find himself, but stayed with his friends around school. The only thing he found was that he loved to drink and party and spend money. Now that he's back in school I don't understand how he's passing. He must be doing some serious cheating. Either way, I thought he was doing better this year until he quit calling me. Now, I don't know what's going on. My phone vibrated in my pocket and it didn't take a psychic to know it was Wren. I held the phone up to Dane's face and he shook his head no.

I rolled my eyes. "You know she is going to keep calling until I pick up, and if I don't she'll just show up."

"I haven't been home fifteen minutes and already she's up my ass." I had to laugh.

"I'll shut my phone off. That will give us about ten minutes to talk before she shows up."

He shifted his head back further so that he could look at me. "What did you want to talk about?"

"So you do get my messages."

"Yes, I get your messages." He huffed. "I've just been really busy."

I stared at him. I could tell he was hiding something from me. I could see it all over his face. He knew that I could tell too, but I didn't push him for information. What good would it do me? "Well, I wanted to talk to you about the lake house."

"What about it?"

"I want to move into it, by myself." I said, shifting the peas up a bit. They were sliding down his face.

"Do you think that's a good idea? You've never been by yourself."

"I know that. I will be twenty-one in two weeks and I need to get out and start living my life. I am only asking because the lake house is yours too. I don't want you being mad at me if I move in there. I want you to tell me that it's okay."

"You're serious aren't you?" There was a questioning look in those dark blue eyes. The way he cocked his head to the side was like he was trying to read my thoughts.

"Well yeah, why do you think I am asking?"

"It just seems weird, that's all." He moved my hand down and the peas with it. "Things have been the same for so long that it will be weird coming home and not having you here."

"I know it will, but you'll get used to it. We have to change. We're both getting older and we can't keep things like this forever. I want to have a life of my own. You can come visit me at the lake. I'll be closer to your school than I am now."

"Good point. So, I guess you'll need my help moving."

"For sure, do you think you can help next weekend?" I asked.

"Yeah, I guess." Don't think I didn't notice the way he rolled his eyes.

"That means no hangovers, Stuart Dane Evans." I practically growled at him. I am in no way, shape, or form, babysitting that boy on moving day. I do it enough already.

"You know I hate when you call me that."

"I know, that's why I do it. You know I mean business." He just shook his head and smiled. I wrapped my arms around him for another hug. Gosh, I've missed him. I was about to ask him about school when the ever expecting knock sounded on the back door. This was record time for Wren. She must have already had her makeup on.

"Hey guys, are you all having a party without me?" She came right in. We have been walking in unannounced to each other's homes for years now. I wouldn't expect anything different.

“I would ask you what you’re doing here, but I’m pretty sure I know,” I winked at her.

“Oh shit, what happened to your eye Dane?” She hurried over to him completely oblivious to me sitting there.

“Well hello to you too Wren baby,” I smacked her on the arm. She rolled her eyes at me.

“Nothing,” he said in his normal bitchy tone.

“It’s not nothing, it’s serious. It’s almost swollen shut. Let me help you.” When she reached over to touch him, he swatted her hand and backed away.

“I told you that I’m fine. I don’t need your help.”

“Quit being so stubborn,” she said and tried to reach for him again.

“LISTEN!” He yelled in her face. I saw her flinch. “I don’t want you helping me. I don’t even fucking like you. When are you gonna get that through your thick skull, and stop annoying me.”

“Dane!” I shouted as he turned around and stomped off. The tears were already flowing down her cheeks. “I’m so sorry Wren. I don’t know what his problem is.” I wrapped my arms around her. She stood there crying her eyes out. “He doesn’t deserve you.”

“I’ve got to go,” she said through her strangled cry.

“Wait Wren,” I yelled after her as she ran out the door. “Just great,” I sighed, watching her run off towards her house.

“What’s all the commotion about?” Uncle Jake yawned.

“Dane’s home,” I said shaking my head. That was all the explanation he needed.

CPSIA information can be obtained
at www.ICGtesting.com
Printed in the USA
LVHW020041240122
709153LV00015B/2176